TROUBLE
~ IN ~
TIMBUKTU

TROUBLE
~ IN ~
TIMBUKTU

CRISTINA KESSLER

Philomel Books

PHILOMEL BOOKS
A division of Penguin Young Readers Group.
Published by The Penguin Group.
Penguin Group (USA) Inc., 375 Hudson Street,
New York, NY 10014, U.S.A.
Penguin Group (Canada), 90 Eglinton Avenue East, Suite 700, Toronto,
Ontario M4P 2Y3, Canada (a division of Pearson Penguin Canada Inc.).
Penguin Books Ltd, 80 Strand, London WC2R 0RL, England.
Penguin Ireland, 25 St. Stephen's Green, Dublin 2, Ireland
(a division of Penguin Books Ltd).
Penguin Group (Australia), 250 Camberwell Road, Camberwell, Victoria 3124,
Australia (a division of Pearson Australia Group Pty Ltd).
Penguin Books India Pvt Ltd, 11 Community Centre, Panchsheel Park,
New Delhi—110 017, India.
Penguin Group (NZ), 67 Apollo Drive, Rosedale, North Shore 0632,
New Zealand (a division of Pearson New Zealand Ltd).
Penguin Books (South Africa) (Pty) Ltd, 24 Sturdee Avenue, Rosebank,
Johannesburg 2196, South Africa.
Penguin Books Ltd, Registered Offices: 80 Strand,
London WC2R 0RL, England.

Published simultaneously in Canada.   Printed in the United States of America.
Design by Semadar Megged.   Text set in Berling.

Library of Congress Cataloging-in-Publication Data
Kessler, Cristina.
Trouble in Timbuktu / Cristina Kessler.
p. cm.
Summary: Ignoring her parents' wishes, as well as the customary place of women
in Timbuktu society, twelve-year-old Ayisha joins her twin brother in trying to
stop a pair of tourists from stealing an ancient manuscript.
[1. Twins—Fiction.   2. Brothers and sisters—Fiction.   3. Sex role—Fiction.
4. Tombouctou (Mali)—Fiction.]   I. Title. PZ7.K4824Tr   2009
[Fic]—dc22   2008008789
ISBN 978-0-399-24451-3
10 9 8 7 6 5 4 3 2 1

This book is dedicated to my true love, Joe,
and to two of my biggest fans and supporters,
my mom, Jeanna, and my mother-in-law, Abby.
Thanks for years of encouragement.
And also to my editor extraordinaire, Patricia Lee Gauch,
for her patience and prodding.
Many people helped with the languages and so I'd like
to thank Sue Rosenfeld, Kent Glenzer,
Aboubacrine Mohamed, Adamou Ganda,
Billa Anassour and Boureima Touré.
Merci and *shukran* to one and all.

Ever since I was a young woman, I wanted to go to Timbuktu. From 1999 to 2001, while living in Bamako, I realized my dream and visited this ancient city three times—by road, by plane and by boat. It truly sits on the edge of the world, far from everywhere but bustling in the Saharan heat. Timbuktu is a character in itself in this book. This spelling is the official English spelling in Mali, while in French it is Tombouctou. As in all of my books, many parts come directly from my journals.

Ahmed, another one of my main characters, is based on a real Bella boy I met on my first trip in 1999. He was an amazing boy, teaching himself English, German, Spanish and Japanese, in addition to speaking Arabic, French and Tamashek. We spent a pleasant week together, meeting every day. About fourteen months later, Joe and I returned to Timbuktu. One day, as I wandered around the town, I heard, "Cristina, author of children's books!" I turned and there was Ahmed. I couldn't believe he remembered me after all that time. Especially when I thought about how many *toubabs* he had guided over that period. I was humbled and impressed.

On my second trip he took me to visit his family, and

that's when I met his sister, the character Ayisha in this book. She was a very sharp girl, asking me endless questions as we drank tea. These two Bella kids, children of the new generation, proud of their city of sand and heritage, inspired me to write this book.

The fourth major character in this book is the ancient manuscripts. The first time I saw one, it took my breath away. Beautiful, precise writing in Arabic, with incredible pen-and-ink sketches and patterns, on brittle, yellowed, ancient parchment. These treasures prove that the written word existed in Africa long before it did in Europe. The effort to protect the manuscripts is relatively new compared to how long ago they were written. Black-market buyers are a real threat to those working to protect these ancient works.

There were many challenges while writing this book, but one that never failed to amuse me was writing for hours, struggling through the Sahara Desert on the page, while listening to the gentle Caribbean waves roll ashore outside my window.

Thanks for joining me on this journey to Timbuktu.

CK
St. John, Virgin Islands

HOT DID NOT ADEQUATELY describe the day. The brittle leaves on the lonely acacia tree dangled like dried insect carcasses caught in a spider's web. There was not a trace of breeze or relief in the still heat. The sun beat down on Timbuktu with no mercy. It was lip-sweating, shin-dripping hot.

Ayisha gazed across the flat sandy plain that spilled northward from the edge of the city into rolling waves of sand dunes. She breathed in short little gulps, for with each breath the dry air left a parched trail down her throat. Raising the hem of her long, rose-colored dress, she wiped her sweaty face. It came away damp with just the faintest hint of brown, remnants of the day's dust and chores.

"Where is he?" she mumbled as she took the two baskets she carried off her head. Turning to the west, the minaret of the Djinguereber Mosque caught her eye. The four mud walls forming a tall rectangle, wide at the bottom and narrow at the top, had sticks poking out of it. A loudspeaker was tucked into the sticks on two faces of the structure. It always struck her as odd—that one of the oldest mosques in Africa had such modern things hanging off it.

Squinting, Ayisha scanned the faces of a group of boys as they left the mosque. Each held the wooden board they wrote on during their Koranic studies in their right hands as they pushed and shoved one another with their left hands. She could see her brother Ahmed was not among the boys. She kept her eye on the rounded portal that led into the outer corridor of the mosque. She could see the sun pouring through a square doorway across from the round entrance, a beautiful bright box of light in the darkness of the mosque's interior.

A loud shout filled the air as a younger boy was pushed into the path of a group of Japanese tourists walking down the road. Ayisha could easily distinguish them from the German, French, American, Australian or any other tourists, for they all wore masks across their noses and mouths and white gloves on their hands. The pushed boy was scrambling to avoid contact with any of them, and they were doing the same. He finally broke loose and ran after the boys that were running away down the sandy street.

Ayisha watched the Japanese tourists. Whatever brought them here, she wondered, when they are afraid to breathe our Timbuktu air or touch anything? She shook her head. *Toubabs!* They don't all look alike, but they do all look like *toubabs*. Timbuktu had a special power for attracting *toubabs*, strangers, from far and wide. She knew it had once been the learning capital of the Islamic world, according to her father, but that was centuries ago. She knew that it was hard to get to—once nearly impossible—her city of sand in the southern reaches of the Sahara. But she also knew that it was even harder to get out of. "When I am old enough," she had said to her twin brother, "I will leave Timbuktu. I will."

"Where would you go?" he always asked. "I like it here. I don't want to go anywhere else."

"But how do you know that, Ahmed?"

"From the *toubabs*. Look how they leave their homes and travel all the way here. If their homes were great, they'd still be there!"

Ayisha hated to admit it, but she was jealous of her brother. His freedom let him talk to the *toubabs* all the time. He even earned money telling them things about Timbuktu's history and guiding them around town. She knew that as a young girl she couldn't walk up to a foreigner and offer her services. Word would travel back to her parents faster than dust during a harmattan storm if she did such a thing.

She shifted her position against the mud wall that she leaned on, getting as much of her body as possible into the meager shade it provided. Again she looked down the wide, sandy road toward the mosque. The buildings in between, all short and square, mimicked the color of the streets. Men in long gowns strolled by. Their indigo turbans told her they were Tuareg as they walked casually along, holding hands. The hooves of a passing herd of goats stirred up little dust devils that rose and fell in the still, hot air. Ayisha wiped her sweaty face with the end of her sleeve. The sun was dipping toward the horizon, but it didn't seem to take the temperature down with its decline.

Suddenly there he was, Ahmed, standing taller than usual and smiling wider than she had ever seen before. He held his wooden tablet in his right hand and raised it high when he saw her. Dangling from his other hand was a white cloth, bordered with two bands of dark blue on each end. He broke into a run to join his twin. It took her a moment to realize that his shadow, Sidi, was running right behind him.

"You look very happy with yourself," she said when Ahmed arrived. "And late as usual." She eyed the cloth as Sidi stopped at her brother's side.

The boy greeted her with a large smile and said, "You'll be proud of your brother."

It irked her that he said that, for she was always proud of Ahmed. Not only was he her brother, but also her womb mate. She was twenty-two minutes older than he, and proud of it.

Her thoughts were interrupted when Ahmed said with a laugh, "I wouldn't be late if you didn't always arrive early." He raised the cloth's end to wrap around his arm. He didn't say anything about the cloth, and she didn't ask.

It was a game they had played their whole life—sharing news or thoughts without speaking. Suddenly Ayisha clapped her hands and cried out, "You did it! You recited your verses perfectly!"

Ahmed held up the blue and white cloth. "Alhaji Musa

gave it to me. He said that all good scholars should have a prayer cloth." Running it through his right hand, he added, "I never expected it."

"So now you're a scholar?" Counting on her fingers, she said, "That makes you a *toubab* guide, a *futbol* star and a scholar." She wanted to congratulate him, in fact knew that she should, but in that moment envy ate at her.

Ahmed put his arm around her shoulders. "And don't forget, the twin brother of the highest-scoring student in the school's history."

That immediately brought a smile to her face. It was true: in their annual final tests she had scored the highest of any student at the school. Her father had been proud, but nothing compared with her mother. Until that day, her mother had groused about Ayisha continuing school after finishing her primary classes. Ayisha's test scores changed her mother's mind in a matter of seconds.

"Someone so smart should keep studying," she surprised the family by announcing that night at dinner. With a little flick of her head, Mother told them, "All the women at the well were very impressed." A smile crawled across her mother's face as she relived the scene in her head. Thanks to the scores and her mother's pride, it was now certain that Ayisha would attend Le Lycée Franco-Arabe high school next year. She not only planned to attend, she planned to shock everyone by staying the number-one student so she could go to university one day. She dreamed of the university in Bamako, the country's capital. It was so wild a dream that she hadn't even told her brother yet. She knew it would sound far-fetched to him.

"Ayisha, are you here?" asked her brother.

She laughed. "Thank you, brother, for reminding me of that. And *chapeau*, congratulations, on your achievement today." She would have carried on if a sudden frown hadn't taken over her brother's face. She turned to look over her shoulder at what had grabbed his attention. A *toubab* couple walked down the wide, sandy street. In places the sand was ankle deep, and deep ruts of vehicle tracks wove down the road. They struggled as they walked.

"Who are they?" she whispered. "Do you know them, Ahmed?"

Ahmed wiped the grimace off his face as the couple spotted him and veered to walk toward him. Sidi came up behind Ahmed. "Are they the *américaines* you met this morning?"

Ahmed nodded and called out, *"Bonjour,* Monsieur Griff, *ça va bien?"*

"Bonjour. Ça va bien, merci," replied the man. Good day. We're fine, thanks.

His longish brown hair licked at his collar. The sweaty tourist wore a turban wrapped awkwardly around his head. His right knee poked through his ripped blue jeans. Big black letters asking, "Got a problem?" covered his T-shirt. He looked at Ayisha and asked, *"Ça va bien?"*

His twangy American accent sounded strongly in his French, but at least he made an effort to speak French. That was something, thought Ayisha.

A *toubab* woman stood at his side, wearing a long flowing skirt that kicked up dust with every step. Ayisha watched Ahmed and Sidi purposely not look at her, and knew exactly why. The woman wore only the skimpiest of tops, not fit for Timbuktu. Her blonde hair, longer than her husband's, was tied back. The loose ends frizzed around her face in the heat. She smiled at Ahmed although he focused on the man, Griff.

Reaching out, the woman grabbed Ahmed's sleeve, really surprising him, Sidi and Ayisha. A smile covered her face as she said in her twangy French, "This has got to be your sister." Then continuing in English, she turned to her husband and said, "Look at them, Griff, they both have the same tilt in their left eyebrow, the exact same smile and the same hair—it fits like a cap on their heads. Do you think they are twins?" Ayisha didn't understand a word she said.

The *toubab* woman suddenly reached out a hand to Ayisha, who slowly reached forward too. She had never touched a *toubab* before, never touched white skin, and it surprised her to learn that white skin really felt no different from her own. The woman smiled as they shook hands, saying, *"Enchantée. Je m'appelle* Trudy."

Ayisha smiled back. *"Je m'appelle* Ayisha."

There were three languages going on; French among the four, English between the *toubabs* and Arabic between the twins and Sidi.

Breaking back into English, Trudy turned to Griff. "Aren't they the cutest? They are like a set of bookends!"

Griff snorted. "That's what they look like, all right." Then he whispered to his wife in English, "And with any luck we'll need some bookends for the manuscripts . . . if we get them . . ."

Alarm suddenly spread across Ahmed's face. The *tou-babs* obviously didn't notice. Ayisha did. She grabbed his arm and said in Arabic, "Let's go, Ahmed. What did they say? Tell me." She laughed, adding, "Obviously they don't know you speak English!"

Ahmed turned to the Americans and said in French, "Nice to see you again. We have some chores to take care of so we'll say *au revoir* now."

"Wait! Can you be our guide again tomorrow?" Griff asked, also in French. "As I mentioned this morning, we want to see the museums. Maybe take a walk in the desert. Visit the mosques. Not all tomorrow, so maybe for the next few days?" He unzipped the pouch across his stomach, taking out a wad of folded money. "We'll pay you well," he said as he pushed a 100 CFA note at Ahmed. "Take this now and if tomorrow is good, then maybe you can help me with some other things too." Griff cocked his head to the side, eyeing Ahmed closely. "I am a bit of a collector; maybe you can help me."

Ahmed hesitated. Ayisha saw that too. "What time?" he finally asked. Usually he jumped on an offer to be a guide.

Trudy spoke quickly to Griff. "How about early, before the unbearable heat begins?"

Griff nodded and said, "The earlier the better, because of this wretched heat."

"*C'est bien*," said Ahmed. "Let's say eight o'clock on the patio of the Bouctou Hotel."

Everyone shook hands all around. Then Trudy turned to Ayisha. "You should come too, one day."

Ayisha wanted to, more than anything. *Toubabs* fascinated her, the way they dressed and talked so loudly and men and women held hands in public. It was strange how all foreigners were *toubabs*, but not all *toubabs* were alike. Here was an American, showing off her shoulders, as different as could be from the Japanese with their masks and gloves. She wanted to spend some time with a *toubab* and ask question after question, but she was sure she wouldn't. Her parents would never agree to her going. "I'll try to come tomorrow," she told Trudy.

They wasted no time. Kicking up plumes of sand, the three young Bellas scurried away. Once they rounded the corner of the long street, Ayisha put her arm out to stop her brother. "Tell me, why did you scowl when you saw them? And why did you nearly jump out of your skin when they said something in English?"

Ahmed shook his head and took a quick breath. "Let's go collect the dung. I'll help you with that if you'll help me. I think I have a problem. Bigger than any problem I've ever had before."

"I'll help too!" chimed in Sidi, but Ayisha said in rapid Arabic, *"La, shukran."* No, thanks.

She turned her back on him and said to her brother only, "It must be bad, if you're volunteering to collect dung with me!"

"It is," he said. "Ayisha, I think those two will only make trouble in Timbuktu."

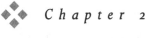 *Chapter 2*

AYISHA WALKED WITH Ahmed to the wide open space near the well. It was her least favorite thing to do—collect dung. Piles of camel, goat and cow dung covered the area from the animals gathered there to drink and pull water from the well. Ayisha usually did this chore alone, every afternoon, collecting enough dung for the cooking fire. Today she carried two baskets, hoping to fill them both so she could take an afternoon off the next day. Ahmed volunteering to help was an offer he seldom made, and one she quickly accepted.

Walking toward the well, Ayisha looked at her brother and asked again, "Ahmed, what was that all about? What sent that worried look all over your face?"

Ahmed stopped in the sand. "Ayisha, I don't trust them. He asked about manuscripts, Ayisha. He's an archaeologist—he must mean the ancient manuscripts. He sounds like he's planning to take some away from here."

"Is that what he said in English just now?"

"I think so. She said we'd make great bookends—whatever that means—and he said, Bookends, that's what we'll need for the manuscripts, if we can get them."

Ayisha's dark brown eyes simmered with anger. Shaking her head, she said in disbelief, "But Ahmed, he can't just go to the market and buy one. He'd need a local person to help him find one. Yes?"

Ahmed just nodded very slowly.

Eyes wide, Ayisha asked, "Could that be what he wants from you? Does he want you to be the person who helps him find some ancient manuscripts?"

Ahmed's eyes drilled into his sister's. Ayisha could feel his distress. She blew out a puff of air, suddenly knowing the *toubabs* would have to steal the ancient manuscripts to get them. And anyone who helped them would also be a thief.

Ayisha grabbed his shoulders, then quickly cleared her throat. "What shall we do?" she said. "These papers *are* Timbuktu! The very heart of Timbuktu. Ahmed, Ahmed, what shall we do? We have to stop them."

"We?" Ahmed asked. "How can you help me?" They both knew that boys and girls didn't share the same freedoms, but Ayisha often forgot that. "Besides, since when have you cared about the ancient manuscripts of Timbuktu?" He stopped when he saw her stricken face.

"I suppose I've just never seen you so upset before," Ayisha said.

She looked down with her deep brown eyes, refusing

to look at him. Ahmed stared at the sister that looked so like him. She had bright black hair, with bangs that hung across her forehead and two long thick braids. Their mother had been very angry when Ayisha had cut those crazy bangs. Ayisha had whacked her hair off because she liked how the bangs looked on a *toubab*. The young girl stood just a breath shorter than Ahmed and usually had a wide smile, but not now.

Her sadness shamed him immediately, and he took her hand, something he had quit doing when they turned thirteen the month before. Ahmed looked around them. They were at the deepest well, where people used their camels to pull the water up. Two thick logs stood on either side of the concrete ring around the well, planted deep into the hard-packed earth. Wooden pulleys on smooth, thick sticks rested across the two forks in the branches of the logs. A long rope, as deep as the well, dropped down into the darkness, connected to a rubber-tire bucket. The other end was tied to a camel.

Ahmed raised his arm and called out a greeting of "*Salaam alakoum*, Boubacar."

Boubacar held a halter draped from his camel's neck. Ayisha looked his way and could see his exhaustion. She knew that for hours Boubacar had been walking the beast back and forth, a distance equal to the well's depth, pulling up full bucket after full bucket. Boubacar waved at Ahmed as he switched the rump of the ambling camel with a long, strong twig.

Ahmed twisted Ayisha's hand back and forth. "Oh

please, don't cry. I know! You can pick the first dung for me to collect. That will certainly cheer you up . . . It just can't still be steaming fresh." Ayisha laughed at the thought of Ahmed trying to scoop a fresh plop into his basket. She looked around for the biggest, freshest dung pile she could see and then pointed to it.

Running with his knees bending high like a dancing camel, he heard his sister laugh. He stopped at the pile of cow dung, still fresh and big enough to cover the bottom of his basket. Trying to act unconcerned about the messy pile, he bent over for a closer look to see just how he could pick it up. A quick tap of the toe on his tire sandal left an indent on the plop's edge. She knew he would never pick this pile up—not yet anyway. Instead without looking up, he said, "All right, then, Ayisha. What do you think we should do? There is something about them. In fact, I didn't trust them from the very beginning this morning. That's why I agreed to be their guide. It's better to know what they are up to, don't you think?"

Ayisha's heart beat fast. He wouldn't ask for help, she thought, if he didn't want it. Grabbing his arm, she said, "We must stop them, Ahmed. No one, especially a *toubab*, has the right to take even one ancient manuscript from Timbuktu. Even I know that they were written hundreds of years ago. Hundreds and hundreds of years ago. Please, brother, tell me everything about the *toubabs* . . . from the very beginning."

Ahmed wandered away from the steaming dung pile without attempting to put the fresh dung in his basket.

"I met them in the usual way. They were sitting on the terrace at the Bouctou Hotel, drinking tea this morning. I walked over and asked if they wanted a guide, but he told me no. I stayed to chat for just a few minutes, and the Tuareg jewelry salesmen started arriving at the terrace."

"'We don't want them crowding around us, offering to be guides or selling us Tuareg jewelry made for tourists,'" the man grumbled.

"So of course I said, 'Hire me and all the rest will stay away. Guides don't steal customers from each other, so once the others see you have a guide, none of them will bother you.' And so I spent the day with them until classes at the mosque."

Ahmed dropped the basket to his feet and then kicked it lightly. It tipped over because it was empty, reminding them both why they were there. Ayisha said, "Talk while we work." Stooping to pick up a hard, dried plop of cow dung, she said, "And don't think I didn't notice that you didn't pick up the nice warm one I chose for you."

Ahmed just went on, "I usually tell people what languages I speak, but these two never asked. They wanted to speak French, and they didn't ask me if I speak English, so I didn't tell them I do. They talk to each other as if I'm not even there."

Stooping to pick up a large dried plop, he asked, "Remember last summer, when the German *toubabs* were fighting in German in front of me about their private life? It was the same today. This morning the American man told the woman in English something about finding the manuscripts as soon as possible so they could get out of this place hotter than hell itself. Then she said something that they repeat all the time. It sounds like 'gotcha!,' and I have no idea what that might mean, but they say it as often as Father says *Inshallah*."

Ahmed picked up another dried dung pile and flung it at the basket. "I'm sure they mean to steal some manuscripts, or buy them, which is the same as stealing."

"Tell me something more about the ancient manuscripts, Ahmed. I want to know more." Ayisha stooped over to pick up a hard, round cow plop. She had seen several manuscripts in the museum, but not up close. She'd never really paid full attention.

"Do you want to hear everything I tell them?"

Ayisha nodded yes, repeating, "Everything, Ahmed. From the beginning."

With a smile, Ahmed switched into French in a singsong voice that showed he'd said it all before. Many times. "Timbuktu is a city rich in history. It is where the canoe met the camel centuries ago. Once located on the banks of the Niger River, it was a thriving port and religious and academic center as far back as the eleventh century." He cocked his eyebrow and said, "Tell me when to stop."

"Keep going. I always wondered what you say to the *toubabs*. But the ancient manuscripts, Ahmed, tell me more about the manuscripts." She threw another plop into her basket, looking at Ahmed all the while.

Pleased, he continued, "West Africa, North Africa and

the Mediterranean all met here. Salt and goods from the north were traded for gold, books and slaves from the south. The thriving commercial center also developed into a city of renowned Islamic studies taught by the most holy of scholars. At one time there were a hundred thousand Islamic students studying here."

Ayisha cut in, "I can't even imagine it." She looked back at the city. "We think it is crowded now, but imagine being here then."

"It would have been great!"

"Humph. So tell me some more, Mr. Talker. A hundred thousand students! How many people are here today?"

Ahmed smiled, clearly enjoying his performance. "There are thirty to forty thousand residents, my dear sister, depending on the season, and we have sixteen libraries that house a small portion of the seven hundred thousand ancient manuscripts of Timbuktu."

Ahmed stopped short. Shaking his head, he said, "Oh no! Now I remember how his interest grew when I mentioned the manuscripts. It was the first question he asked me." Ahmed kicked a dirt clod resting on the hard, dried earth. "I wasn't sure he was listening until then. 'What are these manuscripts about?' he asked me when I told him about the libraries—as if he didn't know."

With a touch of embarrassment, Ahmed said, "May Allah forgive me—I started bragging. I told him they were about science, religion, world peace, diplomacy, astronomy, physics, conflict resolution, geography, history, law. Anything you can think of, I told him, these scholars wrote about it, some four hundred to six hundred years ago . . . Ayisha, what have I done?"

Wincing, as if in pain, he asked, "Remember Father telling us one evening about the *toubab* caught buying the rare old papers from Fatima, the old widow? How he paid her almost nothing compared with what he would sell them for? Father called it stealing of the worst sort, buying family heirlooms from desperately poor people."

"I remember, I remember. He was smoldering with anger, and then he said something about how all families have been touched by this thievery. He still hasn't told us what he meant by that," she said, tugging on her bangs.

"You're right. Father said, 'When you're older, I'll tell you.'"

"Well, we're older now. We should go home and ask him what he meant, Ahmed. Maybe we need to understand better. But please, tell me, did the *toubabs* say anything after you poured forth all the manuscript information like that full bucket over there pouring water?"

Ahmed nodded slowly. Braying donkeys, hobbled near the well, suddenly split the searing dry heat with their bellowing. Neither brother nor sister noticed. Taking a deep breath, he said, "He asked me if I had any of these manuscripts or knew where he could see some. I told him we'd visit the museums in the morning and a few libraries. I thought then that he was interested in a scholarly way, but I don't think so now." Nudging a rock with his toe, he added, "I feel as dumb as a donkey, Ayisha."

He shook his head. "They are the kind of people Alhaji

Musa told us to watch out for. He told us to beware of anyone, especially foreigners, with too much interest or curiosity in our national treasures, especially our ancient writings. We are all protectors, Ayisha."

Ayisha's eyes glowed in the late afternoon sun. Touching Ahmed's shoulder, she announced, "So we have to stop them, Ahmed. Alhaji Musa is wise—a holy man. All of the ancient manuscripts are our heritage, he says. Letting anyone steal even one is a crime against our people and all of Timbuktu." She surprised herself that she cared so much.

Ahmed nodded as his sister said, "It's not your fault they came here to steal. But we will stop them! We will become our own little police force—*les gendarmes des livres anciennes.*" Police of ancient manuscripts.

"That's good, Ayisha. I like it." His voice was suddenly growing louder and stronger. "Let's make a pledge to protect all the ancient manuscripts of Timbuktu."

Ayisha held her right hand over his heart and said, "Repeat after me." Then she placed his right hand over her heart and said, "We promise to protect the ancient manuscripts of Timbuktu from all thieves. The holy ancient papers of Timbuktu."

Ahmed repeated it, adding, "Foreign or local. Till death if need be." Ayisha's eyes popped wide and she asked, "Death? I think that is too much, don't you?"

"*Ça va, ça va,*" he said in French. Okay, Okay. "Repeat after me: till we have tried every method . . . short of death."

Ayisha still wasn't crazy about the death part, but she repeated it anyway. Then, eager for the last word, she added, "We promise all this before Allah and the camels pulling water over there."

They removed their hands from the other's heart, shook hands and touched their own hearts. The pact was sealed.

"So what are we going to do? Shall we ask Father?" he asked.

Ayisha looked over at the braying donkeys. Each carried four heavy tins filled with water, strapped to wooden saddles on their backs. "I don't think so. He'll just tell us to report it and stay away, but we want to catch them. Don't we?"

Ahmed's dark brown eyes widened. "*Mais oui*, we shall certainly catch them." He paused, nodding. "This is serious, Ayisha. Maybe I should talk to Alhaji Musa. He's a man of great wisdom. Do you think he'll stop us too?"

"I think he's the right one to talk to," said Ayisha. "Tell him we want to catch the thieving *toubabs* so they will go to jail." She grabbed Ahmed's arm. "We must, to scare any other thieves away from stealing our manuscripts."

Ahmed bobbed his head up and down as Ayisha spoke. Looking at her, he said, "I'll discuss it with him. He is a man of Allah and I am a Bella boy, so I don't *tell* him anything. I will discuss it with him."

"And if he says we have to stop, what will you say?" asked Ayisha as she stooped to toss a particularly large dried cow plop into her basket. The sun was dipping toward the horizon, and her shadow stretched before her in a long dark puddle.

"I'll say we are dedicated to catching these two. Then ask him if he has any suggestions for us. I'll tell him that we are trying to make a plan, and that I will share it with him before we do anything."

Ayisha nodded. "That's good. He can help us, but please, Ahmed, don't let him forbid us. Or maybe I should say, forbid you. I want to do this, and even if I have to stay in the background because I can't spend the days with the *toubabs* like you can, I . . . I want to catch these two and send them to prison." She stomped her foot to emphasize her words.

"They want to steal our history! And they think we are too dumb to know. It will be just like regular times—I am the brains and you are the action." She thought back to the last plan she had made, to make money by turning the family into a tourist attraction. Her parents hadn't allowed her to leave the tent for days because they knew she was the one who had created the crazy idea. She shook the thought away as Ahmed shook his head and picked up his basket of dung.

"Fine," he said. "I just want to stop the tumbleweed I started rolling today." Then tilting his head, he added, "I still don't understand why you are suddenly so interested in protecting the ancient manuscripts."

"I already told you—I've never seen you so upset before," she replied. "And besides, maybe it's time I learned more about Timbuktu."

The sudden bellow of a camel surprised them both.

Ayisha watched Boubacar yank on his camel's halter, forcing the big beast to its knees. Another loud bellow, *cahaaaaarh, cahaaaaarh,* filled the hot, dusty afternoon.

Ahmed clapped his hands together. "Now I know what that *bookends* word must mean—covers. He must have meant to find a way to steal the manuscripts and then keep them safe. Like book covers, I think."

"We will cover them, all right. So tight they won't get their stealing hands on them," Ayisha said. Her anger was growing, so she took a deep breath and said, "One thing for sure, DON'T let them know you speak English. Let them keep talking like you're invisible. Look what you've learned already."

"You're right. I can't react like I did today. Fortunately they are so busy talking between themselves they don't even think about me being there. I am invisible."

"So that's what we'll call ourselves—*les gendarmes invisibles*—the invisible police."

They looked into each other's eyes, shook hands and touched their hearts again. Stooping over for her basket and taking it to the nearest plop of dung, Ayisha said, "Do you think there is any chance Father and Mother will let me join you tomorrow? If we have enough dung, maybe they will allow me." Ahmed didn't answer.

They walked in opposite directions, each bending and collecting, filling their baskets. Then, as if a bee had stung her behind, Ayisha stood suddenly and yelled, "I know who we need to talk to."

Like lightning passing between the two, they both shouted, "Auntie B!"

❖❖ *Chapter 3*

EARLY THE NEXT MORNING, Ahmed and Ayisha rose at the first hint of sunlight to milk the family's nine female goats. Their tent stood on the far edge of a cluster of tents, north of Timbuktu. A rippled dune rose not far behind them, and on the other side of that the Sahara Desert stretched toward Algeria for more than a thousand hot, sun-baked miles. The tents stood scattered on the desert floor, some made of twigs and rags, belonging to the poorest Bella people, and others were made of fine woven mats belonging to their past masters, the Tuareg.

Ayisha and Ahmed were proud of being Bella, although many other Bella weren't. The Bella had been slaves of the Tuareg for generations, until slavery was outlawed in 1976. Ayisha knew her ancestors were the workforce of the Tuareg life—her women ancestors did all the housework and cooking. Her grandfathers and their grandfathers herded the cattle, fought in wars as foot soldiers, worked in the salt mines of Taoudenni and worked on the salt caravans. All for the Tuareg.

She loved the fact that the Bellas' knowledge of the desert, and how to survive in it, made life after slavery easier for many of them than for their Tuareg masters. "Don't you see, Abdoulaye, we were used to working hard and knew how to do so many things, including growing millet," she had told her little brother one day as she worked with her mother in the family's small millet patch. She was also proud of their father, a successful blacksmith.

Ayisha's family fell in between the extremes of rich and poor. Their tent was almost spacious, its ceiling made of woven mats over where the family slept. A series of cloths draped over the thick, straight branches lashed together made a frame for the cloths and mats. Everything could be taken down and packed if the need to move ever arose. Ayisha hoped that day would never come, for she wanted to stay in school more than anything else in her Bella world. At least until I met those *toubabs* yesterday, she thought.

Behind their tent, before the sand dune rose, they kept their goats in a pen made of dried, thorny branches. Entering the pen where the mother goats spent the night, Ayisha announced, "We need to lead these people into a net like a spider catches its food. They won't know a thing about it until they are snared!" She plopped down on a very short stool, placing a long gourd between her knees. Expertly she reached out for the nearest goat, tugging in the age-old rhythm of milking—yank, yank, yank, yank.

The long gourd held between her knees caught the squirting milk. Her rose cotton dress hugged her body that still looked too much like her brother's. "Yes, like the insects they are, we shall catch them."

Ahmed had to stifle a giggle at his sister's enthusiasm. "You are full of harsh words on a morning that is only just arriving. But I like them. Do you have any idea yet about what we should do, oh Mighty Plan Maker?"

Ayisha stopped milking to tug on her bangs. "Not really," she said slowly, thinking before each word. "Well, one. I think we need to catch them when they are actually buying the manuscripts."

"That may be much easier to say than to do," Ahmed said as he looked south over his shoulder toward the sand city, Timbuktu.

"So go talk to the Alhaji, quickly, and see if he has any ideas. He's a man of great wisdom."

"And Auntie B?"

"Next. But remember, we won't give up until we have caught them."

Ahmed leapt to his feet, nearly knocking over the gourd bowl he had been filling with milk. "You finish milking and I will visit the Alhaji."

Pouring the milk she had collected into Ahmed's bowl, she said, "I am happy to finish and take the milk back, but come see me before you go on to Bouctou Hotel. I may have a serious plan myself by then." As an afterthought she added, "And don't tell Sidi about the pact we made while collecting dung yesterday afternoon. It's just you and me, do you promise?"

Ahmed shifted the bowl of milk on the ground until it was better balanced. As he walked toward the break in the spiny branches of the goat pen, he said, "Another head might be good. And I trust Sidi."

Ayisha didn't say a word. She just shook her head from side to side in an emphatic NO! while she wiggled the first finger on her right hand back and forth, the universal "no" signal.

"*Cuez*," he said. Fine. "It's just us two and the Alhaji and maybe Auntie B if we can find her. But I need to tell you I won't ask the Alhaji to take the oath we made yesterday." With a wave over his shoulder he ran off. Ayisha bent to the job at hand as mother goats with full udders bleated their impatience. Their babies, kept at a distance until the milking was done, bleated back to their mothers, hunger clear in their voices.

"How's a member of Les Gendarmes Invisibles supposed to think with all this noise?" She pulled a little too hard on the goat she was milking, and it kicked at her with one of its back legs. She slowed down on her tugging.

Ayisha yanked with a smooth, fluid motion, her thoughts wandering as the sun fully arrived over the dunes. She knew, with each pull on the whiskery goat, that Auntie B really was the one to talk to. They hadn't seen her for some time, already a year. She lived with the Tuareg because she hated being in the city. Also, she had a lot of business with the nomads of the region, for she was by far the best henna painter around.

Ayisha stopped milking, straightening up to stretch her back. She patted the goat's haunch and told her, "Henna painters hold a special place in our desert world. They can turn the plainest of hands and feet into intricate swirls and designs." Bending over again to continue milking, she thought about Auntie B. Ayisha knew that her auntie was the best henna painter of all. She made her own detailed designs. Plus, wasn't it true that people traveled days by camel and donkey to see Auntie B? Grabbing the goat's teats once again, she said aloud, "Sometimes they even send for her, to do decorations. Only the best are sent for!"

Ayisha closed her eyes tightly as she pulled, yank, yank, yank, yank on the wiggling goat. She could see Auntie B in her mind's eye, standing out in every crowd in her gowns of flamboyant red or orange or green, with a laugh that captured all who heard it. A smile covered Ayisha's face until another thought forced its way in. There was something sad about her too. Maybe it was because she wasn't married. In fact, she was the only unmarried woman her age that Ayisha knew.

When Ayisha no longer saw streams of milk going into the gourd, she switched to another goat. The first mother ran off to join her baby, which was tied to a stick in the wall. With a faraway look in her eye Ayisha started to milk another mother, brown and white except for the black ears that draped down her head.

"Auntie B will know what to do, but she lives far from here," she told the new goat. Once again the goat she was milking kicked at her just like the other had. Letting go of a teat, she patted the goat's side and said, "Sorry, mother.

But it is hard being a milker and a *gendarme* at the same time."

She quickly finished that goat and moved on to another. Auntie B filled her mind as her hands worked efficiently. Closing her eyes again, she could clearly see her—a short, stout woman who could walk as long and as steadily as any camel. Ayisha imagined Auntie's face, a deep brown, with her head always covered in an expertly wrapped head tie that matched whatever colors were in her flowing gown. She stood out in her Tuareg camp, for the others wore the traditional indigo blue of the Tuareg or the black of the Bella and Tuareg. She's like a giant butterfly I saw in a book at school, Ayisha thought.

On Auntie B's last visit, beautiful dark swirls of henna had produced a detailed flower on each of her palms. Five thick gold bracelets rode up her right arm, toward her elbow. Her right hand wore three gold rings and her left, two. Those hands were forever flying wildly as she moved around the camp on the edge of Timbuktu, laughing and bossing everyone in sight.

Ayisha loved her auntie's eyes. They glowed with a twinkle that usually meant she had some wild idea forming. Ayisha was certain that Auntie B was a direct descendant of Buktu, the woman of their tales who was left to guard a *tim*—the word for "well" in the Tuareg language of Tamashek. She believed with all her heart the legend that claimed Buktu was the founder of Timbuktu eleven centuries ago. "She just never got the credit she deserved for protecting the *tim*," she complained to the goat. "Auntie B would have stayed at the well, like a mother lion protecting her cubs, with the same determination and boldness as Buktu." Ayisha was inspired by her auntie, for she was a woman who always loved a challenge. She even stood up to Ayisha's mother, both strong-willed women. Ayisha knew without a doubt that Auntie B would gladly join in making a plan to catch the *toubabs*. If only they could tell her.

She pulled the last goat waiting to be milked in front of her. A look of concentration wrinkled her forehead as she forced her mind to stay on the job of milking instead of daydreaming. A gentle slap on the rump of the goat sent it off to her tethered baby. Finished, finally.

With great care Ayisha carried the two containers of milk back to the tent, the bowl gourd balanced perfectly on her head. Her father was out in front, fanning a small fire upon which a tiny green teapot stood in a wire basket that held white-hot coals. He glanced up at his daughter and said with surprise, "You have been busy very early, my favorite daughter. What is the occasion?"

Ayisha just smiled at her father, always happy to hear his special name for her. It didn't matter that she was his only daughter. Returning his greeting with her special name for him, she said, "*Sabah el khair,* my favorite father." Good morning. With a very smooth motion she bent her knees to set the bowl down beside him. "The goats' milk grows less each day." It was the season.

She was surprised when he didn't respond with the usual greeting, instead asking testily, "Where is your brother? I have called for him, but until now I have not seen him."

"Didn't he tell you, Father? He is working with some *toubabs*, and they want to start early before the sun gets too high."

Just then Ayisha's mother came out of the door, her youngest son, Abdoulaye, riding on her hip. She too looked surprised to see the milking finished, looking first at the brimming long gourd in her daughter's hand and then at the nearly full bowl on the ground. "Good morning," her mother said, cocking her head to one side and eyeing the milk and then Ayisha. "How is it that my daughter's work is already finished when the sun's slant is so slight it spills no real shadow yet?"

Annoyed at their surprise, Ayisha pursed her lips into a thin line. She sucked her teeth loudly, then said, "But Mother and Father, I do it every day. Why are you both so surprised?"

Her father's voice filled the air. "Let's just say, Little Miss Too Busy, that you milking and your brother leaving before the sun's bottom has left the horizon deserves some consideration. You are both good workers, but such an early start makes me wonder what other plans you have for the day."

"Your father is right. What is the hurry?" Mother held up a hand and said, "Don't mistake my words—I like finding the milk waiting for me when I leave the tent to begin the day. But even you must admit it is not your normal style. What is going on?"

Both parents studied their daughter's face, waiting for an answer.

Ayisha said, "Please, let me pour some of this off and then set down the gourd." She entered the tent and took out a large gourd that was tucked beneath a short bench standing against one wall. Calling out to her parents as she worked, she said, "I can tell you nothing is going on." Carefully she poured the milk from her gourd into the slightly uneven bowl that tilted to the right. "Nothing at all."

Her mother was still talking, loud enough for her daughter's ears inside the tent. "The last time she said nothing was happening, she and her brother and your crazy sister B got into big trouble."

"That's right," her father said. He leaned forward and blew on the coals beneath the teapot. Little spurts of tea bubbled out the spout as the coals flared in a burst of white heat. Tilting his head toward the tent, he said, "Fortunately Auntie B is not here, or I would be more worried."

Ayisha popped out of the doorway. "When is Auntie B coming again? Have you heard something?" Ayisha squirmed as she remembered the last time Auntie B had visited. Auntie B had hennaed Ahmed's hands, and Ahmed and Ayisha had switched clothes—his long white shirt, torn pants and green and yellow prayer cap for Ayisha's rose-colored dress and head scarf. It was all my fault we were caught, she thought, for she had stood outside the mosque, where girls are not allowed inside, contemplating trying to enter through the men's door. Alhaji Musa had stopped her with a slow shake of his head, left to right, but that was not the end of it. That night, as the family sat around their food tray, Alhaji Musa had arrived and reported the incident to her parents. Mother had lashed out at Auntie B, shaming her for leading her children astray. Auntie B left with the Tuareg shortly thereafter, yet to return.

Her father, Ibrahim, shook his head. "We have no idea when your aunt will return. As you recall, she didn't leave under the best of circumstances. But it has been a very long time since she's visited, so maybe soon." Then raising his finger toward his daughter's face, he said, "But don't change the subject. What has you and your missing brother as busy as termites in a hill as the day begins?"

Ayisha lifted her shoulders in total innocence. *"Rien!"* Nothing! "I promise you. It's just that it is so hot for almost the entire day and night, we thought to take advantage of the cool, just like the *toubab* woman suggested. We are being smart. Just look at all the dung we—I mean, I—collected yesterday."

"We as in you and your twin?" asked her amazed mother. Miriam turned to her husband and said, "Now I am really worried. Her brother is helping collect dung and I didn't insist!" Nodding, she said, "Something definitely must be up."

"He felt sorry for me, it was so hot. So he helped me."

"Cuez," said her father, just like Ahmed had yesterday when they were making their pledge.

"Just make sure that all this new organization doesn't lead to some new foolishness. We haven't forgotten about you two trying to turn the family into a tourist attraction. Hardly a pleasant memory. You even hung signs near the main market, offering to take tourists to visit the family for only . . . how much was it? What were we worth, Ayisha?"

Ayisha dropped her head. That was one of her plans that had definitely not been well received by her parents. She remembered how her mother's arm froze in the air, the long pestle dangling, her mouth wide open, as she watched her son suddenly arrive with a group of *toubabs*.

As if leading them through the dusty streets of Timbuktu, Ahmed had said, "This is my mother, pounding millet for our dinner." But when Ahmed had stuck his head inside their tent to ask permission to bring the *toubabs* in, he saw his father holding one of their signs.

Without a word he backed out the door. "So sorry," Ahmed said in Italian to the *toubabs*, "but now is not a good time."

Ibrahim had followed him out of the tent, bending slightly to avoid hitting his head. He glared at his son and then said to the visitors in French, "I am sorry, but we do not do this." He ripped the poster into several pieces, and Ahmed and Ayisha had both shivered.

The Italians did not wait around to see what would happen next. They scurried away, offering apologies over their shoulders.

Snapping Ayisha back to the present, her father said, "I am waiting. How much were we worth?"

Ayisha whispered, "Fifteen thousand CFA a visit."

Ibrahim turned to his wife and said, "Remember that, Miriam? We are only worth twenty-five dollars to our children. And we also had the honor of losing our dignity at the same time by acting 'normal' for the tourists." Father clapped his hands. "What a great day that was!"

Ayisha wiped her sweaty palms on her dress and said, "I am so sorry, Father and Mother. And I promise you the next time Ahmed and I do something together, it will make you proud. I must admit that foolish idea was mine. Since you won't let me work with the *toubabs* like Ahmed does, Father . . . I thought it would be a good way for me to meet some." She bit her tongue before blurting out, "This time it's different. This time we're planning something really serious."

"And why do you need to meet some *toubabs*?" her mother asked. "Look what you did to your hair just looking at them from a distance." Her mother huffed as she looked off in the distance at a string of camels being led across the top of the nearest sand dune.

It took all of Ayisha's self-control not to yank on the bangs she had cut across her forehead. She had cut her hair on a whim, whacking it off with the knife used for cooking after seeing a tourist with bangs on her way home from school. Ayisha remembered her mother's angry face when she saw what her daughter had done to her beautiful long black hair.

Her classmates had gawked and laughed for the longest time, so Ayisha began wearing a scarf tied low across her forehead, until last month when the day's heat grew too great. It was when she took off the scarf that she started really tugging on the hair, trying to make it grow, for she knew she looked funny with her face framed by *toubab* bangs. At the sound of her mother clearing her throat, Ayisha snapped back to the conversation. "Honestly, Mother, it's only curiosity that makes me want to meet some *toubabs*. The stories Ahmed shares with me just make me want to hear all the accents and the questions, some too dumb to believe, and I want to ask them about their homes. Where do they come from? What do they eat? Why did they come here?"

The conversation stopped, much to Ayisha's delight, when Ahmed came running up. Sweaty already, his hair matted to his head, he skidded to a stop as his father grabbed him, preventing a crash into his mother and baby brother.

"Hurry seems to be the order of the day." Glaring at his son, he said, "Your sister has just convinced us that you two are not up to any schemes, just trying to avoid getting hot, but look at you. You look like a shepherd after an afternoon out in the sun's hottest hours, and it's only just risen."

"I just forgot something," Ahmed said, glancing toward his sister. "I went to see Alhaji Musa quickly . . . and then . . . and then I wanted to come back and get my writing board for classes this afternoon so I won't have to walk back in the heat of the day to get it."

Ayisha dropped her head and smiled with admiration. What a quick answer. She turned and went into the tent, saying, "I'll get it for you. Then I'll walk with you on my way to the well." Ayisha smiled inside the tent. Ahmed had something to tell her. She could see that.

Ahmed grabbed Abdoulaye's foot, hanging at his mother's side. "Hello, little brother." Abdoulaye was nearly three and still very much the baby of the family. He reached out his arms for Ahmed to take him, which he did. Putting him down on the ground, Ahmed said, "You're getting too big for Mother's hips."

Abdoulaye looked to his mother, worried. She shook her head, saying, "I will decide that."

Ayisha came out of the tent, the wooden writing tablet in her right hand and two water bags in her left. The large one was made from a camel's udder, and the small one, a goatskin. She handed her brother his board and said, "I'll be back soon," to her parents.

"This conversation isn't finished," her father called out.

"And remember—no schemes!" added their mother.

They tried not to run out of the compound, for already they were clearly under suspicion.

When they reached the open space between town and their tent, Ayisha grabbed his arm and asked, "Is it good news?"

"Yes, very good news. First Alhaji Musa asked me how I knew this. And was I certain, for it is a serious thing to suspect someone of this crime." Ahmed lifted his hands up, palms open. "I told him everything, including about my stupid bragging about the manuscripts. He assured me, just like you did, that their intentions are not my fault. He said I might be right, they might have actually come for this reason."

Ayisha could see the relief that swept across her brother's face when he said this. She was glad Alhaji Musa had told Ahmed this, for she knew he had blamed himself for bragging too much about the manuscripts.

Smiling, Ahmed continued, "I told him how the *toubabs* speak English in front of me, and he nodded. Then he put his hand on my shoulder and said, 'You must be my eyes and ears. When you and your sister, who we know is always thinking up things to do, have a plan, come to me again.'" Ahmed wiped the sweat on his forehead just before it hit his eyes. "He said we must not waste any time. He is also thinking of a good way to catch these two."

As if saving the best for last, Ahmed stared into her eyes. "When I was leaving, he grabbed my arm and said, 'I like your sister's idea of setting an example by sending them to prison.' In fact, he said he knew you were smart from your test scores, but that this is a different kind of smart. A very important kind."

Ayisha's eyes lit up. "Maybe if we catch them, it will make Alhaji Musa forgive me for that stupid trick I tried to play on the world."

Ahmed winced at the memory. "It wasn't that we tried to trick the world, it was that you tried to trick Allah when you got the bright idea to switch clothes and try to enter the mosque."

"I know, I know," she said quickly. "Maybe I can earn his forgiveness if we can save some manuscripts." Clapping her hands she asked, "Alhaji Musa really said I am smart?"

Ayisha could not hide her pleasure. Her eyes sparked like hot coals for making tea. Her dimple showed when her twin said, "But I have saved the best for last. He wants you to come with me when we have a plan to discuss, so we three can figure out the best way to deal with it all."

Looking across the sandy plain toward the sun that was on its burning trip westward, he said, "I saw the *toubabs* on the terrace when I ran past. I told them I would be right back, and she yelled out to me, 'Good. The sooner the better. I'm getting hot already.'"

Tilting his head, he asked, "Are you going to join us?"

Ayisha shook her head. "Mother and Father are already wondering what is going on with us. Or me, I should say. I will save it for today and ask them tonight about going with you tomorrow." As an afterthought she added, "Who in their right mind would come to Timbuktu in the hot season if they hate heat?"

"Maybe just someone who has something on their minds beside the weather." With that he turned to leave his sister for the day.

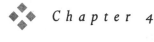 *Chapter 4*

AYISHA STAYED IN HER mother's sight most of the day, to show that nothing unusual was going on. The heat beat down on her back as she swept the family's compound with a broom made of twigs. But her mother knew something was on her daughter's mind when she had to ask the same question three times before receiving an answer.

With her hands on her hips, her mother blurted out, "I said, twice, would you like to spend the afternoon with me at the newest Tuareg camp?"

Mother cocked her head to one side. "Thanks to you and all the talk of Auntie B, your father wants news, if there is any. Many of her friends are at that camp. And I would like to see my old friend Fati. If anyone has news of Auntie B, it will be her."

Ayisha looked across the wide plain that stood empty except for a few scrubby bushes dotting the landscape.

The sun was well past its high point on its drop toward the western horizon. With her back to Timbuktu, she shaded her eyes to look east. In the distance—perhaps a kilometer away—she could just see the rounded tents of the Tuareg, and when the wind was just right, hear the faint *thunk thunk* as the women pounded millet with mortar and pestle. Camels resting looked like dusty brown boulders on the horizon.

Sitting the farthest east of all the tented camps set up on the outskirts of Timbuktu, it was a place Ayisha had yearned to visit. The camp had arrived in the coolness of the full moon, two moons ago, suddenly appearing on the horizon one morning. Ayisha'd asked her not a week after about visiting, and Miriam had snapped back at her, "We'll go when the *soudure*, the unbearable hot season, ends." Now Ayisha couldn't believe that her mother suddenly wanted to go, for if anything the weather was even more scorching than the week before. The heat grew each day, drying the old millet stalks that still stood in the fields.

Fearful her mother would change her mind about going, Ayisha said quickly, "Yes, yes, yes. Shall I get the donkey for you, Mother?"

"No, we'll walk. It should only take thirty minutes at the most." Putting Abdoulaye on her right hip, she looked at her daughter and said, "And we'll talk."

Ayisha tried to ignore the worrisome feeling "we'll talk" gave her. Instead she thought of the opportunity to learn about Auntie B, especially exactly where her camp was.

Eager to get going, she reached out her arms to her little brother. "Come, Little Camel. I will carry you."

Her mother hung on tightly to her son. "I don't like that name," she said. "I have told you that before."

"*Malesh*, Mother." Sorry. Still holding out her arms, she said, "Come, Abdoulaye, I'll carry you."

Hitching her baby up on her hip, Miriam said, "You can have him when I tire." Pointing with her chin to a bundle resting next to the tent's door, she told Ayisha, "Pick that up so we have something to offer when we arrive." Mother looked at the sky and the slant of the sun. "We'll go now, so we have time for our talk, for a visit in the camp, and the walk home in the evening light."

Ayisha picked up the cloth that held tea and sugar knotted into it. They left the compound side by side, neither talking. Ayisha was thrilled to be out with her mother and brother, even if her mother had something she wanted to talk to her about. "Just don't let it be school," she said under her breath as she glanced at her mother.

Miriam wore a black gown adorned by a large silver Tuareg cross dangling from her neck. Auntie B had given it to her some years ago, and it was her finest piece of jewelry. Everyone wore Tuareg silver if they could afford it, for the crosses and bracelets they made were beautiful. Miriam's cross had three triangles off of a circle with the center cut out. This sat atop a three-pointed piece with thick bulbs at the end of each point. It had the finest of lines etched into the face of it, making a geometric design that was pleasing to the eye. The faintest trace of henna still clung to Miriam's palms. Awa, her closest friend, had painted her hands with a spiderweb design, more than a month ago, for a wedding. Ayisha listened to her mother's leather sandals slap her heels as she walked.

The sand held the day's heat, almost burning their feet when they sank in up to their ankles. Fortunately there were many patches of hard, dried ground to walk on, scored with cracks like wrinkles on an old herder's face. Apart from the *slap slap* of sandal on skin, silence that felt as heavy as the heat filled the air. Ayisha threw another quick sideways glance at her mother's face, then just as quickly looked away. I know that look—she's choosing each word very carefully. Maybe it's time for the "we'll talk," she thought.

Clearing her throat, her mother said, "Daughter mine, please tell me what is going on. I see that look in your eye of fierce concentration, and a mind that wanders like a cloud drifting over."

Ayisha wanted to tell her mother about the *toubabs*, but knew that if she did, she and her twin would be forbidden to continue. She searched her thoughts for an answer, something that wouldn't be a total lie. "You know how I love to study. I am helping Ahmed study his Koranic verses, and so the verses are running through my head too." This was true, for she had quizzed Ahmed for days before he was rewarded with the prayer cloth. "You saw his shawl, Mother, that came from us working together as one."

Miriam had to smile, for once again she had a reason to be proud and brag about her children's accomplishments.

"Actually, that brings me to the two things I wanted to talk to you about." Ayisha's shoulders dropped, for clearly the talk was not done.

Miriam stopped on a stretch of hard-packed earth, the heat from the ground rising through her thin sandals, warming the soles of her feet. She reached out and took her daughter's arm slick with sweat. Looking deep into Ayisha's eyes, she said, "Listen. Listen very well."

Ayisha's eyes opened wide. Her mother's stern voice meant only one thing—bad news.

"I have agreed to you going to the *lycée* when the next school year begins, but we need to talk about some important things first. You are a young woman now, and all your male classmates are young men. Young men and young women studying together are different from boys and girls. I know there will be other young women with you, but I need to be sure that you can be trusted to be with the male students all day."

Ayisha let a big sigh of relief escape her lips. "Oh Mother, have no worries about that. *Mafi mushkila!*" No problem! "Going to school is what I want more than anything else on Allah's earth." She thought, Until yesterday it was all I wanted. She continued, "Boys or young men are the very last thing on my mind.

"In fact, they are not even on my mind. I think about healthy camels more, and we both know there is no reason for me to give them a thought."

She wiped her forehead where a film of sweat wet her bangs. They hung down like little daggers, groups of damp hair clinging together and ending in points. Her mother wiped her face too, the sun still strong even as it angled toward the horizon.

Miriam snorted as Abdoulaye reached out for his sister. She handed the little boy, who repeated again and again, "Isha, Isha," into his sister's outstretched arms.

Mother shook her finger in Ayisha's face. "It's what you are up to now that really worries me. I know you well, my daughter. I know when there is something big on your mind. So just know that if you disappoint me with any, and I mean any, crazy schemes, the school door will slam closed to you before you get near it."

Ayisha shifted her brother on her hip, worry lines wrinkling her forehead. She knew that to stop the *toubabs* there had to be some risk—especially the risk of upsetting their parents. Oh Mother, she thought, you could not have laid down a more frightening punishment. Ayisha looked out to the horizon and promised herself that in the end, helping Ahmed catch the *toubabs* and protect the manuscripts would save her from this terrible and ultimate punishment—no *lycée*.

Turning to face her mother, she said, "Mother, I only want to make you proud of me." And that was the truth.

Miriam looked right back at her. Shifting the black cloth that covered her head, she said, "Now, that would make me very happy. But remember"—her mother tilted Ayisha's head back until they really were eye to eye—"If you fail me, you will be exactly where all your girlfriends are, looking at marriage instead of school."

She looked over her daughter's shoulders at a group of kids running from the camp to greet them. Dust flew up from their feet, rising in the air like their excited voices calling, *"Mantole!"* Welcome!

Miriam placed a hand on each of Ayisha's shoulders. "This is the last time we'll talk of this. Don't disappoint me."

"Please don't worry, Mother."

Sliding her hands down to her daughter's wrists, she replied, *"Inshallah!"* Then they continued toward the camp, walking hand in hand.

Ayisha felt ill. She and Ahmed had taken an oath. He had already spoken with Alhaji Musa. There is no way, she thought, that I can or will give up now on making and completing our plan to catch the *toubabs*. She shuddered, thinking of switching clothes with Ahmed, and of the time they had tried to sell the family as a tourist attraction. Both her parents were angry for months. If whatever they did this time went wrong, not going to school was a huge price to pay. Ahmed would probably say it wasn't worth it. But thinking it through right now was not possible, for the whole Tuareg camp lay before them.

❖❖❖ *C h a p t e r 5*

I T WAS A PEACEFUL PLACE. Three tents with walls as high as a woman's waist made from dried millet stalks woven together were covered by large stretched goat-skins sewn together. The most beautiful tent stood to the far west, on the outskirts of the camp. It had finely woven wall mats and a roof made from tightly woven mats with black stripes. A door made from millet stalks lashed to a series of horizontal sticks shut the tent off from the dust blowing from the camp.

Five of the Tuareg women in rich indigo gowns and light blue head ties pounded millet. They laughed and joked with one another as they worked. Groups of men sat around small coal pots, watching the official tea men prepare their favorite drink. They each wore a colored robe with a match-ing turban. All eyes turned toward the visitors.

Fati, supervising her granddaughters' efforts over a mortar and pestle, called out when she spotted them. An old woman, she had wisps of gray hair surrounding her face, poking out from under the black cloth hung loosely over her head. She rushed over to Miriam and Ayisha with surprising speed. *"Mantole,"* she called out in Tamashek, the language of the Tuareg. Welcome. "Visitors at last! Welcome, Miriam. *Isalan?"* What is your news? The old lady held out her hands covered by thick calluses and painted with a fading henna design. Miriam took them, enfolding the old woman into a hug.

"Nan-i," replied Miriam in good Tamashek. I have lots of news. "We are well, and I hope all of you and yours are too."

"Al Humdullah, all are well," said Fati.

Ayisha stepped forward, eager to forget about the sudden heavy burden hanging on her shoulders. "Good afternoon, Grandmother," she said in perfect Tamashek. The old woman, no relation but thankful for the name of respect, said, "Your Tamashek sounds good, Granddaughter. Welcome to our camp. What happened to your hair?" She reached out her arms for Abdoulaye, but he held back, his face pressed into the sweaty place where Ayisha's neck met her face.

It wasn't long before a group of women and kids formed around them. Looking at the glistening sweat on their faces, Fati suddenly said, "Come. Sit and have tea and tell us what brings you here. It must be very important to bring you out on a day with heat that hangs in the air. How is my old friend Auntie B? Still bossy as ever and as busy as a goatherd in a stampede?"

"That's the right Auntie B," quipped Miriam. "We

haven't seen her in more than thirteen moon cycles. We were hoping you might have news of her."

Together they all walked over to the nearest tent. The walls were about four feet high, made of tightly woven mats propped up between giant wooden pegs. A large leather covering of animal skins sewn together was draped over the top of the structure, creating a dark shadow of shade that beckoned.

Miriam sat with her legs crossed, her gown stretched tightly across her lap. She took Abdoulaye from his sister's arms and placed him next to her. He was watching a group of boys not much older than he. His mother was surprised and happy when he rose to his feet and wandered over to them. They all turned and headed out into the bright sunlight.

"Keep an eye on your brother," Miriam told Ayisha as she received a cup of water.

Ayisha gazed out into the sunlight at her brother and his new friends. "Has he ever just walked away like that before?" she asked her mother.

"Never!" With a shake of her head and her eyes rolled heavenward, her mother said, "Please, Allah, don't give me another child to worry about!" Ayisha knew her mother was embarrassed when she looked down again and saw everyone watching her.

"Have you troubles, Miriam?" asked Fati.

"No, no problems! In fact, I have only good news about my children." Ayisha watched as her mother's eyes shone even in the darkened shelter of the tent. Ayisha knew she was gearing up to brag about Ahmed and her.

Miriam pointed at Ayisha and said, "This one has just set a record for the best test scores in her school's history."

Ayisha could see her mother's disappointment when no *oohs* or *aahs* filled the air.

"She goes to school?" someone in the group whispered.

Miriam and Ayisha looked quickly at each other, realizing just how strange it must sound, for these people had rejected the ways of the government—including school—and all sedentary life until very recently. It was a fleeting feeling, but Ayisha felt like a *toubab* must feel when they don't understand something about the talk around them.

The shocked silence lingered until Miriam continued, "Yes, she goes to school."

"But when will she marry? Soon, I hope," added another woman about Miriam's age. Miriam grunted slightly. Clearly this conversation was not going at all as she had expected.

Eager to change the subject quickly, she said, "And her brother, her twin not an hour younger, has been declared a young scholar by Alhaji Musa! He even received a beautiful prayer shawl from him."

Ayisha was glad for the change of subject too, for she didn't need to be reminded of the conversation they had just had. "Mother is right," she added. "And he is not only a scholar but also a *futbol* star. Who speaks many languages."

"But tell us, what is your news? Are you planning to stay here?" Miriam interrupted. "It seems that many Tuareg are settling down these days." Ayisha knew that two major pressures were forcing the Tuareg to face the reality that a nomad's lifestyle was no longer possible. Reluctantly, more Tuaregs were setting up permanent camps. Two full moons ago no one had lived in this very spot, she thought.

Mother Nature was one pressure. Every year the desert seemed to grow, providing less grazing for their herds. The government was the second pressure, trying its best to make the Tuareg settle so they could tax and control them, and so their children could go to school.

With a sudden flush of embarrassment Miriam said, "Oh, but forgive me. I have brought a small *cadeau* for you, sugar and tea." Leaning forward, she placed the bundled gift next to Fati.

With that another woman clapped her hands and two girls came running. "Where are your manners?" she asked them. "How can these visitors have been here long enough to discuss trouble and no trouble and school and scholars and still not been served tea?"

The oldest girl dropped her head and said, "Sorry, Mother, but it's not ready yet." Just then they looked toward the left where a man approached with a small tray holding four short glasses brimming with dark brown tea. A girl ran to him, thanking him as she took the tray. He passed her the tray but continued to walk toward the group.

He squatted when he reached them, just in the entrance of the tent. His hands dangled from his outstretched arms resting on his knees. Fati nodded, saying, "Welcome, Baba Ali. Please join us."

He took one of the small glasses of tea he had just

brought, sipped it noisily, then looked at Miriam and said, "What is the news of Timbuktu?"

It struck Ayisha that he asked about the city as if they had walked days instead of less time than it takes to milk a herd of goats. The tallest of Timbuktu's minarets and its big water tank were visible from the camp, but she was sure that in his mind he still lived far from the bustling city.

The grandmother didn't hesitate to answer, pointing at Ayisha and saying, "The news is that this one goes to school!"

Ayisha couldn't help herself. She blurted out, "That's not the news. The news is that last month I scored ninety-eight percent on the year-end test, the best in the history of the school, and now I am going to the *lycée*!"

She could have kicked herself, for if eyebrows were raised before, now they were rubbing against the roof of the tent! This group might have settled in a more-permanent camp, but school was still far from their minds, she thought. Tugging on her braids, she knew that a girl in school was even further from their minds.

Looking at Miriam, a woman draped in black asked, "But why would she continue to go to school? Hasn't her bleeding started?" She flipped the top of the cloth that hung over her head, clearly a sign of impatience.

"Yes," said the woman who had spoken before. "What about marriage?"

"She shall be married," said Miriam, trying to placate the growing curiosity and consternation of the group. All eyes were on Miriam as she spoke with what sounded like less confidence to Ayisha. "If someone excels as she did, she should have the right to continue. But only if she can prove she is responsible and trustworthy."

The old woman snorted and prepared to say something when Baba Ali asked, "How are the herds? And the *toubabs*? Are there many? Would it be worth a trip into town to sell some jewelry?"

Ayisha couldn't believe her bad luck. The two topics closest to her heart at the moment were all people wanted to talk about—school and *toubabs*. She really regretted spouting off about going to *lycée* because once the topic of *toubabs* came up, she shivered in the heat, knowing there was a good chance she wouldn't be allowed to go to school. But I can't give up Les Gendarmes Invisibles. I can't.

Miriam glanced at her daughter's distressed face and said, "There are *toubabs*. There are always *toubabs*, even when the heat punishes us like it does these long, hot days. My son, the scholar, works with *toubabs*."

Ayisha suddenly said, "I can take your jewelry to my brother, and he can sell it for you so you don't have to make a trip in this dust and heat. Just tell me what your price is—your *toubab* price, I mean—and I'll tell him." She rolled side to side on her rear end.

The man looked at her for the first time. He stood up, towering over all the sitting women. "That is not a bad idea. No wonder you scored so well in this crazy school business. But is your brother strong enough to hold out for the amount I want? Some of those *toubabs* bray about the price like a donkey with a too-heavy load."

51

Sitting tall, Ayisha looked right into Baba Ali's eyes and said, "Don't worry. He won't sell them for a CFA less than what you want."

Miriam's eyes popped wide when her daughter continued, "And what is there for him for his saving you a trip?"

Everyone laughed in sudden little gasps at the nerve of the young Bella girl.

The grandmother, Fati, said, "There is no doubt you are related to Auntie B!"

Once again everyone laughed and the man said, "I will discuss that with your brother when he brings me the money from his first sale." Shaking his head in wonder at Ayisha's boldness, he said, "I hope I don't regret this. But if you and your brother can save me from the bother and unpleasantness of entering the city that never rests, then it will certainly be worth it, whatever the price." Bouncing the red and green leather bag that dangled from his neck on his hand, he said, "It will make me happy to avoid the dust and heat and noise."

Miriam eyed her daughter with a new glimmer of respect as she watched her instantly become a businesswoman. Every tribe, Tuareg, Bella, Hausa, Fulani, knew that every extra CFA anyone could make would be welcome into a family, for day-to-day life was a challenge for all. Miriam gazed at her daughter with pride until Fati clapped her hands and hooted out, "Yes, she's her auntie's niece, all right."

"And her mother's daughter," added Miriam. She leaned forward and gave Ayisha an affectionate pat on the knee, surprising the girl.

As the man turned to go, he said, "I will ask if anyone else wants to send something with you. But how shall you remember what piece belongs to what man and how much each one is? Perhaps I shall send you with only my two necklaces."

"Does anyone have a Bic and paper?" Ayisha asked. All those who could read and write always asked for a Bic, the name given to all pens.

"I'll ask," he said as he left, slowly shaking his head as if wondering if the exchange had really just happened.

They all watched him walk away, his long gown swinging side to side as he strolled over to the group of men drinking tea beneath the largest tree around. Miriam cleared her throat and said, "And so, sister Fati, have you or anyone else news of Auntie B or the Tuareg she travels with?"

"Only old news," said a young woman who was nursing an infant. She shifted the baby, wearing a slim white beaded band around its waist, from her right breast to her left one. "Auntie B's group has settled in the shadow of a giant sand dune, two days' walk from Timbuktu, toward the distant salt mines."

Ayisha wondered if that meant two days and two nights, or one day and night. Trying to be very casual so her mother wouldn't wonder at her curiosity, she asked, "How far is this giant dune?"

Ignoring Ayisha's question, the young woman told Miriam, "They know they will stay there, but we don't know if this is the place for us yet." With her free hand she waved at the landscape they could see through the tent's door.

She made a soft spitting sound as she said, "Tuareg settled . . . Yes, these are very strange times."

Ayisha could feel the woman's disgust. She couldn't think of one Tuareg or Bella used to following their herds who was happy about settling in one place. She thought about the old Bella man settled near their tent. He's as old as the sand, Ayisha had thought the first time she saw him. The skin around his eyes was covered with deep wrinkles, and his hands were covered with scars from hacking salt in the mines far to the north.

The first time she greeted him, his sadness wrapped around them both. He had looked to the north, then back at the ragged collection of cloth and skins draped over a weak twig frame that served as his tent. "I used to be a man of the desert, traveling up and down with the salt caravans." Dismissing his tent with a wave of his hand, he had said, "Now look what I have become. How, I don't know." He shook his head sadly. "The freedom lost is like a knife cut—sudden and painful."

Shaking off the vivid memory, Ayisha asked the young mother who had described Auntie B's camp, "Is it a difficult walk to Auntie B's group?"

Everyone laughed. Then Fati asked, "Is there an easy journey across Allah's hot sand?"

Miriam looked at her daughter for a moment, then turned to Fati. "Do you know if Auntie B's group plans to travel to town soon? Has anyone visited from their camp recently?"

Fati slapped her thigh with a loud smack. "Actually, yes.

How could I forget another visitor already? A stranger was here some days ago, returning from selling a camel near Gao. He traveled alone and arrived here parched, slipping out of the grasp of a mirage much like the one shimmering out there now in the afternoon heat." She gave a short laugh, saying, "You'd think that visitors arrived daily, but they are more sparse than wells in the desert."

They all turned to look out at the horizon, and Ayisha was relieved to see her little brother still playing *erbiki*, hide-and-seek, with his new friends, among the tents and resting camels. She had completely forgotten about him in the many twists and turns the conversation had taken. Miriam asked as they all looked at the dancing horizon, "And so what news did the traveler have?"

"Just that people were settling in to their new place. The things they liked best are that the city is not in sight, like it is here," Fati said, flipping her wrinkled hand in an impatient gesture at Timbuktu on the wavering hot horizon. "And that there is water from a deep well and the land provides enough for the herds. The wide space is also a good place to play *boules*."

Ayisha looked at her mother, for she knew what she thought of grown men playing *boules*. Her mother snorted, for the group of Tuareg Auntie B lived with were the only ones Miriam had ever seen, hour after hour, playing the game brought by the French. Ayisha thought about how it annoyed her mother that they had adopted the game from the same people who had tried to colonize them. For hours the Tuareg men had stood about, throwing colored balls at a smaller black one when the family visited their temporary camp just outside of Timbuktu more than a year ago. It amazed her mother that they had nothing better to do with their time.

At the mention of *boules* Ayisha remembered her parents fighting on the walk back from that camp. Miriam had asked her husband if the men really did have nothing better to do. Ayisha's father answered rather sharply, "What is the difference between sitting in the shade drinking tea and gossiping like bleating goats and having a bit of fun with friends throwing *boules*? Neither puts food in the mouths of anyone!" Then he added, "Life is not only about work."

Ayisha now watched her mother swallow the sharpness she must have felt at the mention of the game. Smoothing her gown across her lap, Miriam asked, "And so where is the traveler? Has he gone home already?"

"Yes," answered Fati. "He stayed with us just for a day and a night, to let his camel rest and himself as well, before continuing on. He had business in Timbuktu, then wanted to get home for a wedding. The trip from Gao had been harder than he expected. He arrived drenched in sweat and parched with thirst from days in this brutal heat. He was in a hurry, so he traveled by day and by night from Gao to here, cutting his travel time in half."

Ayisha thought of the walk they had just made from the outskirts of Timbuktu to the camp. The heat had punished them with every step. She tugged on her bangs, hoping to hear more about how far the stranger had to go to get back to Auntie B's camp. "So he is gone?" she asked Fati.

Fati cleared her throat loudly and said, "What makes you so curious about the traveler?"

Ayisha looked at her mother, who replied, "We were just wondering how my brother's sister is doing. Too much time has passed since we last saw her, and Ibrahim was hoping she was coming to visit soon."

Nodding, Fati said, "Oh yes, now I remember." She reached out and took Miriam's hand, patting the dry skin. Tilting her head, she said, "Auntie B left under a cloud the last time, didn't she?"

Ayisha could see her mother really didn't want to discuss Auntie B's part in the henna-painting, clothes-switching trick of more than a year ago. Ayisha pointed out into the sunshine and said, "Look, here comes the man with the jewelry. He must have a paper and Bic, for he carries at least four necklaces to sell."

Baba Ali squatted, just as before, in the entrance of the tent. He pulled up the sleeve of his dark blue gown and released a paper and Bic pen tucked beneath a leather band that five little *gris-gris* packets dangled from. He handed the paper and pen to Ayisha with a look of challenge in his eyes.

She took them confidently, placing the paper on her left thigh with the pen poised over it. Not a word was spoken as all watched her.

Holding up a silver cross that swung back and forth on its beaded strands, he said, "This is mine. I would like 7,750

CFA for it, not a centime less." He twisted the necklace back and forth, saying proudly, "Look at this fine cut and detailed design."

He held it high for all to see, then gave it to her. The young Bella girl laid it on her right thigh and ran her finger over the thin black lines etched into the face of the piece. Two thin bands of copper outlined a raised centerpiece decorated with etched triangles, surrounding a raised ball made of silver. Ayisha dangled the necklace by the three strands of tiny black beads, adorned with two silver beads and two black glass beads. The *toubabs* would pay a good price for this, she thought.

Ayisha stretched her arm, holding the Bic out straight. She twisted her wrist in a display that all watched. Pulling her arm back in, she carefully put the pen to paper. Acting like she made lists of jewelry to sell every day of her life, Ayisha wrote a "1" and circled it. She wrote something and the amount of 7,750 CFA, about $15, she knew. All wanted to know what it said, but only her mother was brave enough to ask. Running her finger under the line she had written, Ayisha said, "This says, 'the biggest and brightest cross,' and this is Baba Ali's name." Pointing at the numbers, she said, "And here is the price, 7,750 CFA."

Quick little gasps of wonder came from Fati, and the young mother nursing her baby clapped her hands in delight. It was clear that all were impressed with her skills as they finally oohed and aahed as Miriam had expected they would when they first arrived and she had bragged of her daughter's school success.

Ali was the most impressed with the description of his necklace. Ayisha knew he would be. Men and boys were always worried about being the best, she thought. After repeating, "The biggest and the brightest," Baba Ali held the next necklace up, giving the artist's name and price. He watched Ayisha write. She was sure he was anxious for her not to write more about another necklace than his own.

When she wrote the second description down, ready to move on to the third one, Baba Ali cleared his throat and pointed at the paper. Ayisha smiled to herself as she read out loud, "A thick four-point cross with a setting sun on top. A fine piece, 5,000 CFA. Baba Karim's."

Ayisha took the third piece and nodded. As she wrote, she read aloud, "A simpler piece with few details etched into the round face. Four thousand CFA. Baba Karim's."

Handing her the last necklace, Baba Ali watched her carefully. All heard her as she sucked in a quick breath. She knew it was by far the most beautiful, but she didn't know if it was Baba Ali's. Ayisha held the piece high. She hesitated to write, and Ali asked her, "Is something wrong?"

"No, no. Nothing. It's just that this piece is the best, and so I hope that it is yours."

He threw his head back and laughed. "So what will you write?"

Everyone listened as the pen scratched against the paper. Ayisha knew that she had to write the truth, regardless of who had made the necklace. She wrote with a steady hand, then looked up and read, "By far the best piece. Delicate work with a small triangle resting on a curved piece that holds a lovely silver half circle, etched with the finest of lines and tiny circles."

Without lifting her head, she asked for the price and artist. Great relief swept over her as Ali said, "Ten thousand CFA. Baba Ali." He nodded and said, "Your eye is good, for each necklace has a personality and you have spotted it." Almost as an aside, but clear to everyone, he added, "And you can tell the best from the rest."

He took a rag from the small red and green bag that hung down his chest. Carefully he wrapped the four necklaces into the rag and handed it over to Ayisha. "Go well," he said, looking seriously into her eyes. With a nod, he added, "And if your brother is half as smart as you, he will be here soon with the money and maybe we can become partners."

Ayisha tried to hide her pride, but couldn't. "You will see him before the moon is full," she said.

At the mention of the moon Miriam stood. Bent in half, she placed the tea and sugar they had brought onto the mat, then folded the cloth wrapping. Standing straight, she said to Fati, "We'll go before the moon arrives. There is still plenty of daylight, *Inshallah!*"

She tapped her daughter on the back as she made her way to the entrance. Baba Ali rose to clear the doorway, throwing one more glance at Ayisha. "The grandmother is right: you are your Auntie B's niece." At the sound of Miriam clearing her throat, he added, "And your mother's daughter."

He turned to go, then turned back and said, "What happened to your hair?" Everyone laughed, including Ayisha.

The same kids that had walked them into camp followed them out. Ayisha noticed that they laughed and pushed and shoved one another just like the boys had yesterday as they left the mosque. Was it really only yesterday? She glanced at her mother, who had the slightest of smiles twitching her lips. Miriam caught her look and said, "You do not cease to surprise me!"

"But it was not a bad thing to do, was it?" asked Ayisha anxiously.

"Not at all. Not at all," replied her mother.

Ayisha grinned from ear to ear until her mother said, "It was good and bad. Good because your brother stands a chance to make some extra money, *Al Humdullah*!" Bending to pick Abdoulaye up and fitting him onto her hip, she continued, "But bad, because it shows me that there is no knowing what schemes will pop out of that head of yours."

The mention of schemes brought Ayisha crashing right back to earth. She knew that coming up with a plan for the Les Gendarmes Invisibles would have to be the most clever one ever. Shaking her shoulders to lose that thought, she concentrated on the moment. The sun was dipping behind the sand dunes that ran along the western horizon. White clouds that were so thin she could see through them lingered above the parting sun. The first moment without the direct sunlight as it dropped behind a distant sand dune brought a sigh of relief from the two. Ayisha stared at the glowing pink and orange rays that filled the sky. A sudden cough from her mother brought her back, so Ayisha grabbed her mother's hand for the walk home.

There is so much to tell Ahmed, she thought. She reviewed all the information that she had gathered. Auntie B's camp is toward the salt mines, so we know it is to the north. It's at the foot of a giant sand dune, two days' walk from here. It seemed like a lot of information until she gazed at the huge desert running away in all directions.

She swung her mother's hand as they walked toward Timbuktu. The brown city was cast in deep shadow, and the call to prayer from three different speakers drifted across the wide open plain. Abdoulaye, exhausted from his playing, slept soundly on Miriam's right hip, his head bouncing gently on her shoulder as they walked along. Ayisha tried to savor the peaceful walk home, for she knew the odds were great that her mother wouldn't be happy with her for too much longer.

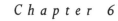 *Chapter 6*

MORE THAN EVER, Ayisha wanted to go with Ahmed the next day.

But there wasn't time to tell him as their mother called everyone to the dinner mat to eat. Ayisha could only ask quickly as they walked together, "Any news of today?"

"No, no news," he answered as they took their places around the food tray.

There was much chatter around the dinner platter that night outside the family tent. The intense heat of the day had been reduced with the setting sun, but a glistening sheen of sweat still covered each face. Miriam looked at Ibrahim and said, "You would not have believed the boldness of your daughter today." It was clear that she was still pleased as she reached forward with her right hand to take some millet and milk. Miriam nodded as she told Ibrahim, "She has brought a business to the family that is not degrading or embarrassing."

Miriam gazed at her daughter and said, "Yes, she has made arrangements for selling, or I should say her brother selling, things that we don't have to buy first."

Her eyes shone with pride as she turned to her son Ahmed and said, "Now it is up to you to see if it can work."

Ahmed's eager smile creased his face. He sat directly opposite his mother, across the food platter. His dusty white pants sported dark spots where he had dripped milk with his first handful of food. Looking from his mother's beaming face to his father's confused one, he said, "So my sister has finally made a plan you like!" He clapped his hands and so did Abdoulaye, who had a hand full of grain that he smashed, then licked off his hands carefully.

"That is the difference," said Mother. "It is not some crazy scheme or idea. There is a big difference."

Ibrahim leaned forward, an elbow resting on each knee. He looked at his daughter and said, "So what have you done, young lady?"

"She has become a vendor of jewelry for the Tuareg," Miriam said. Pointing her bread at her daughter, she explained, "She suggested to a man we met in the camp, Baba Ali, that since Ahmed is a guide, he could save the men a trip to town by selling directly to the people he works with."

Ayisha sat tall. "You see, Father, we can take the money back to them and pick up new pieces as Ahmed sells them. They have their price and we'll have our price, to make it worth my brother's trouble."

Ahmed scooted forward for more food and said casually, "I will try selling to the American *toubabs* tomorrow morning when we meet."

"No, no," said Ayisha, holding up her hand. "Don't try first thing in the morning. Have some fun with them first, doing your tourist things. Then when they are in a good mood at the end of the day, mention that you have jewelry to sell."

All eyes looked at her. Miriam snorted loudly. "Listen to her! She acts like she knows all now. Pity you can't sell them." When she saw Ayisha's eyes pop open, she raised her finger and said, "NO! You will not sell them. It just amuses me that suddenly you know how you want to."

"Actually, she is right." All eyes turned to Ahmed. "The vendors make the people so angry by being pushy and as bothersome as a mosquito on a hot, still night that they don't buy. If we have a good day first, then maybe they will be more willing to buy from me. All *toubabs* eventually buy some Tuareg jewelry, so why not from me, their trusted guide?"

"What did you do with the *toubabs* today?" asked Ibrahim, changing the subject.

"We walked out to the nearest dune, to watch Timbuktu start the day. Visitors like this, and so do I. We hear the animals bleat and bray on their way out to grazing or to the well, and the mortar and pestles thunking with their pounding rhythm. Little smoke trails lift skyward, showing exactly where the women baking bread in their clay ovens are, and we can see market women with their heavy bundles heading to work."

Ibrahim gazed at his son like he had just fallen from

the sky or had three eyes. "Why, you sound like a poet," he exclaimed.

Ahmed dropped his head bashfully and said, "Well, you asked."

"It's good," said his father. "It shows you love your home, which must be obvious when sharing it with the *toubabs*."

"Oh, but I do love Timbuktu," he said.

Silent, Ayisha sat fuming, for she wanted to talk more about the necklaces. She was sure they would provide the opportunity for her to spend a day with the *toubabs*. Almost desperately she blurted out, "Did the *toubab madame* ask for me today?"

Both her parents burst out laughing. "She asked me to join them for today or tomorrow, but we all know that can't happen. Why won't you let me join them for a day? Maybe it would cure me of my *toubab* curiosity if I had to listen to them for a full day." I must spend a day with them, she thought, if we're to catch them. She glared at her brother as he leaned forward for another handful of food, willing him to pick up her thoughts.

Ahmed jolted upright and looking at his parents, he said, "Letting her spend a day with the *toubabs* is a great idea! She would surely tire of them after one day and never bother you again. Let her come with me tomorrow. If she isn't fed up by the end of the day, she can at least try her skill for selling on them."

Ibrahim looked at Miriam, who shrugged back at him. "Your mother and I will talk," he told the twins. "Then what we decide will be final, not open to discussion or argument or insistence."

Ahmed and Ayisha glanced at each other and said in unison, "*Cuez!*" Fine!

"What will you be doing with them tomorrow?" Miriam asked her son.

"We will watch the day begin again, for they enjoyed that very much, and then visit the museums of the white explorers that came here. We'll also visit some of the mosques, and after my Koranic studies, when it's cooler, we'll visit the Flame of Peace and the Garden of Peace." Looking over at Ayisha, he said, "It would be good for you to go too, to learn a little more about your own city."

Ayisha's eyes, as brown as Tuareg tea, sparkled as she said, "That's very true. Mother, Father, please may I go? I know that I can sell the necklaces I have."

"We'll talk," was all her father said in response. "Now let's eat," he almost barked.

Ayisha cleaned the large food tray and stowed it behind the bench along the wall after everyone was finished. She wandered over to where her two brothers sat outside. They were playing a drawing game in the sand, far from the front door of the tent. Ahmed wrote a letter in Arabic and Abdoulaye would try to copy it as his brother guided his hand.

Ahmed looked up as Ayisha plopped down next to them on the hard-packed sand, still warm from the day's heat. Looking around, she asked, "Where are Mother and Father?"

Ahmed held on to Abdoulaye's hand with his finger sticking out straight like a Bic and pointed with his chin toward the back of the family compound. They could see their parents huddled together near the foot of the sand dune that started the wave of dunes northward. "They are there, obviously talking about tomorrow. What do you think? Will they agree?"

Ayisha shrugged. "*Inshallah!* I really don't know . . . The *toubabs*, did they mention the ancient manuscripts today?"

Ahmed continued to write in the sand with Abdoulaye's tiny pointed finger. He tilted his head to look at Ayisha and whispered, "Once or twice. We didn't spend much time together today because he had a bad belly and wanted to stay close to the hotel. We did talk, though, about where we will go tomorrow . . . so they can see some manuscripts."

Ayisha slapped the sand beside her. "I want to see them too, and watch the *toubabs* when they see them. And believe it or not, I want to know much more about the manuscripts for myself—I want to see one and hold one and read one."

Ahmed smiled at Ayisha's enthusiasm. "What brings on this sudden thirst for knowledge, sister mine? Is it really about Timbuktu and her history, or is it about figuring out how to catch these two?"

Ayisha started to get huffy, blowing a loud breath through her tightly closed lips, insulted by the question. Then she realized that maybe it wasn't so odd for her brother to ask, for she really had never displayed much interest in the deeper details of Timbuktu's history before the *toubabs* had come. The only history she'd really wanted to know before was the one her father had hinted at—the one about thieving having touched all families in and around Timbuktu.

Calming down, she said, "You are right to ask, brother. But I can't answer honestly how much is curiosity about Timbuktu's past and how much is determination to catch these two." She raised her shoulders in a shrug. "I so want to catch them doing it, buying the manuscripts to sneak out of the country. But I also want to know more about the manuscripts. They surely have you amazed. And look how far these people traveled to steal some. So it's all those things. Who knows, maybe one day I'll work with the manuscripts . . ."

"Doing what?" asked a shocked Ahmed.

Shaking her head, Ayisha replied, "I don't know. It's just something that came to me now, as we talked. I have a future, brother—of that I am sure—that is more than being a mother."

Ahmed's dropped jaw showed he couldn't believe what he was hearing. It looked like he didn't know where to start with questions when suddenly they heard Sidi shout out a greeting of "*Salaam alakoum.*"

Ahmed jumped to his feet, yanking Abdoulaye's short arm with him. His brother cried out in shock, and quickly Ahmed released him. Bending over to tap his back, he said, "Sorry, Little Camel."

Abdoulaye looked like he was ready to cry, and neither brother nor sister wanted that, so Ayisha reached out to tickle him. He squirmed and laughed as she ran her fingers lightly over his little belly.

Sidi stood beside Ahmed, breathing hard from running. His black hair was sticking up in many different directions, and a thin layer of sweat covered the spot between his nose and his top lip.

Ahmed said, "What is the rush? Are ghosts chasing you?"

Sidi tried to laugh, but he was still breathing hard. He bent in two, his hands on his knees. Taking a few very deep breaths, he finally said, "It's the *toubabs*. The ones you don't like? They asked me to come and get you. Now."

Ahmed looked around to see if his parents were back yet, and when he didn't see them, he asked, "Why? It's late."

"Only Allah knows until we go find out." He ignored Ayisha, who was definitely staring at him.

"Why were you with the *toubabs*?" she asked, clearly suspicious that he was trying to take her brother's job away. That just wouldn't do, for Ahmed had to be their guide if they were to catch them stealing the ancient manuscripts.

Ahmed nodded slightly to Ayisha, and she knew he knew why she had asked. "That's a good question, Sidi. Why were you with the *toubabs*?"

Sidi lifted his hands and shook his head. "What's the problem? Do you own them? Aren't I or anyone else allowed to talk to them?" When he saw the angry looks covering his best friend's face and Ayisha's, he quickly changed his tone.

"I was on my way here when I saw them. You know how that *toubab* woman is; she likes to talk to anyone, and they know we are friends." He held out his hand, which was clutching a crumpled CFA note. "They gave me this to find you, so they must have something important to say. I'll share it with you. We can stop on the way back and buy a cold drink at Abubakar's stall."

Ahmed looked again for his parents, but they had moved out of sight. Ayisha stood and gave his shoulder a little shove. "You'd better go," she whispered loudly. With little pushes she said, "See what they need." Shove. "I will tell Mother and Father where you are if they come back before you." Another shove for encouragement.

She then looked at Sidi, who she really didn't want involved in their business, and said, "Why don't you stay here with Abdoulaye and me? We can play *erbiki* with him. He just learned it today with new friends in the Tuareg camp."

Clearly, Sidi was shocked that Ayisha had asked him to stay. He pulled his head back quickly, as if slapped. Ayisha had never been happy about his friendship with her best friend and brother, and had never encouraged him to spend any time with her. She had even rejected his offer to collect dung just the day before. He squinted at her and said, "You're asking me to stay and play with you two?"

Ahmed clapped his back and said, "That's a very good idea. Who knows, the *toubabs* may want to speak only with me and they might ask you to leave. Stay here and play, and I'll tell you what they wanted when I get back." Pushing Sidi down into a sitting position, he said, "Now, where did you see the *toubabs*? Are they waiting someplace special for me?"

"They are in front of the Azalai Hotel. He looked very agitated about something and eager to talk to you. He said they would walk to the Hotel Bouctou and wait in their usual place. But why should I stay here, playing with a girl and a baby instead of going with you?"

Ayisha grunted at his comment and then forced herself to say, "Because it is good to spend time with girls and babies. You can probably learn something from both of us."

All were shocked when they suddenly heard Abdoulaye whispering to himself, over and over again, *"Erbiki, erbiki, erbiki."*

"He said a Tamashek word," shouted Ayisha. "Little Camel is talking Tamashek!"

Ahmed took advantage of the distraction, jumping and shouting, *"Al Humdullah*, he's talking. Quick, play with him so he will be encouraged, and I'll be back as soon as possible." Without giving Sidi an opportunity to reply, Ahmed took off at a full run.

Ayisha said, "Good. You two hide and I will find you." Looking at Abdoulaye, she said to Sidi, "Take his hand and hide with him. Maybe he will show you a place, and if not, then you can lead him." She looked around the open spaces between the tents. There were many places, including behind a large camel that sat quietly, head high, chewing his cud contentedly. "Just stay close to here," she said.

She turned her back, her eyes closed, and started counting in Arabic, "*Wahid, ethneen . . .*" When she reached fifteen, she turned to look for the boys. Just then her parents emerged from the far side of the compound, rounding the family tent.

She ran over to greet them, hoping they had some good news for her. Her mother looked around, searching for Abdoulaye and Ahmed. She hitched her long black gown up on her right shoulder and then flipped the piece covering her head in a quick snap of her wrists. Still looking left and right, she finally said, "And your brothers?"

"Abdoulaye and Sidi are hiding, and I am going to look for them," Ayisha explained. "And Ahmed will be back soon. Sidi brought a message saying the *toubabs* needed to see him right away."

"This late?" asked her father. "Have they no manners?" He threw the long draping sleeves on his brown *jalabiah* over each shoulder. She could just see the bottom of the leather *gris-gris* packets he wore on his arms for protection from evil talk about his business. He coughed quickly, then said, "And since when does your brother just go off?"

"He asked me to apologize to you, Father, but we didn't know when you would return and he wanted to find out if tomorrow's plans had changed. He'll be back any moment, I'm sure." She looked at her parents and saw the frowns that were moving across their faces. Father's eyes always squint when his anger builds, thought Ayisha. She knew without looking that her mother had sucked her lips in tight, leaving just an angry slash across her face. The last thing they wanted right now was to anger their parents, so Ayisha blurted out, "Would you like some good news?"

"That would be nice for a change," said her mother. Ayisha couldn't help but think about all the recent good news—her test scores, Ahmed's Koran scholarship and the new jewelry business—but she didn't bring any of that up. Instead she said with a wide smile, "Abdoulaye spoke Tamashek! He said '*erbiki, erbiki, erbiki*' as clearly as any Tuareg."

Her mother's eyes lit up at once, and her smile stretched her cheeks tight across her face as she clapped her hands. "Did you ask him to say it? Did you lead him?"

"No, Mother, not at all. He said it himself, and that's why we are playing."

Flapping her hands as if she were fanning a fire, Miriam said, "So go find him! I want to hear this for myself."

As Ayisha ran off, her father called out, "This is just another unfinished conversation."

Ayisha waved her hand to let him know she had heard him. As she looked behind a pile of dried millet stalks, she said to no one but herself, "Oh, how I hate unfinished conversations. I always end up in trouble."

Running over to where the baby goats spent the night, she called out, "Game's over! I see the tail end of Sidi's robe sticking out."

When they emerged, Abdoulaye had a smile as wide as his mother's. Sidi wasn't smiling, though, and groused, "What took you so long?"

"My parents," she said, taking Abdoulaye into her arms.

Sliding her little brother onto her right hip, she told Sidi, "Thanks for playing, but you can go home now."

Sidi looked at her, his head tilted to the left. "You sure are bossy," he said.

"So tell me something new," she said as she walked toward the tent, her left arm swishing back and forth as she hurried along.

"I will." Watching her back as she walked away, he shouted, "The *toubabs* don't want Ahmed anymore; they want me to guide them."

Ayisha stopped dead in her tracks. She whipped around to stare at him and said, "But why? Ahmed knows much more than you do and speaks many more languages than you do."

Sidi was really beginning to irritate her. She shifted Abdoulaye from one hip to the other and said again, "Why?"

Acting like he had just played the trick of the century on her, he said, "They don't. I just made that up. But why do you care so much? Ahmed doesn't even like those two."

"Did you tell them that?" she asked.

"No."

"I care for only one reason—no, two. They pay him well, and he now has jewelry to sell."

Sidi was completely confused by the jewelry comment. "What are you talking about?"

"Ahmed will tell you. I need to get my baby brother to my mother."

Sidi didn't waste any time. He ran toward the town,

waving to Ayisha's parents as he sprinted for the city of sand. Ayisha knew he was going to find Ahmed and ask about the jewelry. She didn't mind that, but she really did want to know what the *toubabs* wanted. Her mother raised her arms out for Abdoulaye as he drew near to her. The little boy eagerly moved from one set of arms to the other.

Ayisha followed her mother and Abdoulaye into the tent. She sat on her sleeping mat, watching her mother get Abdoulaye ready for bed. As her mother worked, she said, "Your brother better be home soon. Night has come and he's not here? Since when is that possible?"

Ayisha didn't answer, for there really was nothing to say. She didn't want to tell her mother of all the things going on, which could explain why Ahmed had to run off after dinner to talk with the *toubabs*. The last thing they wanted was for the *toubabs* to get another guide. She sat quietly, happy to hear her mother start to hum softly as she prepared her youngest son for bed. Miriam lifted his short caftan over his head, then wet the end of her head scarf with spit and washed a smudge off the young boy's face.

The slightest "ugh" escaped Ayisha's lips in disgust, and her mother looked at her quickly.

"Ugh?" repeated her mother. "Is that a *toubab* word? You are quick to criticize, Ayisha." She pointed at her son's face and said, "Look, he's clean now." Then with a sparkle in her eye she lifted her cloth again and said, "Wait, my dear, I see a spot on your cheek." Her laughter followed

Ayisha out the door as she fled from the prospect of her mother's spit rubbed on her face.

She needed to think. The first thing we must do is really establish if they plan to steal some manuscripts, she thought, and if they are, then we need to act quickly. But how? she wondered. How?

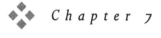 *Chapter 7*

THE MOON WAS UP, spreading a soft golden glow across the land. Her father sat at his morning spot, preparing coals for tea. He sat with a straight back, his knees bent and pointing outward beneath his deep brown *jalabiah*. His hands moved swiftly as he arranged his tea tray. Beside him, the hot coals left from cooking dinner glowed in his wire coal basket, used only for making tea. He looked up as Ayisha squatted beside him. "Your brother should be doing this for me," he grumbled. "You two have become quite independent lately, maybe a little too independent."

"But Father, you and Mother are always telling us to accept responsibility, to face new challenges. And that's what we're trying to do."

"It is a fine line between rudeness and independence. Rudeness is disappearing without permission. True independence is when you ask permission the first time and then pursue your challenges."

"You're right, but there was no chance to ask for permission. In fact, if you must be angry or disappointed, then be so with me. I gave him permission."

Her father threw his head back and laughed. It was a harsh laugh, not one of amusement, and Ayisha shuddered.

Head tilted and eyes opened wide, he asked, "So you give permission now?"

"Only this once. It seemed important for him to check with the *toubabs*, Sidi arrived with such a rush, panting about how they wanted to see Ahmed as soon as possible. Since we want to sell them jewelry, it seemed best that Ahmed go find out if he would still be guiding them tomorrow." As she finished speaking, Ayisha yanked on her bangs and then slapped her hand to her side. With the faintest hint of desperation she asked, "You will let me go tomorrow to help sell the necklaces the first time, won't you, Father?"

Her father fanned the coals that were just beginning to take on a white crusty covering. They sat in the small wire basket, which had a wide mouth for holding them and a teapot that would sit on top of the coals. He counted four fingerfuls of green tea leaves scrunched together, then packed them inside the chipped blue teapot that he had owned longer than Ayisha's lifetime. He picked up the big water container made from a camel's bladder, squirting water into the teapot until it was full. With a final swirl of his finger he mixed the tea and water, then placed it on top of the hot coals.

They both jumped slightly when Ahmed came charging

back from town. He stopped suddenly when he saw his father and sister, obviously waiting for him, sitting in the moonlight out in front of the tent.

Ahmed dropped his head and said, *"Salaam alakoum."*

His father returned the greeting as he patted the ground beside him. "Sit," he said loudly.

Stealing a look at his sister's face, which was mostly in shadow, Ahmed tried to get an idea of just how much trouble he was in. Deciding to break the suspense, he snorted and said, "Those *toubabs*. They get an idea and they want an answer instantly."

"They still want you as their guide, don't they?" Ayisha asked.

"Yes, they still want me to guide them. Sidi told me his joke he played on you, and believe me, that's all it was." Wiping the sweat from his face with his long sleeve, he told them, "They want me to take them to see the elephants of Timbuktu. Tomorrow!"

Ahmed looked at his father and then his sister and continued, "They had dinner with some other *toubabs* who told them about the elephants of Timbuktu. They seem to think they just have to take a short stroll somewhere nearby and there the elephants will be."

"And so what did you tell them? Or am I allowed to ask?" said Ibrahim.

"Certainly you can ask, Father. What makes you even ask that question?"

"Well, now that your sister feels she can give permission for you to just leave at night, I'm not sure what my role is. What do you think, daughter, am I allowed to ask my son about his plans?"

Ayisha could feel her face burning and was thankful for the darkness so they couldn't see just how embarrassed she felt. Ahmed looked from his sister to his father, back and forth, back and forth.

Ayisha knew she had to say something, so she said, "Please, Father, I never would have told him to go if you had been here. We know that's your job and you would have decided. But it sounds like it's good he went. What if they had just left without asking Ahmed's advice? We would have lost them!"

Father tilted his head and said, "*We* would have lost them? Since when do you work with them? Is there something else you haven't told your mother and me?"

Ayisha shook her head. She realized she had to show less interest in the *toubabs* or her father would never let her talk to them. She laughed at herself, showing much more mirth than she actually felt, but she wanted him to see how foolish she had been. "Not we. It's just that I am hopeful that this new business of selling jewelry will work. If it does, then our goat herd will grow and grow, and maybe we can even pay my school fees."

Her father stared at her, clearly not sure he believed her. Just then the spout on the teapot belched out a spurt of hot tea. Her father lifted the pot off the coals and added sugar to the tea. He let it dissolve, then began pouring tea into one of the tiny little glasses that sat on a tray beside him.

He filled the glass, then picked it up and poured the tea directly back into the pot. He did this six times, pouring from a little higher each time. When he was sure the tea was well mixed, he poured again, this time lifting the pot higher and higher as he poured. He filled three glasses and the twins' eyes opened wide when they realized he was including them in his tea ceremony. Only once before had he served them tea, when Ahmed won the *futbol* game and Father's pride had been great.

The two children looked at each other quickly, not sure why they were being included once again.

Each glass was filled to the brim, a white foam topping them. He handed Ayisha a glass and she said, "*Shukran*, Father." Thank you.

Next he passed tea to Ahmed, making sure not to spill a drop from the brimming glass. He then picked up his own, and as one the three took a giant slurp that filled the air. No one spoke as they savored the flavor of the strong sweet tea.

Ayisha took another swallow and said, "It's delicious." A small white mustache from the foam decorated her top lip. She wanted to leave it there, but she saw her mother moving toward them, her loose black gown flowing out around her. Remembering the spit on her brother's face, she quickly licked off the foam.

Her mother laughed when she saw her do it. "Still worried?" she asked her daughter.

"Worried about what?" asked Ibrahim as he poured his wife a glass of tea.

She leaned forward and took it from her husband, answering, "She doesn't approve of me washing a smudge from her little brother's face with the cleaner Allah gave us all—spit."

"Ugh!" said Ahmed.

Both mother and daughter looked at him and laughed. "There's that word again. Where did it come from?" asked Miriam.

"The *toubabs*," he said. "They all say it, whether they are English or Irish or American or Canadian. All the English-speaking ones. It always means the same thing: disgust!"

"So you too are disgusted with your mother?" she asked before taking her first sip of tea.

"Not at all. I just hope you don't try to do it to me!" Ahmed took a sip and then continued. "This American couple has a new word for me—*gotcha*, or something like that. I have not been able to figure out what it means yet."

Ayisha smiled into the darkness, happy for a conversation that held no threat or reprimand. Just the family talking peacefully and happily like old times, she thought. Looking toward her parents, she realized the moment was over.

Ibrahim and Miriam exchanged looks. The moon had risen higher, only a few days away from being full. The parents shook their heads in unison. Miriam looked at her son and asked, "So now you just come and go as you please? Even at night?"

Ayisha scrunched down, hoping her father wouldn't start again, but it was a hope in vain.

He pointed at his daughter with his tea glass and said, "He had permission to go. From her."

Miriam's head swiveled quickly to look at her daughter. "You gave him permission?"

"Yes, Mother. I already told Father that I am sorry for being so, so . . ."

"Bossy? Would that word do?" asked her mother.

"Bossy," she replied, nodding slowly. Hoping to change the subject, she took the final swallow of tea from her glass and then held it out to her father. "Is there enough for a little more?"

He lifted the teapot and poured a steady stream into her glass. As he raised the teapot toward his son, Ahmed gulped the remaining tea in his glass and held it up. Ibrahim poured, raising the pot higher and higher to form the thick foam on top. He then set the teapot on the sand and added water to it, beginning the process again. Miriam leaned forward and blew on the coals, bringing them back to life with red sears of heat streaking the white covering.

In the silence that had fallen, Ayisha suddenly asked, "So what did you tell them about the elephants of Timbuktu?"

Smiling, he said, "I didn't tell them that *Timbouctou le mysterious, avec les elephants de Tombouctou* is just a phrase for *toubabs*, because it sounds good."

Ibrahim snorted at his son's words. "I like that. A daughter who gives permission and a son who criticizes government phrases." He clapped his hands, and the twins didn't know if he was angry or joking.

"It's just the truth, Father," said Ahmed, shrugging and turning his head from side to side.

"*Al Humdullah!* Someone is telling the truth." He looked directly at his daughter and said, "I wish all were telling the truth."

"But Father, I haven't lied to you. I want to spend some time with these *toubabs*, but I haven't yet, except for a moment when we met on the street," said Ayisha.

Ibrahim said, "Maybe you haven't lied, but also maybe you haven't told us everything either. You know omission is as good as a lie. I want some answers now about why you are so obsessed with these particular *toubabs*. I know that look, Ayisha. You and your brother are planning something with these *toubabs* as sure as we sit here before Allah." He leaned forward, an elbow resting on each knee. "Talk!" he barked.

Ayisha dropped her head, knowing her father was right but not willing to give up her desire to catch the two thieving *toubabs*. She was sure her parents would be proud of her brother and her once the deed was accomplished. After all, they would be protecting and saving a part of Timbuktu! "Please trust me, Father," she said.

Her father eyed her for a moment, then looked at his son. The rising moon revealed the worried look on the boy's face. "And so what else did you tell these *toubabs*?" Ibrahim asked.

"I said that the elephants don't actually live here, near

Timbuktu. That they live in the region and pass by here, making the longest migration of all elephants in the world in search of food and water. They could be in Gossi right now, or maybe even as far away as Burkina Faso."

Ahmed looked at the three faces that were listening so intently to him. He sat a little straighter and continued, "It is early June, the time the elephants move south every year. I promised to ask around and find out if they are still in Gossi, and if they are, then with your permission, I could take them there by taxi."

"Take them to Gossi? A full day's travel from here? That's between Mopti and Gao, two places you have never been. No, three places you have never been. How can you be a guide when you need one too?" Ibrahim asked.

"Why are these two so important to you and your sister? More important than any *toubabs* you've worked with before?" Miriam was squinting and shifting her gaze from one twin's face to the other.

"They pay well," Ahmed said. "And if I can sell them jewelry, then I can make even more money for the family."

Miriam huffed slightly as she leaned forward to fan the dying coals. As she brought a bit of life back into them, tea spurted from the spout. Ibrahim grabbed the teapot and began again the process of sweetening the tea. Miriam cleared her throat and said, "We have discussed you going along tomorrow with these people, Ayisha."

Both children held their breaths, waiting for the final answer. Miriam fixed her gaze on Ayisha and said, "At first

I was totally against it, afraid of what plans you might have for becoming a guide on your own, but your father assures me that not even you can be that bold."

"Father is right, Mother." Ayisha leaned forward and said with deep emotion, "And don't forget, Mother, I want to go to *lycée* more than just about anything else in this world. You have already told me what that depends upon."

Trying to sound casual, she added, "Besides, if I go tomorrow, I will sell the jewelry and Ahmed can see how it is done." She cringed, remembering her mother had made and canceled the same suggestion over dinner.

"I know exactly what the Tuareg men out in the camp want, and I have seen Auntie B in action, always getting the price she wants, whether buying or selling something." Looking at her father, Ayisha said, "And she always gets paid the most for her henna painting. Whatever price she asks."

"Auntie B," said her mother with the slightest shake of her head. "Allah help us if she is your shining example."

Ibrahim sat a bit straighter at his wife's words. Pouring tea in a steady stream, he stopped the flow like the water tap near the Grande Marché in town when you twisted it closed. "She could do much worse for an example," he said, defending his long-missing sister.

"You are right, Father. Forgive me," said their mother.

Ibrahim poured again, filling all four glasses that sat on the tray. He lifted the tray this time, holding it out for each to take their freshly filled glasses.

"What do you think, Father, shall she go along tomorrow?" their mother asked.

"Only if they follow the list of places to visit that Ahmed mentioned before." He pointed at his son and said, "And there will be no treks off to Gao or Gossi in search of elephants. Is that clear?"

"Oh yes, Father, very clear."

"Well, it's good to know you have some sense," said his father.

Ayisha couldn't help herself, interrupting the two with a question. "So I am going with Ahmed tomorrow?"

Their father and mother shared a quick glance, and then Ibrahim nodded. "You will go, but only after I meet them."

"That's perfect," said Ahmed. "We can meet them after prayers. Father, we'll go to mosque together and Ayisha can meet us afterward."

Ayisha clapped her hands and instantly regretted it. Both parents looked at her, and her mother said, "I just don't like how happy this makes you."

"It's only for a day, Mother," she said a bit too loudly. All eyes shifted to her face and she said with a giant smile, "And I promise to bring back funny stories that we'll all laugh at."

"Ugh!" was all her mother said as she lifted herself from the ground. They all laughed as she walked away. When she reached the entrance to the tent, she turned and said, "I'm not surprised you look up to your aunt like you do, for you both share one very big thing."

"Bossy!" said Ibrahim and Ahmed and Miriam.

"Very bossy," said her mother as she disappeared inside the tent. Ayisha dropped her head to hide the smile that covered her face. She loved being compared to her Auntie B. And she was going with the *toubabs* tomorrow.

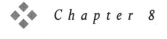 *Chapter 8*

ASHORT COUGH FROM her father brought Ayisha's head up. Finishing his tea, Father swooshed clean water around the glass again and again, until the water ran clear in the moonlight. He was concentrating on his daughter's face, which was obviously bursting with a question or comment she was holding back. Finally Ibrahim said, "Ask it, before your head bursts like a . . ."

Ayisha looked at her brother and without saying a word, he gave her a nod, showing he knew what she would ask. She cleared her throat and tried to ask casually, "Father, remember when you said no family had been left untouched by thievery? What exactly did you mean? You said you would tell us later, so now seems like a good time."

Ibrahim snorted at his daughter's daring. "Now is not a good time. But soon."

"How soon?" asked Ahmed.

"When your Auntie B next visits, then we will tell the tale together. *Inshallah*."

The twins' eyes connected in the moonlight, their stare shortened when Father asked, "What makes you so curious? Why do you ask?"

Ahmed said, "Just curious."

Ibrahim handed the tray to his son and said, "Finish cleaning these things. You two make me tired—more tired than a mother goat with two kids pulling and tugging at her teats."

As he stood, he said, "Don't be out here long. The call to prayer comes quickly." Then he turned to Ayisha and said, "You have some sense, for you look up to your Auntie B. That shows me something very important about you. It makes me have a little more faith in you than I probably should."

He brushed the sand from the back of his *grand boubou* and said, "And thank you for news of my sister from the Tuareg camp. It is good to know she's not somewhere distant like Taoudenni." Taoudenni, the salt mines out in the desert, rested fifteen difficult days, at least, from Timbuktu by camel caravan.

"Let's go see her, Father! How long can it take to reach the giant dune where they stay?" Ayisha asked.

"More days than I have right now for travel. But maybe we shall go one day. It should take two days and one night at the least. But now with the weather hotter than my blacksmith tools is not the time to go." He waved and walked away.

"Sleep well, Father," called Ayisha.

She turned to her brother and said, "Everything is going perfectly, *Al Humdullah!*" Swishing water in one of the glasses he had just filled, she asked, "So what else did the *toubabs* say?"

"Not too much. He is impatient, wanting to leave at first light searching for elephants, even if he has no idea where they are. I am sure that the elephants are already on their way to Burkina Faso because it is late June. I hope so, anyway, because if they have gone, that means rain might fall sometime soon and break this heat that grips the days and nights."

Finishing his work, Ahmed said, "Father is right, dawn comes faster than a camel racing. So tomorrow you milk the goats while I go to mosque with Father, and then we can meet up with the *toubabs*." He lifted the wire coal pot and set it on the tray next to the glasses and blue teapot.

Standing, he said, "Enough talk for one night. I will see you in the morning." He leaned down for the tray of his father's tea set and walked toward the tent.

Ayisha sat another moment, regarding the power of the moon. It wasn't full, but still it filled the air with a soft light. Thinking it looked a bit like the milk gourd with the tilted bottom, she also jumped to her feet. Tomorrow was a big day, and she needed to sleep so she would be as sharp as a thorn on an acacia tree. Staring at the night sky, she thought, Maybe tomorrow we will get an idea of what trap we need to catch these two.

She entered the tent to a chorus of snores and snuffles

from her parents and brothers. She lay on her mat and joined the chorus as soon as her head rested flat and comfortable.

The next morning everyone was moving early, even Miriam and Abdoulaye. Ayisha walked quickly toward the goats, for she thought that if she showed her parents that she could do her chores and accompany Ahmed, maybe they would let her go more than once. One thing she was sure of, if she brought home good money from showing her brother the best way to sell the necklaces, her chances of going again would improve. She nearly tripped over a baby goat as she rushed to milk the mothers, preoccupied with excitement at having a whole day with the *toubabs*.

"Don't be careless in your haste, daughter," called her mother as she watched Ayisha nearly fall. The goats were ready for milking and things went very smoothly. She didn't spill a drop as she milked or as she carried the two containers to the tent. Pouring the milk into the bigger container, she raised the gourd like she had seen her father pour tea the night before. As it splashed, her mother called to her, "Stop playing with the milk."

Ayisha quickly moved the gourd closer to the big clay pot that held the milk. As she finished the second gourd of milk, she rushed to the door to wash them out. Her mother grabbed her shoulders and said, "Slow down, or you won't be going anywhere. Why such a great rush just to meet *toubabs*?"

"I'm sorry, Mother. I just don't want to miss Father and Ahmed when they leave prayers."

Like an old lady, she slowed her pace, carefully cleaning the gourds so that no traces of milk remained while also carefully using as little water as possible.

She placed the gourds next to the milk container and picked up the two water bags, one completely deflated in its emptiness and the other with a little water that she poured into a gourd. "I'll be back soon," she called out as she rushed to finish her second major chore of the day. "Today's the day," she puffed out as she sprinted toward the well. "We have the whole day to learn their intentions."

There was a line at the well, where two men had their camels attached to the spools that fit into the wooden tripods. They alternated sending their camels off to draw the water from the depths of the well. Three girls called out to Ayisha, standing far to the front of the line. She hated people who did not wait their turn, but today she would be rude. She ran up to them like they were her best friends, which they weren't.

The tallest girl, Zaida, took Ayisha's hand and asked, "Is it true you went to the Tuareg camp yesterday?"

Ayisha wasn't totally surprised that they knew, although neither she nor her mother had talked to anyone when they departed or returned. But word traveled very fast in a town filled with people who loved to gossip. "Yes, we did," Ayisha answered. "We went to ask about my Auntie B." She almost included the news about the jewelry when Zaida interrupted her and said, "And what about the jewelry you are going to sell for them?"

Ayisha had no doubt that Sidi was responsible for all this information being passed about. She decided to ignore her annoyance and said, "What's to say, you know it all already." She then prodded the girl on her shoulder, for the line had moved quickly in front of them.

Zaida set her big plastic water jug on the ground for the man to fill. He poured water from the large rubber tire cut into a curved piece making a perfect bucket. There was just enough left to fill Ayisha's two skin bags. They waited as the other man filled the containers of Zaida's two younger sisters.

With the smoothest of motions Zaida lifted the heavy water jug onto her head and Ayisha slung a bag over each shoulder. Together the four girls walked toward the town. Zaida's curiosity continued. "Did Abdoulaye really speak Tamashek last night?"

Now Ayisha knew for sure that Sidi was the walking source of information. This made her more determined to keep him out of their business, for his big mouth could spoil any plan they made to catch the *toubabs*. "Yes, he did. He said *erbiki* three times, all on his own. Did Sidi also tell you that I found them hiding behind the goat enclosure because his big rear end was sticking out?"

Zaida's mouth dropped open, and the three girls all tittered with laughter. "How did you know it was Sidi? And should you talk about his parts like that?" At once all four girls whooped with laughter. Zaida's plastic water jug jiggled on her head, and she grabbed it quickly with both hands, for few things caused more problems than spilled water in their land of heat and dust. Steadying the jug, she heaved a sigh of relief that not a drop had spilled.

Ayisha was glad to see her tent up ahead. She told the

girls good-bye as they walked on, all of their eyes sparkling from the joke they had shared. She placed the water in the darkness of the tent to keep it as cool as possible. Then she went over to her sleeping mat and lifted it up. Tucked beneath it were the four necklaces Ali had given her to sell. She wrapped them carefully in the soft cloth, and dropped them into a small leather bag that she draped over her right shoulder.

Her mother was waiting for her when she stepped out into the bright sunlight and growing heat. "I'm not sure this is such a good idea. You are happier than a bride leaving for her marriage."

Ayisha couldn't believe that she would change her mind this late. "Please, Mother, I have done my chores and I will be home early enough to pound the millet and help you with dinner."

Ayisha watched as her mother pulled up her long gown and unhooked a small leather bag she always kept there. She tipped it over, and more coins than Ayisha could count quickly fell into Miriam's open palm. She carefully selected two 100 CFA coins and held them up. "It's a hot day, so if these *toubabs* do not extend the hospitality of offering you a cold drink, then you and your brother can each buy a cold drink from Aboubakar's stall."

Ayisha couldn't remember the last time her mother had given her money to spend on herself. In fact, she couldn't remember it ever happening before. She held her hand out and said, "Thank you, Mother. May Allah bless you!"

Her mother snorted, just like her husband, and said, "Take them before I change my mind."

Ayisha gave her mother a quick hug, then bent down and patted Abdoulaye's head as he played in the sand. Trying her best not to run, she scurried toward the ancient city.

She waited for her father and brother down the road from the Djinguereber Mosque, built in the 1500s. She loved the lines of the building, built from *banco* mud. A smooth curving staircase led to the roof, and rounded doors opened into the mosque. Her brother and father were among the first to come out, and Ahmed waved as soon as he saw her.

Walking toward her, Ahmed said something that made their father throw back his head and laugh. His eyes shone a bright deep brown in the early morning sunlight. "Tell your sister what you just told me," said their father as she reached them.

Ayisha looked at her brother's face. He was clearly embarrassed by his father's laughter at what he had just told him. She asked, "What is so funny?"

Ahmed stood tall and said, "I told Father it's going to be scorching hot today."

Both Ibrahim and Ayisha looked at Ahmed, who stood before them, his shoulders thrown back and the slightest touch of anger crossing his face. "It will not only be hot today, but hotter than any days that have passed recently."

Their father laughed and said, "So what makes today

any different from yesterday, or all the days before during this very hot month? How can you predict the heat?"

Ahmed surprised himself as he said with confidence, "I can smell the heat coming."

His father threw back his head and laughed with delight. "You smell the heat before it arrives? Before Allah, please tell us what this could mean."

Ahmed stood straighter, his feet planted firmly in the sandy road. He held his head slightly tilted back, his eyes closed. Deeply he breathed, then again, concentrating on the clues his nose gave him. With his eyes still closed, he said, "The hairs in my nose tell me, by how dry they feel. They are as parched as a bone in the sun, as stiff as a turban blown dry in a hot desert wind."

He took another deep breath, and still with his eyes closed tightly, he continued, "Already the dust has lost its night coolness, heavy in my nose." With one final sniff he added, "And the dung on the road again smells fresh, although most of it was left yesterday. The growing heat is warming it up."

When Ahmed finally peeked at them from beneath his thick, dark eyelashes, he saw them both, heads back, eyes closed, breathing deeply. A small smudge of red sand rested on his father's forehead, a souvenir of the prayers they had just said.

Suddenly Ibrahim's eyes flew open, and patting Ahmed's left shoulder, he said, "You just might be right." The three began walking again, Ibrahim's hand still resting on his son's shoulder. As they walked, their sandals softly slapped the ground, and Ibrahim's prayer beads clicked as he passed them quickly through his fingers on his right hand. "I never doubt the wisdom of a desert man."

Ahmed's eyes opened wide with pride. He stared at his father and then his sister, for never before had his father called him a desert man. Ayisha was just as proud, and she held up four fingers for him to see. Ibrahim looked at his daughter and asked, "What does that mean?"

"Koranic scholar, *futbol* star, *toubab* guide and now a desert man."

Their father joined right in and added, "A desert man who forecasts the weather through his nose. That title is more important than all the rest he carries."

All three laughed until Ayisha looked over her brother's shoulder. Amidst roaming goats and kids playing *futbol* with a sock stuffed with rags came the two *toubabs*. They were bustling directly toward them, the man clearly impatient as he walked with stiff legs through the deep sand of the street.

"Ahmed," he cried out, holding his hand high. His turban looked as rumpled as it had two days before, tilted and loose and messy.

Ibrahim watched the man hustling their way and told his son, "I see what you mean about impatient."

"And I see why they need such an early start," giggled Ayisha. "If they move this fast all the time, they will definitely be worn out before midday! Especially in this heat."

All three were chuckling as Griff and Trudy arrived. *"Bonjour, monsieur,"* said Griff, extending his hand to Ibrahim to shake. "My name is Griff Johnson, Dr. Griffin

Johnson, and this is my wife, Trudy." Ibrahim took the offered hand and answered politely, trying not to look at the woman, who wore a sleeveless top. Her white shoulders had the faintest of red dust on them, and both Ahmed and Ayisha were aware of how disturbed their father was.

Ayisha stepped forward and greeted the woman. She couldn't help herself as she said, "*Madame*, you know, women in our culture don't show their shoulders or legs in public." Ayisha heard Ahmed quickly suck in his breath, obviously shocked by what she had just said.

Trudy looked slightly chagrined as she said, "I noticed, but since I am not of your culture, I thought how I dressed didn't matter."

Feeling fearless, Ayisha said, "Oh, but that's not true. It's very offensive to all who live here."

Ayisha removed the scarf draped across her head and handed it to Trudy. "Just wear this and it will be fine."

Trudy took the scarf and draped it over her shoulders. She looked at Ayisha closely and said, "Thank you. For being brave enough to tell me this, saving everyone unnecessary embarrassment."

Ayisha smiled at her, then looked to see what her father was doing. He was just gazing at his daughter as if he had never seen her before.

"I thank you too," he said to her in Arabic. She smiled at the ground, then at her brother. Ahmed turned to Trudy and said, "Please excuse my sister; she is very bossy."

"*Pas de problem,*" said Trudy. No problem. "I think all *toubab* women need to know this."

The twins laughed aloud, and she turned red, saying, "What, what else did I do wrong?"

"You didn't do anything else wrong. You said *toubab!*" Ayisha told her.

"But isn't that what we are? Isn't that what you call us? Every vendor in the street calls out, *'Toubab, achetez vous mon bijou,'* or shoes, or whatever they are selling. Buy, *toubab*, buy!"

Everyone laughed at this, and Ayisha and Ahmed exchanged a quick glance, knowing that they would soon fall into that category, trying to sell them jewelry.

"I'm glad everyone is so happy," burst out Griff, "but I want to know about the elephants. I have been waiting since the sun rose to find out what your friend told you. Are we leaving today in search of the elephants of Timbuktu?"

All eyes shifted to Ahmed's face. He stood tall and said, "I am afraid not. You see, it's late June. I found out the elephants have started their migration south. They may be in Burkina Faso already!"

"So take us there," he almost demanded.

Ayisha watched her father. Ibrahim didn't say a word, but she could see he was curious to see how Ahmed would deal with this pushy man. Ahmed looked at the *toubabs* and said, "It is many miles away. If you want to go, then it will have to be with someone else. I think you should enjoy your time here in Timbuktu, then head south. Then maybe the elephants will be easier to find, having arrived at their grazing and watering grounds a week or ten days from here, rather than still traveling to them and you following behind looking for them."

Griff looked at the boy, then at Ayisha, squinting as he said, "You two think you are pretty smart, don't you?" He pointed at Ayisha and said, "She tells my wife how to dress, and you tell us when to travel where."

Trudy said in French, "But it's a good idea." Turning to Griff, she added in English, "It's so damn hot that the last thing I want to do is go on a wild elephant chase, Griff! Please."

Looking back at Ayisha and Ahmed, she asked, "Are you two smart kids twins by any chance?"

With wide smiles they both nodded, Ayisha asking, "And guess who is the oldest?"

Ibrahim saw a friend down the wide sandy road, waving at him. He put a hand on a shoulder of each of his children and said in Arabic, "I like the respect in the woman's eyes. She knows you are smart. And I am proud of you, Ayisha, for you fearlessly told the woman to cover herself." Turning to his son, he said, "And I am also proud of you, Ahmed. You have given an honest and smart answer."

He waved at his friend and said, "I feel confident leaving you two with these *toubabs* for the day." Slapping his son on the back, he said in French, "Guide well, and take good care of your sister."

"You're coming with us?" asked Trudy, looking at Ayisha. "That's wonderful."

Ayisha touched her father's hand and said, "Thank you, Father."

Ibrahim looked at his children and said, "Have a good day. I'll see you later, *Inshallah*."

In his twangy French, Griff said, "I am disappointed about no elephants, but there are still many things to do here in Timbuktu." He turned to Ibrahim and said, "*Un plaisir* to meet you, but I am sure you must have to get started on the day too."

Then rudely, he turned his back on him, saying to Ahmed, "What do you say we get started?" Switching into English, he added, "We have something important to do, remember? And the boy just passed a very important test."

"Gotcha!" Trudy answered.

Chapter 9

AS THEY WATCHED IBRAHIM walk away, Ayisha said, "Go, Ahmed, and start. I want to ask Father something."

Ahmed turned to the two tourists. "What would you like to begin with? The museums, the monuments or the mosques?"

"I can pass on the monuments," said Griff. "Tell us, Mr. Guide, what you would suggest."

Trying to rearrange his troublesome turban, he said, as if it were just the most casual of side comments, "Wait, though. What about those old manuscripts you were talking about? Where can we see them?"

"They are displayed in museums and private homes, and a place called CEDRAB," Ahmed answered.

"Actually," said Trudy, "I'd like to stop someplace where I can buy a scarf so I can give Ayisha's back. Then I can wear my own and she can wear hers."

"Good idea," said Ayisha. "I'll catch up with you." She was watching her father turn the corner at the end of the wide sandy road. That was perfect for what she wanted to do.

"*Cuez.*" Looking at Griff, Ahmed asked, "So we go to the market first?"

Griff rolled his eyes and gave the quickest of nods.

As the three started walking toward the Grande Marché, the big, busy market, Ayisha followed the road her father had taken. When she got around the corner, she stopped and took out her carefully concealed necklaces from the cloth Ali had wrapped them in. She picked Ali's best one from the pile and hung it around her neck, then tucked it under the top of her faded red dress. She watched her father meet an old friend. They shook hands, snapped their fingers and then each touched their hearts. She knew they were asking about each other's animals, family, health and work.

Her father looked her way, surprised to see her. He raised a hand and she waved back, then patted the top of her dress, making sure that the necklace wasn't showing. She waved again and ran off to join the others. They were just entering the big market when she caught up to them.

Together the four walked inside the large covered market place. Noise filled the air. Radios played the music of Malian stars like Ali Farka Touré and Oumarou Sangare. On one whole side were men selling piles of cloth. Some sat on the counters of their stalls, with legs pulled up and an arm draped over a knee. Each sold the exact same cloths, including colors, quality and design. There was a group of pot-and-pan menders, sitting side by side. Plastic buckets and jerry cans of green, red, blue, white and yellow were stacked up into tilting towers of plastic.

Across the market women sat behind measly piles of old onions, tomatoes and dates. Ahmed turned to the group and said, "*Monsieur, madame,* where would you like to begin? Is a cloth all that you need, or is there something else as well?"

Griff stepped forward and said, "*Oui,* I need some sandals like yours."

They all looked at Ahmed's feet and the tire sandals he wore. They had once been on a car or truck, but now were slabs of rubber cut to foot size. They curved just enough to neatly fold back in front of his toes, giving protection from accidentally walking into a thorn. Ahmed told Ayisha, "You take her to the cloth men and help her get a good price. I will take him to the cobbler."

Trudy tried to take Ayisha's hand as they walked to the wall of cloth sellers, but Ayisha was too shy and too embarrassed. As they walked along, Ayisha asked, "Do you have a color preference?"

The woman stopped and looked at the piles of cloth. There was every color imaginable, and many that defied names. They reminded Ayisha of Auntie B, who took great pleasure from dressing in the boldest colors and patterns she could find. One man, sitting on his stall shelf, chewing on a wooden stick protruding from the corner of his mouth, took it out and said, *"Toubab, achetez ici!"* Buy here. They walked over to him.

He rubbed his teeth with the stick, which had a splayed, soft end on it from much use. Pointing at Trudy, he asked Ayisha in Arabic, "Who is your friend?"

Ayisha responded quickly in Arabic, "She's not my friend. I am her guide."

The man threw his head back and laughed. "A Bella girl guide? What will happen next—a Tuareg on the moon?"

Ayisha was insulted by his questions and laughter, so she walked to the far end of the row of cloth sellers. Trudy followed her.

An old man, his skin as weathered as an old water bag and with several teeth missing, bowed his head and said, *"Bonjour, mademoiselles. Cherche quelque chose?"* Are you looking for something?

Ayisha liked him immediately and replied, *"Bonjour, monsieur.* We are looking for a scarf for this woman, to cover her shoulders."

Trudy joined in the conversation, in her twangy French. *"Bonjour, monsieur,* I am looking for a deep blue cloth, like that one there."

The one she pointed at rested at the bottom of a tall pile of cloth, but the old man quickly began relocating the fabrics. When there were only about ten pieces left on top, he yanked the piece from the bottom, sending a momentary wobble to the pile. He snapped it open, showing them a brilliant indigo piece of cloth, just the right size for a shawl.

Trudy took it from him, shrugging off Ayisha's cloth and exposing her naked shoulders. The old man turned his eyes in modesty at the sight, but several other sellers looked on. She draped the piece over her and smiled at the man. "How much is it?" she asked.

The old man cleared his throat and said, "Fifteen thousand CFA."

Ayisha had to laugh, so absurd was the price. The man shot her a look, meant to shut her up, but instead her dropped jaw and disgusted look stopped him. He turned to Trudy and said, "What are you offering?"

Ayisha cut in, "Four thousand CFA and not a *centime plus*." She placed her hands firmly on her hips, just like she had seen her mother and Auntie B do many times before. Bargaining was as much a part of life as breathing and drinking. No one ever paid the first price asked, for anything. The old man snorted at her, asking in Arabic, "Why would you bargain for her? Don't you know I will pay you something for the business?"

Ayisha looked at him and said, "But why would you ask three times the price?"

"All *toubabs* are rich, even though they may dress like they aren't."

Ayisha lifted her shoulders and said, "If you give her a fair price, I'll bring you more business. Otherwise I will buy things and sell them myself."

The old man looked her over, head to toe. Shaking his head slowly, he said, "*Cuez.*" Fine. "And what would you consider a fair price?"

Ayisha tugged on her bangs as she thought. She really didn't want to anger the old man. But she also didn't want to help him cheat the *toubab*, so she said to Trudy, "Offer him 5,000 CFA."

Trudy did, and the old man shook his head and said, "Ten thousand." Looking over at Ayisha, he finished, "And not a *centime* less."

Lifting her eyebrows, Ayisha said, "Six thousand, five hundred," in French. Finishing in Arabic, she said through tightly clenched teeth, "That's 2,500 more than I would pay. A very good profit for you."

The old man slapped his thigh and laughed. "You are too bold and too bossy. How old are you?"

Ayisha stood taller and said, "Old enough to go to the Lycée Franco-Arabe next school year."

The old man shook his head and said, "This modern world. Allah protect me. Take the cloth for 6,500, and come back later, for I will have a little something for you." Cocking his head to the side, he added, "And it's just a little because of you and your bargaining!"

Turning to Trudy, the man said, "Fine, 6,500 CFA."

Trudy dug into her little shoulder bag that hung at her side. She pulled out a 10,000 CFA note and handed it to the old man. He made a face, for he didn't have change so early in the day. He took the note and handed it to Ayisha, saying, "Here, *mademoiselle*, find me change."

Ayisha scurried off. Holding the bill up for anyone who wanted to do a good deed and change it, she walked over to the women selling chunks of the hard curdled cheese made from goat's milk. She stopped at a young woman there who smiled at her, a Hausa woman wearing a beautiful gown of green and gold, with a matching head tie fixed snugly on her head. "I have been watching you," she said. "The old man is not happy. Good for you!"

She held up five chunks of the cheese and said, "If you buy these, I can change your large bill."

Ayisha knelt and took the five balls of cheese. Each was the size of a large stone, and just as hard, and filled her hand. The strong scent coming off them made her mouth water.

"*Kadash hath?*" she asked. How much, in Arabic.

"Five hundred CFA" was the answer. Ayisha knew that she should bargain, but she didn't want to lose the chance for the change, so she just nodded and handed the woman the money. The woman dug deep into her *grand boubou* gown and pulled out a wad of money that made Ayisha's eyes pop open.

The woman laughed lightly and said, "I had a very good day yesterday. A man going to a wedding party bought all I had, and he will be back today for more."

She unfolded the pile of bills. The money was old and dirty and folded easily as she counted out 9,500 in change. She pulled the bills from the pile and handed them to the girl.

"*Shukran,*" Ayisha said as she folded the money in half. One hand was full of the money and the other cheese balls.

"*Afwan,*" came the reply. You're welcome.

Ayisha rushed back to the old man and Trudy. She held the bills out to him and he took them. He folded the pile in half and counted them off out loud, folding each bill over his thumb as he flicked them down. "You have only 9,500," he told her. Then he eyed the cheese and said, "That comes from your change, not my money."

She nodded and said, *"Bien sûr."* That's true.

He took his 6,500 CFA and turned to give Trudy her change, but she was busy admiring her new shawl. "Excuse me," he said, "but here is your change."

Trudy took her money. Ayisha held out the five pungent cheese balls to her and said, "This is also part of your change."

Trudy wrinkled her nose as she caught a whiff of the cheese. "No thank you," she said. "Just keep that smelly stuff—I know you saved me more money than that on this cloth."

As they turned to leave, Ahmed and Griff walked up. The old man, hoping for another sale, immediately began trying to sell the *toubab* man another turban cloth. He opened his mouth wide when Griff rudely flicked his hand at him, like a person chasing a dog rather than addressing an older man. "Stop! I don't want any cloth, *shukran.* I just want to get out of here."

Ahmed and Ayisha were humiliated by his rudeness. Even Trudy blanched. Ayisha pushed her brother's shoulder and said, "Go! Take them out of here. I'll find you outside. Now go!" She turned to the old man and said in Arabic, "I am so very sorry. He is a very rude man."

The old man watched Trudy, Ahmed and Griff walk away. Shaking his head, he said to Ayisha, "I hope they pay you well. Give me the heat and dust right here any day." Then throwing his hands out like someone swatting flies off of meat, he said, "Go. *Al Humdullah*, they are your problem and not mine."

Ayisha was steaming mad as she left the market. Just outside the entrance she heard Ahmed, angrier than she had ever seen or heard him, telling Griff and Trudy in a steely voice, "I am sorry, but rudeness is not a good thing. If that's how you choose to be, then I think we should finish right here."

Ayisha's eyes popped open wide, for now more than ever she wanted to catch them stealing manuscripts. She stepped in front of Ahmed, eager to calm the scene down, and said to Griff, who was staring at her brother, "I am sure that you were so rude only because you are just too hot. What's next, brother?" Shielding her eyes as she scanned the sky, she added, "The sun is moving quickly and the heat is growing."

She turned to look at Ahmed, her deep brown eyes pleading with him to calm down. Still staring at Griff, Ahmed sucked in a breath and hissed, "I have a feeling this will be a very long day. Let's go to the Ethnological Museum first."

"Will we see ancient manuscripts there?" asked Griff.

"Yes, yes" was all Ahmed replied.

The group started down the wide sandy road, more like a dried riverbed than a city street. The music of their father's favorite musician, Ali Farka Touré, poured out the short door of a squat, square shop the same color as the sand. The twins listened to the words of the song playing on a tinny radio—*"They send our boys off to war, but we don't know the reason why."* The words made Ayisha a bit sad, for the singer had died less than a month before.

Flat-topped mud-brick houses ran the length of the road, and on the corners of the haphazard cross-streets were women baking bread. They stood before their beehive-shaped ovens, conical furnaces into which they fed round, flat bread on long shovel-like tools. The bread baked quickly in the high heat, and only minutes later was pulled from the oven, brown, round and sandy. The group watched one woman slap two hot breads together, like steaming clapping hands, knocking off sand and cooling them down.

Ayisha suddenly remembered the money her mother had given her that morning. Ahmed's look of surprise made her laugh as she announced, "Please, let me buy you some fresh bread. I love it, and the smell is more than I can resist."

Ahmed took the money from Ayisha and stepped forward to buy the bread, thick, crusty, round spheres of baked flour. His hands were not quite as used to handling the hot bread as the woman's, and he almost dropped the flat loaves on contact. Bouncing one on each palm he said, "Ayisha, please tear them in half so we can share them."

She grabbed one by the edge and carefully ripped it

down the middle. She handed a piece to each of the two foreigners, then took the second bread and ripped it in two. As she gave it to Ahmed, Griff burst out, "Hot!"

He chewed a moment and then spit it out into his hand, adding, "And *trop du sable*." Too much sand. "It's like eating the desert."

The woman baker watched in disgust, turning her back on them immediately. Ahmed grabbed what remained in Griff's hand and said to the woman in Arabic, "Sorry, Auntie."

The woman just shook her head in short little moves and said, "I am glad he is your problem and not mine. I hope he pays you well."

Ayisha assured her in Arabic, "Not to worry, he will pay a very high price."

Trudy, grinding away on the hot, sandy bread, turned to Griff and said in English, "If you can get past the sand, it's actually pretty good." She handed him a small section from her bread and said, "Just eat it. A little sand won't kill you." Almost as an afterthought she added, "Besides, that was very rude. If you want them to help us, Griff, then you have to be more decent to everyone."

Griff looked at Ahmed, saying, "Let's go. The sun is growing hotter faster than that woman's bread cooks." The sun was moving steadily on its course west. The heat, trapped by the sandy road and squat buildings, was growing. It was already near midday, and soon it would be too hot to be walking about, the heat emptying Timbuktu's streets.

Once again they walked down the wide sandy street. The houses and shops, all from the same *banco* mud, had different textures. Some had smooth bricks, and others had rough walls with cracks and lines just like the desert floor. A heavy wooden door adorned each building. The very old doors were decorated with metal shapes and figures, different from the newer doors. They had elaborate carvings on them, with geometric metal shapes pounded into the wood. As they strolled past one house, a young boy came running out, calling, *"Toubab, toubab, cadeau! Donnez moi un Bic, s'il vous plaît."* Toubab, toubab, gift! Give me a Bic pen, please.

Griff and Trudy laughed at the boy.

Ayisha looked into the darkness of the house and saw a woman sitting on the floor, rocking a baby back and forth. She waved at her quickly, and then the group moved along. Tuareg men, wearing long flowing *jalabiahs* and turbans of matching green, white, blue and brown, passed them in a steady flow. Many of the men held hands loosely as they walked down the street, headed to the mosque for the second prayers of the day. Each man offered a friendly *bonjour* as they passed by.

Trudy wiped her forehead and asked, "Ahmed, is it a long walk to the museum?" The sun was obviously taking its toll on her. Her face glistened through a layer of sweat as she wiped it again and again with her new shawl.

"It is not so far. You know, this museum has the ancient well where the woman Buktu stayed while the men took the herds to graze in 1100 AD in the courtyard, which is how this city got its name. *Tim* means 'well' in Tamashek. Mixed with *Buktu*, it means 'the well of Buktu.' There are many artifacts to see here, from the days when Timbuktu was a leading learning and trading center."

Looking at Griff, Ahmed added, "With ancient manuscripts on display."

The *toubab* snorted and turned to Trudy. "Now we're getting somewhere." Looking at Ayisha, Griff threw his hands skyward and said, "At last—the manuscripts. Finally. Let's go."

Ahmed clearly didn't like the tone of voice Griff used with his sister. He took a step closer to the *toubab*, standing between the tall man and Ayisha. "On the way we can stop at the German explorer Heinrich Barth's house. There is also the home of the Frenchman René Caillié, who came here in 1862."

Ayisha watched her brother. Ahmed was happiest sharing his knowledge of the city he loved. Walking down the street of deep sand, he said, "Caillié, who studied Arabic and the Koran before arriving, as part of a disguise, pretended to be a Muslim, so he had a safe journey in and out of Timbuktu. I guess you could say he was the first European to reach here and then return home safely."

"Wasn't Caillié the one who described this place, even way back then, as 'a mess of ill-looking houses, built of earth'?"

Ahmed's face showed his surprise that Griff actually knew some history of the city. It wasn't exactly a complimentary quote, but it was still a sign that the man had done some research about Timbuktu.

Trudy answered Ahmed's unspoken question. "You remember Griff's a trained archaeologist. His studies and work have taken him around the world, from the Incan ruins in Peru to the pyramids of Egypt."

Impatiently Griff glanced over at Trudy. Shading his eyes as he looked down the dusty, crowded street filled with animals, people, motorcycles and overloaded tilting trucks, Griff said to Ahmed, "It's good Barth's house is on the way, since it's the only one I really want to see. He's the only explorer I've ever read about who drank his own blood to stay alive in the desert."

Ahmed's, Ayisha's and Trudy's eyes all popped wide at that information. Griff ignored their surprise, raising his hands in question for which way to walk. Ahmed pointed to the right, and Griff took off down the sandy road between bleating goats and a woman who carried her wares on a table turned upside down on her head.

Ayisha dropped back and casually said to Trudy, "Your husband . . . he's an archaeologist? Excuse me, but he doesn't have the look of one."

Trudy laughed. "What is an archaeologist supposed to look like?"

Ayisha shrugged. "Maybe more like a scholar? And you—are you an archaeologist too?"

"Just about," answered Trudy. "I met Griff on a dig in Nazca, Peru. He was second-in-charge and I was a student volunteer." She twirled the end of her new scarf and said, "He left that job . . . early, and I left with him, leaving school at the same time."

"But why would he leave his work early?"

Trudy answered quickly, "They didn't appreciate him enough or pay him enough." Then, as if waking up, she slapped her forehead and said, "Enough. Why am I even answering these questions? It's none of your business."

Ayisha bent over to take an imaginary rock from her worn leather sandal, telling Trudy, "I'll catch up with you." She needed to think. Her mind was running as fast as a racing camel. She wondered why Griff had left the dig early . . . why he had left Peru . . .

Ayisha trudged as fast as she could through the thick sand to catch up with the group. When she reached them, Griff looked at her, then Trudy, saying in staccato English, "What were you two talking about back there?"

Trudy snapped back in English, "Only that you got fired in Nazca for buying artifacts from grave robbers to sell back home." The exchange Ayisha couldn't understand got immediate reactions from both Griff and Ahmed. Griff stopped walking, tension filling his face as he stared at his wife. Ahmed's face took on a deeper shade of dark as anger sneaked across his cheekbones and pursed his lips. He gave the slightest of head shakes as his sister stared at him.

Ahmed looked down a winding alley that ran off the main road. Houses and shops sat below the street level, for the alley was open to the north where the desert began its trek for more than a thousand hot, arid miles. Sand blown in directly from the desert had made the street higher than when the shops and houses were built.

Ayisha placed her hand on her brother's shoulder and said in Arabic, "What is it, Ahmed? Tell me, please."

Griff's voice interrupted them. "Why do you switch into Arabic all the time? Don't you want us to know what you are saying?"

"No, not at all," answered Ayisha. "It's just that it is our first language, and so natural. I guess that's why you speak English, not to hide anything, just to converse easily."

Griff just nodded, saying, "Now let's get going. We've been out since the sun's early arrival and still haven't seen a thing."

Ahmed took a deep breath and said to Griff, "Barth's house is just there, beyond that tree. An old woman lives there, and she has opened her house to the public for a small fee. So please, if you don't want to pay to enter and see the displays, just tell me. Not her."

Griff nodded, dipping his head up and down like a chicken snatching corn from the ground. "I'll pay. I'll pay."

Opening his hand wide as a gesture of welcome, Ahmed said, "Good. Let's go." As his sister stepped up beside him, he whispered into her ear, "Now I know for sure why they are here, and I will do anything to stop them."

She looked into his eyes. "What did he say back there? Tell me, Ahmed."

Ahmed quickly said, "I'll tell you later."

Nearly shaking with excitement, Ayisha whispered, "And I have news for you too."

Chapter 10

THEY ALL STOOD BEFORE Barth's old house, a typical mud structure of flat roof and heavy wooden door covered with round metal pieces. Ahmed knocked loudly on it, and within a moment the door swung open to reveal an old woman, a tangle of wrinkles crisscrossing her face like a spider's web, covered in a black gown that was also thrown over her head.

"*Bonjour,*" she said, smiling slightly to the group.

"*Bonjour, Madame,* I was wondering if the house is open for visitors," said Ahmed politely.

"*Mais oui.*" Yes indeed. "It is 1,000 CFA to enter for the *toubabs,* and you may come for free as the guide."

Ahmed turned to Griff, who was already pulling out the money from the pack he had strapped to his waist.

Ahmed breathed a sigh of relief, seeing there would be no insulting scene. Ayisha dropped her head, for she didn't want to spend her meager stash of Mother's money to enter. Ahmed noticed and said to the woman, "And what is the price for a local?"

Looking at Ayisha, the woman said, "Is this your first visit?"

Ayisha nodded. "It is, but I will wait over there in the shade of that building."

"No, you may visit once for free, but then there will be a charge every time after, of 50 CFA."

Handing over the 2,000 CFA, Griff led the way into the house. It was dark and cool inside, with a low ceiling. An array of glass cases filled the walls of the entryway and into a second smaller room behind. There were signs in Arabic, English, French and German, explaining the little exhibits of Barth's belongings, old tools and jewelry, but no manuscripts. They were silent, moving along quickly as each one read the brief explanations in their preferred language. The room had been the sitting room when Barth lived there. It was small with mud walls cracked like the dry face of the desert.

Heinrich Barth had arrived in Timbuktu in 1853, after spending a long and difficult ten months crossing the desert by camel. He didn't stay long, for the Fulani and Tuareg were fighting for power in Timbuktu, so he escaped on the Niger River in May of 1854. He had left many possessions behind when he fled, which filled the tiny museum.

Ayisha found herself fascinated, but it was clear that the *toubab* was becoming more impatient. After a very quick look around, he headed out to the street. "Interesting," he said, then looked at Ahmed. "A look at some manuscripts would be good now. It's getting hotter and hotter, and so far for me the events of the day haven't been worth the sweat."

Pointing to the north, Ahmed said, "The Ethnological Museum is close, just across the Place de l'Independence, near the Sid Yahiya Mosque. The mosque is the oldest in Africa, dating back to the 1400s, and is named for one of the 333 saints of Timbuktu. It's still a place of prayer." As they strolled by, Ahmed pointed at the building. "No tourists or non-Muslims are allowed inside." He then pointed to the distant minaret towers of another mosque. "The Dinguereber Mosque. For a fee of 1,000 CFA you can enter that mosque and go to the roof for the best view of the town."

"Not now, not now," said Griff. "Later."

Trudy slapped her hands against her thighs, wilted with the heat. "Please, take us to the most manuscripts. Please!"

Griff just started walking, kicking up dust as his feet dragged through the soft red sand. He stopped and looked at Ahmed, pointing at a building larger than the others nearby. "Is that the museum there?" Ahmed nodded. Looking at Trudy, Griff whispered in English, "Finally!"

Trudy just shrugged, the most she could do in the heat, which definitely was taking its toll on her. "Whatever," she replied.

They walked down an alleyway that turned suddenly in a jumble of crooked angles. Beautiful blue indigo cloths, ranging from the deepest of blue to the lightest of blue, hung on a line outside the front of a tailor's shop. The whirring sound of a foot-pedal sewing machine hummed as they passed. Kids were everywhere, playing with cans, moving them like cars through the sand. Two young boys sat in the meager shade of an acacia tree, its branches twisted and bare of leaves, writing lessons from the Koran on their wooden tablets.

Within five minutes they had reached the Ethnological Museum. Trudy said, "I'll pay for Ayisha if she doesn't get to enter for free. I haven't gotten a single dirty look from anyone since I got this shawl, and I owe her for that."

The museum was open, and right away Ayisha went to the well of Buktu. She sighed loudly as she looked down into the circle of darkness. Ahmed laughed and said to the *toubabs*, "She wishes she was related to the old woman who stayed here while the Tuareg took their animals to graze. Why, I don't know, but she does."

"But it's simple. Buktu is a hero."

"Right," said Griff, clearly running short of patience. "Let's go inside."

The museum wasn't very big, but it had a nice variety of exhibits of old furniture, jewelry and games. Griff looked briefly at each one, when suddenly he caught sight of a glass case in the far corner of the room. He wasted no time rushing over to it, bending low to look as closely as he could. The ancient manuscript was about the size of a large book. Its pages, very brittle, lay piled stiffly, one on top of the other. The text had obviously been written by a flowing hand, for it covered the yellowed paper in perfectly spaced lines. No one spoke as they all gazed at the ancient book, glowing golden in a shaft of light from the window.

Ahmed's voice, filled with awe, almost whispered, "This manuscript is from the thirteenth century. It teaches tolerance for all people, religions and types of government." Ayisha looked at her brother as his voice grew louder with obvious pride. "It proves Africans have had written history longer than many other cultures, including European ones." No one said a word for a long moment as they gazed at the ancient manuscript. The silence they shared hung as heavily as the heat in the air.

Finally Griff straightened up. "Amazing. So, they say there are thousands of these. Ever seen one not on display, Ahmed? One that belongs to someone?"

"A few," replied Ahmed. He looked at his sister from the corner of his eye.

Ayisha noticed that the *toubab* archaeologist's eyes had taken on a brightness that hadn't been there before he saw the manuscript. He pointed at it now and told Trudy in English, "They're more impressive than I ever imagined. Look at the beautiful script and the diagrams in the margins. Now I see why they are so valuable." Lowering his voice, he added, "I wouldn't mind buying one for myself."

Ahmed walked slowly away, like he wasn't listening, but he heard Trudy reply, "Please, Griff, I'm getting very tired in this heat."

Griff called to Ahmed, "We are ready to go back to the hotel. We can talk on the terrace. I want to hear more about these manuscripts." Sweat was dripping down the sides of his face, and his shirt was a patchwork of sweat stains. He surprised Ahmed when he said, "Let's save CEDRAB for tomorrow morning."

Ahmed nodded. "I agree. Everything will be closing soon for the afternoon prayer, and so unless we really rush right now, we will be too late today."

Walking toward the museum's exit, Ahmed took Ayisha's hand to slow her down. Dropping his voice, he said, "Did you see how he has changed since seeing that manuscript? He loved it. I'm certain he even plans to steal one for himself! I think the moment of truth is here. What do I say when they ask to not just see, but to buy a manuscript?"

Ayisha stopped and said, "The only thing you can say—yes. If we sell one to them, then we can catch them. It's getting one that will be difficult, but we'll figure it out. We will catch them, I know it." Looking at the *toubabs'* backs, his covered in sweat, she said in a whisper full of awe, "Ahmed, that manuscript really is amazing. I really want to know more about them. How could I be so ignorant of my own history? We absolutely, positively must stop them."

Ahmed eyed his sister and told her, "I'll talk to Alhaji Musa when I go for prayers this afternoon. He's ready to help us."

When the group stepped outside, everyone's eyes squinted against the dusty glare. A passing truck, moving slowly down the sandy road, sent up a cloud of dust. A string of four donkeys being led by an older woman appeared out of the dust. Not far behind was a line of camels, each carrying a load of dried salt, the thick chunks clunking against one another as the tall camels plodded down the dusty street.

Ahmed and Ayisha turned as one toward the north, for it was late in the year for a salt caravan to be arriving. They were both surprised to see, on the horizon, a caravan of ten camels. It was smaller than the caravans that arrived from October to March, usually bringing the forty-five-kilo salt blocks on 70 to 250 camels. The animals and men were just beyond the rounded tents of the Bella living out there and were busily trading what they had carried for 900 kilometers across the scorching desert from Taoudenni.

Pointing at the caravan, Ahmed said, "The trip they just made takes about fifteen days in the cool season. I have never seen one arrive in the hot season."

Griff started walking toward the caravan until Ahmed shouted, "No. No, come back. Those Tuareg have just completed a very difficult journey, and the last thing they need or want to see is some *toubab* visitors accompanied by two Bella." He turned and started walking toward the hotel, and the group followed.

"Tuareg and Bella—what's it all about?" asked Griff as he walked.

"What's it all about?" cut in Ayisha. "When the Tuareg first founded Timbuktu—thanks to Buktu—they captured all the people that lived here already. Everyone they captured became a slave."

"So your ancestors were slaves?" asked Trudy.

Ayisha dropped her head and said softly, "Our father started life as a slave. It was abolished only in 1976."

"But wait. Wait. They weren't slaves like in your country," said Ahmed. "They ate with their Tuareg families, lived in the same camps and stayed in the same types of tents. Maybe not as fine, but not so different either."

"You make slavery sound good," said Griff.

Ayisha looked up. "No one said it was good. When slavery was banned, many Bella took their freedom and moved on to start their own lives, but some stayed because they knew nothing else. Our father moved to Timbuktu and started his own blacksmith shop, something he couldn't have done as a slave."

Ahmed started walking quickly toward the hotel, giving the *toubabs* his tourist speech as he went. "More than 500 years ago Timbuktu was on the river. Goods came from the south and salt from the north. Timbuktu began as a trading center, salt being traded for gold equally, and soon attracted scholars and holy men and students."

Trudy interrupted, "So were they the ones that wrote all these manuscripts?" Sweat trickled down her face as she walked, moving more and more slowly as the heat increased.

"Yes, they were," Ahmed answered. "The books were copied by hand. They sold for more than the salt or gold." Ahmed's eyes shone as he talked about the treasures, unable to stop himself even though he knew that Griff's interest was not completely the same as his.

The four walked down the road. A blind old man, clutching the shoulder of a young boy, walked slowly down the road toward them, calling out for alms. His hand had worn a hole through the boy's shirt, and his face, covered with gray stubble, lifted when he heard the voices of the four approaching. He stopped in his tracks and held out his hand, eyes squinted so tightly shut that they looked like they were being sucked into his head. *"Monsieur, un cadeau, s'il vous plaît."* Sir, a gift, please.

Griff walked right by, not acknowledging him. Trudy looked to the other side of the street as if she didn't want to see him. Ayisha stopped and dug into her cloth that carried the cheese balls. She gave one to the man, saying, "Go with Allah."

The old man raised the cheese over his head and said, *"Inshallah."* God willing. *"Shukran."* Thank you. He shuffled away, still holding tightly to the boy's shoulder while he took the smallest nibble from the cheese ball.

No one spoke as they wandered down the wide, sandy road. When they reached the hotel, three tables were empty. Ahmed and Griff took the one nearest the building and carried it into the little shade the building threw. The sun had long passed its midpoint in the sky, and the shadows were growing.

The four sat, and when a Tuareg jewelry seller approached, Griff waved him off. This reminded Ayisha of her plan, so she casually pulled her necklace from inside her collar. It shone in the sunlight, buffed to a lovely shine. She played with it like she was unaware of what she was doing. Trudy took a closer look, asking, "Where did you get that? From one of these men?"

Trying to act surprised that she was fiddling with it, Ayisha looked down at the necklace and said, "Oh no. It is from a friend who asked me to sell his work for him. He lives far from town, so I said I would try. But I'm afraid I'm not very good at it. I have never tried to sell anything before."

"Do you have more or want to sell that one?"

"Yes. Are you sure you'd like to see them?"

"Yes," answered Trudy.

Griff was watching the whole thing, his head tilted to one side. He lifted his chin and said to Ahmed, "She's good. Look how she pretends she forgot she had something to sell."

Ayisha ignored him as she laid the necklaces out for Trudy. She also took off the one she was wearing and said, "I am supposed to sell this one as well, for even though the price is very good, it is still too expensive for me."

Griff leaned toward Ahmed. "Let me ask you something. Do you ever sell anything?"

"You mean jewelry? Because if you do, then I can say no, I never have."

"What about other things?"

"Like what?"

"Well, just for curiosity's sake, let's say some ancient manuscripts?"

Both Trudy and Ayisha stopped talking and looked directly at Ahmed. He took a deep breath that all could hear, and said, "I never have, but I've also never been asked before."

"So let's say someone is asking you now. What would your answer be?"

Ayisha cut in, "They are not for sale." Then turning to Ahmed, she asked, "Isn't it against the law?" She definitely didn't want Griff to think they were here for that purpose, plus she wanted him to know what great risk it was for them.

Ahmed nodded. No one spoke until he added, "They are our heritage. People don't sell the manuscripts, and if they do, it must be at a very great cost."

Griff asked, "How much?"

Ahmed rubbed his hands on his pants, suddenly clammy with sweat. "I really don't know. These are heirlooms, passed from father to son, mother to daughter, for generations, and to find someone who wants to part with them is very difficult, and I imagine dangerous too. I heard of one old woman last year who sold a manuscript for a cow. But that was to a collector for CEDRAB, a place where they preserve ancient manuscripts. Not to be sold to foreigners."

Griff held his palms up and lifted his shoulders. As if on cue, Trudy sat up straighter and looked around the hotel's terrace. "Look," she said, "Griff's an archae-ologist, whether he looks like one or not. He needs some of these important papers for when we get home. To study."

Ayisha said, "But he won't be able to share his studies

with anyone else, for how can he explain having ancient manuscripts?"

Griff looked at her again, sizing her up. "Let me worry about that. Don't you want the world to know that Africa was much more intellectual than the rest of the world hundreds of years ago? That Timbuktu, remote as it is, has a great history of learning? To prove that, I'd like to buy a manuscript, or more than one . . . I will pay well, money I'm sure your family could use."

Ahmed cleared his throat and shook his head. With great effort he said, "I don't like it, I don't like it, but I can ask around. By tomorrow I will know if there is anyone looking to sell their family treasures."

Standing suddenly, he said, "I must go to the mosque. I want to make up for the midday prayers I missed. Please excuse me."

Griff grabbed his sleeve and asked, "You know what? You passed an important test today."

Confused, Ayisha asked, "What test could that be?"

Griff looked at Ahmed. "I didn't really want to look for elephants. I knew already that the season is wrong, but if you agreed to take me on a wild elephant chase, then I knew you would lie about anything else I asked you. So now I know I can trust you. Do you think you will have manuscripts for me tomorrow?"

Ahmed shook his arm, trying to free it, and said, "*Inshallah*. I will do my best. I will see you in the morning. Then we will go to CEDRAB ourselves, when the curator is there, a man of vast knowledge. He can tell you more than I can about the ancient manuscripts. They open at nine o'clock."

Just then the voice of the muezzin from Djinguereber Mosque filled the air: *"Allahu Akbar!"* God is great! In less than a moment two other voices joined in, each calling over loudspeakers to the faithful that it was time to pray. "Now I really must go, for Allah calls," said Ahmed. "You can plan a time with my sister, and we shall meet here tomorrow morning."

Ayisha said, "Go, brother. I will stay a few minutes longer, in case Madame Trudy wants a necklace or two. We will meet them here before nine o'clock, on this terrace." Both smiled, for Ayisha had never spoken before of a specific hour. She always talked of the sun's slant, the day's shadows, the call to prayer, to mark the time.

Smiling at Ahmed, she said in French, "After Madame Trudy buys some necklaces, I will go home and finish my chores. I will tell Mother that you might be late so you can begin asking around after prayers." She knew she was sounding in charge again, so she added, "Is that a good idea?"

Griff gave Ahmed a slow wave and told the young Bella boy, "Don't worry, this bossy girl will make sure we are where we should be when we should be there. You go look around for manuscripts to buy, but don't be too obvious. I'd hate to end up in a jail in Timbuktu!" Then he laughed, like he didn't think it was even remotely possible.

Ayisha watched her brother's back, stiff as the handle of a camel whip. She could tell he was not happy about anything, especially selling the treasures of Timbuktu. She would assure him when he got home that if things went right, the manuscripts would never leave Timbuktu. That he was helping to protect them, not sell them.

Ayisha turned to Trudy and pointed at the necklaces spread out on the table. "Are you interested in any of these? If you don't want any, *pas de problem*." No problem. She started to scoop them up, but Trudy stopped her. She pointed at two necklaces and asked how much.

Ayisha pulled out the prices, written in Arabic. She quickly multiplied them and asked double what was written. Then she said, "But if you want both, I can give you a little discount."

Trudy thought the price was too great, and offered half of that. After much to-ing and fro-ing they came to a price, 5,000 CFA more than the written prices for the two pieces. Ayisha started to wrap the remaining ones up when Trudy said, "Bring those back with you tomorrow. Maybe I will want more, or someone staying here will."

Smiling, Ayisha carefully wrapped the remaining necklaces and the money into her cloth. She stood and said, "Good. Until tomorrow, *Inshallah*."

"Speaking of tomorrow," said Griff, "we also have other things to do."

"Can you not do them after we visit CEDRAB? We shall go early and that will save us from the fury of the sun. What other things do you need to do? Maybe we can help."

Griff reached up and shifted his unruly turban. "We

really need to start south. We haven't got endless time. We want to find out about traveling south on a *pinasse*, one of those wooden boats, down the river. The road trip was long and dusty, but we hear the river trip is a bit longer but more comfortable." He tapped the tabletop and added, "We have to go to the port at Korioume to get that information. It's six miles from here, so it shouldn't take all that long to go and come back."

"Perfect," replied Ayisha. "CEDRAB is on the way to the port. You can get a bush taxi on the road after we visit the center. Ahmed can continue asking about manuscripts while you are gone. Then when you return, we can visit the Djinguereber Mosque, go to the roof just before the sunset prayer, and he will give you his news, in private."

Griff tilted his head and said, "It doesn't take you long to take over, does it? I have to admit, it sounds like a good plan. Maybe you should be in charge of finding us some manuscripts too."

A Tuareg man walking past stopped suddenly, looking at the group. Ayisha worried that he had heard Griff talking about manuscripts, so she turned to him with a wide smile and said, "*Salaam alakoum*, are you on your way to mosque?"

"*Alakoum wa salaam*," he said. "I am going. What makes you ask?"

Ayisha lifted her shoulders and said, "Nothing, Baba. You just looked like a man eager to pray."

The man nodded slowly, his eyes squinting just slightly as he looked at Ayisha and then at the *toubabs*. "Do your parents know that you are here? Alone with strangers?"

"Yes," she said. "My brother is their guide, and he just left for the mosque. I myself am leaving also in this moment, to help my mother prepare the evening's meal."

"*Cuez,*" he said. Then looking once again at Griff with his ripped jeans, crooked turban and scruffy beard, he said to Ayisha, "So go. Now!" He walked toward the edge of the terrace but turned back to say, "You, young Bella, had better not be here the next time I turn around."

Pushing her chair under the table, Ayisha assured him, "I am going just now."

Ayisha seethed inside, angry with Griff for speaking so loudly that he had gotten this man's attention. She turned to Trudy and hissed between clenched teeth, "It is most important that no one know what we are discussing. It can only mean serious trouble for us all if someone finds out." Not even looking at the *toubab* man, she finished with, "I will see you tomorrow," then walked tall across the terrace toward the cluster of tents on the horizon.

As she left, Trudy called out, "Don't forget to bring the necklaces with you tomorrow."

They couldn't see the smile that covered Ayisha's face as she hurried away. She waved over her shoulder, showing she had heard Trudy, certain that the profits from the day's sale and the promise of more sales the next would give her another day with the *toubabs*.

 *C h a p t e r   11*

DINNER THAT NIGHT went very well. Ahmed recounted how Griff actually knew about Timbuktu and maybe wasn't as unbearable as he had appeared at first. Ayisha beamed throughout, proud of the money she had made and happy to know that Griff thought he had convinced them against their will to find him some manuscripts. What Ayisha needed now was to go with Ahmed tomorrow.

Miriam had looked at her daughter and laughed. "Look at you, so proud. Don't think you'll be spending another full day with them, even if you did make a good amount of money."

Ayisha stopped smiling immediately. "But Mother, tomorrow she wants to look at the remaining two necklaces again. And we won't be meeting until after I finish all my chores, so I can do all of them slowly and thoroughly."

"Well, you promised to tell us some good *toubab* stories, but until now, nothing," said her mother.

Ayisha reached forward for a piece of bread and stuffed it in her mouth. Spitting it out into her hand as if it were burning hot, she shouted, "Oh, sand! My poor little mouth has sand in it! Help! Help!"

Everyone laughed at her imitation. When the laughter had stopped, Ahmed said, "Ayisha was helpful, Mother. She got the woman to dress correctly, and the woman even thanked her hours later."

Miriam just looked at her older children, then looked away, her thoughts as hidden as a Tuareg man's face covered by a turban.

After dinner the twins walked toward the well to collect water. They went to the one on the edge of town, surrounded by gardens. The well was different from the one where the animals were watered, with a long flight of stairs leading down to it. Scooped from the earth was a large sloping hole, planted with terraced vegetables all around it to protect the walls from erosion. Two women were drawing water as they arrived, so they stopped near the top to talk.

"Did you talk to Alhaji Musa after prayers?" she asked him.

Ahmed shook his head. "He left for Goundam this afternoon. The imam there is near death, so he left in a hurry, and no one knows when he shall return."

Ayisha grabbed his shoulder. "So it's up to us, Ahmed."

He sighed a loud and long sigh. "I just wish this was all over. So what is the plan with the *toubabs*? You seem to have taken control of the whole thing."

Ayisha dropped her head and said, "I only did what you asked, brother, to make arrangements for tomorrow."

He sighed again and said, "*Cuez.* So what are they?"

Ayisha couldn't hide her excitement. "We will meet after chores and prayers and go to CEDRAB together. Then they are going to the port to learn about a *pinasse* going south." Looking shyly at Ahmed, she added, "Now more than ever Auntie B is who we need. She'll know what to do. In fact, I'm sure she can find us the manuscript you promised to show them."

"What? So you expect us to walk across the desert? In this heat?" he asked her.

"We'll do as the salt caravans do—travel at night. We'll carry food and water for the night and day to get there, and be back as quickly as possible. Auntie B has always helped us in the past. Please, Ahmed, can we go? I know she can help us find a manuscript."

"And what about Mother and Father? Have you thought of them?" Ahmed asked. "They will never let us go."

Ayisha looked at the two women collecting water. They each grabbed a full container and walked up the dirt stairs that climbed away from the well, to water their garden plots. The terraced crops splashed green in an otherwise brown landscape. As the women worked nearby, Ayisha whispered, "We won't tell them, Ahmed. We just have to believe that what we are going to do is worth the risk of angering Mother and Father beyond anything we've done before."

"Are you willing to give up school? You know that that is the price you will pay."

With great sadness she nodded. "To catch these two who want to steal our history and think we are stupid, yes." She looked up and asked, "What will you tell them about manuscripts you found for sale?"

Ahmed watched the women splashing water on their plots of green beans. Ayisha studied his solemn face, which was suddenly covered with the beginnings of a smile. "*Al Humdullah*, I've just had an idea. Tomorrow I'll tell them that we have to go to a camp outside of town, just you and me, to pick up manuscripts. That will give us time to find Auntie B."

Nodding, she replied, "That's a great idea!"

Ahmed closed his eyes and counted on his fingers. "But Ayisha—it's four days to go and return."

"I know, Ahmed, but we have to risk it."

The next morning seemed to last forever. Ayisha milked the goats, who gave less milk every day as the heat grew. She went to the well to collect dung, more than usual for the four days they would be gone. She knew that her mother's anger at her disappearance would only grow as she took on her daughter's chores. Ayisha didn't even want to think about it, since she knew they had no choice but to go find Auntie B, especially with Alhaji Musa gone.

When she finished her chores of sweeping and milking, then water and dung collection, Ayisha played with her little brother, Abdoulaye. She was nervous about asking her mother again if she could go with Ahmed to meet the *toubabs*, particularly knowing that they planned to leave in search of Auntie B. Her happiness overflowed when her mother suddenly said, "Are you sure you can sell more jewelry?"

Ayisha tugged on her bangs, and her mother reached out and stilled her hand. "You can go with Ahmed, but just today. Tomorrow this foolishness will stop, so sell what you have, if you can, and then we will take the money and remaining necklaces back to Baba Ali."

Ayisha stooped to pick up her cloth that lay in front of the tent. She held it high, showing her mother the small bundle of necklaces tied into the corner of it. "Thank you, Mother. I shall do my best."

She hugged her little brother and then her mother, who said, "You're just going for a few hours. What's the big good-bye for?"

"Nothing special. I am just happy, for these people are so strange and interesting. Thank you, Mother. I'll be back soon." She threw the scarf over her shoulders, and then flipped it up over her head. She left before her mother could change her mind. The late morning heat surrounded her as she ran toward the city of sand. Plumes of smoke rose skyward over Timbuktu wherever a woman was baking bread. She ran across the open space that separated the tented camp where they lived from the city. The Bouctou Hotel sat on the edge of the town, and she could see the *toubabs* waiting on the terrace. Ahmed was arriving at the same time from the other direction.

Ayisha waved at them as she ran up, sweat dripping down her forehead. Griff stood as she stepped onto the terrace. He rubbed his hands together and said, "We're ready to go to CEDRAB. The day is growing hotter." Ahmed didn't say a word. He just turned and started walking back in the direction he had come from.

Griff moved close to Ahmed's side, whispering, "What news do you have? Had any luck?"

"Yes and no," Ahmed replied.

Griff stopped and took his arm. "Look, it's either yes or no, not both. So tell me, and if it's no, then maybe someone else can help me . . . Did I mention that I'll pay you well for helping me?"

"Yes, you did. And that is the only reason I am doing this—to help my family."

"So what is the good news?"

"I have heard of a woman who has three or four manuscripts, but she is not in Timbuktu. It's a day and a night walk there, but Ayisha and I are willing to go, if you promise to wait here for us. It will take a total of four moon risings, including a day and a night to rest for the journey back, but we will come back with two, maybe three, very old and very rare manuscripts. The oldest, more than 350 years old, even has drawings of the night sky in it, showing the stars."

Ayisha watched the struggle on her twin's face not to express his disgust with it all. She stepped forward and said, "Give us four days and we'll get you a better price because we are going directly to the old woman."

"We'll come too," said Griff.

"Oh, but you can't! This is a Tuareg village where we shall blend in, saying we are visiting an old friend, but you will be too obvious, so you should wait here." She hoped that he hadn't heard of the Tuaregs' reputation for granting hospitality to all travelers.

They walked quickly along the edge of the paved road, so different from the sandy Quarter of Badjinde, the heart of the Old Town. Here the wide smooth road was easier to walk on, and the pace of life quicker. Just as Griff opened his mouth to respond to Ayisha, they arrived at CEDRAB. Ahmed held the door open for the group, who were met by a handsome Tuareg man, dressed in a pale blue gown and turban.

"Bienvenue," said the man. Welcome.

They all heard Griff suck in his breath as he looked at the sight of ancient manuscripts, displayed in closed cases and on pedestals all around the room.

Ayisha could see the Tuareg man's eyes glow as he watched Griff. "Would you like a guided tour of our treasures?" he asked.

Griff appeared oblivious to the man as he rushed right past him to stand before an ancient manuscript resting on a wooden stand. The pages of brown, stiff paper were covered in a clean, precise, Arabic script. Clearly in awe, Griff gently lifted the top page to glimpse at another page, but the man stopped him.

He stepped forward, saying, "Please do not touch the displays." Then he held out his hand and said, "I am Khalid Aziz, curator of CEDRAB, the Centre de Recherchés Historiques Ahmed Baba."

Griff shook his hand, his eyes still on the manuscript, and said, "I am very interested in these papers, for I, too, do historic research for several American universities. As an archaeologist I can appreciate their importance."

"So let us begin," said the curator. He turned to the manuscript Griff had touched and laid the book open to show two pages, one covered across the top half with the most intricate design of triangles around a geometric flower, and the other showing a giant starburst surrounded by hexagonal shapes. "This is a work on conflict resolution and jurisprudence. As you can see, the author was also an artist."

Slowly they worked their way around the displays. In one glass box sat a manuscript made of half-eaten pages, stained and brittle. Leaning over the case, the curator said, "This is what we are battling against, destruction from poor care. These fragile papers are victims of dust, bugs, temperature changes and even vibration."

Griff looked closely and asked, "Why are some so damaged and others not?"

"Because some come from safer storage, from homes of people who lived a sedentary life, whereas others wandered the desert with their owners for generations. We are collecting as many as we can, by purchase or trade, or even just a promise of storage, for these manuscripts show the world that Timbuktu was once a learning center where scholars discussed and wrote about every topic important to mankind." He shook his head and sucked his teeth, showing his disgust. "The climate is not their only enemy, for many disappear into the black market of private collectors and sellers."

No one spoke a word, but Ahmed looked at Ayisha,

and she looked at Trudy, who in turn was looking at Griff. The man continued talking, unaware of the tense silence that gripped his visitors. He opened a door into another room, saying, "And this is where we do our preservation work." Four men and one woman were bent over tables, working carefully with ancient manuscripts. One man was gently dusting the pages of a book before him, and another was gingerly placing a cracked leather cover on a thick collection of brittle pages.

When Ayisha saw the woman, she gasped. Was it really only two days ago that she had playfully told Ahmed that that was her dream—to work with the ancient manuscripts? She glanced at her brother, who flashed her a quick smile. He remembers, she thought. Watching the woman hold a page to the light, brushing the last bit of dust off with a fine little brush, Ayisha knew that her dream could come true.

Suddenly, catching these two *toubabs* in the act of buying manuscripts was all she could think about. The call to the midday prayer surprised them all. They had been there for more than two hours. Turning to Griff, Ayisha asked him if it was time he and Trudy headed to the port. Griff looked around the center, nodding. "Yes, I think you are right. We do need to get to the port."

He surprised the twins when he extended his hand to the curator and said, "Thanks for the tour. You are doing very good work."

When they reached the street, Griff turned to Trudy and said in English, "Now I'm more determined than ever to buy some of these manuscripts, especially one for me. There's a market for these, Trudy. Internationally. This could be a really important buy."

Ahmed, trying to flag down a *bâché* to take the two to the port, shuddered visibly before his sister's eyes when he heard what Griff said. A truck loaded with passengers and piled high with gleaming tin washbasins on its roof skidded to a stop in front of the group. A smoldering look covered Ahmed's face as he said to Griff, "Here is a transport for you to the port."

Griff rubbed his hands together, a smile spreading slowly and snidely across his face. "We'll see you in, say, four hours, on the terrace. By then we'll know for sure when we are leaving and where we'll need to meet when you return from the old woman's village."

Ahmed and Ayisha watched them squeeze their way into the bush taxi. As it left, Ahmed turned to his sister. His eyes burned with a new fury. "We must catch these two."

With that, he headed off to the mosque to join his study group. Ayisha called out to him, "We will succeed." He waved over his shoulder and kept walking. She tugged on her bangs and said to herself, "Yes, we shall succeed, *Inshallah.*"

❖❖ *Chapter 12*
❖

AYISHA SPENT THE AFTERNOON on the Hotel
Bouctou terrace, waiting for Griff and Trudy to
return from the port and Ahmed from the
mosque. She had decided not to go home, for she was certain her mother wouldn't let her leave again. She sat on
the far edge of the terrace, afraid to take a seat or meet the
man that had sent her home the previous day. Ayisha
didn't mind the wait, for she loved just to sit and watch.
Off in the distance a group of children stood around a goat
that was bleating loudly. Three young boys, dressed only in
shorts, had protruding gray bellies covered in dust. A bigger boy, wearing a bright red shirt and green shorts, prodded the goat on its side, trying to force it to move along.

A honking horn caught her attention. A giant truck,
tilting left to right with a fully loaded bed, was working its
way slowly across the deep sand, heading right at the children. The big boy picked up the goat, and the kids scattered like flies being brushed off of meat.

The young Bella girl leaned back on her hands, arms out straight behind her. She looked at the city's collection of flat roofs, pointed minarets, wires and TV antennas. Reflecting on what her brother had taught her over the last few days about the only place she knew, she thought about the city's history as a trade and academic crossroads. Modern Timbuktu is very different, she concluded. For today there aren't any great universities or large gatherings of the learned Islamic scholars Ahmed described. Today it is only a crossroads of people: Songhai, Fulani, Tuareg, Bella and Hausa, all living side by side.

Her thoughts were interrupted by the sound of many excited voices. She looked to her right, where a group of young Fulani women, dressed in their finest *grands boubous* for a wedding, passed by. One girl stood out, her head adorned by ten large amber beads, the color of the richest honey. A piece of red yarn ran across the top of her head, supporting large, scalloped earrings made of glimmering, pounded gold.

The young Fulani woman carried herself proudly. She also carried a young infant, his bald head bouncing against her shoulder. She was clearly close in age to Ayisha, who couldn't help but think, That's what my mother really wants me to be—a mother, not a student. The Bella and the Fulani girls' eyes locked, with Ayisha smiling widely and the Fulani girl smiling right back. Her six friends, still laughing and talking as they walked by, all looked Ayisha's way. Smiles filled every face. As they left, Ayisha closed her eyes and asked herself, "I wonder what it's like to be so beautiful?"

She jumped when a voice from behind her answered, asking, "Are you talking to yourself?"

Her eyes flew open and Ayisha stammered, "You scared me!"

Ahmed's eyes shown with pleasure. "It's not often I get the better of you." He stopped talking when he saw his sister's eyes settle on Sidi. He had walked with Ahmed from the mosque, and Ayisha was not happy to see him.

"*Salaam alakoum,*" Sidi said.

Ayisha answered rather rudely, "Hello and good-bye."

Ahmed stared at her, finally saying, "You sound as rude as the *toubab.*"

She knew he was right, so she quickly apologized, then pointed over her brother's shoulder at the approaching Americans. "Here they come, so it's time for Sidi to go."

Ahmed turned to look and said to his friend, "We'll meet later. I need to work right now, and so we'll meet again this evening, *Inshallah.*"

Sidi gave Ayisha a hard look, then turned on his heel and left.

"What were you talking about? You didn't tell him what we are going to do, did you?" Ayisha whispered loudly as the *toubabs* headed their way.

"No, of course not," her brother answered shortly. "He was telling me about the *futbol* game I missed yesterday. We were defeated again, and the team is blaming me."

"*Malesh.*" Sorry, came Ayisha's reply just as the Americans arrived.

Griff wasted no time. "So what have you got for me?" he asked.

Ahmed started walking, telling the group, "Let's go to the Djinguereber Mosque now. We can talk along the way, looking like an innocent guide and his tourists."

As they started toward the city center, Ahmed said, "The old Tuareg woman across the desert definitely has manuscripts to sell. It's dangerous to ask these questions, though, for suspicion grows each time I talk to someone."

Ahmed, clearly uncomfortable with the conversation, walked quickly, weaving his way through a large herd of sheep wandering down the sandy road. Griff walked right at his side, hissing into his ear, "So how soon can you get them?"

"We'll go tomorrow and be back on Monday, four days at the most," Ahmed said.

"That could be cutting it too close. Today is Thursday and our boat leaves on Sunday afternoon from Korioume. And then we're gone," Griff said, looking at the ground as he walked. He bumped into Ahmed's back, for he hadn't seen him stop suddenly to look at him.

"But we can do it," blurted Ayisha. "We'll leave tonight, in the cool, walk all night and most of the next day, arriving there tomorrow night. We'll spend Friday night there, find the manuscripts and start back first thing Saturday morning. We'll travel Saturday night, and we'll meet you Sunday, at Korioume. We won't go home first, we'll go directly to the port and meet you before your boat leaves." She was breathless by the time she finished. The other three just stared at her.

Her heart pounded in her chest as she looked at Ahmed. He blew out a quick breath and said, "Remember we need to look normal. Let's begin with our tour while we work out the details."

Ayisha wiped the sweat from her face as they stood before the north wall of the ancient mosque. Its surface was smoother than that of the other two mosques in the city, and a winding staircase ran up the side. It was shaped like a pyramid at the bottom, with conical towers.

Taking a deep breath, Ahmed spoke loudly as three men walked past, looking at them. "This mosque was first built in 1327, by an architect named Es Saheli. He received 200 kilos of gold to build it from Emperor Kankan Moussa, who had taken the city from the Tuareg." Ahmed rubbed his hand along the smooth, rock-hard clay wall. He pointed to a platform that stood high above the walls of the mosque. "We can go up there and have a fine view of the city. It's said that your friend Caillié, whom you quoted yesterday, wrote many notes up there. You know, he also wrote that all the population of Timbuktu was apparently 'able to read the Koran and even know it by heart.'" Ahmed's smile could not hide the pleasure it gave him to give a positive quote to the *toubabs* by the same man Griff had quoted the day before. Walking quickly, Ahmed said, "So let's visit inside, then go up there."

Griff opened his mouth, but Ahmed held his hand up and said, "It's best if we do everything like regular tourists."

Ayisha agreed immediately. She looked directly at Trudy, who was wiping sweat from her face with her new scarf. The *toubab* woman just nodded, too hot to speak.

Ahmed went in search of the caretaker to ask permission to enter and to climb to the platform. He found the old man in charge filling the water jugs at the main door.

He shuffled over to Ahmed, his head bent forward. Ahmed greeted him and asked, "Baba, may we enter with the *toubabs*? What is the cost?"

The old man looked over at the group and said, "For the man, 1,000 CFA. The women cannot enter, but they can go to the back area where the women pray, for free. If she wants to go on the platform"—he pointed at Trudy— "it will cost her 500 CFA."

Ahmed rushed back to the group, clearly in a hurry. Griff dug into his pocket and pulled out a crumpled 1,000 CFA and a 500 CFA. He handed them to Ahmed, saying, "Let's get this charade over with."

Ahmed quickly led Griff into the mosque. They stopped to take off their shoes and then walked through the dark building. Columns divided the dark interior, where bats swooped and rays of light spilled down from the air holes in the roof. They walked through quickly and joined Trudy and Ayisha in the back, enclosed area. Together the four climbed to the platform.

Ayisha caught her breath, for she had never seen this view before. The town spread before them: a collection of flat rooftops of both one- and two-story buildings, spires of the other two mosques, confusing masses of crooked wires from building to building. Radios blaring below reached the group. Desert dunes rolled away to the north, east and west, and the strip of tarmac road snaked toward the port in the south.

"It's beautiful," said Ayisha.

Ahmed looked at her and said, "It is beautiful, but don't forget, people live out there, and they also die out there."

Griff cleared his throat and said, "You know what—I don't think there's time for you to go"—he pointed at the huge desert sands—"and get back before we leave on Sunday."

"We can do it," Ayisha said. "We'll get the manuscripts and meet you in Korioume on Sunday afternoon. That should work for everyone."

She looked to Ahmed for help and he said, "It's worth the wait. These manuscripts are from the earliest period of Timbuktu, at least 350 years old. We'll meet you right at the boat. Then you can be on your way and we'll go home, richer for our efforts."

"Well, then, you'd better get going," Griff said.

Ayisha turned just before climbing down from the roof and said, "We'll see you on Sunday, at the port." She sounded much more confident than she felt.

When they reached the ground, Ahmed asked, "Should we really just leave, Ayisha? What about Mother and Father?"

Ayisha raised her shoulders and asked right back, "What can we do? If we wait to talk to Mother and Father, they will surely forbid us from going. And the Alhaji is gone, so he can't help us. If we wait, we'll lose a night's travel. So you tell me, what should we do?" She grabbed his hand and said, "Mother and Father will forgive us when they learn why we rushed off. I'm sure they will. We want to catch these *toubabs*, don't we? I'm sure Auntie B can help us set a trap once she gives us a manuscript." Almost pleading, she said, "Mother and Father will forgive us. They will."

Ahmed looked out at the desert that awaited them, and then at his sister. He just shook his head and shrugged right back at her.

"Do you not want to catch the thieves who want to steal the very manuscripts you love? These people driven only by greed?"

Ahmed let out a loud sigh and said, "Yes, I want to catch them. But what will Father and Mother do to us when we return?" Cocking his head to the side, he asked, "Do you really want to forfeit school?"

Ayisha knew they were losing time, so she said seriously, "They will be proud of us once they get over their anger. We aren't defying them for no good reason."

Looking back at the town, they suddenly saw the *toubabs*, walking quickly and laughing. She pointed at them and said, "I will take my chances with Mother and Father to stop two hyenas like them."

Ahmed looked at the two also and said, "You're right. Let's get going and deal with the consequences when we return."

Chapter 13

THE TWINS RAN BACK TO their tent as though a fire were chasing them. With great relief they found their mother gone. Ayisha took the remaining necklaces and laid them on her sleeping mat. She carefully placed 3,000 CFA next to them, tying 1,000 CFA into the end of her scarf. While Ahmed ran to herd back the goats that grazed listlessly within sight of the tent, Ayisha stopped to look around, as if for the last time.

The sand floor was rippled with footprints, some dark where shadows fell and others bright white where light spilled through cracks in the worn mat walls and roof cloths. Her father's tea set, resting beside the big metal box, caught her eye. She smiled at the sight of Abdoulaye's shoes, one red and one green flip-flop, lying on opposite sides of the tent.

The sound of the bleating, returning goats reminded

her that she was in a hurry. She grabbed the only water bag and ran from the tent. Her face was filled with a rush of changing emotions—fear about the trip they were about to start, determination to stop the *toubabs* from buying any manuscripts to sell in America, worry about her parents' anger and anxiety, and some excitement about the adventures that awaited them.

She left the darkness of the tent and squinted at the sudden sunlight. Running over to her brother, she handed him the water bag and they took off together for the nearest well. There was only one man at the well, pulling water for his goats, which were bleating about their thirst in the hot afternoon sun. The man looked at the twins with curiosity.

"*Salaam alakoum,*" said Ahmed. Peace be with you.

"*Alakoum wa salaam,*" he replied. The man pointed to the sun and then to their hot, sweaty faces and asked, "What in Allah's world makes you hurry so?" He eyed their small water bag, finally asking, "What good is something so small?"

"Good afternoon, Uncle," said Ayisha, ignoring the question. "We are just very thirsty from a day of guiding tourists."

Shaking his head, the old man took his large water container made from old tires and hefted it over the lip of the well. He held it high enough to fill the water bag Ahmed carried, and did so without spilling a drop.

"*Shukran,*" Ahmed said as they turned to leave. Ayisha looked at her brother and said, "I think we need to slow down or we will attract attention." Then pulling on the end of her head shawl, she said, "Here is 1,000 CFA from the money I earned yesterday. This will buy us some dates and a few more balls of cheese. If we eat and drink wisely, it should get us to Auntie's camp."

They tried to walk at a normal pace as they entered the center of the Old Town to buy food. Women were firing up their ovens again, and Ayisha wished they had time to wait for bread. The woman who had sold it to them the previous day waved as they passed. "Where are the rude *toubabs*?" she called.

"We are done with them for a short while," Ahmed called back.

Then like a messenger from Allah, she held up two pieces of bread from her morning baking. Ahmed and Ayisha changed course to buy them from her, but she wouldn't sell them. "A gift," she said, "for bringing me business, but more for taking them away from me as quickly as possible."

The woman suddenly noticed the water bag over Ahmed's shoulder and asked, "Where are you going? Are you starting a trip?"

"Oh no, nothing so exciting. We are taking the *toubabs* later to watch the sunset from that dune," said Ayisha. "They get thirsty easily, so we will be prepared."

Ayisha pointed in the opposite direction they were going to leave by. Ahmed was impressed by her quickness. Turning to the bread seller, he said, "We are going to buy some dates also, have a little feast on the dune."

She gave a quick laugh and said, "*Cuez.* Just promise me that you won't bring them back here."

"Not to worry," said Ayisha.

As they hurried down the road to where the women sat against the wall of a small shop selling dates, Ahmed said, "What has made you so quick with the story?"

"I don't know," she said, shrugging and shaking her head. She looked him in the eyes and said, "But it's a good thing, is it not? For I am sure we will have to tell many stories, especially when we get to Auntie's camp. Let's buy these dates with no chatter, for we are wasting time."

The twins bought as many dates as the old woman could bundle into a piece of used newspaper. Ayisha paid her while Ahmed bought as many balls of cheese as possible with the money he had. He held out three of the hard balls of goat cheese to his sister, who wrapped them up with the dates. It certainly didn't look like much food for a two-day trek across the desert, but they knew that wouldn't stop them. They tried not to scurry as they walked toward the edge of town.

As casually as they could, they walked along the border of the cemetery. Overturned clay pots, upside-down gourds and rocks adorned the graves. A large circle drawn in the sand marked the borders of each grave. Turning back, they could see the minarets of the Djinguereber Mosque, the town water tower and the tall antennas for the town's phone service.

As one, they turned to face their journey. A huge expanse of open desert covered by an endless blanket of yellow sand stretched as far as they could see. Way off in the distance, looking very short from where they stood, were the sand dunes that stood between them and their Auntie B.

When he touched his heart with his fingertips, Ayisha knew her brother was saying a quick little prayer. She smiled at him weakly and they began their trek. The sun was still brutally hot, even so late in the day, and when Ayisha stopped after an hour's walk to wipe her face, Ahmed asked, "Are you sure about this?"

"As sure as the woman *toubab* is sure that Timbuktu is the end of the world."

Ahmed pointed to a tall termite hill in the near distance. "Let's walk there and then rest until the sun is lower. We can sit in its shade and talk about what we shall do when we reach Auntie's camp."

She liked the idea a lot, and rather than say so, she just set out walking. She couldn't believe how tired she felt already, and there was still much desert between them and Auntie B. Her pace was rushed, and Ahmed called out, "Slow down. The mound won't move, and already you are tired. We still have a long way to go tonight if we want to keep the schedule we told the *toubabs*."

Ayisha knew he was right, and she slowed once again. The silence of the desert magnified all sounds, and she could hear her brother's breathing, raspy from much dust and no water. They didn't talk, just concentrated on putting one foot in front of the other. Their goal, the dunes, although closer than before, was still a long way off. The flat desert floor changed as they trudged along. Some places were in deep sand that reached to their ankles, and other spots had a hard rock surface covered by a shallow layer of sand. No matter which, it was easy compared with what lay ahead.

When they reached the termite mound almost two hours later, it stood higher than Ahmed's head, narrow at the top and wide at the bottom. It struck Ayisha that it was not so different a shape from the minarets of a mosque, and definitely the same color. She laid out her shawl to sit on, not the least bit worried about getting dirty, but because she thought it was good to do things as close to normal as possible. Leaning back against the tall clay structure, built by millions of termites mixing their saliva with the sand to form the sturdy tower on the desert, she sighed, *"Al Humdullah."*

Ahmed held up his water bag and asked, "Do you want a sip?"

Almost ashamed, wanting some precious water so soon, she nodded. He dripped water carefully into her open mouth, then tilted back his head and did the same for himself. Still no conversation started as they looked at the distant dunes and then back at the place where Timbuktu stood. From their sitting position it was no longer visible, which meant the twins were truly on their own, in a desert that decided who should live and who should perish.

Ayisha handed Ahmed two dates, and he ate them faster than a goat pulling green leaves from a bush. Now it was his turn to be embarrassed, but she only smiled as she slowly chewed her sweet dates. The two swallows and two dates provided a little comfort. Ayisha stood to look back at where they had come from, both hoping and not hoping to see some sign of Timbuktu. She sighed with relief, for the city was not visible—even the tall communications antennas were gone from sight. That meant they had made good progress in their first three hours of walking. A turn to the west erased any relief she was feeling. "Ahmed," she cried, pointing west.

Ahmed jumped to his feet, stepping out from behind the termite mound to look where she was pointing. A sudden ominous silence filled the air. The sky started to turn dark, like the sun had set, but both knew that was not possible. Their eyes opened wide as they looked at each other, for they knew what was happening. A harmattan dust storm was on its way. One never knew when such a storm would start, for their onsets were sudden and raging as the winds gained momentum and power rushing across an empty desert.

A cloud of dust was building, eating the sky as it moved forward. The sun, still a distance from setting, was blotted out by the massive red wall of spiraling dust. Ahmed's white pants began to whip about as he reached for his sister's hand.

"Stay standing," he shouted. "If we are seated, we shall be covered with sand and no one will find us ever again."

Ayisha's skirt whipped about her like laundry hanging on a line as they stood behind the meager protection offered by the termite hill. Ahmed reached forward and took her shoulders, pulling her close. He draped his prayer shawl over their heads and they stood, sand stinging her bare legs and their feet clad only in sandals. The noise of raging winds and whirling sand owned the desert now, and the twins held on to each other tightly, fighting the wind's attempts to push them over, uncertain whether the storm would last hours or minutes. Covered, they didn't see the giant tumbleweeds that bounced past them or the huge dust devils on the edge of the storm, twisting skyward, bright red with dust.

It ended almost as suddenly as it had begun. They didn't take the shawl off right away, for neither was sure that the storm was really finished. Looking eye to eye in the gloom of the cloth over their heads now covered with a fresh, thick layer of red dust, Ayisha felt her eyes sting. She lifted her hand to rub them but Ahmed stopped her. She knew it would only make things worse, but she really needed to clear her eyes at least a little.

They looked down at their feet, buried beneath sand that had piled up around their ankles and shins. When the raging of the storm had stopped for a few minutes and an ominous silence filled the air, they finally lifted off the prayer shawl. The sky looked like someone had set a red gourd over it. Dust devils tore across the land before them, racing toward Timbuktu. The dust wall hung in the air all around them, leaving a circle of blue at the top where the dust hadn't reached. It cut the sun's glare but didn't really cool anything down. Ayisha bent to rub her legs, which had been attacked by the sand. As she bent down, she saw that their stash of dates and bread and cheese had been left on the ground.

Just the corner of the paper they were wrapped in stuck out of the sand. She dropped down to dig them out and found three dates. The rest had blown away. Two big balls of cheese were gone. She flicked the sand around and found, buried beneath it, one piece of bread. She pulled it from its sandy nest. Lifting her feet from the sand pile and slapping the bread against her thigh to remove the sand, she could feel the tears forming in her eyes. The first tear rolled down her cheek and dropped onto her chest. She tried to hide it from Ahmed, but he saw it, and the next one and the next one too.

"Are you all right?" he asked.

She nodded, closing her eyes as she did. Handing him the three dates, she held up the bread and said, "And the *toubab* thought his bread had too much sand?"

The quick laughs that followed surprised them, but also made them each feel a little better. Looking north, south, east and west sent a shiver through Ayisha as she thought, So little food and so far to go. To hide it, she bent over to rub her legs. They were covered in scratches where the sand had rubbed them raw. She smoothed them with her hand and winced slightly at the pain. Ahmed dropped to his knees and said, "Let me help."

With the end of his prayer shawl he gently brushed the sand from her legs. Then he wetted the corner of the cloth with his spit and began to rub her shins. She had to laugh again, for that's exactly what Mother had done and they both had gagged. Ahmed's head shot up when he heard her giggle. She was glad for another laugh. He looked up at her, laughing also.

"Mother," they said together.

The nearly hysterical laughter stopped just as abruptly, for they both saw Ayisha's shawl at the same time. The wind had shredded it, all that wasn't buried in sand. Slowly she pulled it out. Long tears ran the length of the cloth until they reached where it had been trapped beneath their feet. Each stepped to the side as Ayisha pulled the rest out. It was tattered like a drying turban caught in the powerful winds of a harmattan. Six long strands connected to a small remaining swatch of whole cloth. She dangled it down, staring at it and then at her brother. The six strips didn't move, for not a trace of the wind that had ripped them was in the air. If she hadn't just experienced the whole thing, she would have thought they had been cut by a tailor with scissors.

Ahmed just shook his head back and forth in commiseration. Ayisha continued to stare at what had been her head and shoulder cover, plus the carrier of their food stash. It really didn't look like it was good for anything, but Ayisha knew she would find a use. Suddenly an idea popped into her head and she handed the solid end to Ahmed, saying, "Hold this tightly, please."

He grabbed the cloth and held it with both hands. With fingers as nimble as a hair braider in the market, she braided first the three strands on the right and then the three strands on the left. Taking the solid part from her brother's hands, she stretched the unripped piece across her head and then wrapped the braids around it, left to right and right to left, joined in a knot on her forehead. It gave her at least some head cover. She pulled down her bangs as Ahmed gazed at her respectfully. "So not only your tongue is quick," he said. "That was a very good idea."

She smiled in thanks, then looked at the sky burnished red by the dust storm. "Shall we start? There is still some light left in this red sky. I will clean the food that remains when we stop later. You do know what direction to take now that the sun is hidden and the moon has yet to arrive?"

Ahmed walked around the tower of the termites. "The wind came from behind the termite hill. I don't see the dunes right now, but they were to the west of the hill. I'm sure they'll reappear as the dust settles." Pointing directly ahead, he said, "That's the way."

He readjusted his water bag, which had never left his shoulder, while Ayisha took the remains of the newspaper and wrapped it snugly around the bread, dates and three remaining cheese balls. They walked toward what had been a brilliant sun less than an hour ago. Now the sun's power was covered as completely as a camel's hump hidden under a saddle.

Neither said a word as they walked, for there were many things to think about. Ayisha stared ahead of them, willing the dunes to appear. Finally, the very top ridge of a dune was visible through the dusty sky. Excited, she said, "There they are, the dunes! Do you think we'll be there tonight?"

Ahmed shrugged and shook his head. *"Inshallah."* Allah willing. "I really can't say if we will. They aren't a mirage, so high in the sky. It's good to know that they are there and that we are on the right path."

Ayisha didn't say a word. She just glanced up at the first one and then back at the ground to watch her feet. She didn't know how much time passed and did not look up again until she heard her brother gasp. He stopped and she bumped right into his back. Looking up to apologize or receive an apology, she too was stunned by the sight.

Through the dust reaching halfway up the sky, the sun shot its last rays heavenward. Crimson streaks and purple rays filled the sky like pointing fingers. The red dust wall, covering the entire horizon in all directions, glowed where the sun went down, with a brightness that was missing to the north and south of it. Ahmed looked at his sister and said, "I won't stop for prayers, although we need all we can get. But please, let's just take a moment to thank Allah for getting us through that storm."

Standing side by side, they faced the east. Ahmed held his hands, palms up. His bent elbows made his hands shoulder high. Ayisha followed his example, and with a quick whisper like water running over rocks after a strong rain, he thanked Allah. He then placed his right hand over his heart, and Ayisha followed again. He looked at her, nodded, and without saying a word, they both knew to say together, *"Al Humdullah!"*

They walked and walked until darkness overtook the

dimness of the harmattan. The moon, which was a night from fullness, struggled behind the wall of dust to share its light. They couldn't see it, but they could see the faint glow that rose from the top of the wall of sand and dust. Ahmed altered their course just slightly, walking directly away from the moon and toward the spot where the setting sun had slipped unseen.

The darkness that surrounded them was denser than any Ayisha had seen before. Even inside their tent on a night with no moon, starlight filtered in. On a full-moon, light shot through holes in the mat roof or spilled through the fraying blue plastic sheet over one spot. She always counted the holes in the mats to see if the roof was worse than the month before.

Ahmed tilted his head back to look at the center of the sky. About halfway up from the horizon a few stars twinkled, so he pointed them out to his sister. "I'm glad to see them there," he said.

"Not nearly as happy as me, I am sure." To add some fun to the evening, she started a game they had played since they were small. "I'm as happy as a mother with a newborn baby."

"And I'm as happy as a herder with many goats and camels after a downpour."

"Well, I'm as happy as a baby goat at its mother's udder."

"I'm as happy as a camel with a full hump of fat."

"I'm as happy as the day I set the highest test scores in history at our school."

They both stopped suddenly, for that brought to mind what the price would be for making this trip. To remind them of what brought them to the desert, alone and at night, she added, "And Ahmed, I will be happiest of all the day when we catch those two."

Nodding, he said, "You're right about that. Now I would be happy to get going again, for although we can't see the hands in front of our faces in this darkness, we can walk slowly and still make progress. We won't catch anyone if we don't get back in time."

And so they walked, one foot following the other, the night's progress marked by the growing moonlight. Slowly the light grew, like someone moving the wick on a lantern. The higher the moon rose, the weaker the dust and the stronger the golden glow. The twins could see their growing shadows, and it filled Ayisha with pleasure. She interrupted the silence when she said, "Look, Ahmed, we have moon shadows."

Together they turned to the east, just as the top lip of the moon peeked over the red wall of dust. It reflected off small clouds drifting in the sky. The night's brightness grew and grew, spreading across the desert like a growing spill of goat's milk. To the east was nothing but flat horizon, the bottom edge of the thick wall of dust. Turning to the west, they saw the dunes again. They had disappeared in the dust and then the darkness, but the twins were still right on target.

Ayisha looked at Ahmed and said, "Good navigation, brother. How do you know so many things? Like to stand in the dust storm, and exactly which way to walk on a night as dark as the inside of your water bag?"

Ahmed smiled to himself. "I learned about standing in the storm when the *futbol* team went through a harmattan outside of Goundam. Sidi told me, and it definitely works. Think about the sand that crawled up our legs. If we were lying or sitting, it could have covered us, just like the bread and dates and cheese."

"Or torn us apart like it did my headpiece." She patted her head, proud of her invention.

They walked as the moon arced its way above them. When it dipped into the wall of sand in the west, Ayisha stopped. "Brother, is it possible we will make it there"—she pointed at the nearest dune—"early in the morning?" Rubbing her stomach, she said, "I know that this empty belly and these tired legs, still scratchy from the sandstorm, cannot go much farther without a rest. I would prefer to be rested before we start climbing the dunes."

Ahmed nodded. "It's a good idea. We can stop just before the dune so we will be fresh to start in the early morning."

They trudged on for another thirty minutes, each step heavier than the one before. Ayisha could hear her brother whispering prayers under his breath. She was so tired she felt like even whispering would rob her strength to keep walking. She pictured the *toubabs*, him in his crooked turban, spitting out his bread, and her laughing at his rude comments about Timbuktu. She thought of their lies and eagerness to steal some ancient manuscripts, bragging to each other about the wealth they expected to gain. And her worried parents. That thought really fueled her walking, and she picked up the pace dramatically. Ahmed laughed out loud and said, "What has spurred you like a camel smelling water?"

In one breath she said, "I was thinking of the *toubabs*, and what great cost it is to me to stop them. One minute I was so tired I thought the left foot would not follow the right even once more. And then I saw their faces in my mind, and heard their laughing, and then Mother and Father's worried faces, and my feet started moving with morning's freshness instead of the tiredness that weighs them down."

Ahmed's eyes were open wide, listening to this spill of words. A sudden shiver ran through his body, and he took his prayer shawl off his head to give to his sister. "Wrap this around you," he said. "It's cold out here." He looked at his twin's shoulders scrunched up against the cold and said, "Let's stop here. We'll sleep until the sun wakes us, which I am afraid will be very soon."

Almost embarrassed, Ayisha asked, "Is there any water left? Just enough to wet my tongue?"

Ahmed quickly took the bag from around his shoulder and said, "Of course, for all should have a wet tongue when possible." As he dripped a few drops directly on her tongue, he asked, "And hunger? Does your stomach also complain, Ayisha?"

Ayisha nodded as she savored the delicious liquid on her tongue. She swallowed the minuscule amount and said, "Hunger is easier. I have felt it before and know that it always goes away with the smallest amount of food. But this thirst is terrible. And you, brother, is not your thirst great and your hunger strong?"

Ahmed nodded slowly and said, "What have we done?"

"The only thing we could," Ayisha said. "The only thing we could."

THE COLDNESS OF THE night always shocked the twins at home, in the family tent, so being unprotected out on the desert sands sent shivers through their thin clothes. The day's 109 degrees in the shade plunged 50 degrees. Ahmed put his arms inside his shirt to try to hug himself warm. His teeth chattered. He shook his head as he gazed into the darkness lit only by a star-studded sky. A filtered golden light shone through the haze of the western dust. "Remember," Ahmed said, "this was your idea."

Ayisha sucked in her breath, shocked by the bitter cold. Her thin rose-colored dress offered no warmth against the night's harshness. She pulled tighter on Ahmed's prayer cloth draped over her shoulders. "We'll be fine," she reassured him. "It's Mother and Father I'm worried about."

Ahmed peered into her eyes, mainly obscured in the darkness. "Should we turn back in the morning?"

"And forget about Auntie B? Never. She will know what to do." But the thought of her mother and father worrying would not go away.

Ahmed turned a slow circle, craning his neck back and mumbling, "Where is the North Star? Where is the North Star?" Suddenly pulling his right arm out of its nest inside his shirt, he extended it. Pointing, he said, "*Al Humdullah*, there's the North Star, the one that guides all travelers in the desert."

Ayisha dropped to the ground. She felt the sand rub against the back of her raw legs as she collapsed. The afternoon's dust storm had left them both covered in sand, grains so fine that only time would dislodge them. The sand was hard and cold on the ground, but she was so tired she didn't care. Looking up at her brother still scouring the sky, she asked, "Why do you think Auntie B still stays with the Tuareg family she grew up with?"

Ahmed's shoulders made a quick bounce up and down. He dropped down next to his sister and said, "She told me it was the easiest thing to do, especially since she and Mother don't get along. Also, that's how she makes her living, painting the Tuareg with henna. All those swirls and flowers and shapes she's so proud of."

Ayisha's eyes drooped as she said, "We should try to sleep. Today's storm scared me more than anything, and I am feeling weaker than a baby goat freshly born."

Ahmed scooted close to his sister. "Do you want to face the west, or east toward Mecca?" he asked. He continued scooting until their backs were touching.

"You can have Mecca," she replied through a giant yawn. "We both know it means more to you than to me."

Facing the opposite direction from Ayisha, Ahmed said, "Lean against me. Scrunch up your legs so your body heat stays in."

Ayisha wrapped her arms, encased by the prayer shawl, around her knees. On second thought, she raised her arms high and said, "Wrap this across your chest and we'll stay warmer together." The long white cloth with tassels stretched tightly around them both, like a giant belt. Ayisha wrapped her arms around her pointy knees pulled to her chest. Resting her back against Ahmed's, she tilted her head to scan the sky also. Her eyes dropped in total exhaustion as she thought back on the day.

What a day it had been. Rushing through her chores, then convincing Ahmed that seeking out Auntie B was the smartest thing they could do. Then meeting the *tou-babs* and learning they had no time to spare. First they had rushed to the tent to grab the water bag. Then they had rushed off to buy what little food they could for the trip with some of the profits from selling the necklaces the day before. Thinking about the decision to leave without telling Mother and Father . . . Ayisha exhaled.

She pictured her brother and her, wanting to run, but walking slowly out of town at a baby's pace so as not to attract attention. And the dust storm. Never had she been caught on the wide-open desert in a storm before. And now they were a small, freezing, gritty lump on the desert floor, snuggled back-to-back.

"You know, the first one to sleep will topple us over," she warned Ahmed. As her eyes lingered closed longer and longer, she mumbled, "I wish we had brought more water and food."

Ayisha's head started to slowly roll side to side as sleep overtook her. In a whisper meant only for the night, Ahmed said, "Sleep well, sister of dumb ideas." Then with a snort he continued to watch the night so cold and huge. "And may I also sleep—the one dumb enough to love her ideas." Sleep crept over him, and like one of Allah's natural balanced stone sculptures he had read about, they slept, adding gentle snores from the depth of a well-earned sleep to the cricket-filled night.

The sudden drop again in the temperature heralded the coming dawn. Less than two hours after stopping, the dawn arrived. Ayisha's deep shiver brought the two awake. She looked west at the darkness that had not lost any of its intensity. The dune loomed right before them. She was happy to see it, for the thought of their small water bag and their few bits of food set her to tugging on her bangs in worry.

She scooted around to be shoulder to shoulder with her brother. She did it with an ease that could come only from sharing a womb for eight and a half months. The first traces of light, still dimmed by the reduced layer of dust along the horizon, rose in the east. Ahmed pointed at it with his chin, saying, "When the sun rises, I will have to leave our warm cocoon and say the *Alfadjir*, my morning prayers." He smiled and added, "You could always join me . . ."

She laughed, saying, "I told you, I don't need to pray five times a day at special hours. I pray when I thank Allah for the desert's beauty and for Timbuktu's *lycée*." Hugging herself, she said, "And when I give thanks for parents who are letting me continue school, *Inshallah*, if this trip doesn't spoil it all." Shaking off that unpleasant thought, she said, "I also pray for a chance to go to the university."

Ahmed's head shot up. "University? Ayisha, that's news to me. You, a girl? Do you really think Mother and Father would agree to that?"

"*Inshallah*, when I win a scholarship to the university in Bamako, Mother will want to brag about it more than to watch me sulk in Timbuktu if they don't let me go." She sucked in her breath and repeated, "*Inshallah*."

Ahmed cleared his throat and said, "Sister, don't get too many crazy dreams. No wonder they don't want you to talk to too many *toubabs*. I think you got too much dust in your head yesterday during that storm."

"But there are so many things I want to do, Ahmed—want to know." Taking a deep breath, she said, "When we were at CEDRAB, I really knew for the first time, and I mean, knew as surely as Father knows a good goat when he sees one, that I must work with the ancient manuscripts. Work at CEDRAB!" There, it was out. She had told Ahmed playfully three days earlier, but as she said it now, she knew what she would study for. "And I also crave an adventure in life."

She turned to look at her brother and said, "I want to know why these *toubab* women wear clothes that reveal more skin than they cover, in a place like Timbuktu where no local woman would ever do such a thing. What could they be thinking? Look at Trudy. Before I warned her, she had shown you more skin than you had seen in our first thirteen years of life together." Shaking her head resolutely, she said, "She can't be thinking, for no person could be that stupid."

Ahmed held up his hand and said, "Enough. She knows now that her clothing was offensive, thanks to you, and has covered herself ever since. That was good, for it did embarrass me to see her."

Slowly he rose, breaking the seal that had held their body heat in during their deep sleep. Although only sand surrounded them, the whir of the cicadas cranked up a notch. Looking off to the east, he asked her over his shoulder, "Did you sleep well?"

Ayisha smiled and said, "As well as one can, sitting up in the desert, lacking food and water and knowing that Mother and Father are more worried and angry than two parents should ever be. I've a hunger and thirst I've never known before. I don't know how long we slept, but I did sleep like a camel that has walked for days with no rest."

"It wasn't long, but the best news is that we are on course." He pointed east across a landscape dotted with scrub trees and an occasional tall acacia tree and said, "There lies Timbuktu." Then turning to face due west, he pointed at the sand dunes rising on the horizon, glowing as they caught the morning's rising sunlight.

Together they turned back to the east and gazed at the glimmer of sunlight rising above the dusty horizon. They could see the low clouds that would hold down the day's heat rather than drench the parched land, reflecting an orange light, as strong as the sunset the twins had seen. To a background of frenzied chirruping, the sun's top rim peeked above the dust.

"Al Humdullah," whispered Ayisha as they gazed at the day's dawning.

"Now do you see why I face the east and pray five times a day?" Ahmed asked her.

"Yes, brother—yes. But I've already said my prayer. And Allah answers prayers quickly, Ahmed, for if this isn't a life adventure, then I don't know what is."

Chapter 15

WITH THE SUNRISE came the silhouette. It stood alone on a horizon that sucked up the sky in a long straight line. No trees or brush dotted the distant landscape, just the deep black silhouette that could be only one thing—a man on his camel.

"He looks as if he's coming directly from Mecca," breathed Ahmed. The fiery orange sun rose directly behind the wall of dust, outlining him against a blazing orange wall rising from the earth's edge. The backdrop of Mother Nature's bright orange layer of lingering dust outlined sharply the strong neck of a camel, with a man sitting tall behind its head. Four long legs planted it firmly to the earth.

"That is amazing," whispered Ayisha. "He looks like a tourist sign: *'Tombouctou—le Mysterious.'*"

Ahmed began jumping up and down, waving his arms back and forth over his head. The last thing he had expected to see was someone else on the desert so huge. He whooped and jumped, oblivious to his sister's stare and silence. The figure on the horizon suddenly veered more westerly, heading straight toward them.

As suddenly as Ahmed had started yelping and leaping, he stopped. Looking at their sudden lifesaver on the horizon, he said, "I can pray before he arrives so we are ready to go with him."

Bending at the waist, Ahmed began his preparations for the first prayer of the day. Washing his hands symbolically with sand, he looked toward the stranger. "*Al Humdullah*—thank Allah for sending us this man."

Before Ayisha could respond, Ahmed raised his hands, heart height at each side, palms up. Then he bent again, hands resting on his knees, speaking a rapid Arabic just under his breath. In one motion he dropped to his knees, hands out before him, then dropped his head to the sand in total obeisance. He then sat back on his folded legs, leaning just a little to the right as he continued to pray.

Ayisha watched as he once again leaned forward, touching his forehead to the sand. She could see the camel rider over her brother's sloped back, making progress toward them. As Ahmed rose to his feet and began the prayer process again, Ayisha thanked Allah that he would do it four times so she had time to think. She also looked forward to talking to the stranger, but she was sure her questions would be different from her brother's.

She turned back to look toward the west. There was no trace of the moon that had set and dipped into the dust.

There was just a string of sand dunes higher than any she'd seen before. They were in rows, like the millet grown by the Hausas and Songhai in the sand. One row of dunes followed the other, three total, before a distant dune rose high above the others. She knew that the farthest dune was their destination, for Baba Ali had described a giant dune that served as the backbone for the camp. Squinting with her hand over her eyes, she could see that they wouldn't have to climb the first two rows of dunes. Little pockets of flatness lay in between them, standing side by side, exactly the same height, running away from each other north and south, as far as she could see.

Far to the left of the first pass she could see where the next row of dunes separated—a gaping space between two more dunes that stood side by side, exactly the same height, but not touching. She couldn't see any break in the third dune but decided she would worry about that later. One thing she knew for sure, she wasn't going anywhere with the camel man if he gave her the answers she was hoping for.

She turned back to check his progress just as Ahmed finished his prayers. He stood for the fourth time, turning his head quickly from left to right. He smiled as the final words of prayers spilled from his lips. He opened his eyes, happy to see the camel rider bouncing up and down toward them as his pace picked up.

"Here comes food and water and a ride for you," Ahmed said.

"Food and water is what we hope for. I was slightly worried about our meager supplies, but not anymore."

Ahmed glanced over at her, noticing she had failed to mention the part about a ride. "Ayisha," he said with authority, "if he offers you a ride, you must accept it."

She didn't look at her brother or even respond as she waved her arm in welcome to the now galloping camel man. Camel and man looked connected, so smoothly did the man sway with the camel's rocking gait. His arrival left both kids speechless as the man stepped from his mount before the camel had even come to a complete halt.

"Salaam alakoum," said the twins together.

"Alakoum wa salaam," answered the man. He was a Tuareg, wrapped in a dark green turban that covered his nose and mouth. His long loose gown matched the turban, down to the same amount of dust film. A beautiful green and red leather bag with long tassels swung from his neck. His pale yellow backless slippers were also covered with dust.

The man tilted his head to one side, his eyes revealing the worried look that surely crossed his hidden face. "May I ask what, in Allah's name, you are doing out here, so far from everywhere? Do you have water? And where is your food? Why are you here and where are you going?"

Ahmed and Ayisha looked at each other. Then Ayisha stepped forward and said, "We are fools in the desert. Here is our nearly empty water bag, and most of our food was blown away. Thank you for asking, and thank Allah for sending you our way."

She didn't want to be totally rude, but her eyes slid to the saddlebags, green and red, draped behind his saddle. A water pouch also hung there. The stranger's eyes followed hers. He dropped the reins of his camel, whose head stood tall above them, contentedly chewing on his cud that could sustain a camel for days.

The man reached out his hand to Ahmed and said, "I am Abdul Abdullah. Please, help yourself to water and food." He reached back and unhooked the saddlebags. With a fluid motion he dropped into a squat. He pulled dates and dried goat meat from the biggest bag. All four eyes of the young Bellas bulged at the sight, but the ever fearless Ayisha said, "Baba Abdul, that food looks like the finest feast Allah ever provided, but please, may we have a sip of water first?"

In the early morning light Baba Abdul looked at the twins. "You must have been in the desert during the great sandstorm that buffeted Timbuktu yesterday," he said as he reached for the water bag. "Tip your head back and I will quench your thirst carefully. Then you can tell me where you have come from, children, and where—on Allah's earth—you are going."

Ayisha held her head back, mouth opened wide. The cool water trickled down her parched throat as the man skillfully controlled the amount that he poured out. He then held it over Ahmed's face, once again trickling the water slowly. She suddenly giggled as she watched, and the man's eyes shifted quickly from her brother's face to hers. He crooked his head to the side and said, "It seems quite strange to see someone, stranded in a desert only Allah's eyes can see completely, laughing."

She looked right into his eyes, a bold thing for a young

Muslim girl to do with a strange man old enough to be her father. "Excuse me," she said. "But suddenly I felt as if you were watering us like you water your camel and goats."

"It's not so different," the man agreed. But before Ayisha could say anything more, he said, "If you can laugh, then you can certainly talk. Tell me what you are doing here."

Ayisha gave Ahmed no chance to answer as she quickly said, "We are going to find our Auntie B." In the dawn light she pointed off into the distance at the giant sand dune that stood above all the others. "She lives in the Tuareg camp at the base of that dune. *Inshallah*, for we have never been there before and are trusting the words of another that she is there."

Turning to Ahmed, the man asked, "And your parents know where you are? Out here in a heat hot enough to dry a camel's throat, looking like you wear as much sand as the desert itself?"

Ahmed opened his mouth to answer when Ayisha butted in with, "But of course they know. Our father is ill and we are going for his sister."

Still ignoring her, Baba Abdul asked Ahmed, "Your parents really sent you out here on foot? Before Allah, I don't think so."

"Well, actually not sent us. My mother was in such great fear for our father's life that we thought the best thing we could do was go for his sister," answered Ayisha.

Ahmed's eyes focused on the ground as he listened to the lies roll off his sister's tongue. He wasn't sure if it was clever—so quick and sure were the tall tales she was telling. Looking up, he saw Baba Abdul staring at him.

"Don't you speak?" he asked Ahmed, his temper clearly growing shorter.

"Yes, Baba," he said, using the word *Baba* as a sign of respect. "I do when she gives me a chance. We were born about thirty minutes apart, and she thinks being older always means she is in charge. Even if she is only a girl."

Ayisha was shocked at the "only a girl" comment, but more pleased about her brother following her lead. "Excuse me, Uncle," she said politely, "but do you know the Tuareg camp we speak of? Is that where you are going?"

Baba Abdul looked at her, slowly nodding. "I know it, and you are right. It does sit at the foot of that giant dune off behind the others."

"Will we reach there today, walking?" she asked. Gushing, she continued before he could answer, "I love the desert and the way there are no people here, well, except for us three, not like crowded Timbuktu. If we can reach the camp today on foot, I would love to walk the rest of the way."

Baba Abdul tilted his head. He looked at Ahmed and said, "Do you agree with this girl as bossy as a mother with many daughters?"

"It all depends," Ahmed replied. "If we are only hours away by foot, then maybe we can walk there, then find a ride back. But if it's 'maybe by nightfall,' then I don't agree at all."

"When did you leave Timbuktu?"

Ayisha knew right away why he had asked that—to

determine their speed of travel. "We left late yesterday afternoon, before the raging dust storm that sprang up as quickly as a man springs up when sitting on a thorn. We left after the sun had passed its highest point, but it was still very hot. The heat was great so we sat behind a tall termite hill. *Al Humdullah* that we were there, for when the raging wind arrived and the sand began to fly, we were somewhat protected."

Eager to keep the man's attention as well as prove that they knew what they were doing in the desert, she threw the prayer shawl over her and Ahmed's heads, talking all the while. "We stood like this, behind the hill." Staring into her brother's eyes beneath their cloth tent, she added, "Ahmed said it was better to stand so we didn't get buried in sand, and that's exactly what we did."

Coming out from under the cloth, she continued, "Once the storm passed, we sat again to rest, and shake, for never have I been so scared. That's when we discovered that the wind and sand had stolen some of our cheese, dates and bread. When the heat had dropped and the wind was a welcome gentle breeze, we walked into the night."

She stopped for a breath, so Ahmed spoke. "Seeing you on the horizon this morning was like seeing a messenger from Allah. Your silhouette in the east looked as if you'd come directly from Mecca. So, are we near enough to continue walking?"

Baba Abdul didn't answer his question, but instead asked his own. "Your aunt isn't a Tuareg, is she?"

"No," answered Ayisha with a distinct sharpness in her

voice, her shoulders back proudly. "She is Bella, like us. She prefers the quiet of desert living to Timbuktu, so she is still with the Tuareg family she has known since birth."

The Tuareg man laughed, asking, "What makes you so proud? I'm not sure that being Bella is anything to be so proud of."

Ahmed said, "Excuse me, sir, but why not? Isn't Islam based on the idea of social tolerance among diverse ethnic and racial groups?"

Baba Abdul threw his head back and laughed, much like their father. Ayisha's eyes were popping out as she listened to her brother. Baba Abdul asked, "And where did you learn that?"

"From Alhaji Musa. He showed me an ancient manuscript that says just that, from Timbuktu, written four hundred years ago."

"My brother is a Koranic scholar," Ayisha blurted out. "So he is right, I am sure. Alhaji Musa gave him this prayer shawl that protected us during the storm and kept us warm in the night. It was a prize for his perfect reciting of the Koranic verses they were studying."

Ahmed asked, "So do you know our Auntie B? She lives with these people because, like Ayisha said, she prefers desert life, and also because she makes a good living."

"She's an artist. The world's best henna painter," added Ayisha.

Baba Abdul clapped his hands together and said, "I know who she is. She lives in the Tuareg camp that is quickly becoming a village, and she's well known for two things—her artistic skills and her bossiness." Turning to Ayisha, he said, "The second of which you clearly have inherited."

Ayisha and Ahmed stood taller. "That's her!" shouted Ahmed.

The three stood in silence for a moment before Baba Abdul dropped down into a squat. He took dates and dried goat meat from the small piles in front of him, dividing them into three groups. As he worked, he said, "If you have reached this far since yesterday, then you will make it today before sunset, *Inshallah.*"

Looking around the great expanse of sand that surrounded them, he pointed to the east. Already a shimmering rose off the horizon, the first mirage of the day taking shape. The heat was still bearable, but growing every minute. "Eat," he said. "Then we'll go. I cannot leave you here."

"Oh, but you can!" insisted Ayisha.

Ahmed couldn't believe that she was turning down his offer of help. "No, he can't leave us," he contradicted, turning to his sister. "And you can't turn this ride down, Ayisha. You must accept it."

Baba Abdul watched as the two faced off. Ayisha's shoulders were back, her spine straight and stiff. "You can go," she said. "But I shall walk and enjoy the peace and quiet and the challenge of the desert during the day." Tilting her head, she added, "Besides, he can take only one, and I don't—no, I won't—separate from you. But if you want to ride with Baba Abdul and separate from me, fine. Go."

Ahmed's face changed to a deeper shade of dark brown

as he said, "As stubborn as you may be, I would never leave you alone in the desert. Even if you deserved it." Turning to Baba Abdul, he asked, "Are we many hours away?"

Baba Abdul pointed toward the set of three dunes. "You can see from here you don't need to climb those. Just walk through those narrow gaps."

"I saw that already," Ayisha chimed in, still wanting to impress him with her desert knowledge. "But what about the third row? I don't see any break there."

The Tuareg moved his gaze from the dunes to her face and smiled. "I'm sure the way will become clear to you once you get closer."

He took their drooping water bag and held it up. With a snort he asked, "Did you kill a baby goat to make this pitiful water vessel?"

Ahmed dropped his head in embarrassment. It was the first water bag he had made, and it did come from a baby goat that had been killed by a truck crammed with passengers, in Timbuktu.

Ayisha stepped forward, trying to relieve her brother's embarrassment. "We took the smallest one by mistake. It was by the door of the tent, and we were in a hurry. So we left quickly with what was easiest to take." Her pride faltered as she added, "*Al Humdullah* you have come. It clearly was a stupid choice." She tugged on her hair in her own embarrassment.

Baba Abdul could tell the admission pained her. "I'm glad you can admit that. It shows you have some brains and heart in your bossy ways." He filled their water bag, then surprised the twins when he attached it to his camel.

Taking his own bag, once again pulled closed by the leather strap at the throat of it, he hung it across Ahmed's chest, resting down his right shoulder and across his back. The camel's bladder was much bigger than their water carrier and sent a cooling feeling against his thin shirt.

Reaching out, Baba Abdul grabbed Ayisha's hands, turning them palms up, opened flat. With a scoop of the piles, he filled them with dates and dried meat. Selecting pieces of both for his own breakfast, he said, "I will leave you here only if you accept these. If you walk as fast as you talk, you may arrive there before me!"

With that he grabbed his camel's halter, yanking down so the camel dropped to its front knees. Its backside pointed skyward until the back legs folded in and it rested on the ground. Baba Abdul climbed into the camel saddle that had a large three-pronged piece in front and a tall leather back. Looking at both twins, he said, "Follow your shadow until the sun reaches its highest point, then keep the sun over your left shoulder after the midday prayer." He pointed to the spot of dust on Ahmed's forehead. "A fellow believer knows to ask Allah for help."

A quick flick of his wrist sent the camel on his way. Over his shoulder he added, "And you can be sure, if you are not there by dusk, I will be back."

Ayisha blew out a large breath as the camel's gait built to a trot. Ahmed whirled around to her and said, "I hope you don't regret this decision. Knowing you, there's another reason for it. What is it?" he whispered. "What?"

His sister began dividing the dates and meat into two equal piles, then looked at him and said, "You'll see."

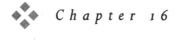 *Chapter 16*

AYISHA COUNTED OUT seven dates each and then five strips of meat each, giving an extra piece to Ahmed. Then she added a date from her pile, saying, "You have the added weight of carrying the water."

"I know how to lighten that load," he said. Lifting the shoulder strap over his head, he told her, "Drink first, one gulp before we eat and one big one before we begin this trek."

Ayisha took a small swallow, tilting her head back. Ahmed took an equally small drink, not wanting to appear needier than his sister. She picked up a date and took a bite. The skin was dried and puckered, but the burst of sweetness from the inside brought a smile to her face.

Ahmed took the biggest piece of meat. The burst of flavor rushed right down to his empty belly. His smile was lopsided as he enjoyed the best meal of his life. While the taste was still strong, he took a large swallow of water, hoping to drive the flavor to all the corners of his stomach. "This must be how everyone felt during the great drought of the seventies."

The drought had been a terrible thing. It had lasted for eight years and changed the life of the Tuareg for good. Herds were lost to starvation as pastures dried up, or to thirst as wells also dried up. Auntie B's Tuareg group had done better than most, for a few camels and goats and even some sheep survived the great *secheress*, the killer drought. Their father and mother had talked of it often, and without fail, each shivered at their memories.

Ayisha thought about that as she took her second drink, then placed the remaining food on the prayer shawl. She pushed it into a corner and then rolled the cloth a few times before tying two knots on either side of the food store. She slung it over her shoulder just like her brother's water bag.

"We'd better get started if you expect to reach that tall dune before nightfall," Ahmed said.

Side by side, they walked toward the dunes straight ahead. They followed their shadows as Baba Abdul had advised, departing from that only when they changed course to pass through the break in the first sand dune. It was a corridor cut between the two dunes running north and south. The dunes were mirror images, standing side by side and stretching away from each other. A flat sandy bottom formed a narrow channel with no top overhead. The slanted sun had not reached the lip of the dune yet, and shade filled it. Though they were both tired and hot, Ayisha shouted a challenge to her brother as they approached the first dune: "I'll race you through the pass!"

Ahmed took off running, catching his sister by surprise. She took off after him, happy for the short diversion from plodding along, planting one foot in front of the other. Ahmed's hurried footsteps kicked up baby dust devils, and the water bag slapped against his back. He stopped just before exiting, to rest in the shade that remained.

Ayisha arrived at his side, holding her left hip and breathing deeply. Her brown eyes searched her brother's face, and she was glad to see that the angry scowl that had covered it most of the morning was finally gone. They had hardly spoken since starting their walk, each attempt she made being waved off by an angry Ahmed.

When she quit huffing and puffing, Ahmed handed her the water bag. She shook her head, saying, "Please hold it up for me. Like Baba Abdul did. I don't feel too strong right now."

Ahmed looked at her closely. "You're not dying out here in a sun made for drying camel and goat dung, are you?"

She laughed briefly and said, "No. I am just very tired." She dropped down on the cool sand in the slight band of shade. Ahmed held the bag over her opened mouth, making a slow, steady stream just like Baba Abdul had. She gulped twice, then held her hand up. "Should I water you?" she asked.

"No," he answered. In one motion he lifted the bag to his mouth and took two gulps, matching her exactly.

"Should we eat again?" she asked.

Ahmed looked at the shrinking shade. The sun's path was moving overhead, which meant midday prayers were almost at hand. "You rest," he said. "After I pray we'll each eat one thing, then carry on." He didn't wait for an answer or take his prayer shawl from her. Instead he began the ceremonial washing of his hands.

Lying back, Ayisha looked at the sky as blue as a *toubab's* eyes—a narrow band of bright blue, straight overhead and far from the dust she was sure still hovered over the horizon. The sun's round hot face was nearly straight above, and as it moved, so did the shade. She rested until the sun glared down on her face. Reluctantly she rose to her feet and took a few steps out of the sand dune pass. She looked left, then right, in search of the next tunnel pass. Relief filled her face as she saw it standing close by. She quietly wandered toward it, not wanting to disturb her brother.

The dunes had the finest of sand ripples covering the front of them. It looked as if a giant had dragged his fingers in a series of squiggles down the sloping sand. The top of the dune had an edge as sharp as a Tuareg sword. She had just noticed the slightest of shadows thrown by the squiggles as the sun continued its relentless hot journey across the sky when Ahmed surprised her at her side.

"I thanked Allah for getting us this far," he told her, "and for sending Baba Abdul." He looked at the sand pass. Just like the other one, it had sloping sides of the exact same height and width. The blue sky provided a roof. He glanced at Ayisha, saying, "Let's eat something and then be on our way."

She sat at the entrance of the pass, carefully unfolding their meager stash of food. She laid it out for Ahmed to take what he wanted. Without hesitation he picked the thickest piece of jerky, biting into it with gusto. Ayisha also took a piece of meat. Sinking her teeth into it brought a smile to her dust- and sweat-streaked face.

They just looked at each other as they chewed. Ahmed's face, deep brown bordering on black, had cheekbones that stood out just below his deep brown eyes. His dark, curly hair was in tight curls as it was after a *futbol* game, with lines of sweat covering his forehead like the lines on the face of the dune. His eyes stared into his sister's, the eyes his mother said were exactly like his.

Ayisha stared right back. Her face was not quite as dark as her brother's, for she spent less time in the sun. She had a dimple in her right cheek, with the same high cheekbones as her twin. Her bangs hung in pointed spikes across her forehead, each with the smallest drop of sweat suspended on its tip. She sucked on the piece of meat in her mouth, caving in her dimple.

Ahmed held up a date and said, "We can share this if you like."

She shook her head, adding, "Let's not. Just in case we end up in the desert again tonight. I don't want to be without any food at all."

"What do you mean? I thought you were sure we would reach the camp! Baba Abdul said we would, or he wouldn't have left us here. What makes you suddenly doubtful?"

"Who knows anything for sure?" she asked. "Maybe there will be another great harmattan that lasts longer than the one yesterday."

Ahmed merely shook his head, and she could see that the good humor that had been restored was quickly disappearing.

Ayisha once again carefully wrapped up what remained of their food. They each took a small swig of water, then started on their way through the sand tunnel. At the halfway point, Ahmed threw back his head and shouted, *"Allahu Akbar!"* God is great! His voice bounced back and forth across the dunes' walls, and the tiniest of sand slides began in the desert silence.

Ayisha joined in, throwing back her head and shouting, *"Al Humdullah!"* Praise Allah! She clapped as her voice echoed around them too. They each shouted their praises once more, then started walking again, reaching the end of the pass.

Together they looked left, for the next dune break, and then right. Nothing was in sight. Nothing broke up the face of the tall wall of sand that stood opposite them. Ahmed looked at Ayisha, who studied the dune that stood farther away than her brother's best kick of a *futbol* ball. Ayisha stepped back and could see the top ridge of the tallest dune they were walking to. She tugged on her bangs, clearly deep in thought. Interrupting her thoughts, Ahmed said, "Walk a bit that way," pointing to his right, "and I'll

walk this way. Call out if you see some way through."
Squinting into the sun, he said, "I hope we haven't made a
big mistake, refusing Baba Abdul's help."

He hadn't even gone two steps when Ayisha shouted,
"I know the way! Remember what Baba Abdul said, to
follow the shadow off your shoulder after midday prayers?
If we go this way, then our shadows are behind us." Twisting around with her arms widespread, she pointed to the
smallest of shadows, falling across her right shoulder to
the ground in front.

Her brother tilted his head and said, "So you actually
do listen sometime—that's good, sister!" Without another
word brother and sister walked north, parallel to the large
dune.

"Have you ever been so hot?" she asked. It hurt to take
a deep breath, so searing was the sun's heat on her dried
throat. Small streams of sweat trickled down from under
her scarf wrapped tightly on her head. Her bangs dripped
water in a slow drip, drip, drip.

"Never," he replied. "Unless you count the day I made
four goals running up and down that field like a camel
with an empty belly heading to water and food." He swiped
at the sweat that stung his eyes.

"That was your greatest game ever," she said, knowing
that the memory would make her brother smile.

The sun beat down and Ayisha licked her lips. She
could suddenly feel little cracks in them like the parched
ground at the driest point of the year. She looked at her
hands, pinching up the skin on the back of her right hand

and watching it slowly fall back down. She closed her eyes and heard her mother's voice telling her, "Always check, daughter mine, for dehydration, because the desert's silent power can suck you dry before you know it."

Ahmed suddenly noticed that his sister wasn't at his side. He walked back to where she was staring at the backs of her hands. She grabbed Ahmed's and pulled up a pinch of skin. It receded a bit more quickly than hers had, which was a good sign for him.

Her brother asked, "Are you okay? Would you like to rest a bit? The sun is still very high and hot."

Ayisha looked at Ahmed and felt the sweat dripping down the back of her neck and the shins of her skinny legs. "Yes," was all she said as she dropped to the hot sand, "for just a few moments I shall rest." Giving a little shake of her shoulders, she said, "I just heard Mother's voice, telling me to check on our body water."

"I knew what you were checking." He held up the water bag and asked, "Do you need a drink now?" She shook her head. Tiredness radiated from her body, as did little heat waves. Trying to change the subject, Ahmed crooked his head and said in all seriousness, "Did you hear anything else from Mother? Like how angry she is?"

"No, but believe me, at this point I think she may be more worried than angry."

"You're worried about school, aren't you, Ayisha?"

"Just a bit, because I knew that school was threatened when we started this journey. I am more worried about the stress we are causing our parents."

Ahmed squatted down and took his sister's hand, something he rarely did now that they had finished primary school. "You're right, we'll be in big trouble."

Air puffed out of Ayisha's lips as she said, "You can be sure of that. You said those *toubabs* meant trouble in Timbuktu, and you were absolutely right." Yanking his hand, she asked, "But what choice did we have? If you had said you wouldn't help, then I'll bet anything your great friend Sidi would have helped them, and would he have stopped them, Ahmed? Would he have? We're doing this to catch them, not to make money. We're out here in Allah's sight to visit Auntie B, who will most definitely help us."

Ahmed stood and pulled her to her feet. "We'll figure this out, Ayisha. We will. Right now let's find our way past this last dune."

They walked silently for the longest while. Their shadows stretched longer as they walked until they finally came to a deep dip in the top of the dune. It wasn't a tunnel, and involved some climbing, but walking indefinitely parallel to the large dune was not what they wanted to do.

"I'll go first," Ahmed said. "You'll push me from behind and then I can pull you up every few steps."

Progress was painfully slow, for it seemed like every step forward filled immediately with sand and then took them nearly a step backward. Their heavy breathing filled an afternoon that was ominously void of voices, animals calling or even the cicadas. It was as if all had stopped to watch their struggle, holding their breaths. Ayisha's face was covered in sweat, and the grit of the sand was rubbing her feet raw where the leather sandals touched her skin. Her brother reached down and took off his sandals, saying, "Try this—it may help."

Ayisha bent down and took her thin sandals off, clutching them in her left hand. The shock of the hot sand almost made her put her shoes back on, but seeing the raw skin under where the straps usually lay stopped her. Determination to finish the climb filled her face. Without standing, she took a step up and found that being bent in half helped. Little drops of sweat spotted the sand. Soon Ahmed was doing the same. If anyone had been passing, they would have seen what looked like two giant dung beetles trying to scurry up the face of a dune that dwarfed them. The sun beat down as if angered by their stupidity to try this climb in the daytime. Step by step, they forced their way up, until finally, sand slipped down both sides of the dune's rigid edge on the top. They had conquered the dune at last!

Ayisha was resting with her hands on her knees, breathing in ragged gasps, when Ahmed suddenly started jumping up and down. "I'm glad to be here too," she said, "but . . ."

She swallowed her words as she saw what had set her brother off. Far below, bouncing along at a very fast trot, was a woman draped in black on a donkey's jolting back. A solitary goat followed.

"It's a miracle!" Ahmed cried out. "This morning it was Baba Abdul's silhouette on the horizon, and in the afternoon it is Auntie B." Raising both hands to wave and whoop, he looked at his sister. The smile covering her face was a combination of relief and not total surprise. He had to laugh as he said, "So that was your plan!"

"Absolutely," she said. "I knew that as soon as Auntie B heard about us, she would come. She would know where the path to the village would leave the dunes."

"But still, she can't offer us both a ride," said her brother.

"Not to worry, that's not why she's here. Remember how hard it is to be alone in her camp? Now we can talk on the way—in privacy."

Chapter 17

AHMED RAN DOWN the face of the large dune they had just struggled up. His arms swirled in the air like windmills. The water bag bounced against his back. "Yeeeeeeeeeai!" he called out in glee as he ran on the verge of out of control down the steep, sandy slope. Ayisha watched, a wide smile just like her mother's covering her face.

"I wish I could roll down!" she called to Mother Nature. She felt the shrinking bundles of dates and goat meat wrapped in the prayer shawl and restrained herself. Her smile widened as she remembered the time she and Ahmed had struggled up a dune simply for the trip down—one long continuous roll that had left her dizzy and weak and happy as could be. That trek up had taken almost five hours, and the roll down less than three minutes. Then it took three months to get rid of all the sand trapped beneath her nails, in her ears, she was sure even in her brain. The memory told her two things: she couldn't risk spoiling their food supply by covering it in sand, but she knew she couldn't just calmly walk down either.

She squinted her left eye shut, deciding on her style of arrival. With a shake of her shoulders she extended her arms out wide and flapped them like one of the moths that gathered at night around any source of light. Imagine flying like a moth—flap, flap, flap, flap, she told herself as she watched her brother run right past their auntie, his speed too great to stop.

When they looked up to see her, Ayisha took off, running and then taking a giant leap, burying her feet deep in the sand and bringing her momentum to a complete halt. Running then jumping, feet digging deep into the sand and stopping her with such force she bent forward at the waist, tipping in half with her rear pointed skyward and her arms flapping like a moth too near the flame.

She found her rhythm easily: five giant steps, then jump. At the last jump she tucked into a roll for the last few feet. Auntie had her right arm around Ahmed's neck and was clapping vigorously. Ahmed's head jerked back and forth like a *jalabiah* drying in the wind, but he didn't mind. Laughter filled the air till Auntie B threw her head back and let loose an endless ululating sound of joy, "Aieaieaie-iiii!" When Ayisha stood from her finishing roll, she could see and hear that her arrival had been a success.

Auntie released Ahmed and pulled Ayisha into her full chest. She continued to ululate, and Ayisha could feel it resonate inside her head pressed to her auntie's breast.

Auntie B grabbed Ahmed again, and the three stood embracing, laughing, celebrating.

Faster than a mosquito biting, Auntie B's mood changed. She held each twin at arm's length and demanded to know, "How is my brother? Did your mother really send you? When did you start?"

Ayisha held up a hand to still the flood of questions. Ahmed made no effort to answer. Without looking directly at her aunt, she mumbled, "Not exactly."

"Not exactly what?" came a quick retort. "Not exactly she sent you? Or not exactly because my brother's so ill?"

"Both," said Ahmed. All eyes shifted to his face.

Ayisha could have hugged him for speaking up until he continued. "It's all her fault we're here," he said, pointing to his twin. All eyes shifted to look at her.

She threw her shoulders back and said, "He's right. Father is fine, not very sick like I told Baba Abdul. He is fine, *Al Humdullah*! Unless you stop to think about how angry and worried he must be." With a visible shiver she added, "I don't even want to think about Mother."

"Whatever brought you out here had better be very, I say, VERY important. Baba Abdul said he met you, with no water and no food. How foolish is that? How stupid?" she corrected herself. "I always brag to any and all about how smart my twin niece and nephew are."

She shook their shoulders, clicking her tongue rapidly and loudly, before saying, "Please explain what looks like madness into sanity—*Al Humdullah* my brother is well— so I will not be shamed when we reach the camp."

Ayisha glanced at Ahmed, who gave her a quick nod to encourage her. She took a deep breath and spewed, one word latching onto another she spoke so fast, "Wewant-tocatchtwothievesofancientmanuscriptsbutweneed-yourhelpfirst!" Her shoulders rose with a quick inhale, but before she could erupt again, her auntie placed her fingers on Ayisha's lips.

Auntie B turned to Ahmed and said, "Can you say it slower than a racing camel?"

Ahmed's big brown eyes looked at his sister, who nodded to him. "We want to catch two manuscript thieves."

A quick gasp came from their Auntie B, who said, "Don't make jokes about that."

The twins were surprised by her quick mood change again. So far she'd been as happy as a mother at her daughter's wedding, then as angry as a camel with a burr beneath its saddle, then very serious, and now almost scared. Ayisha's next comment brought a whole new reaction when she said, "We're police—our own police—trying to catch two *toubab* thieves. We call ourselves Les Gendarmes Invisibles."

Their aunt couldn't help herself. She threw her head back and laughed like they'd never heard before. She bent at the waist, hands on her knees, glancing sideways at the two. She gulped in air, then stood up against her donkey's side and started to launch into a second peal of uncontrollable laughter. Ayisha started laughing as she watched tears trail down her auntie's cheeks. She also began to whoop with rolling waves of laughter while Ahmed watched them both, amazed.

Auntie B pointed at Ahmed, then at his sister and blurted out between bursts of laughter, "Les Gendarmes Invisibles? You two?"

Ayisha's laughter stopped as suddenly as it had started. "Why is that so funny?"

"Promise me something," she gasped. "Tell no one else about this, or my shame will be swamped by embarrassment."

"But we are!" insisted Ayisha.

"According to who?"

"Us!" they both said.

Looking directly at Auntie B, Ayisha added, "And you can be too. We need advice, and who better to ask than the bossiest woman on Allah's earth, who also knows more than any man?" She threw that in because she knew it would please her aunt. "Even Baba Abdul called you bossy!"

Auntie B straightened up from leaning against her donkey's side. Her goat Never nudged her leg, like a dog instead of a goat. She rubbed between his horns, one a broken nub and the other very curved and sharp, and said to her goat, "Do you believe these two? Thief catchers? Invisible police?" Looking at the twins, she asked, "Do you realize how serious this issue is?"

"We do," insisted Ahmed. "Will you help us?"

"You need to take a pledge before we discuss it anymore," Ayisha added.

Once again Auntie B's mood changed. "I will join on one condition only—that Never can also join and be a thief-chasing police goat."

"We're serious, Auntie," Ayisha said with a whine in her voice.

"I am more serious than the dust storm you faced yesterday," replied their aunt.

"You looked nervous there at first," said Ahmed. "Then you laughed like crazy. Now you're serious again. What is making you act so strangely, Auntie B?"

Auntie B tilted her head and said, "You'll find out. Now let's get on with this pledge so I can find out what's going on."

"We want to catch two rotten people," Ayisha said.

Ahmed cut in, "Two miserable, rotten people. If you want to help us, then please repeat, 'I, Auntie B, will work before Allah to catch these two.'"

With her eyes burrowing into Ahmed's, she repeated the oath. She gave Never a little jolt with her knee, and he bleated. "Go on," she said to Ahmed.

Ahmed continued, "We will walk the desert and climb the dunes to succeed, *Inshallah*."

Ayisha's eyes popped wide as her brother added new parts to their pledge. She was praying he wouldn't go into the death part.

Auntie B repeated his words.

Then he said, "We promise to protect the ancient manuscripts of Timbuktu from all thieves, foreign or local, till we have tried every method short of death."

Just like Ayisha, Auntie B's eyes popped wide at the mention of death, but she repeated the sentence. Then she looked at him sideways. "Have you learned something I was planning to tell you about one day?"

Total confusion covered their faces, until Ayisha said, "Is that the story Father has mentioned but never told us?"

"I'm sure," said their aunt.

Ahmed interrupted to say, "We must finish the oath. *Allahu Akbar*—God is great. *Al Humdullah!*"

Both Auntie and Ayisha made the final statement together, with Auntie B adding, "And thank Allah that my little brother is worried and angry—not ill."

Looking toward the setting sun, she slapped her donkey on its hindquarter and started walking toward the camp off in the distance. It was just as it had been described, tucked up against a giant dune that dwarfed the one they had climbed.

"We'll walk and talk slowly, for my stomach muscles hurt from such a good belly laugh," Auntie B said.

Then stopping to look at them both, she added, "And it's good I have had such a laugh, for there is absolutely nothing funny about what we need to do." And then as an afterthought she added, "Or what your father and I have to tell you."

Chapter 18

THEY WALKED IN SILENCE for the first few minutes. It was clear that all were gathering their thoughts, for a small frown covered each face. Ayisha turned to Ahmed and said, "You start. You are the one who first met these two."

Ahmed shifted the water bag dangling down his back. Lifting it over his head, he asked his aunt, "Does your throat need water after such a workout of anger, joy and laughter?"

Auntie B nodded as she reached for the bag. "I'll pour for you," he said proudly. Auntie cupped her hands next to her mouth, sipping loudly as he poured.

Next he turned to Ayisha, who followed her auntie's example. She then poured for Ahmed, who glanced up from his cupped hands and saw the deep shadows slipping across the row of dunes they had crossed through and over that day. He turned to look at the Tuareg camp that was bathed in the last rays of the departing sunlight. He saw in the distance a crowd of kids emerging from the collection of tents, running right at them.

"Talk fast," said Auntie B as she too looked at the kids running, jumping and yelling like a stampeding herd of goats. "We don't want or need everyone knowing our business until it is finished. We have ten or fifteen minutes before they reach us."

Ayisha said again, "You start, Ahmed. You met this troublesome couple first."

Ahmed lost no time. "Auntie B, since the last time we saw you, I have started to work with *toubabs*. As a guide."

Auntie B nodded and said, "Just like your uncle."

Ayisha's eyes popped wide and Ahmed's mouth dropped open. "What uncle?" each one asked.

Auntie waved her hand and shook her head, saying, "We will discuss that later." She watched them open their mouths to ask something, but again she waved her hand and said, "Later. Now tell me exactly why you are here. All the details. It had better be very good or you will meet more than your parents' wrath. Now talk."

Ahmed opened his mouth, but before he could say anything, Auntie B added, "And yes, I know that you are a successful guide that speaks many languages."

Then she turned to Ayisha and said, "And I know that you are the greatest student ever to attend your school. Scoring the highest test scores—whatever that means—in its history."

The twins looked at her, each with jaws gaping open.

Auntie B gave a quick laugh and said, "Those faces, so alike you know they are from the same womb at the same time. Did you think the best henna painter in Timbuktu and beyond doesn't hear news? Have you forgotten my skills at painting . . ."

"And gossip," threw in Ayisha. "It's been more than one salt caravan season since we have seen you." Ayisha couldn't help herself; she grabbed her aunt in a fierce hug. She stretched her arms so her hands could meet and grasp each other and said, "I have missed you so much!"

"The story," called out her aunt as she looked over the girl's shoulder at the running horde of kids. A cloud of dust rose behind them, marking the running crowd's progress in the sky turning red and orange from the sunset still trapped in dust. She gave Ayisha a quick squeeze, then unlocked her arms from around her waist. "Keep talking," she said with no nonsense in her voice.

Ahmed said, "There's a *toubab* couple. He's an archaeologist . . . but we know he and his wife are . . . well . . . they are up to no good, Auntie. They're trouble."

Ayisha butted in, although she had promised herself she wouldn't. "She's a little nicer than he is, but Auntie B, I just don't trust her. She's friendly to me in French, but then says nasty things in English that she doesn't realize Ahmed understands. She definitely has more than one face."

"I don't want a personality report—I just want to know what's going on. How do you know that the *toubabs* are thieves? Have they stolen something?"

Ahmed's face registered his pain at the thought when he said, "Not yet, but they want me to help them steal ancient manuscripts."

Both twins were startled by yet another reaction from their aunt. Her eyes suddenly shone brightly in the departing sunlight, and she quickly blinked back what looked like tears.

"Auntie, what is it?" asked a worried Ayisha.

"Again—just like your uncle."

"What uncle?" Ahmed asked.

"Later. Later. So if you want to stop them, just say NO!"

"But that's it," said Ayisha. "We want more than to just stop them, Auntie. We want to put these two in jail . . . but what uncle?"

Auntie looked at them both in the weakening sunlight. She watched the running pack of kids, who they could now hear shouting and laughing. "Go very, very carefully," she said. "Has your father told you our family history? Is that why you are doing this?"

The two shook their heads, both baffled by the news of a mysterious uncle and some kind of family history that their father had hinted at, then avoided. Still shaking her head, Ayisha said, "Twice he has told us that there is a family story he will tell the next time you are there, to help him."

"And so you are doing this why? Why not just report the *toubabs*?"

Ahmed answered right away and clearly from the heart. "Father once said that no family in Timbuktu has been untouched by the worst kind of thievery: the stealing of ancient manuscripts. Too often from uneducated, poor people. Our people, Auntie B. We thought if we caught them in the act, maybe set a trap of some kind, it would be a warning for all other *toubabs* with the same bad ideas."

Nodding, their aunt took a step back to look the two over from head to toe. Auntie B's eyes moved from Ayisha's scratched legs up to her dusty red dress, then her braids and the bangs she was tugging on below the funny little scarf thing on her head. The prayer shawl still hung over her niece's shoulder, and the packet of food rested against her left hip.

Without saying a word, Auntie B looked at Ahmed, clothed in thin white pants red with dust and a T-shirt that had something in a foreign language blazoned on the front. Shaking her head, she said, "Your serious face looks so much like my brother's, it almost takes my breath away."

Moving her gaze from one face to the other, she told them, "If you are doing this because you care so much, then I would like to help you, any way I can, to the best of my ability." She then cracked the briefest of smiles and added, "And I'd like to take the pledge again, this time from my heart."

"Who is this uncle you keep mentioning?" asked a querulous Ayisha. "Do you and Father have another brother?"

"No." She paused and then said, "No brother . . . I had a husband. But that is all I will tell you right now."

"You were married?" Ayisha eyes were opened wide,

and she kept shifting her gaze from her auntie's face to her brother's—back and forth, back and forth.

"Why didn't we know?" asked an angry Ahmed.

"That's not the topic for now," said Auntie B in an equally sharp voice. "I now understand why you call yourself police, with all these questions, but why the invisible police?"

"You know about Ahmed's languages, right? Well, these *toubabs* are always speaking French with Ahmed—her French like a bleating goat separated from its mother. Anyway, like I told you, Auntie B, they don't know that Ahmed speaks English, so they talk between themselves in English as if he wasn't there."

Their auntie's smile returned as she raised her finger and said, "As if he was invisible . . ." She clapped her hands, her long line of gold bracelets clinking against one another, and said, "How clever!"

They all could clearly hear the arriving kids shouting calls of *"Mantole, mantole,"* welcome, welcome, before the yellers arrived.

Auntie B dropped an arm around her niece's and nephew's shoulders. She clicked to her ever patient donkey and ever faithful goat to follow as the three walked toward the Tuareg camp. Their shadow was long and three times wider than that of a single person as their strides moved as one, joined together by Auntie's arms.

In a quiet but decisive voice she said, "No more talk about this until I get rid of these pesky children. In the meantime we should all pray to Allah for guidance in this most difficult task." The three trudged across the deep sand, followed by their shadow, spreading like a carpet on the desert floor behind them.

Ayisha leaned around her aunt to look directly at her brother, triumph in her voice. "I knew we needed to come here. We need a plan, one that can work. And we need an ancient manuscript, Auntie B. Is it possible to find one?"

Auntie B's head jerked up to look at her niece. "Oh, is that all? Just a precious manuscript?" She blew an exasperated puff of breath through her pursed lips.

"I'm worried about your parents," Auntie B said as the village kids descended on them. One little boy started running, bending his knees high, just like Ahmed had done only days before. As Ayisha watched the boy and thought of Ahmed collecting dung, she thought, *Was that really only four days ago?*

Even with no words exchanged, Ahmed nodded at his sister. "Yes, only four days ago at the well."

Releasing Ahmed's and Ayisha's shoulders from her protective hug, Auntie B held her arms opened wide to the arriving kids. They pushed and shoved to get a hug, then began asking questions as fast as sand travels down a dune. "Why are you here?" asked a boy wearing a long gray shirt that touched his calves.

"Where did you come from?" shouted another. He was easily their age, with a smile filling his face. "Did your parents really send you here?"

Finally a young girl stepped forward and asked, "What happened to your hair?"

Auntie laughed out loud, saying, "I like her hair."

Ayisha's eyes opened wide in appreciation. "*Shukran*, Auntie B. You are the first, adult or child, to say you like my hair."

Auntie held her hands high, signaling all to stop talking. The boys were shoving each other and playing with pure joy at having children visitors to their camp. Auntie looked at the four boys and five girls. "You'll know why they are here when the time is right. Now let's get going, for the sun departs and I hear the drums announcing that the wedding's final night is starting."

Ayisha clapped. "There's a wedding? We'll be welcome, won't we?"

Auntie B raised her left eyebrow and tilted her head. "You are making a joke," she said. "And coming from, what was it, the school's smartest ever?"

Ayisha's face glowed like the lingering sunset colors. A warmth of pride traveled directly to her deep brown cheeks, her smile spreading from her eyes to her ears to her chin.

Taking each twin by the hand, Auntie B said, "Have you ever heard of any Tuareg, or Puehl, Fulani or Bella not extending a warm welcome to all visitors? It just doesn't happen among desert people."

"It was just a joke, a very bad one," insisted Ayisha. She couldn't take her eyes off the activity in the camp. A large fire sent flames dancing high in the darkening sky, shining on the bustle of action. As they arrived, Ayisha stopped just to watch. Women in every variation of the beautiful blue indigo walked in groups, clapping and singing, swaying side to side. Their heads were covered with head cloths matching their blue gowns. Some were just draped across the head, and others were tied with elaborate fancy knots either in front or back. Each *grand boubou* had its own embedded damask pattern that shone in the firelight on the heavily starched and ironed gowns. Every clapping hand had a detailed henna design on it.

Men also walked in groups, all moving toward the fire and the ululating women—crying "Aieaieaieiiii" just like Auntie had when they had met in the desert. Their voices rang as one, and it didn't take Auntie a moment to join in. The men wore long gowns and matching turbans of green, blue, spotless white, red and deep purple. Detailed, complicated embroidery of a contrasting color decorated the chest of almost every man. Excitement filled the air as all knew that dancing would soon begin.

To make her aunt as happy as she had made Ayisha moments ago, the young girl said, "I know who painted all the hands covered in beautiful henna."

Like a lantern, Auntie B's face lit up. "You are right about that," she said, patting her own breast. "What a busy time," she reflected happily. "And you couldn't have arrived at a better moment, for the work is finished and my purse is full."

Then reaching to take off the black gown she wore, she revealed a *grand boubou* of reds and greens and yellow beneath. Intricate gold thread embroidered on the front of her gown dazzled Ayisha and Ahmed, it was so obviously the best that could be bought.

Auntie handed Ayisha the black robe and laughed as she saw their awed faces. With a quick tug she undid a head tie that had been cinched around her waist. With hands that had done the task more times than anyone could count, she wound the cloth around her head. Patting it into place, she said, "Let's join the party, for tomorrow we will be very serious."

Ahmed and Ayisha's eyes met. The last thing they had expected upon their arrival was a party, but the thought of leaving behind all their worries, even if only for a few hours, was irresistible.

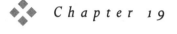 *Chapter 19*

AYISHA AND AHMED stood in awe, watching the hustle and bustle of the camp in full swing. Dust rose everywhere as kids ran between the adults and women shuffled along in a slow dance called the *takamba*. A rolling beat filled the air as the women swayed, arms floating on air in their slow-motion dance. The licking flames sent their shadows falling every which way.

Two women dressed in black worked at stretching a goatskin tightly over the head of their wide, wooden mortar—the same one that they pounded grain in every day. The older woman held down the sides of the skin stretched over the mortar's mouth while the younger woman wrapped a supple long rope made of goatskin around the drumhead again and again and again. When she finished off the rope by tucking it tightly into the wrapped band, the older woman took off her leather sandal and pounded the drum, testing the tautness and sound. Satisfied, she picked up the newly made instrument, and together the two went to join the other women drummers.

Suddenly a girl Ayisha's age stood before the twins. *"Mantole,"* she said as she held out two small cups of water. "Welcome. I am Fatimata. Did you really walk here by yourselves?" She wore a finely woven white blouse covered with intersecting straight lines of red embroidery. Her hair made Ayisha jealous, for it was done up in five thick braids—one down the center of her forehead, one in front of each ear and two down her back.

Before Ayisha could answer, the girl added, "And why would you do that?"

Ayisha opened her mouth, but the girl continued, "And your parents let you?"

Taking the offered cups of water, Ahmed threw his head back and laughed, for it was rare to see someone outtalk his sister. He handed one cup to his sister, then held his empty hand, palm open, toward the girl and said, "Please, why don't you let her answer your questions?"

Ayisha tugged on her bangs, then quickly dropped her hand when she saw the girl look closely at her *toubab* hairstyle. "We've come for our Auntie B, on family business. But enough of that. Who is getting married?"

The girl's mouth dropped. She asked Ayisha in a loud whisper, "Do you really think a wedding is more interesting than the never-before, ever-before arrival of two children across the desert on their own?"

Ayisha didn't answer. Instead she watched her Auntie B talking excitedly with the crowd that had formed around her. Auntie B, throwing up her hands and slapping her thighs, finally made the crowd burst into laughter. Ayisha decided to try being just as dramatic. "I hate to be rude, but do you know how hungry we are?" she asked the group of children forming around them.

All eyes, staring intently, were on her face. Some young girls shook their heads to say no, so Ayisha looked deep into the eyes of the girl who had first approached them, then tilted her head back and drank the whole cup in one gulp, something that should have been savored slowly. "I am as hungry as I am thirsty, and if someone was to put a whole roasted goat before my brother and me, we would finish eating it without even sitting down." For added emphasis she patted her flat stomach.

Cries of "I'll get you food!" or "Let me help!" or "Follow me" were suddenly interrupted when a racing camel came into the camp area. The man charged right up to where the line of women drummers were playing and singing, and in one fluid motion his camel halted and he stepped off, right into a dance before the singers. Ahmed and Ayisha looked at each other in surprise and grinned, for they recognized the entry from that morning. Baba Abdul lifted his legs high, knees bent sharply, and then stomped hard on the earth, sending up small clouds of dust around his dancing footsteps.

His eyes hooked on the twins when he turned their way. With a final stomp, he strode away from the group of women ululating and clapping and laughing. His mouthpiece was pulled tightly across his face, but the wrinkles at the corners of his eyes revealed his smile.

Baba Abdul looked at Ahmed and said, "Welcome. I am glad you are here safely. I hope you enjoy tonight, for I am sure there will be serious talk about your foolishness tomorrow."

He held his hand out and Ahmed took it in a loose handshake. They shook limply, snapped fingers and touched their hearts. Ahmed was shy and nervous, for he had never been greeted as a man before. To hide his embarrassment he said, "*Al Humdullah!* Thanks for the water and food, and for telling Auntie B."

Baba Abdul snorted shortly and turned to greet Ayisha as he said, "That's exactly what you expected, wasn't it, Mademoiselle Bossy? You knew I would tell her, and I knew I would tell her. That's the only reason I left you there."

Ayisha smiled right at him and said, "That is very true. And now we are here, hungry, thirsty and greatly relieved. Do you always make such a dramatic entrance when you arrive somewhere?"

Baba Abdul slowly shook his head from side to side and said, "Maybe I left you out there for two reasons—the second one being that you need some modesty. But arriving here has made you more bold rather than less. And yes, when my youngest daughter is getting married, I am a happy and proud father." Then tilting his head as if imparting a secret, he said, "And it feels good and looks good too. You are impressed, admit it."

"It is impressive. I really don't mean to be rude, and I thank you also, from the bottom of my heart, for telling Auntie B. Seeing her coming across the desert was almost like a mirage, too good to be true. In fact, exactly like seeing you this morning. *Al Humdullah!"*

Ahmed's voice suddenly cut in. "So you knew all along that we would be here tonight?"

"Absolutely, whether it was under your own power or a camel rescue." Abdul looked around the activity for Auntie B and laughed when he saw her entertaining the group of women Ayisha had seen her with. "And what did your auntie have to say? She doesn't look like a woman worried for the health of her brother."

"Oh, but she is," insisted Ayisha. "We have had a good talk and we know we are not finished yet, but she said we should have fun tonight while we can."

Looking around, Ahmed asked, "Did you say your youngest daughter? Is this her wedding? You almost missed it if you just arrived today."

Baba Abdul nodded. "A sick camel held me up. I had traveled to Gao to sell a camel for the wedding and got delayed. My camel got the catarrh and I had to stop twice on the return."

Ayisha tugged on her bangs, which were coated with sweat and dust. "Were you out in the camp of Baba Ali and the grandmother Fati? Did you spend time in Timbuktu?" She clearly looked nervous as she asked that, wondering if he had heard more than he'd mentioned that morning. "Did you know we were out here?"

"There was talk all over Timbuktu, for the desert is huge and harsh, and disaster is always at hand. I told the man who told me about two missing Bella children that I would watch for you, and that if I didn't find you on the desert or in the camp, we would start a search immediately. He said your parents thought maybe you were headed this way, looking for your auntie, or perhaps south, after the elephants, so another man left in that direction."

"So you knew Father wasn't sick?" Ayisha said, feeling ill at the moment. "And you knew that they didn't send us?"

Just a nod of Baba Abdul's head answered her questions. "And so guess what that also means? I will be sitting in with your auntie tomorrow to hear why you are here, and then we will start back."

An irritated "humph" blew through Baba Abdul's lips, so Ayisha asked with embarrassment, "Did Auntie know when she came to find us?"

"No. The woman didn't give me a chance to finish; she just called that goat of hers, jumped on her donkey and bounced out of the camp. No matter how much I yelled at her to stop and listen, she only waved an arm over her head and bounced off toward the dune. I figured she would learn soon enough, if you didn't lie to her like you did to me."

Ayisha felt uncomfortable, for she could feel his gaze resting on her dropped head. "We're not really such terrible liars. We are on a very serious and important mission."

Baba Abdul held his hand up to stop her. "Save it for tomorrow, and it had better be the truth, and all of it. To see your aunt dancing and singing and laughing makes me think she may agree with you, and that really worries me. She's a grown woman and should know better than to encourage acts of foolishness, even after they have occurred."

Saying not another word, nor allowing another word to be said, he turned on his heel and left. Ayisha could feel her cheeks burning at her embarrassment of telling lies to someone who knew they were definitely lies. She suddenly didn't feel as clever as she had at the time. She glanced at Ahmed, who was watching her closely.

"Embarrassed?" he asked.

She nodded without saying a word. "I felt so clever this morning, and now I only feel sick."

Ahmed looked at Fatimata, who was clearly trying to take in every word they said. Grabbing Ayisha's hand, he walked away from the Tuareg girl, whispering as they walked. "Well, maybe clever isn't always a good thing. Al-haji Musa told me that to be clever is a great gift, and the world needs some clever. But to be kind is what matters the most. To be generous of heart and spirit is more important, and that's why you're here. You want to stop these thieves from your heart."

Ayisha looked at her brother and said, "So being clever to achieve a thing from the heart is not so bad?"

Ahmed shrugged. "Who knows? Maybe when lies are made to achieve some good, they aren't as bad, I don't know. I'll talk to Alhaji Musa about it when we finish this business."

Just then the girls arrived with a platter of food, big enough for all to share if the two didn't eat it as fast as Ayisha promised. They carried it over to where the twins talked, and all dropped to the ground to sit in a circle and share the hot, juicy goat and couscous with dates. Ahmed bent over to clean the sand out of his sandal when suddenly Auntie B called out to them. He turned his head just in time to see her goat Never running right at him. With amazing speed Never crashed his horned head into Ahmed's backside, sending the young Bella boy flying toward the platter of food that sat at the center of the circle.

Not a soul made a sound as they watched Ahmed's right hand, as if in slow motion, reach out for his sister's shoulder. His outstretched left hand, never used near food, headed straight for the platter of dinner in the center of the circle.

Without losing a beat, Ayisha reached out and pushed Ahmed's right shoulder, sending him into the oldest girl's lap. A loud sigh of relief poured from everyone's mouths as he missed the dinner platter.

"Aye yae yae!" cried Fatimata. Her scramble to get Ahmed off her lap made it clear she was not too happy about being so close to a strange boy. Blowing out like a blacksmith's bellows, Ahmed tried to get righted so he could get away from her.

The youngest girl in the circle leaned forward for a handful of food and said, "Good push."

"Lucky push," said Ayisha, laughing as she elbowed the goat that was crowding his way into the circle.

Huffing from her run over to them, Auntie B added, "That's the truth. One touch of that unclean left hand and the food would be spoiled. And that, my dear, would be a disaster, for I am as hungry as a camel four days into the desert."

Like royalty, she extended her hand covered with dark brown spirals and stars surrounding a flower with six petals to Ahmed and pulled him to his feet. He hugged her hard, then dropped to the ground, pulling her down with him.

Looking at Ayisha, Auntie B asked, "Are all young boys so clumsy, or just your twin brother?" Not waiting for an answer, she reached forward and scooped up a handful of food. The meat's fat dripped down her arm, so she quickly stuffed the food into her mouth. A nudge on her shoulder reminded her that her goat was still there. Auntie B punched back with her elbow into his chest. *"Allez, Jamais!"* she told him. Go, Never. "I'm sure you don't want to see what's on this plate. It may not be a brother, but it could be an old friend."

"Why do you call him *Jamais?*" asked Fatimata.

"Well," said the older woman, "it's a long story that can be made short. Who has the time to hear it?"

All the kids shouted, "Me! Me! Me!"

Auntie B flipped the end of her head tie over her shoulder, leaned forward for another handful of food and said, before putting it into her mouth, "We were in the market in Korioume, the place where the boats come from Mopti and sometimes Gao. The market is a very busy place: people selling huge baskets of millet and sorghum, blocks of salt sitting before men, and women selling some vegetables and dried fish. There are also lots of animals for sale."

She stopped to put the food in her mouth, cupping her fingers in a tight curve so as not to drop anything. Her eyes caught Ayisha's, who had to smile, for clearly this wasn't to be the short version.

Auntie shifted on her bottom, leaning left, then right to get more comfortable. "It's a place full of cars and trucks, and much noise and dust. People calling out their wares and greetings to one another, and horns honking, radios blaring, and *Inshallah*, I shall never have to go there again." She turned to her niece and nephew and asked them directly, "Have you ever been there with your father?"

Ahmed and Ayisha shook their heads, and finally Ayisha said, "Never, Auntie."

Tilting her head to the side, Ayisha suddenly clapped and asked, "Is that why you call him Never? Because you got him there and then decided to never go back?"

Auntie B's eyes shone in the bright moonlight. "You are too clever! But no, that's not the reason." Then looking around the group of children from the camp, she asked, "How many of you have been there?" Three young girls raised their hands, including Fatimata. She was obviously happy that she had done something the twins hadn't, after their feat of walking across the desert on their own. "How would you describe it?" Auntie B asked the girls.

Fatimata spoke right up. "It's everything you said, as well as dirty and smelly."

Auntie B beamed at her, for she spoke like a true nomad. "And so, I was there one day, waiting for a *pinasse*— one of those long wooden boats that you will never get me into—bringing the finest henna available from Mopti. I had a big wedding party that I was going to, where business would be brisk and I was sure to need many kilos of the fine dried leaves from the south. I was planning to try a never-seen-before design on a young Fulani bride, and was looking forward to getting fresh supplies."

Ayisha softly cleared her throat as her auntie leaned forward for more food. No one spoke a word, for they were all eating steadily, their eyes fastened on the storyteller. Auntie B looked quickly at her niece and asked her, "Are you in a hurry?"

"No, no!"

"*Cuez,*" said Auntie B, shifting again side to side on her wide bottom. "Fine. It was just before Tabaski, our huge feast at the end of Ramadan. Tempers were short because people were hungry and in a great heat, weary from daytime fasting for nearly thirty days. There was a *fou,* truly a crazy man, walking through the crowds, shoving people and insulting others, just being unpleasant and difficult and rude. I had my mother goat, Chérie, at my side, with a baby goat at her side. She had been my goat for many seasons, and Chérie had raised and I had sold many of her kid goats over the years."

Auntie B stopped talking as she remembered the exact moment. Her face took on a sad look. Then she shook herself and continued, "I saw the *fou* working his way toward us in the crowd, which had many too many people in one space." She glanced around at the dunes in the distance and the giant one behind them and the space around them all. "Nothing at all like this," she said, waving her hand, palm upturned and bracelets clinking together, at the surrounding space bathed in moonlight.

"People were pushing and shoving, mainly porters trying to get work carrying bundles to and from the boats, for money. There were high stacks of shining aluminum washbasins, boxes of canned—I'll never eat it—food. *Toubab* food to me." She looked at the faces staring at her, entranced by how far she could wander in telling a story.

As if on cue, Never the goat wandered over to his friend. Auntie B rested her arm over his shoulders, like others would with a dog or a favorite sitting camel. It made everyone smile at the strange sight, and Auntie B snapped out of her funk and said, "Now to make a long story short, the *fou* smacked Chérie over the head for his Ramadan feast! My old faithful goat. Of all the animals there for sale or with their owners, mine was the one he picked. Chérie dropped to the ground like a load falling off a camel, and I knew that she was dead."

Hugging Never tightly to her chest, she said, "I went as crazy as the *fou*. The people nearby were aghast at what he had done and grabbed onto him before I could. He was lucky, I can promise you that, for two strong men held me back. I was fighting to get free when I heard the baby goat bleating at his dead mother's side. He nudged her and it broke my heart, so I told the men to release me, I would not injure the *fou*, I had a baby to attend to."

Her hug must have tightened a bit, for Never bleated, again as if on cue. Auntie's eyes glimmered as she said,

"And so I made the baby goat a promise, and I named him. 'Never,' I said, 'shall you be a Ramadan feast goat. Never."

She gave her goat another squeeze and he bleated again, and Auntie B said, "He did that right then, after I said *never*, like he was answering to his name, and so that's how he got his name."

The sound of sucking teeth and clapping from her audience filled the night air. Auntie B dropped her head in acknowledgment of their praise, smiling as she did. Never squirmed at her side, still pressed close and slightly agitated by the sudden noise. He bleated, and she kissed his forehead right between the horns on his twitching head. It required good timing to do that unscratched, thought Ayisha. She also thought it strange that this story took place in Korioume—exactly where she and Ahmed needed to go next to meet the *toubabs*.

Auntie B looked at her audience and added, "It also reminds me of my promise to him every time I think of him or call him."

"Is that another reason you never want to go back to Korioume?" asked Ahmed.

"Yes, it is. All the activity only holds bad memories for me, and since Never goes everywhere I do, I can't take him into such a dangerous place. Look what happened to his mother."

Ayisha couldn't believe they were talking about Korioume, and she asked, "And why will you never go in that wooden boat, the *pinasse*?"

Auntie B said, "You wouldn't ask me that if you had seen one. Or if you'd seen water bigger than a puddle. Put my life in a *pinasse* with sixty or more people, cheek to cheek for days and nights on water that rocks back and forth like a heavily laden camel? *Jamais!"* Never!

"I'm sure I would love it," Ayisha sighed.

"Humph. Go see one and then give me the same answer, and I'll begin to wonder how someone so smart can also be so dim." Flitting her hand back and forth, she said, "But there's a wedding happening without us. Without me. Quick, help me up, and Never and I shall join the singing and dancing."

Ayisha and Ahmed each took an upper arm and heaved their auntie up. She smoothed down the creases in her *grand boubou* gown and patted her head tie to make sure there were no loose ends.

"You can do what you want tonight, but I suggest you not stay up too late, for troublesome times are coming tomorrow."

A shiver ran down the back of each twin, and Fatimata asked, "Are you in trouble?"

Both nodded, and Ayisha added, "Big, big trouble in Timbuktu."

"With your parents, I am sure," said Fatimata. Both nodded again. Fatimata surprised them by taking the hand of each one, telling them, "Well, then, let's join the others now." Ayisha shrugged, as if trying to leave her troubles there. She glanced at Ahmed, but he was watching all the activity moving on around the camp. Blowing out a long breath, Ayisha let Fatimata lead them to the wedding, followed by the younger kids that had shared the meal and story with them.

When they stopped on the edge of a line of singing women, Ahmed pulled his hand free and said, "Thanks for the food. You are very kind. No offense, but I think I will have more fun with boys. Too much time with too many girls is not a good thing for a man." Ayisha snorted as he raised his hand and waved at a group of seven or eight boys, all watching him on the other side of the giant bonfire. He recognized two of them from their previous visits to Timbuktu and called out, "Tarik! Khalid! I am coming." When they waved back, he turned to Ayisha and said, "Sleep when you must. I will be with them for the rest of the night. And remember, have fun tonight because tomorrow our worries return." He ran off to join his friends, old and new, before she could say a thing.

"You don't mind, do you?" asked Fatimata.

"Not at all," said Ayisha. "Look at my Auntie B." The girls watched the round, short woman as she did a very slow dance down the front of a group of women clapping along with the drumbeats. She dipped, but mainly moved her hands about in fluid movements, telling a story with her face and hands. Who would know that she just told us what must be the saddest story of her life, and now she's dancing with not a care in the whole wide desert, thought Ayisha.

When the dance was finished, Ayisha and Fatimata joined the women in a loud ululating cry, "Aiyaiayaiyaiyaiyai . . ." As she shouted with joy, Ayisha turned to look for her brother. The air was filled with dust and trembled with the deep *thump thump, thump thump* of drums. Ahmed danced with

Tarik, side by side, stomping the ground as hard as he could to the drumbeats of the women.

Ayisha danced and laughed and twirled in the dust and sand, letting loose the tension that had gripped her since they had started their Gendarmes Invisibles. She whooped for the great pleasure she felt to be reunited with Auntie B, and the hope of making a plan with Auntie B to trap the two *toubab* thieves. She shouted from her toes, *"Al Humdullah,"* thanking Allah for getting them there safely. And then she shuddered right back down to those toes when she thought of her parents. Suddenly it was clear to her that they couldn't return home without the arrested *toubabs*. That accomplishment would be the only hope they had of not being punished for life. And maybe even saving her school dreams.

As the full moon tipped toward the western horizon, the newly married couple passed through the dancers, touching hands and then their hearts. Ayisha knew the party would go on and on. When she couldn't clap another clap or ululate another time, she went to find her auntie.

Auntie B was in a deep conversation with six women, tracing the henna pattern she had made on her own hands. Clearly they were asking her something about the design she had painted when she spotted her niece. Slapping herself on her forehead, she rushed to meet the exhausted girl.

"Je suis fatiguée," Ayisha told her auntie. I am so tired.

Embarrassed, Auntie B took her into a hug and said, "Let's get you to bed right now. I am sure you have no idea what difficult days lie ahead. We may celebrate tonight, but tomorrow we will face the desert and the challenge you have brought with you."

Together, Ayisha and her favorite aunt walked to the tent Auntie B shared with as many as six women and countless kids. Ducking to enter, they crossed to the far wall to Auntie B's sleeping platform, covered with oblong pillows of leather dyed red and green. "Sleep well. I'll join you soon, so be ready to roll over when I come."

She leaned forward and kissed the tired girl's forehead, just like she had kissed Never. A smile crawled across the young girl's face while her eyes remained closed. In the softest of whispers Ayisha said, "I am so glad that you are going to help us, Auntie B, for then we shall surely make a trap to catch the *toubabs*."

"Allah help us," responded her auntie as she bustled out of the tent.

Chapter 20

AYISHA'S EYES POPPED open in the early dawn light. Auntie B shook her shoulder, whispering, "Get up. We need an early start on the day."

Ayisha rose on her elbows to look about the dusky interior of the tent. Little rays of light that spilled between gaps in the tent's woven sides danced with dust motes across the collection of bodies packed tightly together. Ayisha had to smile, for this was exactly how her auntie had described the boat she would never get on. Bodies pressed tight like dried, hard goatskins stacked and tied for market.

Her auntie looked at her closely and asked, "Are you really smiling just now? Before the call to pray is finished and before the sun has even left its resting place completely? At what?" Auntie B surveyed the crowded tent. She knew immediately what Ayisha found so amusing and turned to her to say, "At least we are not rocking back and forth in a carved piece of wood floating on the Niger River. Here I can get up and leave. Just like this."

Auntie B caught Ayisha's hand as she stood up, pulling her with her. "Does your mind ever stop?"

Straightening her bangs, Ayisha shook her head a definite no. "Never."

They worked their way out of the tent, stepping over sleeping kids and waking women. When they stepped outside, the strong smell of smoke filled the air. Last night's fire was a giant smoldering pile of beautiful coals, excellent for cooking tea. Two men were at one side of the fire, picking white-hot and glowing red coals out with long metal tongs used by a blacksmith. On the other side of the fire four women were also bent over, picking hot coals up with their bare hands, holding them just long enough to flip them into their coal pots, then reaching for another.

They all greeted Auntie B and Ayisha as they approached. One, named Tara, lifted her chin to point at Ayisha and said, "She's very relaxed for someone far from home and most definitely in deep trouble."

"Good morning to you too," retorted Auntie B. "We will get some coals, eat and pack to be on our way before you have finished your breakfast." Auntie B whipped her black covering tighter, revealing the anger she did not express. Ayisha's head snapped around to look at her, and she knew not to say a word when she saw the anger in her auntie's eyes. "Whether she's relaxed or not, in trouble or not, is, I believe, none of your business."

Lailai, an old friend of Auntie B's, stood up and said, "You're just in time. Here are your coals."

Auntie B bowed quickly and accepted the unexpected pot brimming with white-hot coals. She looked at her friend, a smile replacing the frown as quickly as a candle spreads light in a dark tent, and said, "Thank you, *ma soeur*, you are a true sister and friend."

As they walked back toward the tent, Ayisha asked, "Are we really leaving right away? What about making our plan to catch the thieves before we leave?"

Her aunt stopped dead in her tracks, turned to her and said, "Have you already forgotten how long it takes to get here? We won't just be walking; we'll talk as we travel." Pointing back at the women they had just left, she asked, "Do you think we'd find any privacy here? Do you want everyone wondering what our business is and making their own stories?"

"No, not at all! But . . ." What she wanted to ask was about the manuscript. Auntie had not said a word about it. What use was anything without a manuscript?

Auntie B held up her hand and said, "Now don't argue with me. In fact, you should be thankful, for Baba Abdul has offered to take us back, on two camels and my donkey and a donkey for you."

"But if he comes, then he'll know our secret!"

"Not to worry. He knows more secrets about this family than we have forgotten."

Trying to hide the hurt and anger she felt about this stranger knowing more about her family than she did, Ayisha asked in a miffed tone of voice, "Does that mean he knows of this uncle we've only heard of?"

"Exactly!"

"*Al Humdullah*," said Ayisha. "Maybe he'll finally tell us the story."

Her auntie snorted, then started walking again, saying over her shoulder, "Your father and I shall tell that story. Now go find your brother so we can prepare to leave. I would rather start earlier, slowly, just to escape this camp that thrives on rumor and curiosity. We'll be gone before the sun's heat has begun for the day."

Ayisha took off running. For the first time, she was glad to be away from the tenseness of her aunt. She saw a group of boys playing *boules* in the dawn coolness. She thought of her mother, who found the game ridiculous. Her brother must have been embarrassed to be caught playing, for when she came running up, he dropped the blue ball in his hand to the ground, as if it held a hot coal inside.

Ayisha was shocked to see him playing *boules* when there were so many important things to do. "Play if you must, but do it quickly. We are going to eat and prepare to go, sooner rather than later."

Ahmed bent to pick up the ball, whispering to her as he did, "Are we really leaving soon? We must if we want to reach Korioume in time."

His sister nodded and said, "Right away, as soon as we pack Auntie's things and prepare our food. So throw that ball so we can get started, eating first, because I am very hungry."

Ahmed held the ball up to his face, eyeing the small black ball that five other balls were gathered around, about twenty feet away. He squinted one eye for a better line of sight, then swung his right arm back, stepped forward on his left leg and let the ball fly. It flew over all the balls around the target ball, just like a vulture flying into a kill. It landed directly on top of the black ball and buried it into the sand. The boys erupted in shouts of joy, for no one had ever seen such a throw before. They pounded Ahmed on the back and raised his arms high, and the smile that covered his face sent Ayisha into a salute of the best kind, shouting a joyful "Aiaiaiaiaieee" ululation.

Ahmed took a deep bow to his friends and said, "I know when to quit!" He shook hands with each boy, touching his heart after each shake. "I will see you again, I am sure."

Tarik said, "That is a great way to leave. Now we will never forget you." Turning to his younger brother, who was watching the whole thing, he said, "Collect the *boules*. We are going with the *Champion du Boules!*"

Ayisha turned to Tarik, putting her hand up. "Please join us, but after breakfast. Auntie B is a bit bothered this morning and she'll only send you away. Come when we've eaten and I know she will welcome you."

Ahmed said, "I am sure Ayisha is right. But please, let me lift the ball myself." They all walked over with the slightest of reluctance, almost physically awed by what they would find.

A collective sigh of appreciation filled the air as Ahmed lifted the blue ball to reveal the black one, resting so deep that sand started to fill in on top of it. Quickly Ahmed placed the ball back on top. "Maybe you should share this first, if it's never really happened before."

"It's never happened," said Tarik, looking around at the

others for confirmation. Every boy, eyes wide, confirmed Tarik's words with a spontaneous chorus of *"Jamais!"* Never!

With long steps backward, suddenly afraid of spoiling the feat before it could be shared and bragged about, the group moved away.

"Now we must go," said Ayisha.

"Yes, *Champion du Boules*, go!" shouted Tarik. "We'll join you later. Nobody leaves here in a hurry."

"Oh, yes they would if they had just had the encounter Auntie B had," Ayisha told Ahmed as they hurried away. Her breathing turned ragged as she tried to keep up with her brother and tell the whole story.

Finally Ahmed took pity on his sister and stopped, saying, "Tell me quickly what's going on, then we'll run the rest of the way."

In gasps Ayisha related the fight at the coals with Tara and their auntie's burning black eyes, looking as hot as the smoldering embers. Ahmed listened with his head down, watching a dung beetle that was struggling along with a chunk of camel dung twice its size. Blowing out a loud puff of breath, she finished with, "And so we leave this morning with Baba Abdul, in the sun's heat, to get away from the busybodies. Auntie B will help us figure out how to trap the two *toubabs* while we walk."

Ahmed nodded, saying, "That's good. Did you ask again if she could find an ancient manuscript before we go?"

"Thank you, brother, for I haven't asked again, but now I surely will."

Ahmed looked deep into his sister's eyes. "And I am very happy that Baba Abdul will be with us. I will ask him as we walk about the uncle we are learning of only now." He would have said more, but a group of kids rushing their way made him grab Ayisha's hand and say, "Quick, let's go."

Ayisha looked back and said, "It is only your worshippers from *boules*." Then she pointed at a group of men, heading to where the boys had been playing. Tarik was running in front, jumping up and down in excitement. "You are already famous and it's been only ten minutes since the throw. I cannot keep up with all of your titles, brother."

Ahmed took off running, telling her, "The only title I really want is manuscript-thieves catcher! Now run, fast!"

When they reached the tent, Auntie B was busy packing a large saddlebag with food. Dates and dried goat meat were in stacks in front of her, and without looking up, she said, "I know. Now he is the *Champion du Boules* besides a Koranic scholar, *futbol* star and famous guide." She picked up a long piece of dried meat and pointed it at the twins. "We're leaving as soon as possible after breakfast. In fact, eat so you can pack the food and collect the water while I gather my goods together. I think I'll stay awhile in Timbuktu, and when your mother sends me away, I might go stay with my old friend Fati in the camp outside of town."

Ayisha clapped in joy. "You're going to stay with us for a while? *Al Humdullah!*"

Auntie B tilted her head up and said, "Don't get too excited too soon. No one knows what type of welcome we shall get, and I may not be welcome at all."

"They can't blame you for our coming here," Ayisha blurted out.

"Eat," said their auntie. "And then pack so we can go. You heard how fast word traveled about your brother's *boule* throw. Think what they would do if they really knew what brought you here."

The twins sat by the food tray loaded with millet and goat milk. They scooped handfuls into their mouths and slurped the hot, sweet tea their auntie's friend brought to them. Once finished, Ayisha stepped over to Auntie B where she sorted what to take and what to leave. She packed her henna tools and supplies first.

Taking special care, she wrapped her clay mixing bowl that she had used since her first henna painting seventeen years before. It had a dark burnished shine to it. Next she took her drawing tools, one a plastic sheet rolled around a long, old trader's glass bead that served as the funnel for drawing thicker lines. She placed beside it her treasured porcupine quill that a client had given her years ago, for drawing the finer lines. Taking her bag of fragrant green henna powder and the tea leaves she boiled to add to the henna to make a paste, she tied them in a tight bundle. She put the bowl and the bundle in the corner of a long, worn towel for the trip and rolled it up around the items. Carefully she placed them in the far corner of the leather trunk she always traveled with. Next to the bundle went her gowns, of deep indigo blue, rich purple with yellow embroidery, and her favorite one made of a pale green cloth covered with small blue circles and white bands on the sleeves.

Each was newly pressed and almost crackled with all the starch in it. She placed them next to the henna tools and then added her head ties, another pair of sandals and an old worn bag, red and green with fancy stitching. She opened it wide and pulled out a flat-shaped thing, covered with a blue cloth. Too small to be a manuscript. She peeked under the cloth and then placed it in the trunk.

"This is my business and your nosiness, so don't ask." She must have heard the sharpness in her own voice, for she looked at Ayisha and smiled. "You'll know soon enough. I think you and your brother should go get the water. Here is my bag, and Baba Abdul will be filling his own bags. Take yours also, although I hear it is only large enough for a swallow of the tiniest baby."

Ahmed reached down and took all the bags. "I'll get the water. Ayisha, you pack the food. Auntie, we'll be ready before you."

Taking a deep breath, Ayisha asked, "Can you find an ancient manuscript, Auntie? Before we leave?"

The look in Auntie B's eyes sent a shiver down Ayisha's spine, so she bent quickly to begin packing.

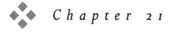

AYISHA BEGAN ROLLING three sleeping mats
into a large bundle. As she did, the same women
who had been at the hot coals arrived. Tara went
directly up to Auntie B and said, "Please forgive my rudeness this morning. But you must admit, their sudden arrival is most unusual."

Ayisha watched her auntie suck in her lips, then release
them with a loud smacking sound. Not another thing, not
any word, could have expressed better Auntie's anger and
impatience. She looked at her niece and said, "The rope for
tying the sleeping mats is over there." Then she greeted
every woman, except Tara, one by one, by name. "And how
is your morning, Lailai? *Al Humdullah*, I am packing for a
trip and shall soon be out in the desert's dunes and spaces,
beneath a sky rather than a tent, traveling with my two
favorite relatives, my good friend Baba Abdul and my goat
Never."

Pointing at them all, she said, "And you shall be stuck here, talking about whoever is not present, so I am sure that we four will provide you with plenty to talk about as you look at the same faces you see daily and hear the same chatter over and over again."

Grabbing a beautiful old brown leather box sitting near her, Auntie B snapped it closed, fastening the tying belts that ran around it. When she was done, she patted it like an old friend and said, "Now all we await is the water boy and the camel man. And in the meantime, we will load the donkeys with what we can, so excuse me, but we have much work to do."

Her friend Lailai stepped forward and said, "I have brought you extra dates for the journey."

Auntie hugged her after taking the offered dates. "*Al Humdullah*, you are a true sister and friend."

Then another woman stepped forward, the oldest in the group that had joined them from the nearest tent. She held out a beautiful worn indigo cloth. "I think Ayisha should take this so she can give the prayer shawl back to her brother to use as a turban. And take that foolish rag off her head."

Ayisha took the cloth with bowed head, then hugged the old woman around her waist. "Thanks, Grandmother, one thousand times. I shall use it proudly and feel you with me, and when Auntie B returns, I'll send it back with her."

"No, don't send it back." The old woman wound the cloth around the girl's shoulders and neck. "It is connected to a very important time in your life, for crossing the desert with only your brother is a major life moment, and so it should stay with you."

Then turning to Auntie B, the grandmother said, "I am sorry that you don't wish to share your worry and troubles with us, but you must have your reasons." Not waiting for an answer, she dropped gracefully to the ground, making it clear that she would be there until their departure. One by one, the rest of the women sat beside her.

Auntie B looked at the group. "There is nothing to share. My brother is ill and I must go." She pointed at Ayisha, who was slinging the mats over the donkey's rear end, and then to Ahmed walking toward them with Baba Abdul and a crowd of men and boys. They were leading two camels loaded with water, a teapot, a bag of dried dung and saddlebags filled with tea, sugar and food. Looking back at the group of women, she continued, "And who sent these children or who didn't is of no importance to any of you. The only thing that matters is that they arrived safely to bring their message."

Bending to pick up a bundle of food, Auntie said, "Now please excuse me, for I have much to do." Just then Baba Abdul and Ahmed joined the group. Baba Abdul announced to the women gathered, "He has thrown a *boules* ball as never seen before. It was the *très carreau.*" The very most perfect shot. "And it shall remain in its place for all time, as a salute to its rareness."

The women all sucked in their breaths at the news, for to sacrifice two *boule* balls was big indeed. Tugging on the camels' halters, Ahmed and Baba Abdul each brought their animal to its knees. Ahmed went to his auntie's trunk and asked, "Is this ready to load?"

Auntie B nodded. Then she pointed at the food bags Ayisha had packed and said, "And those also. When they are ready, we'll eat what's left from breakfast, drink our fill and begin."

Ayisha and Ahmed watched Baba Abdul put his hands on his hips and stare at Auntie B. After looking at her for some moments, he cleared his throat and said, "I beg your pardon, but you are not in charge."

All the women snickered, and Tara's laugh rang out. Instead of delaying their departure with a public argument, or worse yet, angering Baba Abdul into changing his mind about the trip, Auntie B dropped her head and said, "You are most right, Baba Abdul. We will go as soon as you say, which by the looks of things could be very soon."

Baba Abdul shook his head and looked at Ayisha. "Two bossy women in the desert. It may be too much."

When he saw the alarm that filled the girl's face, he had to laugh. "Not to worry, I shall get you home, for your parents' sake." Then turning to Ahmed, he said, "But to make sure the trip is as pleasant as possible, the two bossy women will walk on their own. Bossing each other."

Auntie B smiled and said, "That is fine with us." She smoothed her black gown and looked at Ayisha.

Ayisha, eager to show that she would be no trouble, promised Baba Abdul, "I will contribute words only when asked."

Ahmed patted her shoulder and said, "Knowing you,

you consider everything you have to say important. Let's just pack and go."

He cinched up the ropes that held the trunk close to the camel's hide. Baba Abdul checked the straps to make sure they wouldn't chafe the animal's sides and then said, "You may just be a camel man one day."

Ahmed's smile, already stretched as tight as a drum-head across his face, filled his face even more. Ayisha was sure he was thinking of his father calling him a desert man. Was it really only three days ago?

Baba Abdul looked at his traveling companions and said, "We are ready except for one thing: the departure prayer asking for a safe journey." As he spoke, they saw the imam from the village rushing toward them. Everyone greeted him with the greatest of respect, and he dropped his head to Auntie B and Baba Abdul and said, "Forgive my late arrival. I hope that I have not held you up."

Auntie B raised her hand and said, "We are just ready. All the preparations are finished, and the only thing left is your blessing." Bending down, she picked up a beautiful red and green bag, thick with something inside, and draped it over her shoulder. As she patted it, Ayisha wondered— Maybe that's the manuscript.

Baba Abdul stepped forward and said to the imam, "One always rushes toward Allah, not away, and so we would have waited for you if it had required two sunsets or a whole moon's cycle."

Standing before Auntie B's tent, the men and boys immediately fell into two lines, stretched ten feet long and facing the imam's back. The women stood in two rows behind the men. In one motion they all squatted, turned their palms upward and prayed to Allah, asking for a safe journey. With the blessing finished, Auntie B grabbed the harness of her donkey, clicked her tongue for Never to follow and started walking. Wasting no time, Ahmed pulled down on the camel's halter to make it sit so he could climb into the saddle.

Ayisha mounted her donkey. She had not ridden one in a very long while. She was happy until she looked at her brother, six feet above her head on the camel. He had his feet braced against the neck and looked as if he did it every day. Like Auntie B, Baba Abdul held his camel's halter, and he walked along at her auntie's side.

"Go with Allah," called the imam and voices from the group.

"*Inshallah*" filled the air four times. Once from each traveler.

The group didn't disperse, but instead stood watching them leave. About a dozen boys and girls ran behind the travelers, excited by the change from the day's regular activities. The men and women walked with them nearly all the way to the nearest dune. The women finally called out, "Good trip, safe travels," in Arabic, Tamashek and French.

As the four carried on, the twins on their animals and the adults walking, each waved an arm over their head, saying good-bye and thanks as they entered the vastness of the desert. There was a moment of silence from the watching group.

The four travelers walked on when the stifling desert

air was suddenly filled with the voice, first only of the grandmother, then all the women: "Aieaieaieiiii!!!" As one, Auntie B and Ayisha returned the call. The trip officially began as the ululation of the women drifted faintly away and the desert's silence took over.

No one said a word. Ayisha looked ahead at the large dune awaiting them, shimmering in the growing heat. She looked around the group and knew that all were saying one last prayer, offered up individually to Allah, asking for a safe journey across his giant, difficult desert.

THE BOY ON A CAMEL, the girl on a donkey, the older woman leading her donkey, the man walking with his camel and the goat moved across the desert floor toward their first big hurdle—the dune Ahmed and Ayisha had struggled up the day before. Ayisha couldn't believe that just yesterday afternoon they had approached the giant sand mountain from the other side.

Ayisha opened her mouth, but Baba Abdul raised his hand. "Don't talk. Save your breath and strength for this large dune that stands before us. We'll talk at the top, and you will both tell us everything, and I do mean everything, that has happened."

And so they trudged in silence, upward and onward. Ayisha's breathing grew loud and ragged as she struggled up the sliding sand. She had followed Auntie B's lead and dismounted from her donkey to save its strength for the long journey ahead. As she held her side, she looked at

Auntie B, who had also stopped. Her aunt looked up ahead and then back down, as if checking their progress. Sweat covered her face. Abdul and Ahmed were first to reach the summit. Ahmed ran back down the dune's face to take Auntie's donkey for her. The sun continued its daily march west, rising higher and higher in the sky as finally, together, sister, brother and auntie reached the top of the sand dune.

All four turned to look back at the camp, snuggled up against the giant dune behind it. They could see groups of people resting in any pool of shade they could find, looking as small as termites. Men sat in four different small groups around teapots and coal pots. Some women pounded millet while others cleaned up from the wedding the night before. Children ran about, some helping and others playing tag.

Ayisha looked at Auntie B and noticed the streaks of red dirt that ran down her face. She was sure her face looked the same, for the climb up the dune to the pass had been hot and difficult. She wiped her face with her cloth, then looked at the rich streaks of the color indigo in her new shawl. She didn't want to dirty it, but she also found the sheen of sweat covering her face very irritating. Swiping her face again, Ayisha looked at the cloth. In the lightest streak of blue there was a slight darkness, almost with a purple tint, created by the red dust and blue cloth.

The descent from the dune was going to be more brutal, for the first half of the climb up there had been in a large patch of shade spilling down from the top, shortening as the sun rose. It had been hot, even in the slight shade, and the final hour of climbing had been exhausting. The next part of the trip would be straight into the sun's path, with no chance of shade unless a cloud suddenly appeared. Baba Abdul looked at the three and said, "Let's rest here a bit." It had been an easier trip on a camel than a donkey. In fact, both Auntie B and Ayisha had walked up the slope.

The sun was reaching its highest point, and Ayisha could see that Ahmed and Baba Abdul wanted to say their midday prayers. Auntie B and Ayisha sat on the western edge of the pass that sat fifteen feet lower than the rest of the dune. The man and boy stood side by side, facing east. They began their prayers together.

Ayisha whispered to her auntie, "I am so tired, but so glad to be away." She tilted back her head and rolled it from side to side. Auntie B had her arm around Never, feeding him some of the fodder that Fatimata had given her.

"We have only just begun the journey," Auntie B whispered back. "But it's always good to get the hardest part done first, like that climb, while we're still fresh rather than do it at the end. But then, the end means you are almost arrived." With a deep sigh she said, "Oh, I'm just not sure which is better."

"I think the best part of a journey is when it's finished, coming or going."

Her auntie squinted at her niece. Slowly shaking her head, she said, "You have all the answers. I hope you have one for this challenge we are facing."

Ayisha did have an idea, but she wanted to wait until they all sat together to discuss it. "I hope we can sit and talk a bit while the sun still stands overhead."

As the boy and man bent for the fourth time, Auntie B took the red and green bag off her shoulder and hung it on the corner of the trunk attached to Ahmed's camel. "Don't worry. I have no intention of leaving right away. But watch: Baba Abdul will think it's his idea to wait, which will make him very happy."

When Ahmed and Baba Abdul joined them, Auntie B said, "I think some water would be good, but you are in charge. Also, the child is tired and hot and asked if we must start right away, but I told her we must ask you what is best."

Baba Abdul eyed them. "You think you are so clever, but yes, before your leading question I had decided to sit out the heat of the day. We can rest a bit, and drink a bit, and eat a little. Then we can walk into the night, for the moon is only one night past its fullness, and the desert shall be as bright as a cloudy day." Looking first at Ahmed and then at Ayisha, he added, "If we walk through the night and six or seven hours tomorrow, then we should reach Timbuktu by late afternoon."

"But we can't go to Timbuktu," Ayisha blurted out, "for we must reach Korioume tomorrow before the *toubabs* leave at sunset."

Baba Abdul looked sternly at the young Bellas and said, "Obviously we need to talk. NOW!"

It was very hot, with the sun falling directly on them

on the dune's summit. Ayisha looked at Baba Abdul and asked, "I can make us some shade. Should I?" One day when herding goats, she and a friend had seen others do what she planned to do.

Baba Abdul nodded quickly and said, "Fine, do it. But be quick, for we obviously need to know exactly what is going on."

Ayisha got right to work. She pulled her donkey over and asked Auntie B to hold its halter. Then she pulled her auntie's donkey next to it. She gave Auntie B that halter too. Without telling anyone what she had in mind, she then untied the mats.

Her auntie spoke out, "We're not here for good. What are you doing, child?"

Ayisha just smiled and said, "Watch."

She took the second-longest mat and stretched it out on the desert pass. Then she asked Auntie B to sit on one end, still holding the halter of her donkey. Taking the reins of her donkey, she asked Ahmed to sit at the other end of the mat and then handed him her donkey's halter. Ayisha then took the longest mat and draped it over the back of Auntie's animal, asking her hold on to a corner of it. Finally she ran the mat to the back of the other donkey, draping a roof over the mat below and creating instant shade beneath.

"Uh, uh, uh," said Auntie B. "You are just too smart."

Just then Never bumped her aside and moved into the shade. Everyone laughed at the cheeky goat. Ahmed helped Ayisha finish the job by running the long hemp rope that had held the bundled mats over the donkeys' backs and across their bellies, securing the makeshift roof. It would stay tight as long as the donkeys didn't move toward each other. When the job was done, Ahmed, Ayisha and Auntie B stared out from the newly created shade at Baba Abdul's legs, from the knees down.

"Come inside," called Auntie B. "There is plenty of shade for all, including a goat."

As the legs turned and Baba Abdul started to walk away, he said, "I will get some water and a bag of food. If we are going to camp now so we can walk most of the night, this is good."

He bent to look inside when he returned. The three were resting comfortably, Auntie on her side, legs stretched out, resting on her elbow. She was short enough to fit beside her donkey. Brother and sister were in their nighttime position, resting back-to-back. Baba Abdul's perpendicular smile made everyone encourage him to enter. Auntie started to move, but he stilled her with his hand on her foot, scrunching down and stretching out across the edge of shade on the width. He held up the water bag and Ahmed took it. He poured water for his sister in her cupped hands, then crawled on his knees to his auntie and poured water for her too.

Holding out his hands as the boy scooted over to him, Baba Abdul drank, then took the bag and poured for Ahmed. No one had taken more than two gulps, so the bag still looked very full. With efficient hands, Baba Abdul twisted the thin rope around the bag's neck again and again, closing it tightly. Stretching, he hung it from the donkey on his right. While Ahmed had been delivering water, Ayisha had placed part of the food out. Taking the separate package of dates that Lailai had given them, wrapped in red cloth, she spread the dried black fruit on the mat, counting out three each. That left twenty, just in that pack alone. Gazing at their own date bundle, which was twice as large, and the meat also in a bulging bundle, Ayisha felt rich at the thought of all the food they carried.

Auntie B unwound the cloth holding the dried meat and was making little stacks of it for four.

She looks like someone at a party instead of someone just starting a two-day trip, out in the huge expanse of the southern Sahara Desert, thought Ayisha. She looks at home.

Twisting to sit upright, Baba Abdul leaned on his wide-spread knees, his eyes directly on Ayisha's face, then Ahmed's. Under the power of the man's look the young girl remembered why they were there, and what they needed to do, and felt foolish for having party thoughts.

Auntie B looked at Ahmed and said, "It's time to start talking about everything going on." She turned to Baba Abdul and said, "We want you to join our group, but you must promise not to take us lightly."

Baba Abdul looked around at everyone and said, "Your group? What is this group called, Two Bossy Females and a Boy?"

All started to argue until Baba Abdul raised his hand to silence everyone and said, "So tell me what this group is."

"Les Gendarmes Invisibles," said Ayisha in her most serious voice.

He threw his head back and laughed, loud and long.

"How dare you LAUGH?" Auntie B shouted, stopping when she saw her niece and nephew looking at her. "Oh, right, I did that too."

Ayisha pushed her brother's shoulder. "Please, tell him everything."

Ahmed sat forward, his elbows on his bent knees, a smaller mirror image of Baba Abdul sitting across from him in the shade. His dark brown face took on a serious look as he told his story from the first day he had met the tourists, to the suspicion that they wanted one of the ancient manuscripts, to the last day when they agreed to meet at the port of Korioume on the quickly approaching Sunday. He also explained how the *toubabs* always talked in English, not knowing that he could understand them. This, Ahmed told him, was how he discovered what they did. Baba Abdul could not hide his smile. Finally, he said, "And so that makes you the Gendarmes Invisibles. Very clever."

He turned to Ayisha and asked, "And what do you have to add? Why are you here instead of at home with your worried parents?"

Ayisha sat up straight, her back rigid and her face stern. "Because I want to catch these *toubabs*! They have insulted again and again our heritage, city and cultures."

Snorting quickly, Baba Abdul asked, "And how is this your problem? You are not a guide. You're only a young Bella girl with too much nerve, running away from home and scaring your parents like no parent deserves to be scared."

"But don't you see? They are rude, stealing people that want our traditional treasures. I want to catch these two, more than . . . yes, more than . . . going to school."

Everyone gasped, including Ayisha, when she made this announcement. At last the worst had been spoken aloud: following this quest of Les Gendarmes Invisibles would end her school dreams. It was the choice she had made when they took their first step into the desert two days before. Perhaps Ayisha was fooling herself—they didn't even have an ancient manuscript and she was beginning to fear they'd never have one.

Auntie B tapped Ayisha on the shoulder and said, "Please, bring me my treasure bag hanging beside my trunk."

Scooting her way out from the shade, Ayisha straightened up and walked around to the far side of her donkey, patting his hindquarter as she passed it. As she untied the hanging bag, she looked at the camels, chomping their cuds peacefully. A sudden feeling of jealousy swept over her, for she felt anything but peaceful inside. Taking her auntie's bag, she dropped it to the ground, then got on her hands and knees and scooted back into the group. Auntie B reached deep into the red and green leather bag and carefully pulled out a packet wrapped in a deep blue indigo cloth. It made the slightest clanging sound as she set it down. Slowly she untied the bundle. An old, burnished metal box was revealed.

Digging into her robes, she pulled forth a long, thin leather strap, which held a single key. With all eyes watching, she fit the key into the lock and turned it once, pulling the lid open slowly. Ahmed's breath caught and Ayisha's eyes widened at the sight of an ancient manuscript.

Ayisha clapped, relief washing over her. Like magic, the manuscript was finally here—in their hands. She hugged her auntie. "I knew you would help us find one!"

The manuscript was written on yellowing, brittle paper, and little holes were scattered about, places where insects had eaten it. The Arabic writing, written by a sure hand long ago, flowed across the top page of text. Baba Abdul looked quickly at Auntie B and asked, "How did you get this?"

"Alhaji Musa gave it to my husband many years ago. Your uncle, children. He said that a scholar deserved to have at least one manuscript of his own." Patting the small box, she added, "We bought this metal box to keep it in and buried it outside our tent for safekeeping."

"Uncle!"

"Yes, Ayisha, your uncle, my husband."

Ayisha wanted to touch the yellowed manuscript, but was afraid to, so instead she held her hand over it and asked, "Do you know what it's about?" Then looking confused, she added, "Why would Alhaji Musa give . . . your husband an ancient manuscript?"

Auntie B rubbed her hands along her thighs. Ignoring the second question, she said, "I only know what I was told it says," she replied. Then looking at each twin, she said, "You two read Arabic—you tell me."

She laid it out on the cloth that had held the box, laying six piles of ten pages each, side by side. As she worked, she said, "They told me it's about politics, from more years ago than we can count."

Ahmed, Baba Abdul and Ayisha all leaned forward, their heads nearly touching as they read the words. Baba Abdul didn't say anything, just nodded as he read. Ahmed held his breath as he read, and Ayisha gasped aloud.

"Oh, Auntie, this is amazing." She ran her finger right to left under each line without touching the brittle page. Looking up at her auntie, she whispered, "The first page says, 'The day the world realizes that everyone needs somebody else, that no one can be completely alone, peace will come to the world.'" Nodding, she said, "It's a beautiful message, and one that is even more important today."

Baba Abdul shifted his eyes up to look at Ayisha and said, "You read well. And comprehend also. It does say that. That we all should work together for a better world."

He sat up straight and let out a slight whistle between his teeth. "Why have we not figured this out yet, when the scholars of centuries ago gave us the path to follow?"

Ahmed still had not said a word as his eyes traveled from page to page. His finger ran down the pages without touching them as he quickly scanned the ancient document. Finally, leaning back on his heels, he said, "It's true. From what I've quickly read, this entire manuscript is a document dedicated to world peace. We still know nothing about getting along, when the ancient scholars did. But I guess no one listened back then either, for how many invading powers took over Timbuktu?"

"All good questions," said Auntie B. "But let's get to the questions and answers that count right now."

And as the sun marched across the sky, the plan was hatched to catch the thieves. Ahmed and Ayisha had the bait they had come for, a manuscript to tempt the *toubabs* into buying more, and a trap for catching them that took Ayisha's breath away just to think about. Everyone had a role, even Baba Abdul—and everyone had contributed, she thought, and now a trap like a spider's web that catches a fly had all the necessary parts to make it work. Her thoughts were cut short when Baba Abdul pointed to the dipping sun, tilting toward the distant dune behind the Tuareg camp. He raised his hand and said, "To successfully complete this plan, we need rest, food and Allah's blessing. I think it would be best if we all rested before the final prayer of the day. Then we shall eat and begin our walk to put this plan into action."

Finally, a plan. And an uncle too.

Chapter 23

AYISHA JERKED AWAKE as she felt the movement about her. Auntie B was struggling to get out from under the draping prayer mats, and the donkeys were restless from standing still for hours. Ahmed and Baba Abdul were just beginning their prayers, facing east into a darkening sky, the last remaining rays of sun shining on their backs.

Ayisha scrambled out from beneath the shade and helped her aunt untie the mat draped between the donkey backs, rolling it as it dropped down. Bending over, she pulled the mat that they had sat on and followed her auntie over to a place behind the man and boy already praying, heads to sand. Without a word Auntie B and Ayisha started their hand washing with sand, then raised their palms upward and followed the ritual for prayers. The gentle murmuring of four soft voices, reciting prayers, filled the air.

"We will walk for a few hours and then stop for tea and food. Here," said Auntie B, handing each a collection of dates. "We can walk and eat." Then pointing to the sky, she said, "The moon will rise there, and when it is high enough to throw shadows, we shall rest."

Baba Abdul looked at her, squinting slightly as he did. "I see you have taken over again."

Auntie dropped her head and said, "Forgive me. Like a true desert woman, when I travel, I am always figuring the way of least strain and challenge. I don't mean to be pushy or bossy, just organized."

Ayisha dropped her head and smiled, for she was sure Auntie would say anything to keep the peace.

It worked, for Baba Abdul said, "Well, it's a good idea, so I will agree to it without further delay. Let me suggest that we walk down the dune to save our animals extra work, and then ride at the bottom."

As one, the group started down the hill, each leading an animal, all followed by the goat named Never.

When they reached the flat, Baba Abdul yanked on his camel's halter, and it quickly bent down to its front knees. With a graceful step he slung his leg over its back, missing the tall back piece of the saddle as he settled into the seat. Ahmed repeated every move of the older man, like a shadow.

Auntie B and Ayisha sat tall on their donkeys, and slowly the caravan started the trek toward the break in the dune that awaited them. Their progress was steady as their animals slowly worked their way through the deep sand. Each rider looked deep in thought. Ayisha's mind clamored with all the plans they had discussed and discarded that afternoon, finally settling upon the best one.

The trap was really quite simple, thought Ayisha. The four would separate when they reached the road: Auntie B and Baba Abdul would take the extra donkey and camel and go north to Timbuktu. Ayisha and Ahmed would go south, to the port at Korioume, where the *toubabs* would be waiting for them. While the twins traveled with the *toubabs* by boat to Niafunke, Baba Abdul would collect two more manuscripts and the police in Timbuktu, then take the road to Niafunke to await their arrival.

Ayisha smiled as she thought about how she and Ahmed would lure the *toubabs* with Auntie B's manuscript to Niafunke: they'd travel downriver on the *pinasse*, promising to provide them two more manuscripts for sale in that river town. Baba Abdul had told them it would take at least a day to travel to Niafunke by boat, which would give him time to go to Timbuktu to get the two other manuscripts and inform the police. Then he would travel to Niafunke by road with the *gendarmes* and the two ancient manuscripts, and they would all meet there, to snap closed the trap to catch the *toubabs*.

Ayisha couldn't believe all the things she was doing for the first time, and most likely the last time too. She found it hard to picture that the next day she would go from a trotting donkey on the desert, to a public transport flying down a paved road in the afternoon, to a *pinasse* in the evening, traveling by river on the wobbling wooden boat that even brave Auntie B was afraid to go on.

For a moment she imagined herself to be braver than

her auntie, until she thought of her auntie's job, by far the most difficult—explaining to their parents where she and Ahmed were. That was brave.

Suddenly Ahmed broke the silence as he asked, "Now, why do we tell them we're going to Niafunke? Why don't we just catch them when they take this manuscript?"

Ayisha looked at him in surprise. "Did you already forget? It's because we won't have the police there in Korioume when we get on the boat. This way Baba Abdul can make sure the police are there when we arrive in Niafunke and catch them in the act of buying national treasures."

Auntie B snorted slightly and said, "You just want to ride on one of those tilting, tipping transports on the Niger River. Wait till you see one—that may change your mind."

Ayisha looked at her auntie. "But don't you agree? Mother and Father will be happy to know where we are, and the police can be warned and ready to meet us."

Auntie B said quickly, "Happy, I doubt. Relieved, maybe, but happy, no. And, *Inshallah*, not too angry to appreciate the courageous task you are undertaking."

Holding her hand up to slap her donkey on its rear end, Ayisha added, "And the thieving *toubabs* will be arrested and made an example of for all that follow." Her hand dropped on the donkey's rear and it spurted into a short run. Ahmed kicked his camel's sides as his sister shot past, and he took off in a long, loping run. They didn't go far, for they didn't want to wear out the animals that they needed to get them where they were going.

The glow of the rising moon filled the dusk. Its light reached upward from the dune they traveled toward, and when its first rim climbed over the sand wall before them, Ayisha clapped "It's beautiful, *Al Humdullah*!" she cried out. Auntie B exchanged a quick glance with Baba Abdul, both smiling at the young girl's genuine shout of pleasure.

Traveling at night was definitely the way to go. The rising moon filled the night's darkness with a soft golden light, spilling across the expansive desert. It looked as full as the night before. The slightest flat edge became obvious, but did nothing to diminish the moon's light.

No one spoke for more than an hour as the animals trudged along. Each rider swayed in a personal pattern on their animal's back, moving toward the rising moon. It was hard to see the stars in the moon's brilliance. Ayisha was content as she swayed along on her animal, for this time they had food and water, and most important of all, knowledgeable company.

The moon had almost reached its zenith by the time they reached the pass in the middle dune. It was the second dune they had met on their trip to the Tuareg camp. A deep shadow was cast across the pass now, welcoming to one and all. Baba Abdul rode into the dark slash, and the three others followed. When all had entered, he dismounted in one easy motion. Then Ahmed dismounted and ran to help Auntie B get off her donkey. Ayisha filed in last and slipped from her donkey's back, rubbing her backside as she did.

Baba Abdul unhooked a bag from his camel and began

putting out his equipment for making tea. Auntie undid the bag of dried dung on her donkey, and Ahmed unrolled a mat for them all to sit on. Baba Abdul listened to the soft voices of Ahmed and Ayisha as they laid out the balls of hardened cheese like those Ayisha had bought in the market only days before. She looked at her brother and asked, "Is it really only two days since I bought cheese in the market?"

Ahmed just shook his head. "I don't know. Does it really matter how many days ago?"

"No, not really. But now I know for sure, Ahmed, life is full of surprises these days."

Baba Abdul took his small smoking kit from around his neck. He tipped out a handful of matches and a hard stone to strike one against. He lit the dung and a few straws from Never's food that Auntie had piled in his wire-basket teapot holder. Briskly, he fanned it with one of his leather sandals. It didn't take long for the wispiest plume of smoke to rise, and soon a fire was going.

Ahmed pulled his tiny water bag from his camel and filled the teapot. Baba Abdul had to smile as he said, "I see it's good for something." When the fire was hot enough, he added a few chunks of charcoal and fanned them until they began to glow with a white heat. Just in that same moment the moon made its presence known, sending a bright light along the top of the wall facing them inside the sand pass. Auntie B added dates to the cheese balls in front of each person.

"Eat," said Baba Abdul, "for we shall leave as soon as we

drink some tea for strength as we take advantage of the night's coolness."

Everyone chewed as the tea cooked. Not a word slipped from Ayisha's lips as she concentrated on eating.

Like a man sitting in his home, Baba Abdul smoothly went through the process of preparing the tea and finally served the first round to each one. A collective *"Al Humdullah"* filled the air as they each savored the strong, sweet brew. They all ate and drank silently, relishing their first real meal since breakfast.

When they had drunk their three rounds of tea and finished eating, Auntie B asked Baba Abdul, "Is it possible to rest for just the shortest time? I feel like my age is catching up to me after such a long and busy day."

Baba Abdul nodded and said, "Rest while the children repack everything. If we want to reach the road with time to spare, we shouldn't spend too much idle time here. I am sorry, but that's what is best for the schedule we have to meet. Remember, the *toubabs* plan to leave on the boat tomorrow evening."

Looking off at the remaining dune between them and the desert that spilled toward the paved road, Baba Abdul said, "We'll leave as soon as the things are loaded. Sorry."

Ahmed and Ayisha quickly collected all the things that had been unpacked and buried the dead coals in the sand. Ayisha bundled up the remaining food while Ahmed washed the tea glasses. Baba Abdul prayed in a loud whisper as he stowed his teapot, coal pot and the clean glasses Ahmed handed him. When they finished, all could hear

Auntie B, filling the night's silence with her gentle snores. As they finished the last preparations for leaving, louder snores rose from the exhausted Bella woman.

Baba Abdul gently nudged Auntie B on her shoulder. She jerked awake and set right to work, acting as if she hadn't been asleep at all. Ayisha stared at the sky that was visible over the pass and gave herself a hug. For the first time in her life, she felt like she owned the whole world.

❖ *C h a p t e r   2 4*

BABA ABDUL YANKED on his camel's halter, saying, "It's time to go. We don't want to waste the
night's coolness."

"Should we water the camels before we start?" asked
Ahmed.

Auntie B choked back a laugh at what must have been
his very earnest tone and expression. "You look so much
like your father; it makes me catch my breath." His large
dark eyes set in rich brown skin. His black hair curled
along his neck. Twisted curls sprang out from the sides,
just like on his sister's and father's heads. "It won't be long
before you have a little beard on your chin to tug on, just
like Ibrahim," Auntie B said.

Patting his shoulder, Baba Abdul said, "Not to worry.
The camels drank their fill before we began. Surely a camel
man knows that a camel can go for another week without
water. We'll be there long before that, *Inshallah.*"

Quietly they each mounted their animal. They began again, the trek across the desert bathed in moonlight. Auntie B sang softly as they moved along. Ayisha listened to her sing their tale of crossing the desert alone and planning to catch the thieves. Auntie B stopped short when she sang, "And their uncle . . ."

Snapping her head around, Ayisha looked at her auntie's face, so soft looking in the moon's spilling light. Auntie B shook her head, saying, "You'll learn soon enough."

Once again, all slipped into silence. The animals' hooves softly plopped on the sand as they plodded along the flat desert floor, hour after hour. Silently the group traveled through the sand tunnel of the first, or last, dune, depending on which direction one was going. As the moon moved west, their shadows lengthened. The desert's vast silence was once again filled with the gentle snores of Auntie B, swaying side to side on her trudging donkey. Not long after, the louder snores of Baba Abdul drifted down from his camel. The brother and sister looked each other's way. Ayisha smiled in the moonlight. First she pointed at their auntie's relaxed figure on her donkey, then at Baba Abdul.

"How do they sleep?" she whispered to Ahmed. "I guess we need more experience riding animals. I know if I even close my eyes, I will fall off instead of fall asleep."

Ahmed reached forward and patted his camel's long, strong neck. "Just think of how many salt caravans they traveled to Taoudenni and back. Fifteen days, each way, traveling at night. You would be sleeping too, right now, if you had spent so much time on a donkey or camel."

And so they went on for the rest of the night. Ayisha, tired as she had never been before, swayed side to side on her donkey, which seemed to be walking in his sleep. She and Ahmed had stopped talking, for there seemed nothing left to say. She was shocked by that, for they always had something to share, something to say. But after nearly five days of constant companionship it seemed as if they had finally run out of things to talk about.

Breaking the silence that had accompanied their trek for hours, Ayisha suddenly asked, "How do Mother and Father do it?"

Ahmed was surprised by the sudden voice, but also confused by her question. "How do they do what?"

"Find something to talk about day after day, for they have been together longer than we've been alive."

Auntie B surprised them when she interrupted to say, "I wish I'd had the chance to find out."

Ayisha asked, "What, Auntie B? What did you say?"

Auntie B snorted and said, "Oh, nothing. I just awoke suddenly and entered your private conversation. Forgive me."

As the sun finally made its early morning appearance, Baba Abdul awoke. He looked like someone trying to act as if he had been awake the whole time, but Ayisha, tired and getting grumpy, greeted him with a snappy, "Good morning! Did you sleep well?"

"Very well, thank you," he replied. He looked ahead at the wide expanse of desert that lay before them. The sun's golden rim was peeking over the horizon, sending glorious rays of shooting orange light skyward. He pointed at the rising sun and said to Ahmed, "You've kept us on the true path through the night. I do believe you are a camel man."

Ahmed couldn't contain his smile, and when Baba Abdul saw Ayisha's face fall, he added, "And I am sure that you helped."

She smiled at him for the recognition that she too had spent the night awake, unlike himself and Auntie B.

Then pointing at a stand of dried trees in the near distance, Baba Abdul announced, "We will stop there, in the shade, for tea and food and prayers. We shall rest a short time and then head slightly southeast so that you can find these robbing *toubabs* and get on with our plan."

Ayisha had to ask, "Will we be there in time?"

"*Inshallah*" was his only reply.

When they finally reached the shade of the spindly, dried-out trees, Ahmed was the first off his beast. He slid off the camel as it sank to its knees, almost as gracefully as Baba Abdul. Ayisha looked at him with pride, for they both had changed during this trip. Ahmed had shown his knowledge of the desert during the storm, and now he was riding a camel as if he had been born to it.

With more exhaustion than she'd ever known in her short life, she slid off her donkey's back. I wonder, she thought, if being independent and being bossy are often confused, especially if I am involved? She rubbed her donkey's back, then took a gourd hanging off its side to fill with water for the tired beast. As she worked, she thought, Perhaps if I listen more often, trying my best to follow some instructions instead of always giving them, people will think I am independent instead of bossy. It seemed to be working with Baba Abdul, who had not called her bossy since the beginning of the trip. She liked that.

They all worked quietly. Auntie B provided the fuel for the coal pot for tea while Ayisha laid out the mats and Ahmed fed Never and the camels. Baba Abdul wasted no time getting the tea under way, for they all knew that tea would bring them back to life.

Ayisha just couldn't believe her luck. Here she sat with her brother, who was as much a part of her as her left leg; Auntie B, whom she admired and loved deeply; and Baba Abdul, a stranger only forty-eight hours before but now a trusted and loyal friend and a member of Les Gendarmes Invisibles. Best of all, they had a plan that could not fail. What more could one ask for? she wondered.

The morning began with a gentleness that would fool a person with no experience of the desert and its power. Or the sun and its power. Reds and oranges filled the sky, with shots of white light bursting through. The kids watched as the sky went from a colorful explosion to a growing paleness. They knew that as the day passed and the heat grew, the moment's bright white would fade to a muted, beaten white. They didn't want to be on the desert floor, no matter how flat, when that occurred.

"Are we far from Korioume?" asked Ayisha.

"Still a fair distance," replied Baba Abdul. He pointed to where the slightest wisp of dust marked the fury of a desert dust devil twisting upward. It was small compared with the horizon, and looked many days away to Ayisha's untrained eye.

"That is a vehicle traveling across the desert floor to meet the road to the port. We will walk that way and hail a *bâché* for you when we reach the paved road. We should reach there before afternoon prayers." Ayisha watched several dust devils now that Baba Abdul had pointed out the first one. Each vehicle made its own sand road, criss-crossing tire marks of vehicles racing against getting stuck in the sand. A dust trail always followed each car and truck. They were the source of the dust devils, not Mother Nature.

Ayisha looked at him and said with a wavering voice, "We'll really be hailing a vehicle?"

He nodded and looked at her with an expression of curiosity. "Is there a problem? I thought that's what we agreed upon yesterday."

She took a deep breath, not sure if she would tell the truth or a lie. The idea of telling another lie did not appeal to her, for she remembered with a flash of embarrass-ment the first lies she had told him. The truth was the only answer.

"I've never ridden in a vehicle," she said softly.

Auntie B piped up with, "Neither have I. But then I have no desire to, just like I will never ride in a *pinasse* on the Niger River." She looked closely at her niece's face and asked, "Are you afraid of riding in a vehicle?"

Ayisha nodded.

"So what would you rather do?"

Ayisha held her hands out, like a beggar in the town, then pointed at a dust devil and said, "Could you drop us close enough for us to walk the rest of the way, instead of swerving and racing across the sand in one of those?"

Auntie laughed suddenly in the stifling heat. Talking to Baba Abdul as if the twins weren't there, she said, "Here is a girl who set out across the Sahara with her equally inexperienced brother and arrived safely at our desert camp. She is the smartest in her school and most amazingly wants to ride in a *pinasse*. And still she is afraid of a vehicle swerving and racing across the desert?"

Turning to Ayisha, Auntie B asked, "You'll risk your life on a carved piece of wood on a tumbling water path, but don't want to get in a vehicle on the road?"

"That's right," said Ayisha. "But if I have to, I will." She shrugged and said, "Just the speed in town scares me." Then looking at the dust devil Baba Abdul had pointed out she said, "Look how fast that dust is traveling! It's true, I am afraid."

Auntie B looked at Baba Abdul. "Would it be possible to drop them where they can walk to the noisy, crowded port?"

Sighing loudly, he nodded. Following the racing dust devil with his eyes, he said, "We should start now." Tilting his head, he looked at Ayisha and said, "Since you won't take a bush taxi, we'll walk you closer to the road, to that scrawny tree there, the one with no leaves. There we shall split up, and you and Ahmed will walk south to the port and we will turn north, for Timbuktu."

Ayisha jumped up, eager to pack so they could get on their way. The closer to Korioume the better, as far as she was concerned. She looked at Ahmed, who had also gotten right to work. Auntie B and Baba Abdul exchanged quick looks. Nothing could have expressed Ayisha's fear more profoundly than the speed with which she worked.

They plodded along throughout the morning. Ayisha could tell that her donkey was tired, so she spoke soft words of encouragement to it. She leaned forward and whispered in its ear, "You're a beautiful, strong donkey." They trudged along in the heat that rose with each degree the sun ascended in the sky. Ayisha looked back at the last dune and the corridor they had passed through. She was happy to see it had shrunk in size, a sure sign of their progress.

When the sun had nearly reached its highest point in the sky, Baba Abdul stopped. They could hear the racing engine of a *bâché*, one of the bush taxis. They scared Ayisha the most, for she had seen many leave Timbuktu, packed tight with customers and tilting with the ruts in the road under their heavy loads.

Baba Abdul pointed to their left, where all the dust devils seemed to congregate while they slowly shrank in size. "There is the port—you can see where the dust finally settles." He commanded his camel to sit with a squeeze of his knees, and the giant brown animal quickly dropped onto its front kneepads. He stepped off with his usual grace as the animal's back end settled on the ground. Brushing the dust from his gown, he said, "We'll drop you here, far from the road, so you don't have to fear being struck by one of the vehicles. If you walk due south, you will reach the port before the sun sets."

Shielding his eyes from the sun's glare, Ahmed said, "We have traveled well, for they said the boat would not leave until sunset, so now all we have to do is find them there."

Auntie B looked toward the port. Ayisha could see the shudder that ran through her auntie's body as she shook her head. "Not to worry," said Auntie B. "The place is crowded and busier than three weddings at once, but just go down to the river's edge and I am sure you will find your stealing *toubabs*." With a loud sigh Auntie B got off her donkey. She solemnly handed the green and red saddle bag, her treasure bag, to Ahmed. "Here is the manuscript. Carry it in this for safety so that none will know what you have."

Then turning to Ayisha, she dug deep into her robe. Finally she pulled out a little woven bag, bulging at the sides. Slowly she pulled from it a large roll of CFA notes. "Thank Allah for all the business I had just before your arrival. Now put out your hand," commanded Auntie B.

Ayisha did, palm up.

Auntie B began counting bills into her hand, snapping each bill straight, but not too hard, for the bills were old and could rip easily. There were notes of 500 CFA and 1,000. Auntie counted slowly, "Four thousand, four thousand five hundred." She stopped at ten thousand.

Ayisha was staring at the money, for never had she held

so much. Auntie wrapped her fingers closed around the pile and said, "This is for passage on the boat, if the *toubabs* won't pay for it. And food. And a drink or two if you get tired of river water."

Ahmed said, "Thank you, Auntie. We'll take it just in case, but I heard him tell her that he expected to make much money by selling these manuscripts at home, so I will say he must pay our way."

His eyes were steely, and Ayisha liked the look of a returning anger. Ayisha wrapped the money in the corner of her scarf and then threw that end of the scarf around her neck, landing the small bundle against the front of her right shoulder. She gave her auntie a big hug and then stepped back. She tried to hide the fear growing over her, but all could see it.

Auntie held her by the shoulders at arm's length. She looked deep into her niece's eyes and said, "Are you sure about this?"

"*Bien sûr,*" Ayisha responded. She had never been surer about anything in her life. Auntie then handed her a few dates and said, "Eat these on your way, for strength. Then you can buy food once you reach the market area, for there are many food stalls."

Ahmed, anxious to get the difficult good-bye over with, stepped forward and hugged his aunt too. "We'll see you in Timbuktu," he told her. Turning to Baba Abdul, he said, "And we'll see you in Niafunke."

They shook hands, snapping fingers and touching their hearts. "Take good care of your sister," Baba Abdul said.

Then, turning to Ayisha, he added, "Not that she needs much help."

She hugged him around his waist, surprising everyone. He tugged on her braids in a gentle fashion and said, "Go with Allah. We'll meet again in Niafunke."

Then together all four said, *"Inshallah."*

Chapter 25

NOTHING COULD HAVE prepared Ayisha and Ahmed for Korioume, packed with bellowing camels and bleating goats, barking dogs and crowing roosters. *Bâchés* raced their engines and honked their horns while their touts screamed at passing people, looking for passengers. Little stalls made from crooked poles and stretched tarps sold everything from canned to-mato paste to rubber-tire sandals. Tuareg men wandered about, selling swords and necklaces, leather boxes with beautiful tooled work and camels. Groups of men sat about, relaxing on their chairs made of thick plastic string, drinking tea.

Ayisha held her hands over her ears, for never had she heard such noise. Kids ran about, playing tag around the legs of men strolling hand in hand and women carrying tall baskets of millet on their heads. She jumped high off the ground when a Land Rover, loaded with people, suddenly honked behind her. Ayisha scurried to the side of the road and was embarrassed and surprised to see Trudy and Griff get out when the vehicle stopped.

Ahmed said, "And so we begin." Looking at his sister, he added, "I think things will go well, for Allah has dropped them right at our feet in all this madness."

Griff was laughing when they met. He pointed at Ayisha and said, "Are you part gazelle? You sure jumped back there."

He turned to Trudy and said in English, "Miss In Charge sure is nervous."

Trudy replied, "That's good to know she can be scared."

Ayisha saw Ahmed scowl before he dropped his head. She didn't know what they had said, but it clearly wasn't good. Trying to get things off to a good start, she said, "*Bonjour.* Good day, how are you?"

Trudy smiled and said all was well. Griff didn't want to waste time with niceties so he pointed at Ahmed and asked, "What's in the bag?"

Ahmed said, "*Bonjour,* Griff. *Ça va bien?*" Are you well?

Griff ignored the question and said again, "What's in the bag?"

All eyes were fixed on the smooth red and green leather bag that hung from Ahmed's shoulder. Ahmed rubbed it, then looked at his sister, who nodded quickly. Taking a deep breath, Ahmed finally said, "It's what you are looking for, but I can't show you here." Looking around, he spotted a row of tall trucks parked in the far corner of the market.

He pointed with his chin and said, "Let's go there. I will show you what we have behind those big trucks if no one is around."

As they walked over to the transport area, Griff asked Trudy, "Have you ever seen a more disgusting place?" He kicked at tin cans in the road and then pointed at a herd of cows grazing on a pile of plastic bags. Ahmed listened as he told his wife, "If I get hurt here, please just shoot me. I don't want to die a slow death from infection in this country."

"Gotcha" was her quick reply. "Now let's see this thing and determine if all the sweating and dust has been worth it."

Once they rounded the trucks, they found a quiet spot. Carefully, Ahmed started to reach down into the red and green leather sack. He stopped and looked at Griff. "The seller will sell only a set of three manuscripts. You can have this one only if you buy two more in Niafunke, just down-river. It's on your way."

Griff flexed his hands, clearly eager to have a look at what Ahmed had. The young Bella boy carefully lifted the metal box from the bag. Ayisha held out her hands, palms up, and he rested the box on them. Deliberately he dug into the bag and pulled out the large metal key Auntie B had used.

Ahmed looked first into his sister's eyes, then at the greedy *toubab*, who suddenly blurted out, "So show me!" Again Ayisha gave a silent nod, so Ahmed turned the key. Opening the metal box slowly, he displayed the first page of the ancient manuscript, yellowed with age and brittle around the edges. Griff whistled between his teeth and reached out to touch it, but Ahmed stopped his hand while quickly closing the box Ayisha held. "You cannot touch it until you own it for it is very fragile. And you cannot own it until you buy all three."

"So where is this Nia-whatever place you're talking about?" asked an excited Griff.

"It's about a day's trip from here, *en pinasse*."

"And how do we know who to talk to once we reach there?" asked Trudy. Suddenly she was very bossy herself, pushing her way in front of Ayisha.

Ayisha pushed her way back in front of Trudy and said, "We'll go with you. We know where to go and whom to ask for once we reach there."

Griff tilted his head and said, "You're going on the boat too? And who is paying for it?"

Trudy turned to him and said in fast English, "Let's pay and get this over with. I'm hot and tired of Timbuktu, of Korioume and of Mali. I'm tired of being nice, and quite honestly ready to get rid of this cloth slung over my shoulders."

Ahmed turned to Ayisha and explained in Arabic everything they were saying. His sister started to turn when Ahmed grabbed her arm. Ayisha looked at Ahmed as he said to Griff, "So do you want this or not? If not, we will take it to Timbuktu and get it back to the owner. If yes, then you must buy our boat tickets. We'll get the other two manuscripts in Niafunke, and you'll pay us a fair price for our hard work and for the three ancient manu-scripts."

Ayisha could no longer contain her tongue and said, "And then you can go south to find your airplane to America, and we'll return north to our home, Timbuktu, and all will be happy."

Griff only nodded and then turned on his heel, saying, "Let's find the boat captain I spoke to the other day."

Usually Ahmed led the way, but this time they all followed Griff as he wound his way through the market. They passed women sitting behind small piles of rotting tomatoes, dried-up oranges, used clothes and meat, covered in flies. The women's gowns of red, green, purple, blue, yellow and mixtures of each contrasted brightly with the hard dry earth they sat on. Some market women sat behind large pots covered in burlap, selling millet and rice and sorghum. The noise of people shouting and goats bleating was unbelievable.

Off to the left, on the edge of the sprawling market-place, Ayisha saw a man yanking on a camel's halter. At first the animal made a deep gurgle, but as the pulling continued, the gurgle turned to a roar, and still the man pulled. He let go when the roar erupted in a great spew of green, sticky slime that dripped down the man's white *jalabiah*. Everyone around laughed at the man, for all knew that an angry camel would spit, just like it had.

Ayisha crashed into her brother's back since she wasn't watching where she was going. Before she could complain, her mouth dropped in amazement. There before her stood the Niger River. She had never seen so much water in one place in her life. Boats sat crammed against the shoreline at odd angles, some filled with giant bags of grain and others with people. The river, a deep brown, was nothing like the clear water that came from the wells in Timbuktu. And it really was moving—if she could believe her eyes.

Ahmed stood with his jaw dropped, clearly stunned. In a voice filled with awe, he told his sister, "Now I know why they call it the Strong Brown God." He looked at his sister, and they both broke into wide smiles at the new and amazing sight. Griff was pushing his way through a line of porters carrying heavy loads on their shoulders and heads from the water to the land or land to water. The large pack the *toubab* wore on his back smacked others as he twisted and turned through the crowd. Ayisha hoped that he was heading to the largest boat there, not the tiny little ones like the one that carried four men, three women and a bicycle.

When he reached the riverbank, Griff squatted on his heels next to a man who was washing a long white shirt in the brown water. The man had a small white cap on his head, showing he had made the pilgrimage to Mecca. He dropped his shirt in the water, wiped his hand on his brown pants, then shook Griff's hand. They talked for a moment, and then Griff pointed at the twins, who stood next to Trudy farther up the riverbank.

It was clear that they were arguing over the price, but finally Griff reached into the small bag he always wore around his waist and pulled out money. He dropped the heavy pack off his back and waved for the others to follow. Trudy, carrying a pack smaller than Griff's, clambered down the gentle slope to the river. Ahmed and Ayisha looked at each other, and then made the trip down too as Ahmed pressed the red and green bag tightly against his chest.

Although the boat wasn't leaving for hours, people were already boarding. Ayisha could see the seats, flat boards across the width of the boat, many with large bundles stuffed beneath them. When finished with Griff, the captain of the boat climbed over the passengers sitting on the boat, settling behind a tiny steering wheel at the front. Ayisha watched the man as he proudly sat at the bow, painted with bright stripes, circles, triangles and giant dots of yellow, blue, red and white. The man rested against his seat back, a tall wooden slab, made of four rounded pieces painted in the same colors with the same designs as the bow. A plastic yellow and orange pitcher sat beside him, next to a large orange plastic glass. He sat in the sun, with three men directly behind him. An old man with a scraggly gray beard and turban held a radio to his ear as he patiently waited for the trip to begin. The other two watched the shoreline, their prayer beads passing through their fingers automatically.

The boat, fifty or sixty feet long, had six benches in front of a large open space in the middle, where three women sat, tending fires in two giant coal pots, stirring two big metal containers of cooking food. A group of men sat to the side, tending their teapot and talking, chewing tobacco and spitting on the already messy floor. A chain of ten men in a line passed fifty-kilo bags of millet one to another, the last man inside the boat finally dropping each one on a large, growing pile on the floor. Each thunk of a bag made the boat sink lower in the water. There were six men huddled over the giant engine that sat behind the kitchen and cargo areas.

Not even looking, Griff hauled his pack on board and slung it toward an empty space, totally unconcerned about whom he might hit. He headed to the covered area that stretched from just behind the men sitting in front to just in front of the giant engine that sat at the back of the boat. Thick poles ran from one side to the other, and above them were layers of mats that spread shade across the board seats. Griff pushed and shoved and finally made his way to a bench that had only an old lady on it. He stuffed his pack under the seat, then stuffed Trudy's. When he reached for the red and green bag slung over Ahmed's shoulder, the boy leaned away from him, shaking his head.

Griff pointed at Ayisha and said, "I still don't know why we need you or why I paid for you, but you're here, so sit."

Ayisha was shocked by his rudeness and would have said something, but Ahmed just gave his head the quickest of shakes and she held her tongue. She moved in next to the old woman, who wore a gown of bright red with gold embroidery. Ayisha greeted her and asked permission to sit beside her, which the woman instantly granted by patting the board next to her.

Ahmed plopped down next to Ayisha and bent around

her to greet the older woman. He had to scrunch closer to Ayisha when Trudy sat down beside him, and even closer when Griff finally dropped down onto the wooden plank.

"How far are you going, Grandmother?" Ahmed asked.

"To Mopti, *Inshallah*." She had no teeth and her cheeks caved in on her empty gums. She bounced her hands together in a silent clap as she looked at Ayisha and Ahmed. "And you. Where are you traveling to?"

Ayisha joined the conversation and said, "To Niafunke. Do you know how long that will take?"

The old woman smoothed her beautiful gown across her knees and said, "One day, not long." And then she added again, *"Inshallah."* God willing.

Ayisha couldn't take in all that was happening around her. Men washing goats and cows in the water; women doing laundry, great piles heaped up beside them. Kids played, splashing and laughing, while men in long lines carried goods to and from the boats. Even cars and trucks were parked at crazy angles, half in and half out of the water, receiving a good wash.

Radios blared from all sides. She could hear Ali Farka Touré and said to Ahmed, "At least Father's favorite singer is with us on this trip."

Ahmed smiled. "Did you know he is from Niafunke— the singer, not Father?"

Ayisha shook her head in slow motion, side to side. She couldn't take in all she was seeing, hearing, learning. The boat suddenly tipped to one side. She grabbed her brother's hand, and together they looked behind them. They could see two men struggling with a moped motorcycle, the front wheel twisting and turning as they tried to lift it up to the roof of the boat. Ahmed saw hands grab it from above and it disappeared. Suddenly thick ropes were being tied around the roof from the outside, run across and over the top again as they tied down the motorcycle.

Trudy began squirming, saying in English, "I'm hot and sweaty and this boat stinks."

Griff gave her the slightest of smiles and said, "It's that load of dried smelly fish someone just hung from the roof over there."

He patted her knee and said, "It will all be worth it. Trust me. We'll get the manuscripts, lose these dumb kids and head home with our treasures. The rewards this time, dear Trudy, will be great." After a short pause he added, "I can't wait to see these other two manuscripts. If they are anything like the one Ahmed has, then there's money to be made." Bouncing his hands on his knees, he added, "I'm telling you right now, though, I have to keep one of these manuscripts for myself. They really are amazing."

Wiping her brow with the end of her head scarf, Trudy said, "Whatever, Griff."

Ahmed turned to Ayisha, who was watching his face as he listened to the two *toubabs* talk. She noticed the little furrow in his brow as he struggled to hide a grimace.

"What?" she asked, looking innocently at the bustling shoreline. "What did they say?"

Smiling widely, he answered, "Just talking again about

how rich they'll be when they get home. But we know that they won't be rich, and they won't be home soon. Oh yes," he said, his eyes shining, "and he called us dumb."

Ayisha let out a long, loud breath. So much had happened in less than a week. She could feel the boat sink again and again as men heaved large sacks of salt and millet on top of the *pinasse* and into the cargo area. The slightest of breezes started blowing, so she leaned forward to catch what relief from it she could. Her back already ached, from riding a donkey, sleeping on the desert floor and now sitting on a wooden plank with no back. Rubbing her back, she whispered to herself, "You asked for an adventure . . ."

The engine rumbling to life suddenly filled the air. A black cloud of smoke drifted forward, under the roof and over the people. Everyone pulled their head scarves and prayer shawls over their mouths and noses to protect them from the exhaust that slowly drifted through the boat. The pointed tip of the boat nosed out into the river while men on shore pushed on the equally pointed stern. Ayisha could see that everyone but the *toubabs* were saying a silent prayer as the journey began.

She looked at Ahmed and said with great relief, "We should thank Allah that we arrived in time, for this boat is leaving early." They both looked at the sun, which was still far off the horizon.

Ayisha was a mix of emotions. The first moment when the boat was set free from land, it rocked back and forth and sent a shiver of fear and excitement through her. The next, when it was gliding smoothly across the water, she felt a rush of excitement. Her smile was huge as she turned to her brother and said in Arabic, "I can't believe we are on this boat! And heading to another place we've never been before." Then looking down the bench, she added, "And best of all, we're about to catch two thieves."

Ahmed glanced at his sister's happy face. "I'm glad to be under way, for the sooner we arrive in Niafunke, the sooner this whole thing will be over." He patted Ayisha's knee. "Was it three or four days ago you told me you always pray to Allah, asking for an adventure?" Looking at the red and green bag hanging from his shoulder and pressed between their thighs on the bench, he added, "Maybe you should be more careful about what you pray for."

Chapter 26

THE RIVER WAS AS BUSY as the streets of Timbuktu, with boats of all sizes. There were long pointed ones with a man in front and another in back walking against long poles planted on the river's bottom to move them along. They passed passenger boats like theirs, making their way to Korioume, heavily laden with sacks on the roof. Ayisha pointed at one and told Ahmed, "That must be what we look like."

The shoreline stood farther away than Ayisha liked as they motored toward the center of the river, but she knew it didn't really matter. She had never been in water deeper than her ankles, so if the boat suddenly sank for any reason, she knew she would not survive. She shook her shoulders, anxious to get rid of the bad thoughts. Just then the river made a slight bend to the left, and as they made a turn, what she saw took her breath away. A brilliant green as far as the eye could see ran from the river's edge up to the white sand dunes that stood in the distance. She had never seen anything like it. The brightness of the green tested her eyes, and the distance it covered amazed her. The old woman, enjoying the young girl's reactions, leaned over to her and said, "*C'est la riz.*" It's the rice fields.

Ayisha could only stare, for never had she seen such color or anything so green growing in the desert. And so huge. As the boat chugged along, the rice fields continued until they came to a small village. The rice stood out in brilliant contrast to the mud-brick walls and the two small minarets of the mud mosque that dominated the village. Kids were running along the shoreline, jumping and waving at the passing boat. Ayisha found herself waving right back. When the kids ran out of land, they stopped, and the giant wooden boat chugged along around another gentle bend. She noticed that they had moved closer to the shore, for a large sandbank stood exposed in the middle of the river. Up close to the verdant green rice fields she could see giant locusts sitting on the green stems of the plants.

The dipping sun marked the passing of time. Ayisha stood up to stretch her back and look around the boat. The workers lying spread out on the bags of millet and rice watched the women cooking, laughing and chatting as they scaled small fish, cut onions and stirred the big pot. Ayisha looked at Ahmed and said, "Do you think we can walk back there?"

He turned to look at the benches between them and the cooking area, the people crowded on the benches and the bundles lying everywhere. He shrugged, not sure that it would be worth it. "Up to you," he shouted over the constant thumping of the engine. Just then the boat lurched and came to a complete halt.

She fell into Ahmed's lap and looked at him, eyes wide. The crew scrambled from their beds of grain and looked over the side. Chatter and shouts filled the air as someone cut the engine. The captain sprang up and climbed back over passengers and bundles to see what was going on. There they sat, perched on a sandbar. One by one, the men started climbing out. One walked in water up to his knees to the river's edge, obviously looking for something. He walked ahead of where they sat and finally waved his woven cap of green and red, signaling something.

Before they knew it, the same chain formed from boat to shore, to unload as much as necessary to free the grounded boat. The captain looked at Ahmed and said in Arabic, "You must get off also. The old grandmother can stay, but you four must get off until we free the boat." Pointing at the big sandbar in the river's middle and then at the smaller one they sat on, he told the boy, "These sandbars suddenly appear as the water level drops. Close to shore we can off-load until we are free enough to move off this unexpected sandbar."

Ahmed relayed the message to Griff and Trudy, who took the news with surprisingly good humor. Griff laid his hand on Trudy's shoulder and told Ahmed, "She needs to pee anyway, and now she can."

Ayisha and Ahmed really didn't need to know that, but it was true, this was a good opportunity, for there was nowhere to take care of personal business on the boat.

They joined the line of the other twenty-seven passengers to get off, asking the old woman if she needed anything before they left. She just waved her hand at them and shook her head, no, a smile dimpling her collapsed cheeks.

Ayisha wandered up and down the narrow paths running beside a channel of water that separated the rice fields. It was still the strangest sight she had ever seen. Fields of green, sparkling in the quickly diminishing sunlight, filled the landscape until the desert took over once again in the distance. At different intervals little channels poured out of the big channel, irrigating the fields.

She looked back at the boat. Most of the passengers stretched out on the narrow bank, just down from where the men piled the huge sacks of grain on a low, flat area. Like camels in a caravan, one man followed another, bent low under the heavy millet sack each carried. And still, even with the growing pile of sacks on the shoreline, the boat sat lodged, not moving, which meant they would keep off-loading until the boat shifted. Ayisha could see Ahmed and Griff talking in the end of the day's light and decided to join them.

"But it's not my fault," she heard her brother say as she walked up.

Griff was agitated, rubbing his hand through his long dirty hair, his dirty turban cloth wrapped around his neck and shoulders. He paced back and forth, and she was sure that he would start spitting like a camel if he didn't get his way soon.

"We've been here, what, two hours, and still the boat is

stuck." Then turning to the growing pile of sacks, he said, "And then once the boat moves, they have to reload all that?"

Ahmed shrugged and said, "I guess so. Like you, I have never been on this river before."

Griff glared at the captain, who sat with a group of men, drinking tea. The captain lifted his glass in a salute, then called out to invite the angry *toubab* to join them. "You'd think he was on vacation," huffed Griff. Then he made a sweeping gesture with his arms and said, "They all look like they are. What's with all these lazy people? Why can't they all help so we can hurry it up?"

"Maybe it's you with the problem," Ayisha blurted out. "Those men are working very hard. Why don't you help if you're in such a hurry?" As an afterthought she added something she had read once, a sign on a small café in town. She straightened her shoulders and said to Griff, "We appreciate hurry, but hurry takes time."

Ahmed dropped his head to hide his smile. He heard Trudy snort a short laugh before she said to Griff in English, "The little smart mouth has a point. You pacing and shouting won't speed anything up, Griff. And you aren't exactly helping move things."

Griff waved her off and went to talk to the captain. He showed his rudeness by refusing to sit, so all had to crane their necks to look up at him. He looked like a vulture, his shoulders hunched, his hands up, his head shrinking into his neck. "How many days will this take?" Ayisha heard him ask.

"How many days, perhaps five or ten. *Inshallah*," replied the captain. Then he turned back to the group and drank another slurp of his tea. The men laughed, for they knew he was teasing the impatient *toubab*.

Griff dropped down to a squat and said, "You're kidding, right?"

The captain shook his head slowly. "You *toubabs*, always in such a hurry. My boat carries sixty tons of goods, and however many tons need to be removed to let her float again will be removed."

He scooted to his left and said, "May I suggest you relax, drink some tea, chat? Pacing and shouting won't get the job done any faster."

But Griff wasn't interested in drinking their tea. He had seen the tea man fill his pot with the murky river water. Instead of accepting, he said, "I'm going to carry some bags."

All watched: the men drinking tea, the old grandmother still on the boat with the women cooking, the other passengers relaxing along the bank, Trudy, Ahmed and Ayisha. Griff stomped over to the line of men waiting to carry bags away. They were in water knee-deep and chattering and laughing among themselves. They all stopped too, to watch the skinny *toubab* try to carry a fifty-kilo bag of millet.

The man with the green, red and white knitted cap was next in line for a bag. He stepped aside and let Griff move ahead. Two men in the boat pointed to his head or shoulder. He chose his shoulder. They bent to lift the bag by either end and placed it on his shoulder, draping it down his back. Griff's knees buckled when the weight hit him, and then he slowly straightened up. All eyes were on him as he tried to step away from the boat. Two men stood on either side of him, and it was a good thing, for with the first step he began a slow collapse. The men grabbed the bag before it went underwater, but they let Griff go. He tumbled back into the water, which had grown murkier and murkier with every step taken in it. Ayisha was sure he must have heard the laughter just before his head went under.

He came up spluttering and spitting, thrashing his arms to get rebalanced. He slogged over to where two men were off-loading the sacks from their shoulders. When the next bag arrived, he elbowed one of the men off-loading aside, then reached up to grab the tied-off ends on one end of the waiting bundle. His shame was obvious when he couldn't lift the heavy thing up high enough to reach the top of the growing pile and dropped it instead. He fell headfirst into the river again, trying to save the bag from getting wet. The man he had pushed aside grabbed the bag just before it hit the water. He held it high as Griff shot to the surface again. His scowl was murderous until he saw one man reach out a hand to help him ashore. A woman took the cloth that was draped over her baby and handed it to him to dry his face. Little giggles rippled through the group, and finally he had to laugh too. Holding his arms out wide, he said, "Okay, so I'm not the strongest man here."

He splashed to the edge of the river and took the towel

Trudy had pulled from her pack. He looked around at the flat horizon of green and said, "I'll go change." He pulled from his pack a dry T-shirt and another pair of torn jeans. With his shoes sloshing with water, he walked up the nearest irrigation canal path.

The work to off-load the boat continued as the sun dropped below the horizon. As many bags were onshore as still in the boat, and still the boat did not budge. Mosquitoes arrived en masse with the dusk. Griff had calmed down until the arrival of the gnats and mosquitoes. They were thick, forming little buzzing clouds around all heads and eyes and ears. He swiped with full swinging motions, and Trudy slapped at the air and whined, "I hate this place!"

"I agree, it's not an easy place—damn boat. But neither was the bush taxi. It'll all be a funny story back home, especially after we sell the manuscripts. Remember, Trudy, the manuscripts. Stay focused."

"Don't tell me again how happy I'll be. I'm not now, Griff, and I'm tired of hearing it. In fact, I'm fed up with everything."

She saw the scowl start to cross his face. His mood had lightened since his public humiliation, and she didn't want to change that, so she said, "Sorry. Oh my God—a snake, behind you!"

Griff leapt up as if his pants were on fire. He was looking right and left while still slapping mosquitoes.

"Where? Where?" He stopped when he heard Trudy laughing.

"Oh no, not a snake. Just a stick." Then with a smirk covering her face, she said, "Gotcha!"

There was that word again. Ayisha looked at her brother, who was smiling. She pointed up the bank with her chin, so they rose and walked to the edge of the rice. In Arabic she asked him, "What was that all about?" She was also fanning the cloud of bugs surrounding her face with the end of the beautiful cloth the old Tuareg woman had given her in Auntie B's camp.

Ahmed's eyes were bright with amusement as he said, "She told him there was a snake, and he jumped up. Then she told him, 'Oh, it's just a stick,' he glared at her and she said that word again, *Gotcha!* I think I know what it means now."

He leaned over and whispered in her ear. Ayisha's eyes lit up just like her brother's as he explained, and then they laughed. When he stepped back to look at her face, he could see the wheels turning in her head. "What? What?"

She just looked at him and said, "Teach me to say it."

And so they practiced in the closing day. Ahmed said it and Ayisha repeated it, "Gotcha! Gotcha!" again and again, until the sky turned a soft rose color with golden streaks piercing it. Ahmed saw all the men, both crew and passengers, begin their preparations for the sunset prayer.

Ayisha said, "I'll stay here and say my own little prayer for success tomorrow, when we reach Niafunke. You do think Baba Abdul will wait for us, don't you?" Then turning him to face the others, she said, "Go. Allah is expecting you."

❖ *Chapter 27*

THE EVENING ARRIVED with a rousing chorus of cicadas and frogs. Ayisha and Ahmed had never heard a frog before, and it was Griff who explained it to them. He seemed very subdued to Ayisha after his afternoon of public humiliation and the bad snake joke he thought only he and Trudy shared. They all sat together but not talking too much. Red welts covered their arms and faces. The mosquitoes had been reduced in number with the setting of the sun. Some still buzzed about, but not like the clouds that had formed at the day's end.

Shortly after prayers, but before total darkness claimed the night, the fifty-seventh bag was lifted from the boat and a loud sucking noise filled the air. A man standing at the stern pushed on the long pointed end, and the boat shifted. Soon all were pushing and the boat floated free in the shallow water. A chorus of *"Al Humdullah!"* and *"Bisimallah"* filled the night. All spirits lifted with the boat.

Ayisha clapped in relief, then turned to the captain. "This means we'll still reach Niafunke tomorrow, doesn't it?"

"*Inshallah,*" came a chorus of replies.

All evening long the thought of her angry parents had never left the young girl's mind. Auntie B must be sitting with them now, she thought, assuring Ibrahim and Miriam that their children were safe. In her mind's eye Ayisha could clearly see her mother's stern face, staring at a very uncomfortable Auntie B.

The moon rose, later than the night before, in a clear sky. Smaller in size, with a flattened right edge, it still cast a fair amount of light. Standing in a little group around the cooking women, Ayisha paid 100 CFA for two bowls of food. The aroma had set her mouth watering. She couldn't wait to eat, for a sudden hunger made her stomach growl.

Ayisha almost felt like Griff as she had her first taste of fish. Never before had she eaten it. Goat, yes, and lamb and beef, but never, ever fish. She wanted to spit it out but knew how rude that would be after having seen Griff do the same with the sandy bread. She swallowed the first bite of the salty sauce, poured over a heap of rice. Her brother was having the same problem, for he almost squinted in pain as the foreign fish went down his throat.

Looking closely into her bowl, she could see a few chunks of fish on top. There were also onions, which she had eaten before. Her eye caught Ahmed's in the firelight. He shrugged, clearly not knowing what to do with the fish either. The captain, sitting near them, suddenly laughed out loud and said to the group in Arabic, "Look, our Bella guests don't like their food!"

Ayisha, shamed to her toenails, said, "That's not quite true, Baba. I am just not used to this food, but I can learn. Just like a *toubab*!"

At that everyone laughed, except for Griff and Trudy. The woman pinched Ayisha's arm and said, "Are you making fun of us? I heard that word *toubab*."

Ayisha quickly pulled her arm away. *"Qu'est-ce que c'est?"* What is this? "Why are you hurting me?"

Scowling at her, Trudy asked, "So what did you say? What was so funny about *toubabs*?"

"They could see that I didn't like the food too much. So I told them that it was different, but that I could learn to like it just like a *toubab* learns to like our food. *C'est toute*." That's all.

"Fine. So tell me, when does this trip get going again?"

The captain heard Trudy's question and said, "I thought you both understood. We will stay the night here. We will reload most of the bags tonight and finish at the very first light, then be on our way. You should be in Niafunke by tomorrow afternoon, Allah willing."

He stood and pointed to the boat, the land, the pile of bags, the roof of the boat. "Find a place to sleep, and in the morning we will go."

With that the captain lifted his long white cotton shirt to his chest and walked out to the boat, now floating in water up to his waist. He hefted himself aboard, said good night to the old woman and the cooking women and climbed onto his seat by the steering wheel. He disappeared from sight as he lay on his side.

Griff stretched out, his head on his pack. Trudy did the same. For once neither had a rude comment to make. Casually, Griff said to Ahmed, "Your good friend Sidi tried to steal your job while you were gone."

Ahmed leaned forward and asked, "He did? Did you also ask him about the manuscripts?" Ahmed couldn't hide his concern.

"No," said Griff. "I'm not stupid. He talks too much. He told us all kinds of things, like the way you are always best at whatever you do."

Trudy sat up on her elbow and pointed at Ayisha. "And he told us how you are getting to be as bossy and crazy as some old aunt of yours." The *toubab* laughed then, adding, "I believed that."

Ayisha was ready to lash out a response when Griff said, "He also said that you speak English, Ahmed, but I know that's not true. I'm sure you would have told us if that was the case. You are a proud young man, with an even prouder sister who likes to brag about you."

Ayisha stood suddenly. She didn't like the turn in the conversation, plus she was fuming about anybody calling her Auntie B crazy. She pointed to the roof of the boat and said to Ahmed, "That's where I want to sleep. Let's go." Without a word of good night to the *toubabs*, she walked to the river's edge, not caring in the least if she was being rude.

Two workers who had just dropped two bags into the

boat said, "Come, we'll help you." One picked up Ayisha and placed her into the boat. Ahmed tried to resist being carried, but Ayisha called out, "Do it. It's better to be dry!"

Once he was on board, they climbed up to the roof of thick, layered mats. The motorcycle, tied to the sacks at the far end, lay near three people already stretched out on the piles, all sleeping. Ahmed and Ayisha walked over an around them as best they could, then finally settled on their own section of the load. Ahmed let out a real sigh of relief. He was wrapped in his prayer shawl, with his green and red bag, Auntie B's treasure bag, resting across his chest. He started to nod off when he suddenly asked his sister, "Are you warm enough?"

"I am," she said. She was sure that he was snoring before she finished her answer. Gazing at the stars and the moon, she thought, I'm under the same sky as in Timbuktu and the desert we just crossed, but in a whole different world. She smiled into the darkness, reviewing all her adventures of the last few days. They had crossed the desert twice, once on foot and once on a camel and a donkey. They had survived a harmattan storm in the desert. They had formed a plan with Auntie B and Baba Abdul that was sure to catch these thieves. And they were members of Les Gendarmes Invisibles. Plus, an uncle—they had an uncle! It all sounded so great until her mother and father's faces floated before her eyes. She shook her head to send them away, hoping that having Auntie B with them had calmed their fears.

She lay on her back, staring at more stars than she'd

ever seen before. The sky had regained its clarity after the dust storm and reached from east to west and north to south. She hugged herself and said a silent prayer for the next day. She thought of three fragile, priceless manuscripts the *toubabs* wanted to buy and shuddered. They had to stop them from stealing them. She also thought about Sidi and knew that his friendship with Ahmed would be over after what he had said to the *toubabs*. Maybe that was what had made them so unpleasant again. She couldn't believe she'd almost liked them at one point.

She knew it was good that the trip was taking longer, for that meant for sure Baba Abdul would have all in place tomorrow for the event that was to change the *toubabs'* lives. And hers too, she suddenly thought. She knew they had to succeed, for it would be the only thing that could help her keep her school dream. Another shudder ran down her spine, for she could see in her mind's eye the gates of the *lycée* swing shut before she could enter. Shaking that image from her head, she felt all of her aching muscles and an exhaustion that ran from her head to her toes. She gave herself into the gentle rocking of the boat and finally slipped off to sleep.

C h a p t e r 2 8

A SUDDEN TILT OF THE boat and loud voices woke the twins. Both hunched under their cloths, faces covered to protect them from the mosquitoes and gnats that were greeting the sunrise like they had the sunset. The men, already hard at work, loaded bags from the shoreline. There were only about twenty left on the shore. Ayisha rubbed her eyes, which still held grit from the desert, and smiled at her brother. "Today's the day," she said.

"Inshallah" was all he answered as he sat up.

The *toubabs* were on the shoreline, doing their mosquito dance and thrash. Griff saw the twins and waved them to come ashore. Ayisha said, "You can go, but I am not. Let the men work on loading the sacks instead of unloading us."

"I need to pray," he said.

"So what is wrong with right here? I will get out of

your way." She walked to the far end of the boat's roof and called to Trudy and Griff, "We'll see you on board."

As Ahmed prepared to pray, Ayisha went below to see if she could help the women cooking, or the old grandmother. Activity filled the dawn's air. A fire burned nicely under another pot of fish stew. One woman was rinsing bowls out, swirling water around and around inside them one by one. Talk and laughter filled the air from the men working as they reloaded the heavy sacks of grain. The grandmother lay stretched out across the wooden bench, and she waved at Ayisha as she stepped into the boat's interior.

She greeted each person she met, and then one woman handed Ayisha a plastic cup filled with steaming tea. She sipped it with every taste bud in her mouth. It was hard to know which was better—the sweetness of the tea or the warmth that ran down her throat. She looked up and saw Trudy being carried to the boat like a fifty-kilo sack of millet by two workers. She tried not to smile at the woman's surprised face when they dumped her on board like just another piece of baggage.

When Trudy's angry face turned her way, Ayisha held up her cup and said, "Come have some tea. It will do you good."

Trudy rolled onto her side so she could slowly lift herself. Her pack was still on her back and had softened the blow of her hard landing. She got onto her knees and hands when one of the crew reached out to help her right herself. She took his hand long enough to stand up, then snatched hers back.

Ayisha turned her attention to Griff. Carrying his bag and dry jeans over his head and wearing his wet jeans from the day before, he waded toward them. The water rose to his waist as he reached the side of the boat. He threw the bag and jeans in and hefted himself up the side. He rested for a moment when his backside touched the edge of the boat, then slowly let himself fall backward into the growing pile of millet sacks in the boat.

When he reached Ayisha and Trudy, he looked into the bubbling open pot of tea the women were cooking. Then he looked more closely, as if he were checking for bugs or something. "It's very good," said Ayisha. "And cheap. Have some."

Just then Ahmed joined the group. He gratefully took the cup Ayisha held out to him and slurped loudly, his enjoyment interrupted by Griff asking his wife, "So do you think it would kill us to drink some of that?"

Dirty from sweating and sleeping on the ground, she was grumpy and full of bites that already had scabs after a night of scratching. "Who knows?" she blurted out. "If this rotten trip hasn't killed me, Griff, I'm sure the tea won't either." She looked into the big pot and added, "It's certainly boiling hard enough to kill any critters that might be in it."

Griff took out a pile of coins and asked for two cups. Neither one could stifle the sighs of pleasure that escaped when they took their first sips.

Just as the sun lifted over the tallest sand dune in the distance, the throbbing of the engine started again. People clapped, and murmurs of *"Al Humdullah"* ran through the boat. A belch of black smoke filled the boat, but this time Ayisha, Ahmed, Griff and Trudy were sitting on top of the loaded roof. Two men sat at the front of the roof, watching for sandbars.

The view was much better and they could almost recline against the sacks rather than sit rigid on the bench. The old woman happily stretched along the bench they had left empty, watching and resting and rolling her prayer beads through her fingers.

The time seemed to fly. The breeze blowing across the top of the boat was fresh and welcomed. The sun's rays danced upon the surface of the water like diamonds. Griff looked at the treasure bag Ahmed held tightly to his chest. He started to say something, then clearly thought better of it and bit his words off.

Turning to Trudy, Griff said, "He holds that thing like a baby."

She was lying back, watching the sky pass and flocks of egrets fly overhead. Their long white necks stretched out while their white wings flapped gracefully. She looked as if she was relaxing for the first time since the trip had started. "Let's just get the stupid manuscripts and then get out of here, Griff."

Ahmed looked at Ayisha, but she was clearly off in her own world. He followed her gaze and watched the shoreline also. After having grown up in Timbuktu and the desert surrounding it, they found the sights on the shore to be sometimes familiar and sometimes so far from what they knew. As the morning passed, the shore changed again and again. Once there was a small oasis, covered with date palms, and then a short while later a collection of tents. A man sitting up front pointed with his chin and called out to Ayisha, "Those are Bozo tents. The Bozo people are the fishermen of Mali."

Ayisha had heard of them and knew they called themselves "the masters of the waters," but she had never seen their tents or boats. She didn't think she'd ever seen a Bozo before. At the water's edge, women, as black as could be, washed clothes and waved at the passing boat. Ayisha waved at them, a giant smile filling her face. Farther along there were barren lands, hot, dried and parched, with an occasional acacia tree, and then cities of mammoth termite hills.

When they saw the collection of termite hills, the brother and sister looked at each other and smiled. These were bigger than the one that had protected them during the sandstorm. They knew that a village must be somewhere nearby, for there was a lot of foot traffic on the shoreline. Women in *grands boubous* were lovely spots of color on an otherwise monochromatic landscape. Tuareg men walked along, some hand in hand and others draping their arms over a sword across their shoulders. All walked in the same direction, wind whipping their robes around their ankles.

Ahmed caught his breath when a large town suddenly appeared. He called out to the men, "Is this Niafunke?"

One man turned and said, "No, this is Dire. Niafunke is maybe two or four hours more, *Inshallah*."

All breathed a sigh of relief when the boat didn't turn into the town. They could see the minarets of the mosque standing above all the other buildings of *banco*. The man turned again and said, "Your *toubab* friends are lucky, for our cargo and other passengers are going to Mopti. We don't have to stop here. We will collect new passengers in Niafunke when we drop you two there."

Looking first at the *toubabs* and then at the two Bellas, he asked, "What takes you all to Niafunke? It is not the most visited town along this river."

Ayisha cut in. "They love the music of Ali Farka Touré. And so do we. And so does our father." Ahmed looked at her with his eyes wide, amazed once again at her swiftness telling only part of the truth. Ancient manuscripts did not even get a mention.

Ayisha continued, "We want to show them where Ali Farka Touré lived. Then they will go on with you so they can go home, and we will head back to Timbuktu."

The man laughed quickly, shook his head and said, "I hope the travel is worth it. Just to look at the house of a man recently departed you travel this far?"

Ayisha smiled and said, "Not just look—we want to pay our respects too." Smiling wider, she added, "I love to travel. I am just learning that." She raised her arm and waved at kids running along the shore. A small wooden pirogue, much smaller than the *pinasse* they were on, suddenly passed between them and the shoreline. Sitting in the front of the boat was a small boy wearing the strangest hat Ayisha had ever seen. It was green and orange and had seven points sticking out from his forehead. Trudy clapped and cried, "That's the crown on the Statue of Liberty."

Griff turned, looking ready to scoff until he saw it too. "You're right. How bizarre is that?"

Ayisha asked Trudy, "Excuse me, but what did you say?"

Trudy pointed at the boy, who had a smile as bright as the sun. "That crown is what the Statue of Liberty, a famous monument in America, wears. Where did he get it?"

Ahmed joined the conversation. "Probably in the Dead Man's Market."

Both Griff and Trudy stared at him. Ayisha continued, "That's what we call the market where they sell used clothes and things. The clothes come from America, and we always thought that whoever owned them must be dead, otherwise they would still be wearing them."

The *toubabs* threw back their heads and laughed. "The Dead Man's Market! What a hoot!" shouted Griff.

Ayisha looked at Ahmed, who didn't appear offended by what they were saying. She waved at the boy with the statue's crown and continued to watch the shoreline. Boys plowed barren fields with camels pulling the single-bladed plows. Every town, no matter how small, had a mud mosque. In one town the mosque looked only big enough for two men. In another town, women stood down along the banks, working together pounding millet in their tall mortars. The *thunk thunk* rhythm reminded Ayisha of home.

Finally, just as the afternoon call to prayer floated on the air from the shoreline, the boat turned in. The men up front jumped to their feet, and the one they had talked to earlier said, "Welcome to Niafunke."

As they pulled into the shoreline, he pointed to a large,

flat-roofed building right at the water's edge. A thick wall stood in front of it, the same color as the land around it. Pointing, he said, "There's the house of Ali Farka Touré."

Griff was standing already. He asked Ahmed, "Who is this Ali Farka you're talking about? Does he have what we need?"

"No, no. He was a famous singer in Mali. He is our father's favorite, and ours too. Unfortunately, he died recently, but his music will be with us forever."

"I hope you're not going to waste our time going there. Let's take care of business so we can get back on this thing and finish our trip to Mopti, where we'll catch a bush taxi to Bamako and finally our plane home."

Griff was right. Once they reached Mopti, the two Americans would have to change to road transport. A mix of rapids and shallow water prevented big boats from traveling between Mopti and the capital, Bamako, where they would find the airport.

Ahmed looked at Griff and said, "Actually, I think you should bring your things. It is not sure when we will meet the man we are looking for." Pointing at a *bâché* moving through town, he said, "There is plenty of transport here. And look at all these other boats."

Griff wasn't happy. "But I paid for all the way to Mopti."

"Well, I believe you should bring your things. As you can see, the town is not too large, but maybe the man hasn't arrived yet. Or maybe he got tired of waiting for us, for we are late." Ahmed shaded his eyes and searched the shoreline for Baba Abdul. He scratched his cheek covered with mosquito bites, then said, "I don't see him yet. We left his camp at the same time, but he went all the way back to Timbuktu to collect the other two ancient manuscripts. He was going to come to Niafunke by road . . . Oh, Ayisha. What if he turned back?"

Ayisha stood tall on the boat's roof, scanning the shoreline in both directions. She stared hard at the town, willing Baba Abdul and the *gendarmes* to appear. Blowing out a little puff of breath, she whispered to herself, "Please, Allah, let them still be here." Turning to the group, she pasted a confident look on her face and said, "I'm sure he's near, maybe waiting for us in the shade of that large tree back there. Let us go look, for he too wants this business finished quickly."

Once they were all off the roof, the two foreigners gathered their packs and Ayisha and Ahmed shook hands with all they had met. As Ayisha started down the wooden plank that led to the shore, she suddenly saw Baba Abdul walk quickly around the corner of a short *banco* building. He looked back over his shoulder, making the briefest of eye contact with Ayisha, who nodded, confirming she knew where to go. Releasing a giant sigh of relief, the nervous young Bella girl looked at Ahmed and pointed to the left. "Let's look this way first."

❖❖ *C h a p t e r   2 9*

SWEAT WAS POURING DOWN each face, for once they left the roof of the boat, not a breeze stirred. The heat hung heavy as the dust they stirred up as they walked. Griff stayed right at Ahmed's shoulder, muttering something in his ear. All jumped when a *bâché* taxi leaned on its horn behind them, then swerved past, sending up a cloud of dust, thick and choking. Trudy bent with her hands on her knees, coughing and complaining. She yelled at her husband, "Oh, Griff, I hate this place."

Griff threw a look her way, then asked in loud, jarring French, "So where is this guy, Ahmed?" He tilted his head and squinted and said, "If there even is a guy . . ."

Quickly, Ayisha said, "Let's go. We won't know where he is until we look." She pointed at the short building, then started walking. "Please, just follow us."

Finally the group reached the small building Ayisha had seen Baba Abdul go behind. As they turned the corner, Ayisha shouted in fake surprise, "There he is!"

Baba Abdul was talking with two other men, all dressed in *jalabiahs*. He looked up at the sound of her voice, acting surprised to see the group. He shook hands with the two men, snapped his fingers and touched his heart, then coolly walked toward Ayisha, Ahmed and the *toubabs*. He had a wrapped package held tightly in his arms.

"It's lucky we meet so quickly," he said in Arabic as he shook Ahmed's hand. Baba Abdul sneaked a quick look at the *toubabs*, then looked away. Seeing the exiting boat passengers, he said to Ahmed, "We need to go someplace less open. I am not comfortable, and neither should you be. Come with me."

When all started to follow, he pointed at Ahmed and said, "No—just you." Ahmed waved the *toubabs* and his sister off. The Tuareg man and Bella boy walked behind a small shop and stopped. Ayisha loosened the hem of her dress, which was stuck to her sweaty, dusty brown legs. She leaned forward and saw Baba Abdul give Ahmed the package he carried. He also pointed toward the two men he had been chatting with. Those must be the police, she thought.

She glanced at the *toubabs* to see if they could see Ahmed. Trudy was flailing at a fly buzzing around her face. Griff stood tapping his foot, pulling on the T-shirt stuck to his flat chest. He looked up and caught her gaze. "So where is he? And what are you looking at?"

Fortunately she didn't have to answer him, for Ahmed came back to the street carrying a large package wrapped in a green cloth. Sweat covered his face, and she could feel his nervousness. He said to the three waiting for him, "Let's go over there, by the stand of trees. No one is there just now, and we can finish this business finally."

Pointing at the new package Ahmed held, Griff anxiously asked, "What did you get?"

Ahmed pressed the package against his heart and said, "I haven't looked yet, but I trust the man." He shifted the red and green bag hanging against his chest and said, "I'm sure it's what we came for. Let's go." When they reached the trees, Ahmed looked directly at Griff and said, "The price is set, so no bargaining. You accept it or forget it." He looked at Baba Abdul, who was standing down the street in the scraggily shade of a leafless acacia tree, watching them. The two men stood a short distance behind him, talking as if they hadn't a care in the world. A very nervous Ahmed looked at his sister, then lifted the old red and green bag over his head, off his shoulder. He pressed it against his heart with the new package Baba Abdul had just given him. Ahmed took a deep breath, then pointed at Baba Abdul and told the two *toubabs*, "He is there to watch us. If he sees you arguing, I am to go right back to him and that will be that."

Griff said, "I don't like having so many rules, but if these manuscripts look as old as the first one, we'll pay and be on our way."

Trudy added in English, "And will be done with the two of you!"

The four walked over to the place where flat-topped acacia trees stood. There were empty little wooden stalls scattered around. They could all tell that it was the marketplace, abandoned because it wasn't market day. Looking around cautiously, Ahmed slowly unwrapped the two manuscripts Baba Abdul had collected in Timbuktu. They were as fragile as the one in his bag. Griff eagerly held his hands out in a "give me" motion, palms up and fingers opening and closing.

Shaking his head, Ahmed told Griff, "You cannot touch them until you pay for them." Ahmed dropped his eyes, looking for Baba Abdul. He stood in the same place under the tree, but the other two men were gone.

Ayisha had watched them leave. One wore a brown *jalabiah* and the other a green one. They walked casually across the empty marketplace, gesticulating with their arms like two men caught up in a deep conversation. Ayisha was sure they must be the police.

"How much?" Griff's eyes were glued to the parchment papers.

"Remember, no bargaining. He wants 55,000 CFA for each one."

Griff looked at him, tearing his eyes away from the ancient papers. "How much?"

Trudy cut in and said, "You must be kidding."

Griff blew a breath out and said to Trudy in rushed English, "Let's just do it. That's about a hundred dollars each, a fraction of what we'll sell them for. A fraction. If we do this quickly, then maybe we can catch the boat if it hasn't left yet and get out of Dodge."

That obviously appealed to Trudy, for she took out a roll of bills and began counting. Griff clearly didn't want to waste time, so he unzipped the pack on his waist and also took out a roll of bills. He counted as quickly as he could, stopping at 90,000. He looked at Trudy. She held up her roll and said, "Here's 120,000 CFA. That will leave us with 40,000 CFA to get back to Bamako, where we can change money if we have to until our flight home leaves."

Griff took her money and told Ayisha to open her hand. He carefully, but quickly, counted out 165,000 CFA. Ayisha's eyes were wide as she watched, for never, ever had she seen so much money. It made the 10,000 CFA Auntie B had given her look like small change.

When she had the money, Griff turned to Ahmed and said, "Fine. Give me the manuscripts, all three, so we can go."

Ayisha didn't want the *toubabs* to even touch the precious manuscripts, so she blurted out, "But wait. What about paying for our services? We have done a lot for you and taken great risks, crossing the desert and finding manuscripts that could send us all to jail, so we should be paid well."

Griff looked at Trudy, who took 10,000 CFA off the bills still in his hand. She turned to Ahmed and Ayisha and said, "Here it is. Take it or leave it. No bargaining."

Ayisha took the money, praying that the real police would appear soon. She couldn't bear to watch Griff take the manuscripts into his hands, so she quickly looked in all directions for the policemen but didn't see them. She wanted to cry when she saw Griff take two of the manuscripts and zip them into his small pack, then hand Trudy the third manuscript after a reluctant Ahmed took it out of its metal box. Ahmed cringed when he saw the *toubab* woman jam the brittle manuscript into her pack.

Ayisha looked around once more for the *gendarmes*, trying her best to hide her growing panic. She knew they didn't have a plan in case the police didn't arrive. No sooner had she thought this than a sudden shout filled the air. The two men ran out from behind a broken-down truck across the deserted marketplace, yelling, *"Police! Arrêtez vous!"* Police! Stop!

The *toubabs* looked at each other in shock. "Run!" yelled Griff. He took off in the opposite direction of the police as Trudy threw off her pack with the manuscript inside and took off after him. Ayisha looked at the pack, then looked at the running woman. Pack. Woman. She swiped up the pack, heavier to run with, but she knew she couldn't leave the precious manuscript behind. Slinging it over one shoulder, she took off after Trudy. She ran with a strength and speed she didn't know she had. The distance closed between the runners as Ayisha ran like the wind with the pack bouncing against her back. She had no doubt that she would catch the fleeing thief. She could hear the *gendarmes* running and shouting not too far behind her.

Griff and Ahmed were racing far ahead of them, throwing up dust devils just like trucks on the desert. Trudy struggled to follow the husband who had forgotten all about her. The *toubabs* ran toward a dusty *futbol* game on the outskirts of town. One of the players looked up, clearly annoyed, then saw all the people running toward them.

He stared at the strange sight of two running *toubabs*, followed by two local kids who were in turn followed by two adults. He quickly shouted to his players, and they all stretched out in a line, forming a human wall.

Trudy saw them and tried to change directions. That slight hesitation gave Ayisha just the chance she needed. Like the gazelle Griff had called her just the day before, Ayisha dodged to her left and cut the woman off. The woman and girl fell to the ground, the pack falling off Ayisha's shoulder. Trudy's long skirt was twisted around her legs, and her shoulder scarf was nowhere in sight. With a single leap Ayisha sat on Trudy's back. Griff stopped running when he saw the *futbol* players fanned out across the field. Puffing hard, he bent with his hands on his knees. Suddenly he tossed the bag far away, as if that would disassociate him from the two precious manuscripts tucked inside it.

The *gendarme* in brown ran to grab the bag. It was covered with dust, and the zipper stuck when he tried to open it. Blowing on it, then brushing the zipper quickly with his fingertips, he finally got the bag open. The two manuscripts, in total disarray, were inside. He looked at Griff and then at Ahmed, who were both looking at Ayisha and Trudy and the policeman in green.

The *gendarme* was pulling on Ayisha's arm as she sat proudly on the woman's back. "Get off now," he said with a yank. "She is not a camel, though she may wish she were one soon."

Ayisha had her right hand planted squarely in the middle of Trudy's back. As she leaned forward to get off, her full weight fell forward, and the woman gasped in surprise. A huge sigh of relief escaped from Ayisha's mouth as she stood up.

"You did a good job. A brave young woman you are," said the policeman. A smile, filled with relief and exhaustion, could not hide the pleasure and pride she felt from the policeman's praise. Ayisha stood with a leg on either side, carefully flicking sand off her dress, looking at the back of the *toubab* woman who had caused so much trouble.

Impatiently the policeman told Ayisha, "Move, move." She raised her left foot over her captive's back. She looked at the policeman and said in French, making sure Trudy would understand, "Do you have any idea how many times this woman has insulted our culture, our country, our heritage? You and me and all who call Timbuktu home?"

"No, but I am sure you will tell us all more than once. Now let's get over to the others." He leaned down and grabbed Trudy's right arm, pulling her to her feet. As soon as she stood, he dropped her arm and wiped his hand on his gown. Picking up her pack with his left hand, he pointed with his right hand toward the others and said, "Go!"

Trudy scuffed her feet as she moved off toward Griff. She looked at her partner in crime and said in English, "Still worth it?"

Ahmed held Griff by his right arm while the policeman in brown held his left arm. All Griff could do was look at his wife, blow air between his tight lips and shake his head. Disbelief filled his face. Ahmed dropped Griff's arm when the other two arrived. Shooting her eyes skyward, Ayisha silently signaled her brother to join her. She stepped back from the group and waited for Ahmed to reach her. Grabbing his shoulder, she stretched up and whispered in his ear. He nodded, a smile growing as he did.

As one, they walked up to the two *toubabs* and shouted in unison, "Gotcha!"

Chapter 30

THEY ALL SAT IN a circle around Ibrahim's tea set that evening, under a sky filled with raging sunset colors of orange and pink. Extra glasses had been added for Baba Abdul, Auntie B and Alhaji Musa. Ayisha sat between her mother and her father, looking across at her brother, who sat between their father and the Alhaji. Trying to keep her distance from her angry sister-in-law, Auntie B sat between Baba Abdul and Alhaji Musa. Not a smile was to be seen on any of the seven faces.

Their mother asked the first question, speaking to the children but looking at Auntie B. "So what do you know about your uncle?"

"Nothing," said Ayisha.

Ahmed looked at his fuming mother. "She's right, Mother, we only learned that there was an uncle—is it three or four days ago?—in Auntie's village."

Their mother's head rotated to look at them. "Then why did you go to your auntie's village for help? Why didn't you come and talk to your parents who live right here?" She slapped the ground in front of her, just to make sure that all knew the level of her anger. Pointing toward the horizon, she added, "But no, you leave like dust devils yourselves, across a scorching desert attacked by sudden sandstorms." Just the thought made her shiver, and Ahmed and Ayisha shared a look of regret at making their mother worry so.

Ayisha reached out to touch her mother's shoulder, but her mother pulled away. Looking first at Auntie B, she asked the twins again, "If you knew nothing of your uncle, then why did you run off to your aunt instead of your father or me to catch these thieves?"

The question confused Ayisha, for what could having a missing uncle and catching thieves have to do with each other? Burning under her mother's piercing gaze, Ayisha said, "It's my fault. I was afraid you would not let us go, and there was nothing more I have wanted in life than to catch these two thieves."

Her mother snorted and said, "You seem to only want, want, want in this life. You want to go to school. You want to talk to *toubabs*. You want to sell jewelry. Are you telling me you wanted to catch these two more than you wanted to go to school?"

Nodding, Ayisha said, "I must have, because I couldn't stop myself, even though I worried about school while we were gone." All eyes were on the young girl as she continued. "I am so sorry, Mother, for the worry and strain we have caused you and Father. But can't you see what a good thing we did?"

Miriam sat forward, pulling the black cloth farther over her head. She shook her head, as if in wonderment. "What really amazes me is that you just left, started off alone across the desert, after our discussion on our walk to the Tuareg camp."

Ayisha's eyes popped wide open, and a trembling veil of liquid covered them. She looked at the ground and said, "So I did give up school?"

Ibrahim reached out to touch his daughter's knee, patting it gently. "Answer your mother's question. Why were you so determined to catch these two by yourselves?"

Raising her eyes, she said, "Many reasons, Father, but two main ones. These people thought that everyone around them were fools. They had no respect for our town and our culture, and that made me angry. But worse—they wanted to steal treasures from our heritage."

She sat straighter as she said, "They needed to learn a lesson that would spread to all who follow with the same idea." She bounced her hands on her thighs. "That's why we had to catch them in the act."

Ibrahim turned to Ahmed and said, "And why were we excluded from all of this?"

Ahmed was happy to take some of the pressure off his sister. Slow tears were dripping down her cheeks as she realized that not all dreams come true. "We didn't come to you because we were afraid you would forbid us to continue, just like Ayisha said. And you would have forbidden us, Father, is that not so?"

His father rolled his eyes toward the bright red, green, yellow and blue prayer cap on his head.

"And so first you went to Alhaji Musa?"

"Yes, Father."

"And did he agree with your plan to leave for the Tuareg camp you've never been to before, across the desert in the hot season?"

All eyes shifted to look at the Alhaji. Shaking his head slowly, he told Ibrahim, "I was gone when they needed me most. And that's when they should have been smart enough to come to you." The Alhaji looked down at the blue and yellow plastic mat he sat on, picking at a loose thread. "I see now that I should have come to you myself before leaving, to tell you what your children were up to. But I left in a great hurry, to reach my friend's bedside before death arrived. Thank Allah I made it." Then he looked into Ibrahim's eyes and said, *"Malesh, mon ami."* Sorry, my friend.

Ibrahim shifted his gaze back to his son's face. "And when you reached the camp, did your auntie tell you our family history?"

"No, Father, no history was shared. She told us we had had an uncle, but that's all. Just like you, she said this is a story you two should tell together."

Ayisha spoke, although she probably shouldn't have. "Oh, Father, we would love to know what it is. You said you'd tell us only when Auntie was here again, and she said she would tell us only when we were all together again. Now we're all here, so please, please, tell us the story of this mystery uncle."

Ibrahim looked at Miriam and raised his eyebrows in question. She shrugged, and they both looked at Auntie B across the circle. She had been quiet a long time, thought Ayisha. Auntie B gave Miriam and Ibrahim a very slow nod, eyes closed and head tilted, across the small dung fire that burned between them. Chirping cicadas filled the darkening sky, as if announcing the day's first break from the sun's punishing heat.

Miriam cleared her throat. "I think now is the time, but the discussion in general is not finished."

Ibrahim nodded as he turned to his sister and said, "Well, Buktu, this is your story. I think it's time to tell it and to reclaim the city you lived in for a short while, and the name you gave yourself as a child."

"Buktu is your name, Auntie B? I've always dreamed you were related to the first Buktu, the woman at the well. Are you?" asked an astonished Ayisha.

"Only in spirit, my dear, only in spirit." Auntie Buktu twisted the big gold ring on her right thumb, cleared her throat and plunged in. Tilting her head, she looked at the twins and, with a thick sadness they could each feel, she said, "Are you ready to learn about your uncle? The time has come to tell our family history."

With very solemn faces they nodded. Ayisha whispered under her breath, over and over again, savoring the sound of "Auntie Buktu, Auntie Buktu . . ."

Reaching under her gown, Auntie Buktu pulled out the flat package wrapped in the blue cloth she had tucked into her trunk in the Tuareg camp. Ayisha watched closely as her aunt slowly unwrapped it. Inside was a beautiful leather folder, with a delicate pattern carved into its cover. Auntie Buktu opened it and slowly took out an old photo and held it to her breast.

"My husband was an honorable man in a very dishonorable situation." Her tongue worked inside her mouth and she let loose small *"toc, toc, toc"* sounds. Ahmed recognized them as her nervous noise, and so he got up and sat in front of her. Ayisha did the same, with their backs to the others, face-to-face with their Auntie Buktu. Ahmed reached out and took her hand and said, "Please tell us, Auntie Buktu. What is his name? And where is he?"

Ayisha could contain herself no longer. "Auntie Buktu, oh, how I love to say that! Please, when can we meet him?"

Auntie Buktu raised her hand. "Sorry, but you will not ever meet him. It was not his choice or decision not to be here. He was in prison in Mopti for something he did not do. Malaria killed him before he could come home."

Ahmed's eyes were wide, and Ayisha's jaw dropped, as they took in all this news at one time. An uncle? In Mopti—in prison?

Auntie Buktu looked at the photo, then slowly handed it to Ayisha. Ahmed leaned over her shoulder to look. There stood a young Auntie B, next to a tall, proud man with eyes that seemed to spark with life, even in the faded black-and-white photo. Ayisha turned the photo over and read aloud an inscription in French. "To our Malian friend, Jamal. Thanks for a great tour of Timbuktu. From your American friends, Dianne and Rodney."

Auntie put out her hand for the photo. She looked at the writing on the back and said, "These were very good people. Not all *toubabs* are bad." Then she turned the photo and laid it on her knee, where she could gaze upon it as she spoke. Touching his face, she said, "His name was Jamal." A small hiccup of pain filled the air and Auntie Buktu's shoulders sagged. Ahmed jumped to his knees and wrapped his arms around his auntie.

Ayisha wrapped her arms around her too. "Please don't cry. I know Uncle Jamal was innocent. He had to be if he was married to you." Patting her auntie's shoulder, Ayisha added, "I want more than anything to know more. So please, when the sadness passes, tell us the rest of the story."

Ahmed leaned back on his heels, his brown eyes opened wide, and Auntie Buktu laughed with a sudden chuckle. She patted his knee and said, "You are so much like your father. And your uncle too. I have thought it again and again, and then one day on my last visit thirteen months, two weeks and five and a half days ago I knew it for sure. I saw you from afar in the market and knew that you and your uncle would be very close if he were still here.

"You were with two men tourists, *toubabs* from wherever the white people come from. You were helping them shop, bargaining for them with the old man selling sandals made from car tires, just like yours. I moved closer and could hear you, talking French to the *toubabs* and Arabic with the trader. That day I went back to the camp and wept, for my husband had the same skill with languages and foreigners that you have."

A slight hint of a smile lit the dark brown pupils of her eyes. With pride she said, "He was very smart, just like you and your sister. He taught himself to read and write, for Bella slaves did not go to school. When we were given our freedom, many Bella stayed with their Tuareg families, but not my Jamal. He moved to town and got a job at the mosque. First he was just supposed to sweep and keep the water containers full. But he met an Alhaji, a holy man his own age, who was much taken with your uncle's eagerness to learn." Looking to her left, she caught the eyes of the Alhaji, and she said, "The generous holy man was called Alhaji Musa."

The Alhaji dipped his head in acknowledgment of the compliment and to confirm the story. Ayisha and Ahmed turned to stare at the holy man. Alhaji Musa rubbed his chin, then nodded quickly to the twins. Auntie continued, "He soon had your uncle working with the ancient manuscripts, as his assistant."

Auntie Buktu leaned back, a wide smile covering her face, suddenly lit by a burst of flame from the fire Miriam fanned. "For years Jamal had worked as the guardian of the mosque and loved his work. But when he began working with Alhaji Musa and his papers, your uncle blossomed like a desert flower."

Patting her gown smooth across her folded knees, Auntie B took a quick breath and continued, "I had never seen him so happy. In fact, I complained because some dusty old papers made him happier than I did. Can you imagine? We were newly married. Not even two hot seasons had passed since our wedding when our short life together came to a halt, as suddenly as the first whipping winds of a harmattan."

She sat straighter and told her niece and nephew proudly, "I was a very beautiful young woman, much sought after. I did not always look like an old hag. And your uncle—what a handsome man." She slipped into a silence, looking at the photo, until Ahmed cleared his throat and brought her back to the moment.

"Your uncle would leave the tent for the first prayer of the day and not return until after the last prayer. The whole day he spent reading the ancient manuscripts written generations ago, then debating about politics or religion and talk, talk, talking with Alhaji Musa. They would sit in the patio of Djinguereber Mosque, binding books, reading text, discussing all the finest details of the knowledge he was gleaning from the ancient manuscripts he treasured."

Stopping with her eyes closed, she looked as if she was remembering a special scene. "I watched them at work once, so many years ago, through the door from the street." Auntie Buktu opened her eyes and stared right at Alhaji Musa. "You sat on a mat in the shade, and with the gentleness a mother reserves for a newborn, you both smoothed the ancient manuscripts made of fragile parchment. Not a night passed that Jamal didn't return home more energized than when he had left. And always wanting to talk about all he had seen and learned that day."

Alhaji Musa cleared his throat. "And don't forget, Buktu, we also studied the greatest book of all, the Koran."

Auntie Buktu nodded as she rocked from side to side in slow motion, closing her eyes again, as if looking back in time. Softly she said, "Soon word began to spread that Jamal was becoming quite the scholar on these papers and the Koran and was eager to share his knowledge."

Proudly she looked at Ahmed and Ayisha. "People would seek him out for recommended Koranic verses for their *gris-gris* packets, to protect them from all sorts of things. On his way home at night, they asked him for advice on all subjects, from how to find a mate for a son or daughter to what prayers to say for the firstborn." She shrugged. "Jamal was becoming known, and some people didn't like that."

She looked at Ahmed. "He even had *toubabs* that visited the mosque ask him to take them around when he had time." Shaking her head, she said, "Men. Always worried about who is better, who is smarter, who is more noble. Suddenly people, mainly Tuareg, were saying, 'How can an ex-slave be so revered? This is embarrassing. And just not right!'

"My husband tried his best not to attract attention, but he also could not refuse someone seeking help. Then one night, as we sat listening to our little radio, the local *gendarmes* suddenly appeared at our tent."

She slipped again into a sad silence until the sound of

a bleating goat filled the air. Ayisha said, "Please carry on, Auntie. You were listening to your little radio when the *gendarmes* appeared . . ."

Auntie Buktu's eyes closed briefly, then opened again, and she sat straighter, continuing. "I will never forget that night. The older policeman, Mohamed, had asked your uncle, just that day, for advice about a wife who could not conceive. Your uncle gave him two tracts from the Koran to put into his *gris-gris* packets to wear around his upper arm. When they arrived, my husband thought it had something to do with that.

"He leapt up from the mat and offered his hand in greeting, but neither policeman reached back. They looked very uncomfortable, that much I will say for them. Ashen like coals gone cold."

Auntie B looked into her hennaed hands. She sucked her teeth twice quickly. *"Thitch. Thitch."* The twins could feel her pain, so they each reached out for a hand. Three quicker *"Thitch, thitch, thitches"* filled the air, followed by a long puff of Auntie's breath.

She squeezed their hands and said, "My husband asked, 'Mohamed, is something wrong? Is Alhaji Musa not well? Why these faces as long as a goat's beard?'

"I will never forget how the policemen slid their eyes to look at each other, seeing who would speak first. The silence stretched, and your uncle slapped his hands together and almost shouted, 'Have vultures pulled out your tongues?'

"Finally the younger one, not the man Mohamed, who

had asked for advice that very same day, cleared his throat and said, 'Baba Jamal, we are here on very important business—very serious. I am afraid to say we are here to arrest you.'

"Your uncle's eyes opened wide, and his jaw dropped. It was if he had been kicked by a donkey, no sound but a deep breath of air, and then a laughter that shook the woven roof. He placed his hand on the young man's arm and said, 'That is very funny. And exactly what crime have I committed?'"

Auntie Buktu looked into Ahmed's eyes, then Ayisha's. She breathed noisily and said, "Your uncle scratched his head like a man thinking deep into his brain, saying, 'I can't remember the last camel I stole, so that can't be the problem. And I have not broken any of the Koranic laws, so I am sure that you are here in jest.'

"But the silence that followed filled the tent like dense smoke while both policemen looked at the ground. Not a hint of laughter or the slightest chuckle came from either man. My husband finally could take the silence no longer, so he snapped out, 'So what is your business here? What is my crime?'"

Auntie B smoothed the creases in her long gown, running her hands up and down her thighs. She looked at her niece and nephew and said, "The youngest *gendarme* cleared his throat again, staring at his dusty shoes. Then in almost a whisper he said, 'Theft is your crime.'

"Jamal grabbed the man's chin, pulling him up face-to-face, and told him, 'Look me in my eyes and tell me I am a thief. Tell my wife, Buktu, that she is married to a thief. And also tell her exactly what I have stolen, for that is a total mystery to me.'

"The policeman turned to his partner and said, 'You tell him. I have said enough.'

"His answer could not have shocked us more, or made your uncle more amazed. The pain in Mohamed's eyes was very obvious. His pupils shone in the glow of the candles, like the watery eyes of a cow. He must have been crying before they arrived, for they were as red as a man's eyes that has just looked into a harmattan wind. He glanced at your uncle, looked away, then flinched when I stepped forward and told him, 'Speak up or leave.'

"My husband held my hand, something reserved for only private moments, giving me the gentlest of squeezes. Finally the policeman Mohamed said, 'You have stolen sacred manuscripts.'

"Your Uncle Jamal sat with a great thud upon the mat. He shook his head, then finally looked up and said, 'I have stolen the manuscripts I would give my life to protect?'

'*Oui*, that is what we have been told. We must take you to the *gendarmerie* after we search your tent for the missing manuscripts. We want to find them before you can sell them to a *toubab*.'"

Auntie Buktu stopped her story, and *"Thitch, thitch, thitch"* filled the air like a hen cackling.

Ahmed leaned forward and asked, "Auntie Buktu, can I get you some water? Do you want to stop, rest a bit, before finishing?"

Auntie Buktu shook her head firmly, left right left right. "I will finish now. One time. But first I will have some water."

Ahmed jumped up to get the water bag that sat beside his father's tea set. It was nearly empty, hanging flat. She cupped her hands and Ahmed filled them. She sipped and then tilted back her head, letting the few sips flow down her throat.

Sitting straight again, she continued, "It is as clear in my mind as if it happened yesterday. Your uncle leaned over to his right from where he sat and pulled his shoulder bag across the floor. It was a leather bag worn smooth from much use, in fact, the same bag I gave to you on this trip. His mother had made it for him when his father's favorite camel died. Beautiful cross-stitches of white ran down the straps, and soft leather, painted green and red, hung down the front."

Ahmed jumped to his knees and said, "You told me it was your treasure bag, so I thought you meant it held treasures. But maybe you treasure it because it belonged to Uncle Jamal."

Auntie Buktu cocked her head to the side and regarded her nephew. "You are very clever for so clumsy and anxious a boy. Yes. Definitely, I treasure it because it was your uncle's. But please. Let me finish this painful tale."

She leaned forward and picked up the empty water bag, bouncing it nervously on her lap. "Your uncle dragged his bag over to his side. With a flashing anger in his eyes, he handed it to Mohamed and said, 'Let's start the search right here. If I am guilty, then I'm sure you'll find the holy manuscripts that I revere more than life right here in my bag, cleverly hidden.'

"We all gasped when Jamal turned the bag over, shook it, and two ancient parchment manuscripts, rolled tightly, fell onto the mat. The giant key for the mosque storeroom fell out, as did his well-worn copy of the Koran. We all just stared at the little pile, all eyes locked on the manuscripts like a baby's eyes locked on a mother's breast. Your uncle's face could not have been more shocked if gold coins had dropped from his bag. Finally, with the slowest of motions, Mohamed bent down and picked up the rolled scrolls.

"He tapped them against the palm of his hand and then said, 'I have seen for myself that these papers were with you, but before Allah I must say I don't believe that you stole them. There must be an explanation, but we must go to the police station to sort this all out.'

"Your uncle rose slowly to his feet. He looked into my eyes and said, 'I will be back soon. They will know I am innocent because all know I would never roll up a fragile ancient manuscript. Fear not, I will be back before our favorite radio program is over.' It was then that I realized that the radio still droned on. I bent to shut it off and said, 'I will go with you,' but your uncle and the policemen all said at once, 'No, you stay here.'

"And with that, your uncle, my beloved husband, left the tent for the very last time."

Ayisha's voice rose in total indignation. "But who put those manuscripts there, Auntie Buktu?"

Auntie's shoulders sagged, and she dropped her head so her chin nearly touched her chest. Blowing out a short puff of breath, she said, "Your uncle died in prison, an innocent man. Two months after Jamal was dead, the *gendarmes* here caught a man, a neighbor called Ag, selling manuscripts to a *toubab* from France."

Looking at her brother Ibrahim, who had not said a word since she had started her story, she said, "I am tired. You tell the rest."

Ibrahim sat tall. He pulled on his short beard and said, "I went to talk to this man Ag at the *gendarmerie*, before they sent him to Mopti. He had asked for me, and I knew right away why. For more months than a goat carries a kid, this miserable man Ag had taunted your uncle, about everything, before Jamal went to prison."

Ibrahim sucked on his teeth in disgust. "This wretched man, who had many missing teeth and always the dirtiest of clothes and turban, was certain he was better than your uncle, calling him a lowly Bella."

Ibrahim looked at his sister's eyes across the circle, shining with anger in the firelight. "He told me that terrible afternoon that he sent for me that he had placed the manuscripts in your uncle's bag, because he was jealous of him.

"I'll never forget this man's whining voice when he told me, 'All the *toubabs* wanted to talk to Jamal. And all the people went to him for advice, a lowly ex-slave, when they should have come to me, Ag, a Tuareg.'

"It shocked me when Ag said, 'A good man died in prison. I thought he would only be gone a short while and return humble, as he should have been. But then he died and I asked Allah for forgiveness. Now I ask you.'"

"Did you forgive him?" asked Ahmed.

"Not yet," said his father, "although I pray for it every day."

Just then Miriam spoke up. She turned to look at Alhaji Musa. "I don't mean to insult you, but did you never tell these two about your friend, their uncle?"

Alhaji Musa dipped his head to acknowledge the question. "You have a right to ask, and I can say, as Allah is my witness, I never said a word to them about Jamal."

Ayisha rose from in front of Auntie Buktu and squatted down in front of her mother. She looked into her mother's eyes as she said, "We knew nothing at all when we did all those things to catch the thieves. It was not an act of revenge, Mother. It was an act of loyalty to our city and heritage. And now it feels like the only thing that we could have done. Knowing about our uncle, I'm even happier that we did it."

Ahmed joined in, "We became involved with stopping the stealing trade when we didn't even know about our family's sad history."

Baba Abdul, who had remained silent, cleared his throat, and all eyes looked his way. "I knew your uncle well. We knew your uncle was an innocent man, so Alhaji Musa and I went to his trial to speak for him. But no good words could save him, for the manuscripts in the bag were impossible to ignore, and so the judge found him guilty."

Suddenly Auntie Buktu spoke up. "The day they took him away, I dropped the rest of my name. I had named myself for the woman who founded Timbuktu, but when the government of Timbuktu found Jamal guilty, I left Timbuktu—for more than seven years. And I stopped using that name, calling myself only B instead. I finally came back here when I learned that I had a niece and a nephew."

Looking first at her niece and nephew, then at her sister-in-law, Auntie Buktu said proudly, "When they came to me in the desert and told me their story and need, I knew that I had to encourage them. Don't you see, my sister? They were bringing a bit of justice to the memory of their uncle." She reached out and patted each twin on the knee, saying, "And now when they hear of this, perhaps those that may not have believed in Jamal's innocence because he was a Bella, or for whatever reason, finally will. For when they regard the risks Jamal's own niece and nephew took to protect the exact same things he revered—and they didn't even know of him—finally honor will come to this family."

Miriam's eyes shone as she looked at her children. "So you really did take these risks solely to protect the manuscripts of Timbuktu?"

Ayisha nodded silently.

"That's the only reason," said her brother.

Miriam looked at Alhaji Musa and said, "And have these two brought honor to the family? Do you agree?"

The Alhaji nodded with enthusiasm. "They have brought great honor indeed. Despite all their mistakes, which you have mentioned, they have shown their willingness and dedication to protect Allah's papers even at great risk to their own safety."

Baba Abdul cleared his throat. "I have not been asked, but I would like to say something." He looked directly at the twins. "These two deserve respect, for they have faced a large challenge and met it. Maybe better choices could have been made before striking out across Allah's parched land, but they chose to act, which is admirable." Smiling with the smallest hint of embarrassment, he added, "And we worked well together, Tuareg and Bella."

Miriam nodded. "I like that," she said. Then she turned to her husband. "And what do you say, Father?"

Ibrahim didn't answer right away. He tugged at his beard and looked at his daughter, who sat with her eyes closed. He smiled at her and then at Ahmed and said, "They have brought us honor overall, for they acted out of integrity, and not revenge."

They dropped their heads, smiling brightly until Father added, "I may not agree with all their methods, but I am pleased with their results."

Ahmed laughed out loud, trying to lighten the mood as he said, "Mother, Father, you should have seen Ayisha. She jumped on that *toubab* woman like a vulture on a carcass. She was so angry, and she didn't even know about Uncle Jamal! That woman was lucky Ayisha didn't know about him!"

Like the sudden bleating of a goat on a scorching afternoon, laughter filled the night—for the first time since Ayisha and Ahmed had returned.

Ayisha jumped up and grabbed her brother's arm, wrenching it until he stood up. "Ahmed was not exactly gentle. He had that man's right arm in a grip as tight as a baby goat on a teat."

Her mother whooped with laughter at her daughter's brashness. "As tight as what? No, never mind, don't repeat it."

Baba Abdul couldn't resist the light mood. "And what about your son? Throwing the best *boule* ever thrown?"

Ahmed and Ayisha looked in alarm at their mother, for they knew she hated the game. She surprised them all when she said, "But of course, if he is going to waste his time playing the game, he should at least be the best."

Then Auntie Buktu said, "And you can also be very proud of your daughter, for she showed those girls in our camp that one can be both the smartest in school and the bravest."

Ayisha cleared her throat, and all looked her way. She turned to her parents. Smoothing her bangs instead of tugging on them, she said, "Actually, Mother and Father, maybe you should thank the *toubabs*. Before this experience I did nothing but dream of leaving Timbuktu."

Her mother started to say something, but Ibrahim stopped her with a hand on her knee. Taking a deep breath, Ayisha continued. "Now more and more I want to stay here in my city and finish my studies. I still have dreams. I don't know. Maybe I will work with the ancient manuscripts myself. Maybe so."

Smiling brightly now, she added, "So maybe the *toubabs* did us all a great favor!"

In the silence that filled the air, Auntie B tilted her head and asked her sister-in-law, Miriam, "And what about Ayisha? You didn't really say she won't be going to school, did you?"

Miriam looked at Ibrahim, who was smiling with pleasure and pride at his children. Then she looked at the pleading eyes of her daughter and Ahmed. "Yes, yes. I guess she can go, if she promises never to repeat this act."

Ayisha released her brother's arm and ran to hug her mother. Ahmed joined her, and Miriam laughed with pleasure as they hugged her hard, both shouting, *"Al Humdullah!"* Praise Allah!

Then Auntie Buktu began the cry, and without a moment's hesitation Ayisha and Miriam added their voices in a loud, joyous "Aiaiaiaiaieee!!!"

They all laughed as Abdoulaye came running, being chased by the girl Houyti, who had been watching him. Abdoulaye threw back his head and let loose an "Aiaiaiaiaieee!!!" that filled the sky.

Ayisha looked around her family. Her mother's smile radiated from her face, and Auntie Buktu ululated again. Ayisha grabbed Ahmed's hands and turned in circles, calling out again and again, "I'm going to Lycée Franco-Arabe!"

When she stopped, they looked at each other and said as one, *"Al Humdullah!"*

French Glossary

Allez, Jamais!—Go, Never!

Au revoir—Good-bye.

Bâché—Taxi, public transport, usually a converted pickup truck with seats in back.

Banco—Dried mud used for building.

Bic—The common name given to all pens, taken from Bic pens.

Bien sûr—Of course.

Bienvenue—Welcome.

Bonjour. Ça va bien, merci—Good day. We're fine, thanks.

Bonjour, mademoiselles. Cherche quelque chose?—Good morning. Are you looking for something?

Boules—A game where players throw larger balls at a small ball a short distance away.

Cadeau—Gift.

Ça va bien?—How are you? Are you well?

Ça va, ça va—Okay, okay.

Centime plus—Not one more cent.

Centre de Recherchés Historiques Ahmed Baba—The Ahmed Baba Center of Ancient Research.

C'est bien—Good, fine.

C'est la riz.—It's the rice fields.

C'est toute—That's all.

CFA—The monetary unit for French West Africa.

Chapeau—Congratulations.

Enchantée. Je m'appelle—Pleased to meet you. My name is . . .

Fou—A crazy person.

Grand boubou—The long flowing gown worn by men and women.

Grande Marché—The big market.

Gris-gris—Little leather packets worn on the upper arm filled with verses from the Koran for protection.

Je suis fatigué—I am tired.

Les gendarmes invisibles—The invisible police.

Les gendarmes des livres anciennes—Police of the ancient manuscripts.

Lycée—High school.

Ma soeur—My sister.

Mais oui—But of course.

Mon ami—My friend.

Monsieur, un cadeau, s'il vous plaît.—Sir, a gift, please.

Pas de problem—No problem.

Pinasse—A long wooden boat.

Place de l'Independence—Independence Square.

Police! Arrêtez vous!—Police! Stop!

Qu'est-ce-que CEDRAB?—What is CEDRAB?

Rien—Nothing.

Secheress—A killer drought.

Soudure—The hottest part of the hot season.

Toubab—Stranger. The origin of this word is unclear, but

it is not insulting. It is used widely throughout French-speaking West Africa, particularly the Sahel region.

Toubab, achetez ici!—Stranger, buy here.

Toubab, achetez vous mon bijou!—Stranger, buy my jewelry!

Toubab, toubab, cadeau! Donnez moi un Bic, s'il vous plaît.—Stranger, gift! Give me a Bic pen, please.

Trop du sable—Too much sand.

Un plaisir—A pleasure.

Arabic Glossary

Afwan—Thank you.

Al Humdullah—Praise Allah.

Alakoum wa salaam—Peace be with you.

Allahu Akbar!—God is great!

Bisimallah!—In the name of God!

Cuez—Fine.

Harmattan—A dust storm with strong winds blowing off the Sahara Desert.

Inshallah—Allah willing, God willing.

Jalabiah—Long-sleeved gown worn by men.

Kadash hath?—How much?

La, shukran—No, thanks.

Mafi mushkila—No problem.

Malesh—Sorry.

Sabah el khair—Good morning.

Salaam alakoum—Peace be with you.

Shukran—Thank you.

Tabaski—The big celebration feast at the end of the fasting month of Ramadan.

Takamba—One, two.

Wahid, ethneen—One, two.

Tamashek Glossary

Erbiki—The game of hide-and-seek.
Isalan—What is your news?
Mantole!—Welcome!
Nan-i—I have lots of news.
Tim—Water well.